#1 *New York Times* Bestselling Author

DEBBIE MACOMBER

THE COWBOY'S LADY

**HARLEQUIN
BESTSELLING
AUTHOR
COLLECTION**

**HARLEQUIN®
BESTSELLING
AUTHOR
COLLECTION**

Recycling programs
for this product may
not exist in your area.

ISBN-13: 978-1-335-97993-3

The Cowboy's Lady
First published in 1990. This edition published in 2020.
Copyright © 1990 by Debbie Macomber

Small-Town Nanny
First published in 2016. This edition published in 2020.
Copyright © 2016 by Lee Tobin McClain

This edition published by arrangement with Harlequin Books S.A.

For questions and comments about the quality of this book, please contact us at CustomerService@Harlequin.com.

Harlequin Enterprises ULC
22 Adelaide St. West, 40th Floor
Toronto, Ontario M5H 4E3, Canada
www.Harlequin.com

Printed in U.S.A.

CONTENTS

Also available from Debbie Macomber

MIRA

Visit her Author Profile page on Harlequin.com,
or debbiemacomber.com, for more titles!

THE COWBOY'S LADY

Debbie Macomber

To Merrily Boone
Friend
Title Finder
Speller of Impossible Words
Discoverer of Great Restaurants

Chapter 1

Everyone in Cougar Point, Montana, knew the bowling alley had the best breakfast in town. For a buck ninety-five they served up eggs, sausage, hash browns and toast, plus all the coffee a body could drink. Russ Palmer was hungrier than a bear in springtime, but food wasn't the only thing on his mind.

He wanted company—of the female variety.

"Mornin', Russ," Mary Andrews, the lone waitress, called out when he walked into the restaurant. Her greeting was followed by a chorus from several other ranchers.

Russ removed his black Stetson and hooked it on the peg by the door. Although it was only a few days into September, the air was decidedly cool and he'd worn his blanket-lined denim jacket.

Sliding into the booth with a couple of friends, Russ picked up the tail end of what Bill Shepherd was saying.

"Pretty as a picture."

Russ's interest was instantly piqued. "Who?"

"The new schoolteacher, Taylor Manning," Harry Donovan answered eagerly. At twenty-three Harry still had the peach-faced immaturity of youth and fine, blond hair he couldn't seem to control.

A schoolteacher. Russ's curiosity level fell several notches. "Taylor's a funny name for a woman," he muttered, reaching for the menu, which was tucked between the sugar container and the salt and pepper shakers.

"The missus and I met her yesterday," Bill went on to say. "She rented old man Halloran's place on the edge of town."

Russ nodded as he scanned the menu. He ordered the "special" every Saturday morning, but he liked to see what was offered in case something else struck his fancy.

"She moved here from Seattle," Harry informed Russ enthusiastically.

"Then she's a city girl," Russ said, and a hint of sarcasm slipped into his voice. The kid had it bad. Personally Russ didn't hold out much hope of the new teacher sticking it out past Christmas. Seattle was known for its mild climate. At best Taylor Manning could deal with four or five days of drizzle, but he'd bet his ranch and five hundred head of cattle that she had no idea what a Montana winter could be like.

"Whether she's a city slicker or not, I couldn't rightly say," Harry said with no lack of fervor, "but I can tell you one thing. She's real pretty. I swear she's got the bluest eyes I've ever seen and dark, silky hair that falls to about here." He gestured with his hand to a point well below his shoulder blades. "A man could see himself running his fingers through hair that soft," he said dreamily. Pink tinged Harry's cheeks as he stopped abruptly and cast a self-conscious look at his two friends.

Russ laughed outright. "Hell, Harry, she hasn't even been in town a week and already you're sweet on her."

"I can't help myself." Harry grabbed his mug so fast he nearly spilled his coffee. "Wait until you meet her yourself, then you'll know what I mean."

"I'm not going to be mooning over any schoolmarm," Russ told the two men. He hadn't gotten to the age of thirty-four safely unmarried only to be taken in by the charms of a citified schoolteacher. Especially one Harry Donovan would fantasize about.

Bill and Harry exchanged glances, then Harry snickered loudly, apparently amused by Russ's attitude. "You just wait till you see her yourself," he said again.

"What do you mean I can't use my American Express card here?" Taylor Manning demanded of the clerk at the small store. "I could use this card in Kodiak, Alaska!"

"I'm really sorry," the older woman said, "but as far as I know, no one in town takes American Express."

Shaking her head, Taylor pulled her Visa card from her wallet and set it on the counter. "I'll use this one instead." She pushed her chocolate-brown hair over her shoulder and looked around. This situation was becoming embarrassing. Taylor had used her meager savings to rent the house. She'd gone shopping for some kitchen things she was going to need, thinking she could use

her credit card and pay for them when it was more con-
venient.

She was grateful there were only two other people
in the store. A cowboy and his daughter. No, Taylor decided on second thought. The teenage girl was too old
to be his daughter, but too young to be his girlfriend.

"I'm very sorry, but we don't take Visa, either."

"You don't take Visa," Taylor echoed in shocked disbelief. "*Everyone* takes Visa."

"No one in Cougar Point," the woman said apologetically.

Taylor smiled blandly. "Then what *do* you take?"

"Cash would work."

Taylor rummaged through her purse, drawing out a
checkbook. She studied the meager balance and sighed
inwardly. "I don't suppose you take out-of-state checks,
do you? Don't answer that," she said quickly. "Anyone
who doesn't honor American Express or Visa isn't going
to take a check from a Seattle bank." She stared down
at the few items longingly and made her decision. "I'll
simply put everything back and wait until the checks
come through from my new account." She'd also have to
wait until she'd deposited her first pay two weeks from
now, but she didn't feel announcing that was necessary.

"I'm really sorry, miss."

Taylor nodded. "No problem," she murmured, and
even managed a respectable smile. She turned, nearly
colliding with the cowboy she'd noticed earlier.

"Oh, sorry," she said, slipping past him.

"Just a minute. Did I hear you mention Seattle?" His
voice was deep and masculine. Without giving her a
chance to respond, he added, "You wouldn't happen to
be Taylor Manning, would you?"

"Yes. How'd you know?" Not that she should be surprised. Folks had been introducing themselves all week, telling her how pleased they were that she'd accepted the teaching assignment in their town.

Setting his black Stetson farther back on his head, the rancher explained. "The kid mentioned something about you this morning over breakfast."

"The kid?"

"Harry Donovan."

Taylor didn't recall meeting any youngster by that name, but there'd been so many names and so many faces that she'd long since lost track.

The cowboy smiled, and their eyes held for a moment. His reaction hinted at curiosity, but for her part, Taylor had no feelings one way or the other. Oh, he was good-looking enough. His head was covered with a crisp black Stetson; all the men in town seemed to wear them. His dark hair curled along the nape of his sun-bronzed neck as if he'd delayed getting a haircut a couple of weeks too long. He was tall, easily six-three, and he wore tight-fitting blue jeans and a plaid shirt beneath a thick denim jacket.

"Mabel," the rancher said, looking past Taylor. "This is the new schoolteacher."

"Well, for goodness' sake, miss, why didn't you come right out and say so?" Without a second's delay the clerk reached beneath the counter and brought out a tablet and started listing the items Taylor had wanted to purchase.

"Does this mean you'll accept my American Express? My Visa? My check?"

"No, I feel bad about that, but most of the commercial people in these parts don't do credit card business with those big banks. I'll just write down these items here and send you a bill at the end of the month the way I do with most folks."

"But...you don't know me." The woman hadn't so much as requested identification.

Mabel waved her hand, dismissing Taylor's concern. "I feel terrible about this."

Taylor turned her gaze to the cowboy once more. "Thank you."

He touched the brim of his hat in a quick salute and started down the aisle toward the younger girl.

While Mabel was writing up the sale, Taylor watched the exchange at the rear of the store. The teenager was standing beside a cosmetic display, gesturing wildly.

"If you could just sign here," Mabel instructed, turning the tablet around for Taylor. "I can't tell you how pleased we are that you've come to Cougar Point. There won't be much of a social life for you, but we have our moments."

"Yes, I know," Taylor murmured. She hadn't accepted this teaching assignment because of the potential nightlife. She'd specifically chosen the backwoods of Montana in an effort to give herself the necessary time to heal after her disastrous affair with Mark Brooks. She'd moved to Cougar Point so she could immerse herself in her chosen profession—and deal with the bitterness of losing Mark. Next year she'd leave Cougar Point again, rejuvenated and whole. Her family, especially her father, had assumed she'd taken this job on impulse, and although her actions were often spontaneous, for once her father was wrong. The decision to spend a year in Montana had been well thought out, the pros and cons carefully weighed. She was taking this time to mend a badly broken heart, hoping twelve months in the country would do what six months in the city hadn't.

"I want a second opinion," the teenager cried as she rushed toward the front of the store. "Excuse me," she said brightly, holding out her hand. "I'm Mandy Palmer and this is my brother, Russ, who happens to be obstinate and stubborn and completely unreasonable and—"

"Mandy," Russ threatened in a voice few would challenge, "I said no."

"That's just too bad," the girl returned. Tears glistened in her green eyes. She was petite and very pretty, and wore her thick blond hair in a long French braid. It swayed when she jerked her head toward her brother.

"Mandy," Russ threatened again.

The girl ignored him with a defiant tilt of her chin and looked at Taylor. "When a girl's fourteen years old and going into her first year of high school, she's old enough to wear a little makeup, isn't she?"

"Uh…" Taylor hesitated. Mandy was staring at her with imploring eyes while her brother glared heatedly, silently demanding that Taylor mind her own business. "What does your mother say?"

"Our parents are dead," Russ said gruffly. "I'm Mandy's legal guardian and I say she's too young to be painting her face with all that garbage. She's only fourteen!"

"Were you wearing makeup when *you* were my age?" Mandy asked Taylor, the appeal in her eyes desperate.

"A little," Taylor admitted reluctantly. She clutched her purchases tightly, not wanting to get caught in the middle of this family fight.

"Mascara?"

"Yes," Taylor confessed.

"Blush?"

Taylor nodded, ignoring the fierce scowl being directed at her by the girl's brother.

"How about lip gloss?"

"I was wearing that in junior high," Taylor said, gaining a bit more confidence. In Taylor's opinion—although it clearly wasn't wanted or appreciated by the male faction here—Mandy should be allowed to experiment with a little makeup.

"See," the girl said enthusiastically. "And you turned out to be a fine, upstanding citizen, didn't you? I mean a little lip gloss at fourteen didn't automatically turn you into a…a lady of the night, did it?"

Taylor couldn't help laughing; that was the most ridiculous thing she'd ever heard. "No. But it was close. It all started with too much mascara, followed by blue eye shadow. Before I realized what I was doing, I was into perfumes." She hesitated and lowered her voice to a whisper. "The French kind."

Mandy gasped for effect.

Taylor didn't hide a smug smile as she continued. "From there it was a natural descent. I found myself standing on street corners…"

"It's time to go," Russ ordered. He gave Taylor a look that could have curdled milk. "We've heard more than enough."

Still amused, Taylor left the store. She sure hadn't made a friend of the rancher, but Russ was being too strict with his younger sister. It wasn't like her to take sides in something that didn't involve her, but his attitude had struck a familiar chord. Taylor's own father was often hard-nosed and outdated in his views. More than once the two of them had fought over the most ridiculous issues. If her mother hadn't been there to run interference, Taylor didn't know what would have happened. The crazy part was, she thought the world of her father. They could argue until the cows came home, but that never dampened the deep affection they shared.

Till the cows came home! Taylor paused midstep. Good grief, she was already beginning to think like a cowgirl. If this was the way she sounded after ten days, heaven only knew what she'd be like in a year's time.

Taylor was walking to her car when she ran into Mary Beth Morgan, another teacher. They'd met earlier in the week during a staff meeting. Mary Beth was in her mid-fifties, friendly and a country girl through and through. She was the type of woman who personified everything good about small towns.

"You're looking pleased about something."

Taylor nodded. "I just met Russ and Mandy Palmer. They were debating whether Mandy's old enough to wear makeup and somehow I got stuck in the middle. That man is certainly opinionated."

"Mandy can give as good as she gets. I once heard Russ say that even Napoleon couldn't stand up to Mandy when she truly wanted something."

That seemed like a comment the cowboy would make and, despite herself, Taylor discovered she was smiling.

"Russ has a good heart, so don't judge him too harshly," Mary Beth said as they strolled down the sidewalk together. "He's raising Mandy on his own and genuinely cares about her. His views may be kind of outdated, but he tries hard to be fair."

"What happened to their parents?"

"Actually Mandy's his half sister. Russ's mother ran off when he was a toddler. I doubt Russ even remembers her. Fred Palmer took his wife's leaving really hard.

I'm sure there are two sides to that story, though. Fred could be ornery and was as pigheaded as they come."

"Russ must take after his father then."

"He does," Mary Beth said, missing Taylor's joke. "Most folks around here would rather tangle with a grizzly bear than mess with Russ when he's in one of his moods. I suppose that has a lot to do with his living all these years without a woman's influence. Once Betty died…"

"Betty must be Mandy's mother?"

"Right. To everyone's surprise, Fred up and married again. Betty was the sweetest thing, and just the right kind of woman for someone like Fred. She was sweet and kindhearted and as good as the day is long. Mandy arrived a year later.

"Fred and Betty were happy. I don't think there was a dry eye in town when she died. Not long afterward Fred died, too. The doctors may have a complicated name for what killed him, but I'll tell you right now, Fred Palmer died of a broken heart."

"How sad." The humor drained from Taylor. No one could be unaffected by that story.

"Russ reminds me of his father when Fred was around that age. What Russ needs is a wife—someone like Betty who'll cater to his whims and pamper him and let him have his way."

That left her out. The thought startled her. She would no more consider marrying a rancher than she'd entertain the idea of riding a horse. As far as she was concerned, cows smelled, hay made her sneeze and the sight of a horse sent her scurrying in the opposite direction.

"I'm sure if Russ said anything offensive…"

"He didn't," Taylor was quick to assure the other woman. But not because he didn't want to, judging by the look in his eyes. If ever there was a man who longed to put her in her place, it was this formidable rancher. Unfortunately, or fortunately as the case might be, it would take a lot more than one cowpoke to do it.

Mary Beth and Taylor said goodbye at the corner, and Taylor went to the grocery store. With a limited budget and a distinct lack of imagination when it came to cooking, she headed for the frozen food section.

Without much enthusiasm she tossed a frozen entrée into her grocery cart. The local supermarket didn't carry a large selection, and it was either the salisbury steak or the country fried chicken.

"Was that really necessary?" a gruff male voice asked from behind her.

"The country fried chicken?" she asked, turning to face the very man she and Mary Beth had been discussing.

"I'm not talking about your pathetic choice for dinner. I'm referring to my sister. She's going through a rebellious stage, and I don't appreciate your taking her side on an issue. We can settle our differences without any help from you."

Taylor was about to argue when she noticed the teenager coming down the aisle.

"Oh, hi," Mandy greeted her, brightening. She hurried to Taylor and her brother. "You're not eating that for dinner, are you?" the girl asked, eyeing the frozen meal in Taylor's cart. A horrified look spread across her face.

"It seemed the least amount of trouble," Taylor admitted. She'd spent a full day unpacking and cleaning, and even a frozen dinner was more appealing than being

forced to cook for herself. As far as she could see, there
wasn't a single fast-food place in town. The nearest
McDonald's was a hundred miles from Cougar Point.

"I've got a big pot of stew simmering at home,"
Mandy said eagerly. "Why don't you come over and
have dinner with Russ and me? We'd love to have you,
wouldn't we, Russ?"

Her brother's hesitation was just long enough to con-
vey his message.

"It's the neighborly thing to do," Mandy prompted.

"You're welcome to come, if you want," Russ said
finally, and Taylor had the impression it took a great
deal of resolve to echo his sister's invitation.

There wasn't any question that Taylor should refuse.
But something perverse in her, something obstinate and
a bit foolish, wouldn't allow her to do so. Perhaps it was
because she recognized the same mulish streak in him
that she knew so well in her father. Whatever the reason, Taylor decided she was going to enjoy this dinner.
"Why, thank you. I'd be honored."

"Great." Mandy beamed. "We live about ten miles
east of town."

"East?" Taylor repeated, turning in a full circle in
an effort to orient herself. She wasn't sure which way
was east, at least not from where she was standing in
the grocery store.

"Take the main road and go left at the stand of sycamore trees," Mandy continued. "That's just past Cole
Creek, only don't look for any water because it's dried
out at this time of year."

Further directions only served to confuse Taylor. She
wasn't even all that confident she could tell a sycamore
from an oak. And how was she supposed to identify a

dried-out creek bed? Usually Taylor was given directions that said she should go to the third stoplight and take a left at the Wal-Mart.

"Why don't you ride along with us?" Mandy suggested next, apparently sensing Taylor's confusion. "Russ can drive you back into town later."

"It'll probably work better if I follow you," Taylor said. "My car's at the house, but it would only take a minute for me to swing by and get it."

"It wouldn't be any trouble. Russ has to come back, anyway. Besides, I wouldn't want you to get lost once it turns dark."

Taylor noted that Russ didn't echo his sister's suggestion. The temptation was too great to ignore, and once more Taylor found herself agreeing to Mandy's plan.

"My truck's parked outside," Russ grumbled. He didn't seem very pleased by this turn of events. But then he hadn't looked all that thrilled about anything from the moment they'd met.

Russ's truck was a twenty-year-old dented Ford that most folks would have hauled to the scrap heap a year earlier. The bed was filled with supplies. Grain sacks were stacked in one corner, fertilizer in another.

The front fender was badly bent and had begun to rust. The license plate was missing, and Russ had to completely remove the passenger door for the two women to climb inside. Once they were seated he replaced the door and latched it shut.

Taylor squirmed around in the bench seat, searching for the seat belt.

"There aren't any," Russ explained as he slipped in next to her and started the engine.

The seat was cramped, and Taylor had to dig her el-

bows into her ribs. Her shoulders were touching his on
the left side, his younger sister's on the right. It had been
a long time since Taylor had sat this close to a man. At
first she tried to keep her thigh from grazing his, but it
was nearly impossible. So their thighs touched. Big deal.

Only it soon got to be.

There must've been something in all that fresh country air that was adversely affecting her brain cells.
Without much difficulty, Taylor could actually imagine herself smitten with this man. *Smitten?* Oh dear,
her mind was doing it again, tormenting her with this
old-fashioned country jargon....

Suddenly they turned off the main road and headed
down a lengthy rut-filled section that tossed her up and
then down. Every time they hit a dip, Taylor would
bounce off the seat as if it were greased. It was all she
could do not to land on top of Russ or Mandy. They
were obviously accustomed to this thrashing about, and
each managed to stay neatly in place. Taylor, on the
other hand, was all over the inside of the cab.

Whenever the truck hit an uneven patch, some part
of Taylor's anatomy came into intimate contact with
Russ's. Their thighs stroked each other. Their shoulders collided and their waists jostled together. Again
and again their bodies were slammed against each other.

Taylor couldn't help noticing how firm and muscular Russ felt. She didn't want to acknowledge it. Nor
did she want to experience the heat of his body and the
warm muskiness of his skin. He felt solid. Strong. Vir-
ile. A host of sensations, long dormant, sprang to life
inside her.

Not once had Russ Palmer purposely touched her,

and yet Taylor felt as though his hands had caressed her everywhere.

"Would you mind slowing down?" she cried. She hated having to ask.

"Why?" Russ asked, his voice filled with amusement.

"Russ," Mandy snapped, "Taylor's not used to this."

Amused or not, Russ slowed the vehicle, and Taylor went weak with relief. She could feel a headache coming on, but she wasn't sure it had anything to do with the skipping, hopping and jumping she'd been subjected to for the past ten minutes.

They arrived at the ranch house a couple of minutes later, at just about dusk. The first thing Taylor noticed was the huge red barn. It was the largest she'd ever seen, but that wasn't saying much. She knew next to nothing about barns, although this one seemed enormous. The house was sizable, as well. Four gables stood out against the roof of the huge white structure, and the windows were framed by bright red shutters.

Taylor climbed out of the truck on the driver's side after Russ, not wanting to be trapped inside while he walked around to remove the passenger door. It took her a minute to steady her legs.

Mandy bolted ahead of them. She raced up the back steps that led into the kitchen, holding open the door for Taylor. "The stew's in the Crock-Pot."

Taylor saw that Russ had gone in the opposite direction, toward the barn, probably to see about unloading the contents of the truck bed. Her gaze followed him, and she wondered briefly if the close confines of the truck had affected him the same way they had her.

Probably not. He looked a lot more in control of himself than Taylor felt.

A thin sheen of perspiration moistened her upper lip. What the hell was the matter with her? Groaning silently, Taylor closed her eyes. She knew precisely what was wrong, and she didn't like it one bit.

Chapter 2

Russ remained silent for most of the meal. He didn't like this schoolteacher. But he didn't exactly dislike her, either. She was as pretty as Harry had claimed, and her hair was thick and rich. A couple of times he'd been tempted to lift a strand and let it slip through his fingers, but that would've been impossible. And what she did to a pair of jeans ought to be illegal. On the ride to the ranch he'd purposely driven over every pothole he could just because he liked the way her body had moved against his.

"You're from Seattle?" Russ asked. He'd been trying to ignore her for most of the meal, not because he wasn't interested in learning what he could about her, but because—dammit—he was as taken with her as Harry had been.

Taylor nodded, smiling. "I was born and raised in the shadow of the Space Needle."

"Ever had snow there?"

"Some."

The thought of her smooth pale skin exposed to the elements knotted his stomach.

"I understand winters are harsher here than in western Washington," she said stiffly. "I came prepared."

"I doubt that you have a clue how severe winters can get in these parts." Russ had seen too many cases of frostbite to have any illusions.

It was clear that Taylor resented the way he was talking to her. He didn't mean to imply that she was stupid, only unaware, and he didn't want her learning harsh lessons because no one had warned her.

One quick look told him he'd raised Taylor's hackles. She seemed to need several minutes to compose her response, then she set her fork next to her plate, placed her elbows on the table and joined her hands. Staring directly at him, she smiled with deceptive warmth and said, "You needn't worry, Mr. Palmer. I'm perfectly capable of taking care of myself. I've been doing so for many years. I may be a city girl, but let me assure you, I'm both intelligent and resourceful."

"Do you know what happens to skin when it's exposed to temperatures below thirty degrees? How about the symptoms for hypothermia? Would you be able to recognize them in yourself or others?"

"Mr. Palmer, please."

"Russ." Mandy's outraged eyes shot from him to Taylor and then back again. "You're being rude to our guest."

Russ mumbled under his breath and resumed eating. Maybe he was overreacting. Perhaps his motives weren't so lily-white. Perhaps he was more angry with her than concerned about her welfare. She'd certainly done enough to upset him in the past few hours. Taking Mandy's side on that makeup issue had bothered him, but that hardly mattered after the way she'd pressed herself against him during the ride from town. He couldn't get the feel of her out of his mind. Her skin was soft and she smelled like wildflowers. That thought led to another. If she smelled so good, he couldn't help wondering how she'd taste. Like honey, he decided, fresh from the comb, thick and sweet. The knot in his stomach tightened. If he didn't curb his mind soon, he'd end up kissing her before the night was through.

"You're an excellent cook," Taylor said to Mandy in a blatant effort to lighten the strained atmosphere.

Mandy beamed at the compliment. "I try. Rosa and her husband retired last year, and I talked Russ into letting me do the cooking, and it's worked out pretty well, hasn't it, Russ?"

He nodded. "There've been a few nights best forgotten, but for the most part you've done an excellent job."

"She took over all the cooking at age thirteen?" Taylor asked, obviously astonished, although Russ had trouble figuring out why. He'd long suspected that city kids didn't carry anywhere near the responsibility country kids did.

Mandy eyed Russ. He knew that look well by now, and it meant trouble. He bit his tongue as she opened her mouth to speak.

"It seems to me that any girl who can rustle up a decent meal every night is old enough to buy her own clothes without her older brother tagging along, don't you think?"

The way things were going, Mandy was angling to be sent to her room without finishing dinner. "That's none of Taylor's concern," he said tightly, daring their guest to challenge his authority with his younger sister.

"You agree with me, don't you, Taylor?" Mandy pressed.

"Uh…" Taylor hedged, looking uncomfortable. "I have a limit of answering only one leading question per day," she explained, reaching for another piece of bread. "I don't think it's a good idea to get on Russ's bad side twice in only a few hours. I might end up walking back to town."

"Russ would never do that."

Want to bet? Russ mused. Okay, so he wouldn't make her walk, but he'd sure as hell hit every pothole he could. The problem there was that he'd be the one likely to suffer most.

"What do you honestly think?" Mandy repeated.

"*I* think you should eat your dinner and leave Taylor out of this," Russ ordered harshly. The girl had turned willfulness into an art form.

"I… Your brother's right, Mandy," Taylor said, lowering her gaze to the steaming bowl of rich stew. "This is something the two of you should settle between yourselves."

"Russ and I'll settle it all right," Mandy responded defiantly, "but he won't like the outcome."

Russ didn't take the bait. "More stew, Taylor?"

"Ah…no, thanks. My bowl's nearly full."

"When did you start buying your own clothes?" Mandy asked, clearly unwilling to drop the issue.

Russ stared at Taylor, daring her to question his authority a second time. She glanced nervously away. "As I recall, I had the same problem with my father at this age. I got around him by taking a sewing class and making my clothes."

"When was this?"

"Oh, about the eighth grade or so. To this day I enjoy sewing most of my own things. It's economical, too."

"The eighth grade?" Mandy cast Russ a triumphant look. "You were basically choosing and sewing your own clothes when you were only thirteen, then."

"It's not a good idea for me to get involved in a matter that's between you and your brother, Mandy. I did earlier and I don't think it was the right thing to do."

Russ felt a little better knowing that.

Mandy's shoulders sagged, and Russ was pleased to note that she was gracious enough to accept Taylor's word. Finally.

"I didn't mean to cause such a scene in the variety store," Mandy murmured apologetically. "All I wanted was Russ's okay to buy some lip gloss."

Russ set his napkin on the table. "I wouldn't mind letting you wear some lip gloss, but you insist on overdoing it. I walked past your bedroom the other night and I swear your lips were glowing in the dark."

Mandy glared at him, her eyes filled with indignation. What had he said *now*? Before he could ask her what was so all-fired insulting, she threw her fork and napkin onto the table and promptly rushed out of the room.

"Amanda Palmer, get back here this minute," he shouted in the same steely tone that sent his men scurrying to obey. When Mandy didn't immediately comply, he stormed to his feet, ready to follow her.

"Russ," Taylor said softly, stopping him. He turned toward her, wanting to blame her for this latest display of pique.

Taylor sighed and pushed aside her bowl. "Give her a few minutes. She'll be back once she's composed herself."

"What did I say?" he demanded, sitting back down, genuinely perplexed.

Taylor hesitated, then said, "It might've had something to do with the joke about her lips glowing in the dark."

"It's true. I told her she couldn't wear any of that war paint you women are so fond of, so she defied me and started putting it on before she went to bed."

"She's exercising her rights as a person."

"By spurning my rules? I swear that girl drives me to the edge of insanity. What's gotten into her the past couple of years? She used to be an all-right kid. Now it seems I can't say a word without setting her off."

"She's a teenager."

"What's that supposed to mean?" he barked.

"Don't you remember what you felt like at fourteen? How important it was to dress and act like everyone around you?"

"No," Russ stated flatly. His features tensed. He didn't want to discuss his sister with Taylor. She didn't know any more about raising kids than he did. The problem with Mandy was that she was getting too big for her britches.

Standing, Taylor reached for her bowl and glass. "I'll clear the table."

"Leave it for Mandy," Russ insisted.

Taylor ignored him, which was getting to be a habit with her. Russ had yet to understand what it was about women that made them constantly want to challenge him—especially in his own home.

"Why?" Taylor demanded, startling him out of his reverie. Even more astonishing was the fact that she looked angry.

"Why what?"

"Why would you want to leave the dishes for Mandy?"

"Because that's woman's work," he explained.

"You're possibly the worst male chauvinist I've ever encountered," she said, carrying what remained of the plates to the sink. "In my opinion, those who cook shouldn't have to wash dishes."

"It'll be a cold day in hell before you'll ever see me washing dishes, lady." He found the thought comical. He hadn't taken kindly to being called a chauvinist, but he refused to argue with her. They were having enough trouble being civil to each other without further provocation from him.

Taylor hurried to the sink, filling it with hot water and squirting in soap. "Since the task apparently belongs to a woman, I'll do the dishes."

"No guest of mine is washing dirty dishes."

"Fine then," she said, motioning toward the sink. "Everything's ready for you."

Although he was struggling against it, Russ was thoroughly irritated. He was standing directly in front of her. Not more than two inches separated them.

Taylor stared up at him and must have recognized his mood, because she swallowed hard. It wasn't consternation he saw in her eyes, but something that stabbed him as sharply as a pitchfork. Longing and need. The same emotions he'd been battling from the moment he'd laid eyes on her.

He saw something else. She didn't want to experience it any more than Russ wanted to feel the things he'd been feeling for her. When they'd sat next to each other in the truck, he'd never been more profoundly aware of a woman in his life. The air had been alive with tension—a tension that seemed to throb between them all evening long.

Russ felt it.

Taylor felt it.

Both seemed determined to ignore it.

Bracing her hands on the edge of the sink, she anxiously moistened her lips. Russ's eyes fell to her mouth. Her eyes reluctantly met his, and the look they exchanged was as powerful as a caress.

"I…I should be going," she whispered.

"You called me a chauvinist."

"I…apologize." Her pride was obviously crumbling at her feet. The fight had gone out of her.

He pulled his gaze back to her mouth, experiencing a small sense of triumph at the power of his will. "Where'd you ever get a name like Taylor?"

"It was my mother's…maiden name."

Once more her voice came out sounding whispery and soft. Too soft. Too whispery for comfort.

"My mother's from Atlanta, and it was an old Southern tradition to give the first daughter her mother's maiden name." By the time she finished, her voice was a mere thread of sound.

Neither of them spoke for the longest moment of

Russ's life. Taking a deep, shaky breath, he was about to suggest he drive her home. Instead, Russ found himself leaning toward her.

"I'm sorry I ran out of the kitchen like that," Mandy announced, coming back into the room.

Russ frowned at his younger sister, irritated. The girl couldn't have chosen a worse time to make her entrance. For her part, Taylor appeared ready to leap across the room and hug Mandy for interrupting them.

"I was about to take Taylor back to town," Russ announced gruffly.

"Do you have to leave so soon?" Mandy asked. "It's barely even dark."

"It'll get dark anytime, and I still have a lot to do before school starts. Thank you so much for having me—both of you. You're a wonderful cook… I really appreciate this."

"You'll come again, won't you?" Mandy asked.

"If you'd like."

"Oh, we would, wouldn't we, Russ?"

He made a response that could have been taken either way.

Mandy walked to the door and down the porch steps with them. Her arms hugged her waist against the evening chill. "You're driving the Lincoln, aren't you?"

Russ gave another noncommittal reply. His truck was in the shop, having the transmission worked on, and he'd been forced to take the older one into town that morning. Mandy's implication that he'd bring Taylor home in that dilapidated thing was an insult. The look he gave her suggested as much.

"I was just asking," she said with an innocent smile. Taylor and Mandy chatted while Russ went around to the garage and pulled out the luxury sedan. The two women hugged goodbye, and Taylor got inside the car and ran her fingertips over the leather upholstery before snapping the seat belt into place.

"You ready?" he asked more brusquely than he intended.

"Yes."

They drove a few minutes in uncomfortable silence. "How large a spread do you have here?" she eventually asked.

"A thousand acres and about that many head of cattle."

"A thousand acres," Taylor echoed.

The awe and surprise in her voice filled him with pride. He could have gone on to tell her that the Lazy P was anything but lazy. His ranch was among the largest in the southern half of the state. He could also mention that he operated one of the most progressive ranches in the entire country, but he didn't want to sound as if he was bragging.

They chatted amicably about nothing important until they got to town. Russ turned off the side street to old man Halloran's house without even having to ask where Taylor was living. If she was surprised he knew, she didn't say.

When he pulled in to her driveway, he cut the engine and rested his arm over the back of her seat. Part of him wanted her to invite him inside for coffee, but it wasn't coffee that interested him. Another part of him demanded he stay away from this schoolteacher.

"Thank you again," she said softly, staring down at her purse, which she held tightly in her lap.

"No problem."

She raised her eyes to his, and despite all his good intentions, Russ's hungry gaze fixed on her lips. He became aware that he was going to kiss her about the same time he realized he'd die if he didn't. He reached for her, half expecting her to protest. Instead she whimpered and wrapped her arms around him, offering him her mouth. The sense of triumph and jubilation that Russ experienced was stronger than any aphrodisiac. He wrapped her in his arms and dragged her against him, savoring the pure womanly feel of her.

His kiss was wild. His callused hands framed the smooth skin of her face as he slanted his mouth over hers. He kissed her again and again and again.

Her throaty plea reluctantly brought him back to reason. For an instant Russ worried that he'd frightened her, until he heard his name fall from her lips in a low, frantic whisper. It was then that he knew she'd enjoyed their kisses as much as he had.

"Do you want me to stop?" he asked, his voice a husky murmur. He spread damp kisses down her neck and up her chin until he reached her mouth. Drawing her lower lip between his teeth, he sucked gently.

"Please…stop," she pleaded, yet her hands grasped his hair, holding him against her.

But then Taylor lowered her hands to his shoulders and pulled herself away, leaving only an inch or so between them. Her shoulders heaved.

"I can't believe that happened," she whispered.

"Do you want an apology?"

"No," she answered starkly. Then, after a moment, she added, "I wanted it as much as you did. I can't imagine why. We're about as opposite as any two people can get."

"Maybe so, but I think we just discovered one way we're compatible, and it beats the heck out of everything else."

"Oh, please, don't even say that," she moaned, and pushed him away. She leaned against the back of the seat and ran a hand down her face as if to wipe away all evidence of their kissing. "This was a fluke. I think it might be best to pretend it never happened."

Russ went still, his thoughts muddled and unclear. What she'd said was true. He had no business being attracted to her. No business kissing her. She was from the city and didn't understand the complexities of his life. Not only that, she was the new schoolteacher, and not a woman the community would approve of him dallying with.

That they *were* attracted to each other was a given. Why seemed to be a question neither of them could answer. One thing Russ knew: Taylor was right. It was best to forget this ever happened.

For the next week Taylor did an admirable job of pushing Russ Palmer from her mind. It helped somewhat that she didn't have any contact with either member of the Palmer family.

Taylor didn't question what had come over her or why she'd allowed Russ to kiss her like that. Instead she'd resolutely ignored the memory of their kiss, attributing it to a bad case of repressed hormones. That was the only thing it could've been, and analyzing it would accomplish nothing.

Now that school had started, Taylor threw herself into her work with gusto, more convinced than ever that she was born to be a teacher. She was an immediate hit with her third- and fourth-grade students.

On Wednesday afternoon at about four, an hour after her class had been dismissed, Taylor was sitting at her desk, cutting out letters for her bulletin board, when there was a polite knock at her door. Suspecting it was one of her students, she glanced up to discover Mandy standing there, her books pressed against her.

"Mandy, hello," Taylor said, genuinely pleased to see the girl. "Take a seat." She waved the scissors at the chair next to her desk.

"I'm not bothering you, am I? Russ said I wasn't to visit you after school if you were busy. He thinks I'll be a pest."

"You can come and visit me anytime you want," Taylor said, as she continued to cut out blunt letters from the bright sheets of colored paper.

Plopping down on the chair, Mandy crossed her legs and smiled cheerfully. "Notice anything different about me?"

Taylor nodded. "Isn't that war paint you're wearing? And that sweater looks new. Very nice—that light green suits you."

Russ's sister giggled shyly. "I came to thank you. I don't know what you said to my brother, but it worked. The next morning he said he'd thought about it overnight and decided that if I was old enough to cook dinner and wear a little makeup, then I was mature enough to choose my own clothes without him tagging along."

Taylor wasn't convinced that Russ's change of heart had anything to do with her, but nevertheless, she was pleased. "That's great."

"I heard from Cassie Jackson that you're a really good teacher."

Cassie was a fourth-grader in Taylor's class. She smiled at the compliment.

"I hear half the boys in your class are in love with you already," Mandy told her. "I told Russ that, and I think he's a little jealous because he frowned and grabbed the paper and read it for ten minutes before he noticed it was one from last week."

The last person Taylor wanted to discuss was Russ Palmer. "I don't suppose you'd like to help me cut out letters, would you?" she asked, more to change the subject than because she needed any assistance.

"Sure, I'd love to." Within a half hour she and Mandy had assembled a bright brown, yellow and orange autumn leaf bulletin board festooned with the names of every child in the class.

Once they'd finished, Taylor stepped back, threw her arm around her young friend's shoulders and nodded happily. "We do good work."

Mandy grinned. "We do, don't we?"

Noting the time, Taylor felt guilty for having taken up so much of the girl's afternoon. "It's almost five. Do you need me to give you a ride home?"

"That's all right. Russ said he'd pick me up. He's coming into town for grain and I'm supposed to meet him at Burn's Feed Store. It's only a block from here."

Mandy left soon afterward. Taylor gathered up the assignments she needed to grade and her purse and headed toward the school parking lot. Her blue Cabriolet was there all by itself. She was halfway to the car when a loud pickup barreled into the lot behind her. From the sick sounds the truck was making, Taylor knew it had to belong to Russ.

He rolled to a stop, his elbow draped over the side window. "Have you seen Mandy?"

She nodded, her eyes avoiding his. "You just missed her. She's walking over to the feed store."

"Thanks." His gears ground as he switched them, and he looked over his shoulder, about to back out, when he paused. "Is that your car?"

"Yes." Normally Taylor walked to and from school. It was less than a mile and she liked the exercise, but it had been raining that morning, so she'd brought her car.

"Did you know your back tire's flat?"

Taylor's eyes flew to her Cabriolet, and sure enough the rear tire on the driver's side was completely flat. "Oh, great," she moaned. She was tired and hungry and in no mood to deal with this problem.

"I'll change it for you," Russ volunteered, immediately vaulting from his truck.

It was kind of him, and Taylor was about to tell him so when he ruined it.

"You independent women," he said with a chuckle. "You claim you can take care of yourselves and you're too damn proud to think you need a man. But every now and then we have our uses. Now admit it, Taylor. You couldn't possibly handle this without me." He was walking toward her trunk, as haughty as could be.

"Hold it!" Taylor raised one hand. "I don't need you to change my tire. I can take care of this myself."

Russ gave her a patronizing look and then chose to antagonize her even more. This time he laughed. "Now that's something I'd like to see." He leaned against her fender and crossed his arms over his broad chest. "Feel free," he said, gesturing toward the flat.

"Don't look so smug, Palmer. I said I could take care of it myself and I meant it."

"You wouldn't know one end of the jack from the other."

Taylor wasn't going to argue with him about that. "Would you like to make a small wager on my ability to deal with this?"

Russ snickered, looking more pompous every minute. "It would be like taking candy from a baby. The problem with you is that you're too stubborn to admit when a man's right."

"I say I can deal with a flat tire any day of the week."

"And I say you can't. You haven't got enough strength to turn the tire iron. Fact is, lady, you couldn't get to first base without a man here to help you."

"Oh, come off it. It's about time you men understood that women aren't the weaker sex."

"Sure," Russ said, without disguising his amusement.

"All right," Taylor said slowly. She deliberately walked past him, then turned to give him a sultry smile. She narrowed her eyes. "Perhaps you don't care to place a small wager on my ability. Having to admit you're wrong would probably be more than a guy like you could take."

His dark eyes flared briefly. "I didn't want to do this, but unfortunately you've asked for it. What shall we bet?"

Now that he'd agreed, Taylor wasn't sure. "If I win…"

"I'd be willing to do something I consider women's work?" he suggested.

"Such as?"

Russ took a moment to think it over. "I'll cook dinner for you next Saturday night."

"Who'll do the dishes?"

Russ hesitated. "I will. You thought I'd have trouble going along with that, didn't you? But I don't have a thing to worry about."

"Dream on, Palmer. If I were you, I'd be sweating."

He snickered, seeming to derive a good deal of pleasure from their conversation. "Now let's figure out what you'll owe me when you realize how sadly mistaken you are."

"All right," she said, "I'd be willing to do something you consider completely masculine."

"I'd rather have you grill me a steak."

"No way. That wouldn't be a fair exchange. How about if I...do whatever you do around the ranch for a day?" Taylor felt perfectly safe making the proposal, just as safe as he'd felt offering to make her dinner.

"That wouldn't work."

"I'd be willing to try."

Russ shrugged. "If you insist."

"I do," Taylor said.

Still leaning smugly against the side of her car, Russ pointed at the trunk. "All right, Ms. Goodwrench, go to it."

Taylor opened her front door, placed her papers and purse inside and got out the key to her trunk.

"You might want to roll up your sleeves," Russ suggested. "It'd be a shame to ruin that pretty blouse with a grease stain. It's silk, isn't it?"

Taylor glared at him defiantly.

Russ chuckled and raised both arms. "Sorry. I won't say any more."

Opening the trunk, Taylor systematically searched through it until she found what she was looking for.

"A tire iron is about this size," he said, holding his hands a couple of feet apart, mocking her.

Carrying the spray can, Taylor walked around to the flat tire and squatted down in front of it. "I like my steak medium rare and barbecued over a hot charcoal grill. My baked potato should have sour cream and chives and the broccoli should be fresh with a touch of hollandaise sauce drizzled over the top." Having given him those instructions, she proceeded to fill her deflated tire with the spray can.

"What's that?" Russ asked, his hands set challengingly on his hips.

"You did say this Saturday, didn't you?" she taunted.

He scowled when she handed over the spray can for him to examine. "Fix-it Flat Tire?" he said, reading the label.

"That's exactly what it is," Taylor informed him primly. "Whatever this marvelous invention is, it fills up the tire enough so I can drive it to a service station and have the attendant deal with it."

"Now wait a minute," Russ muttered. "That's cheating."

"I never said I'd *change* the tire," Taylor reminded him. "I told you I could deal with the situation myself. And I have."

"But it's a man who'll be changing the tire."

"Could be a woman. In Seattle some women work for service stations."

"In Seattle, maybe, but not in Cougar Point."

"Come on, Russ, admit it. I outsmarted you."

He glared at her, and despite his irritation, or perhaps because of it, Taylor laughed. She got inside her car, started the engine and drove out of the parking lot. Then she circled back, returning to Russ who was standing beside his pickup.

"What do you want now?" he demanded.

"I just came to tell you I like blue cheese dressing on my salad." With that she zipped out of the lot. She was still smiling when she happened to glance in her rearview mirror in time to see Russ slam his black Stetson onto the asphalt.

Chapter 3

No doubt psychologists had a term for the attraction Taylor felt for this rancher, she decided early Saturday evening. Why else would a woman, who was determined to avoid a certain man, go out of her way to goad him into a wager she was sure to win? Taylor couldn't fathom it herself. Maybe it was some perverse method of inflicting self-punishment. Perhaps her disastrous relationship with Mark had lowered her to this level. Taylor didn't know anymore.

She'd prefer to place all the blame on Russ. If he hadn't made her so furious with his nonsense about a woman needing a man, she probably would've been able to stand aside and smile sweetly while he changed her tire. But he'd had to ruin everything.

During dinner at least, Mandy would be there to act as a buffer.

* * *

"What do you mean you're going over to Chris's?" Russ asked his sister.

"I told you about it Thursday, remember?"

Russ frowned. Hell, no, he didn't remember. He needed Mandy to help him with this stupid dinner wager he'd made with Taylor. The woman had tricked him. In his view, she should be cooking, not the other way around. He would've been happy to take her to dinner in town and be done with it, but he knew better than to even suggest that. She'd insisted he make dinner himself.

"What's so important at Chris's that you have to do it now?"

"We're practicing. Drill team tryouts are next week, and I've got to make it. I've just got to."

She made it sound like a matter of life or death. "Couldn't the two of you practice some other time?"

"No," Mandy said. "I want to see Taylor, but I can't. Not tonight."

Grumbling under his breath, Russ opened the refrigerator and stared inside, wondering where the hell he should start. Make the salad first? Cook the broccoli? Earlier in the day he'd bought everything he was going to need, including a packet of hollandaise sauce mix.

"I'm sorry, Russ," Mandy said. "I'd offer to help…"

His spirits lifted. "You will? Great. Just don't let Taylor know. If she found out, she'd have me strung from the highest tree for allowing another woman to slice lettuce for me."

"I *can't* help you, Russ. That would be cheating."

"All I want you to do is give me a few pointers."

"It wouldn't be right." She lowered her voice to a

whisper. "Don't slice the lettuce, and I shouldn't even be telling you that."

"What do you do with salad if you don't chop it?" Russ asked wearily. He followed Mandy into the living room where she collected her homemade pom-poms. "What am I supposed to do with the lettuce?"

"I can't answer that," she said, looking apologetic.

"You can't tell me how to make a salad?" he roared. His temper was wearing precariously thin. "Why not?"

"It'd be unfair. You're supposed to prepare this meal entirely on your own. If I gave you any help, you'd be breaking your agreement with Taylor." A car horn blared from the backyard, and Mandy grabbed her jacket. "That's Chris's mom now. I've got to go. See you later, and good luck with dinner."

She was out the door before Russ could protest.

Russ wandered around the kitchen for the next five minutes, debating what to do first. Grilling the steaks wouldn't be a problem. Anyone with half a brain knew how to cook a decent T-bone. The baked potato wasn't a concern, either. It was everything else. He took the head of lettuce and a bunch of other vegetables from the refrigerator and set them on the counter. Without giving it much thought, he reached for an apron and tied it around his waist. God help him if any of the ranch hands walked in now.

Taylor was impressed with the effort Russ had made when she arrived at the Lazy P. He opened the door for her and jerked the apron from his waist.

"I hope you're happy," he muttered, looking anything but.

"I am. Thanks for asking," she said, but inwardly

she was struggling not to laugh. This entire scene was almost too good to be true. Next to her own father, Russ was the biggest chauvinist she'd ever met. The sight of him working in a kitchen, wearing an apron, was priceless.

"Something smells delicious," she said.

"I'll tell you it isn't the hollandaise sauce. That stuff tastes like sh—" He stopped himself just in time. "You can figure it out."

"I can," she said. Smiling, she strolled across the kitchen and set a bottle of wine on the counter. "A small token of my appreciation."

She couldn't hear his reply as he furiously whipped the sauce simmering on the front burner. "Maybe it'll taste better once it's boiled," Russ said, concentrating on the task at hand.

The table was set. Well, sort of. The silverware was piled in the center between the two place settings. The water glasses were filled.

"The broccoli's done." Russ turned off the burner. "It looks all right from what I can tell." He drained the water and sprinkled a dash of salt and pepper over the contents of the pan.

"I'll open the wine, if you like."

"Sure," Russ said absently. He opened the oven door, and Taylor felt the blast of heat clear from the other side of the room.

"What's in there?"

"The baked potatoes," he said, slamming the door. "How long does it take to cook these things, anyway? They've been in there fifteen minutes and they're still hard as rocks."

"Normally they bake in about an hour."

"An hour?" he echoed. "Dammit, the sauce!" he cried. Grabbing a dish towel, he yanked the saucepan from the burner. He stirred frantically. "I hope it didn't burn."

"I'm sure it'll be just fine. Where's Mandy?"

"Gone," he grumbled. He stuck his finger in the sauce and licked it, then nodded, apparently surprised. "She's over at Chris's practicing for drill team. And before you ask, she didn't help me any."

"Mandy's not here?" Taylor said. A sense of uneasiness gripped her hard. After what had happened the first time she was alone with Russ, she had reason to be apprehensive.

She was overreacting, she told herself. It wasn't as if she was going to fall spontaneously into Russ's arms simply because his sister wasn't there to act as chaperone. They were both mature adults, and furthermore, they'd agreed to forget the night they'd kissed. The whole thing was as much of an embarrassment to Russ as it was to her. *She* certainly wasn't going to bring it up.

"Don't think I had anything to do with Mandy being gone, either."

"I didn't," she said with a shrug of indifference, implying that it hadn't even crossed her mind—which was true, at least before Russ mentioned it.

He was scowling as if he expected her to argue with him.

"Can I do anything to help?" she asked in an effort to subdue her nervousness.

"No, thanks. This meal is completely under control," he boasted. "I'm a man of my word, and when I said I was going to cook you the best steak you've ever eaten, I meant it."

"I'm looking forward to it." Wordlessly she opened a series of drawers until she located the corkscrew and proceeded to agilely remove the cork from the wine.

"I know it's traditional to serve red wine with beef, but I prefer white. This is an excellent chardonnay."

"Whatever you brought is fine," he mumbled as he swung open the refrigerator and took out a huge green salad.

It looked as if there was enough lettuce to feed the entire town, but Taylor refused to antagonize him by commenting on the fact.

"I want you to know I didn't slice the lettuce," he said proudly as he set the wooden bowl in the center of the table, shoving aside the silverware.

"Oh, good," Taylor responded, hoping she sounded appropriately impressed. The second cupboard she inspected contained crystal wineglasses. Standing on tiptoe, she brought down two. They were both thick with dust, so she washed and rinsed them before pouring the wine.

"I wanted to bring dessert, but there isn't a deli in Cougar Point," she said conversationally as she handed Russ his wineglass.

He stepped away from the stove to accept the wine. Scowling, he asked, "You were going to buy dessert at a deli?"

"It's the best place I know to get New York cheesecake."

Russ muttered something she didn't quite catch before returning to the stove. He turned down the burners and took a sip of his wine. "Since it's going to take the potatoes a little longer than I realized, we might as well sit down."

"Okay," Taylor agreed readily, following him into the living room. The furniture consisted of large, bulky pieces that looked as if they'd been lifted from the set of an old western series on television. *Bonanza,* maybe.

A row of silver-framed photographs lined the fireplace and, interested, Taylor walked over to examine them. A picture of Russ, probably from his high school graduation, caught her attention immediately. He'd been a handsome young man. Boyishly good-looking, but she could easily tell that his appeal was potent enough to cause many a young woman more than one sleepless night.

"That's my dad and Betty," he said, pointing out the second large portrait. "It was taken shortly after they were married." The resemblance between father and son was striking. They possessed the same brooding, dark eyes, and their full mouths were identical. She looked at Russ's high school picture again and found herself zeroing in on his youthful features. Even back then, there'd been a wildness about him that challenged a woman. No man had provoked, defied or taunted her the way Russ had, and she barely knew him. By all rights she should stay as far away from him as possible, yet here she was in his home, studying his picture and theorizing about his secrets.

She turned away from the fireplace and sat in an overstuffed chair. "You were telling me before that you've got a thousand cattle," Taylor said, making conversation while her fingers moved nervously against the padded arm of the chair.

"I've sold half the herd. I'm wintering five hundred head, but by summer the numbers will be much higher."

"I see." She didn't really understand what he meant

but didn't know enough to ask intelligent questions. Thankfully Russ seemed to grasp her dilemma and explained of his own accord.

"The men are rounding up the cattle now. We keep them in a feed ground."

"A feed ground?"

"It's a fenced pasture with no irrigation ditches."

"Why? I mean, don't they need water?"

"Of course, but the heavy snows start in December, sometimes earlier. When the ground's covered, the cattle can't see the ditches, and if a steer falls into one, he often can't get out, and I've lost a valuable animal."

"If the snow's that high, how do you get the feed to them?"

"Sometimes by sleigh."

Taylor smiled at the thought of riding through a snow-covered field. She could almost hear the bells jingling and Christmas music playing while she snuggled under a warm blanket, holding tight to Russ.

Shaking her head to dispel the romantic fantasy, Taylor swallowed, furious with the path her daydreams had taken. She drank some of her wine, hoping to set her thoughts in order before they became so confused that she lost all reason. "That sounds like fun."

"It's demanding physical labor," Russ told her gruffly.

His tone surprised her, and she raised her eyes to meet his.

He might be saying one thing, but Taylor would bet her first paycheck that he was battling the same fiery attraction she'd struggled with from the moment he'd first kissed her. He continued to stare at her in that restless, penetrating way that unnerved her.

He seemed impatient to escape from her, and unexpectedly vaulted to his feet. "I'd better check on dinner."

Once he was out of the room, Taylor closed her eyes and sagged against the back of the cushion. This evening had seemed safe enough until she'd learned Mandy was gone. The air seemed to crackle with electricity despite even the blandest conversation.

Taylor heard Russ move back into the room, and assuming dinner was ready, she leapt to her feet. "Let me help," she said.

Russ caught her by the shoulders.

"The potatoes aren't done."

As she tilted her head, her hair fell over her shoulder and down her back. Mark had liked it styled and short, and in an act of defiance, she'd allowed it to grow longer than at any other time in her life.

"You have beautiful hair," Russ murmured, apparently unable to take his eyes from it. He slid his hand from her shoulder to the dark curly mass, and ran his fingers through its length. The action, so slow and deliberate, was highly exciting. Against every dictate of her will, Taylor's heart quickened.

Soon his other hand joined the first and he continued to let his fingers glide through her hair, as if acquainting himself with its softness. Taylor seemed to be falling into a trance. His hands, buried deep in her hair, were more sensual than anything she'd ever experienced. Her eyes drifted shut, and when she felt herself being tugged toward him, she offered no resistance. His mouth met hers in a gentle brushing of lips. Their breaths merged as they each released a broken sigh.

"Tell me to stop," Russ said. "Tell me to take my hands away from you."

Taylor knew she should, but emotions that had been hiding just below the surface overwhelmed her. She meant to push him away, extract them both from this temptation—and yet the instant her hands made contact with his hard, muscular chest, they lost their purpose.

"Russ…"

His answer was to kiss her, a kiss that felt anything but gentle. His hands were tangled in the wavy bulk of dark hair as he bent her head to one side and slanted his demanding mouth over hers.

Their kisses were tempestuous, intense, exciting, and soon they were both panting and breathless.

Suddenly Russ tore his mouth from hers. His eyes remained closed. "I haven't stopped thinking of you all week," he confessed, not sounding very pleased about it. "I didn't want to, but you're there every night when I close my eyes. I can't get rid of the taste of you. Why *you?*" he asked harshly. "Why do I have to feel these things for a city girl? You don't belong here and you never will."

Taylor's head fell forward for a moment while she thought about his words. He was right. She was as out of place in this cattle town as…as a trout in a swimming pool. She raised her head while she had the courage to confront him. Anger was her friend; it took away the guilt she felt for being so willing to fall into his arms.

"You think I'm happy about this?" she cried. "Trust me, a cowpoke is the last person in the world I want to get involved with. A woman in your life is there for your convenience, to cook your meals and pleasure you in bed. I knew exactly what you were the minute we met and I could never align my thinking with yours."

"Fine then, don't," he barked.

"I don't have any intention of getting involved with you."

"Listen, lady, I'm not all that thrilled with you, either. Go back to the big city where you belong, because in these parts men are men and women are women. We don't much take to all that feminist talk."

Taylor was becoming more outraged by the minute. Russ clearly had no conception that they weren't living in the nineteenth century anymore.

"Let's eat," he snarled.

Taylor had half a mind to gather her things and leave. She would have if she'd thought she could get away with it. But Russ had made this dinner on a wager, and Taylor strongly suspected he'd see to it that she ate every bite. Knowing what she did about Russ, Taylor wouldn't put it past him to feed her himself if she backed out now.

Taylor wasn't sure how she managed to force down a single bite. Yet the salad was undeniably good. The broccoli was excellent, the sauce marginal, the baked potato raw, but the steak was succulent and exactly the way she liked it—medium rare.

Silence stretched between them like a tightrope, and neither seemed inclined to cross it. At least ten minutes passed before Russ spoke.

"I shouldn't have said that about you not belonging here," he murmured, stabbing the lettuce with his fork.

"Why not?" she asked. "It's true and we both know it. I *am* a city girl."

"From everything I hear, you're a fine teacher," he admitted grudgingly. "The kids are crazy about you and I don't blame them."

She lifted her eyes to his, uncertain if she should believe him, feeling both surprise and pleasure.

"Word has it you're enthusiastic and energetic, and everyone who's met you says nothing but good. I don't want you thinking folks don't appreciate what you're doing. That was just me running off at the mouth."

Her voice dropped to a raspy whisper. "I didn't mean what I said either, about not wanting anything to do with you because you're a cowpoke."

Their eyes met, and they each fought a smile. Knowing she was about to lose, Taylor lowered her gaze. "I will confess to being a little shocked at how well you managed dinner."

Russ chuckled softly. "It wasn't that difficult."

"Does that mean you'd be willing to tackle it again?"

"No way. Once in a man's lifetime is more than enough. I may have lost the wager, but I still consider cooking a woman's job."

"I thought for a moment that our wager would change your mind. But at this point, why do anything to spoil your reputation as a world-class chauvinist?"

Russ chuckled again, and the sound wasn't extraordinary, but it gladdened Taylor's heart. Something about this cowboy intrigued her. He wasn't like any other man she'd ever dated. His opinions were diametrically opposed to her own on just about every subject she could mention. Yet whenever he touched her, she all but melted in his arms. There wasn't any logic to this attraction they shared. No reason for it.

Russ helped himself to more salad and replenished their wineglasses. "Now that you know what Cougar Point thinks about you, how are you adjusting to us?"

"It's been more of a change than I expected," she said, holding the wineglass with both hands. She rotated the stem between her palms. "It's the lack of conveniences I notice the most."

He arched his brows in question. "Give me an example."

"Well, I came home from work the other night, exhausted. All I wanted to do was sit down, put my feet up and hibernate until morning. The problem was, I was starving. My first impulse was to order a pepperoni pizza, and when I realized I couldn't, I felt like crying with frustration."

"The bowling alley serves a decent pizza."

"But they don't deliver."

"No," Russ agreed, "they don't."

Feeling a twinge of homesickness, Taylor finished her wine and stood. "I'll help you with the dishes," she said, feeling sad and weary as she glanced at Russ. Even in the friendliest conversation their differences were impossible to ignore.

"I'll do them," he responded, standing himself.

"Nope, you made dinner," she said firmly. "You're exempt from washing dishes—this time." She turned on the tap and squirted a dash of liquid soap into the rushing water. Monster bubbles quickly formed, and she lowered the water pressure.

She was clearing off the table when Russ suggested, "How about a cup of coffee?"

"Please," she said, smiling over at him.

He busied himself with that while Taylor loaded the dishwasher with plates and serving dishes, leaving the pots and pans to wash by hand.

"Here," he said from behind her, "you might want this."

She turned around to discover Russ holding the very

apron he'd been so quick to remove when she'd arrived. Her hands were covered with soapsuds. She glanced at them and then at Russ.

"I'll put it on for you," he said.

She smiled her appreciation and lifted her arms so he could loop the ties around her waist and knot them behind her back.

Russ moved to within two steps of her and hesitated. Slowly he raised his eyes to her face. Hungry eyes. They delved into hers and then lowered just as slowly until they centered on her lips.

Unable to resist, Taylor swayed toward him. Once more she found herself a willing victim to his spell.

Their eyes held for a long moment before Russ roughly pushed the apron at her. "You do it."

With trembling hands, Taylor shook the suds into the sink and deftly tied the apron behind her. "I wish Mandy was here," she murmured, shocked by how close they'd come to walking into each other's arms again. Obviously they both enjoyed the lure of the forbidden. Whatever the attraction, it was explosive, and she felt as though they'd been stumbling around a keg of lit gunpowder all evening.

"I think I'll call her and tell her to come home," Russ said, but he didn't reach for the phone.

Once the dishwasher was loaded, Taylor vigorously scrubbed the first pan, venting her frustration on it.

"Are you going to the dance?" Russ asked her next, grabbing a dish towel and slapping it over his shoulder.

"I...don't think so."

"Why not? It'll give you a chance to meet all the young guys in town and you can flirt to your heart's content."

"I'm far beyond the flirting stage," she returned coolly.

He shrugged. "Could've fooled me. Fact is, you've been doing an admirable job of trifling with *me* from the moment we met."

Taylor's hand stilled. "I beg your pardon?"

"Take those jeans your wearing."

"What's wrong with these jeans?"

"They're too tight. Stretched across your fanny like that, they give a man ideas."

Closing her eyes, Taylor counted to ten. The effort to control her temper was in vain, however, and she whirled around to face him.

"How *dare* you suggest anything so ridiculous? You nearly kissed me a minute ago and now you're blaming *me* because *you* can't control yourself. Obviously it's all my fault."

He grunted and looked away.

"My jeans are too tight!" she echoed, her voice still outraged. "What about my sweater? Is that too revealing?" She bunched her breasts together and cast a meaningful look in their direction. "Did you notice how far the V-neck goes down? Why, a mere glimpse of cleavage is enough to drive a man to drink. Maybe I should have you censor my perfume, as well. It's a wonder the good people of Cougar Point would allow such a brazen hussy near their children. And one with a big-city attitude, no less."

"Taylor—"

"Don't you say another word to me," she cried, and jerked off the apron. Tears sprang to her eyes as she hurriedly located her purse. "Good night, Mr. Palmer. I won't say it's been a pleasure."

"Taylor, dammit, listen to me."

She raced down the stairs to her car, barely able to see through the tears in her eyes. The whole world looked blurred and watery, but Taylor was in too much of a hurry to care. This man said the most ridiculous things she'd ever heard. Only a fool would have anything more to do with him. Taylor had been a fool once.

Never, never again.

Russ sat in the living room, calling himself every foul name he could think of, and the list was a long one. When the back door opened, he knew it would be Mandy and reached for a newspaper, pretending to read.

"Hi!" She waltzed into the room. "How'd dinner go?"

"Great," he mumbled, not taking his eyes off the front page.

"Has Taylor already left?"

"Yeah."

"Oh, shucks, I wanted to talk to her. Do you want to see the routine Chris and I made up?"

Russ's interest in his sister's drill team efforts was less than nil. Nevertheless, he grinned and nodded. "Sure."

"Okay, but remember it's not the same without the music." She held the pom-poms to her waist, arms akimbo, then let loose with a high kick and shot her arms toward the ceiling. She danced left, she leaped right, her arms and legs moving with an instinctive grace that astonished Russ. This was Mandy? Fourteen-year-old Mandy? She was really quite good at this.

She finished down on one knee, her pom-poms raised above her head. Her smiling eyes met his, seeking his approval. "So?"

"There isn't a single doubt in my mind that my sister's going to make the high school drill team."

"Oh, Russ," she shouted, "thank you!" She vaulted to her feet and threw her arms around his neck. "Just for that I'll finish the dishes."

"Thanks," Russ said absently. He didn't want to think about dinner or anything else connected with this disastrous evening. That would only bring Taylor to mind, and she was the one person he was determined to forget. He'd suffered enough. All week she'd been nagging at his conscience. He'd even dreamed of her. He hadn't felt this way about a woman since he was sixteen years old.

Then he had to go and say those stupid things. The reason was even worse. He'd been jealous. The thought of her attending the Grange event and dancing with all the men in town was more than he could bear. Other men putting their arms around her. Someone else laughing with her.

If anyone was going to dance with Taylor Manning, it would be him. Not Harry Donovan. Not Les Benjamin. Not Cody Franklin.

Him.

"Russ?"

He turned and found his sister staring at him. "What?"

"You've been pacing for the past five minutes. Is something wrong?"

"Hell, no," he growled, then quickly changed his mind. "Hell, yes." He marched across the kitchen and grabbed his hat, bluntly setting it on his head.

"Where are you going?" Mandy demanded, following him.

"To town," he muttered. "I owe Taylor an apology."

Mandy giggled, seeming to find that amusing. "You going to ask her to the dance?"

"I might," he said, his strides long and purposeful.

"All right!" his sister cheered from behind him.

Chapter 4

"Taylor!" Russ pounded on the front door with his fist. This woman sure was stubborn. "I know you're in there. Answer the door, will you?"

"I can't," a soft, feminine voice purred from the other side. "I'm wearing something much too revealing." The purr quickly became an angry shout. "Army boots and fatigues!"

"I need to talk to you," Russ insisted.

"Go away."

Exhaling loudly, Russ pressed his palms against the door. "Please," he added persuasively, knowing few women could resist him when he used that imploring tone.

"If you don't leave, I'm calling the police."

"The deputy's name is Cody Franklin, and we went to school together."

"That doesn't mean he won't arrest you."

"On what charge? Wanting to apologize to my lady?"

The door flew open with such force that Russ was surprised it stayed on its hinges. Taylor's index finger poked him in the chest and he stumbled back a step.

"I am not your lady! Understand?" Deep blue eyes sliced straight through him.

Russ's grin was so big, his face ached. "I figured that comment would get a reaction out of you. I just didn't think it would be quite this zealous. Did anyone ever tell you you've got one hell of a temper?"

"No." She obviously resented being tricked. She crossed her arms protectively around her waist and glared at him. "There's only one other man in this world who can make me as angry as you do and I'm related to him."

"Which means you can't avoid him, but you *can* avoid me."

Taylor rolled her eyes skyward. "The cowboy's a genius."

Russ removed his hat and rotated the rim between his fingers. "I'm here to apologize for what I said earlier. I don't know what came over me," he hesitated, realizing that wasn't entirely true. "All right, I have a good guess. I was jealous."

"Jealous," she exploded. "Of what?"

This wasn't easy. Confronting her was one thing, but admitting how he'd been feeling... An uncomfortable sensation tightened his chest. "I was thinking about other men dancing with you and it bothered the hell out of me," he said in a low murmur, none too proud of it.

"That makes as much sense as my jeans being too tight. I already told you I wasn't going to the dance."

"Yes, you are," he countered swiftly. "You're going with me."

To his consternation, Taylor threw back her head and laughed. "In your dreams, Palmer."

There were any number of women in town who'd leap at an invitation to attend the Grange dance with him; he could name four off the top of his head. So it didn't sit right that the one woman he really wanted to take had mocked his invitation. He could feel the red burning his ears, but he swallowed his protest. Still, he supposed he and Taylor were even now.

"Some women might appreciate those caveman tactics of yours," she informed him, smiling much too broadly to suit his already wounded pride. "But I'm not one of them."

"What do you want me to do? Get down on one knee and beg? Because if that's the case, you've got a hell of a long wait!" He slammed his hat back on his head.

Some of the amusement and indignation left her eyes.

Russ tried once more, softening his voice. "There isn't anyone in Cougar Point I'd rather attend the dance with," he said. Their eyes held for a few seconds longer before Russ added, "Will you go with me, Taylor? Please?" That wasn't a word he said often; he hoped she realized that.

It was clear she was wavering. Maybe she needed some inducement, Russ decided. He settled his hands on her shoulders and brought her against him. She remained as stiff as a branding iron, refusing to relax. He could kiss her; that might help with her decision. Every time his mouth settled over hers it was like drinking rainwater, sweet and fresh from the heavens. He rested his chin on the crown of her head and felt some of the fight go out of her. A smile twitched at the edges of his mouth. He knew she'd come around once she'd had a chance to think about it.

"Taylor?" he whispered, lifting her chin so he could look into her eyes. What he saw puzzled him. Russ expected to find submission, perhaps even a hint of desire. Instead he discovered bewilderment and distress.

When she spoke, her voice was a little shaky. "I... It'd be best if you asked someone else, Russ."

"You're going to the Grange dance, aren't you?" Mary Beth Morgan asked, popping into Taylor's room after class on Wednesday afternoon.

Taylor shook her head and riffled through a stack of papers on her desk. "I don't think so."

"But, Taylor," the other teacher said, "everyone in town will be there."

"So I heard." Taylor stood and placed the papers inside her folder to take home and grade that evening.

"Why wouldn't you want to go?"

Taylor hedged, wondering how she could explain. "First, I don't have anything appropriate to wear, and second—" she hesitated and lifted one shoulder in a half shrug "—I don't know how to square dance."

Mary Beth smiled and shook her head. "You don't have a thing to worry about. You could show up at the Grange in a burlap bag and you'd have more offers to dance than you'd know what to do with. As for the square dancing part, put that out of your head. This isn't a square dance."

"I'll think about it," Taylor promised.

"You'd better do more than that," Mary Beth said. "I

personally know of three young men who'll be mighty disappointed if you aren't at that dance."

"I suppose I could sew a dress," Taylor said, her spirits lifting. She knew the minute she arrived that Russ would believe she was there because of him, but the thought of staying home while everyone else was having fun was fast losing its appeal.

"Listen, Taylor, there aren't that many social functions in Cougar Point. Take my advice and enjoy yourself while you can because there probably won't be another one until Christmas."

"Christmas?"

"Right," Mary Beth said with a solid nod. "Now I'll tell you what I'll do. My husband and I will pick you up at seven."

"I know where the Grange Hall is," Taylor said, brightening. "You don't need to give me a ride."

Mary Beth laughed. "I just want to see if it's Russ Palmer, Cody Franklin or Harry Donovan who takes you home."

True to her word, Mary Beth and Charles Morgan came by to pick up Taylor promptly at seven on Saturday night.

"Oh, my, we're in for a fun evening," Mary Beth said as she walked a full circle around Taylor. Slowly she shook her head. "That dress is absolutely gorgeous."

Taylor had been up until midnight two evenings straight, sewing. There was an old-fashioned dry goods store in town, where she'd found a respectable—and surprisingly inexpensive—assortment of fabrics and notions. She'd chosen a pattern for a western-style dress with a tight-fitting lace-up bodice and snug waist. The skirt flared out gently at her hips and fell to midcalf. An eyelet-ruffled petticoat of white dropped three inches below the lavender dress. Brown boots complemented the outfit.

"Yup, we're in for a really good time tonight." Mary Beth chuckled as she slipped her arm through Taylor's and led her out the door.

The music coming from the Grange Hall could be heard even before they parked the car. Bright lights poured out from the large brick structure on the highway outside town. The parking lot was filled with trucks and four-wheel-drive vehicles. Without meaning to, Taylor started looking for Russ's truck, then quickly chastised herself.

She was hardly in the door when Mandy flew to her side. The girl's face was glowing with a warm smile.

"I knew you'd come! Russ said you wouldn't be here, but I was sure you would. Oh, Taylor," she whispered wide-eyed when Taylor removed her coat. "Where did you ever find a dress that pretty?"

Taylor whirled around once to give her the full effect. "You like it? Well, I told you before there are advantages in knowing how to use a sewing machine."

"You *made* your dress?"

"Don't look so shocked."

"Could I ever sew anything that complicated?"

"With practice."

"If I took all the money I've been saving for a new saddle and bought a sewing machine, would you teach me to sew? I'm not taking home economics until next term, and I don't want to wait that long to learn. Not when I can make clothes as pretty as yours."

"I'd be happy to teach you."

"Howdy, Taylor." A young man with soft ash-blond hair stepped in front of her, hands tucked into the small front pockets of his jeans.

"Hello," she said, not recognizing him, although he apparently knew her.

"I was wondering if I could have the next dance?"

"Ah…" Taylor hadn't even hung up her coat yet, and she would've liked to find her way around and talk to a few people before heading for the dance floor.

"For crying out loud," Mandy muttered. "Give Taylor a minute, will you, Harry? She just got here."

Harry's cheeks flushed with instant color. "If I don't ask her now," he said, "someone else will and I won't get a chance the rest of the evening." He blushed some more. "So can I have this dance?"

"Ah…sure," Taylor said, not knowing what else to do. Mandy took her coat and Harry led her to the dance floor, smiling broadly as if he'd pulled off a major coup.

Once they reached the dance floor, Harry slipped his arm around her waist and guided her through a simple two-step. They hadn't been on the floor more than a few minutes when the music ended. Reluctantly Harry let his arm drop.

"I don't suppose you'd consider dancing the next one with me?" he asked hopefully.

Taylor hesitated. The room was growing more crowded, and she still hadn't talked to anyone.

"I believe the next dance is mine," a deep masculine voice said from behind her. Taylor didn't need a detective to know it was Russ. She stiffened instinctively before turning to face him.

Russ stood directly in front of her in a gray western-tailored suit with a suede yoke, his gaze challenging hers. His look alone was enough to silence the denial on her tongue. His eyes moved over her like a warm caress, tiny glints of mischief sparking in their depths.

The music started again, and as Harry stepped away, Russ placed his arms around her. There wasn't an ounce of protest left in Taylor as he caressed the small of her back. She closed her eyes and pretended to be engrossed in the music when it was Russ who held her senses captive.

Several minutes passed before he spoke. His mouth was close to her ear. "I knew you'd come."

Taylor's eyes shot open, and she jerked away from him, putting several inches between them. "Let me tell you right now that my being here has absolutely nothing to do with you, and—"

He pressed a finger over her lips, stopping her in midsentence.

Slowly Taylor lifted her gaze to his. Deeply etched lines from long hours in the sun crinkled around his eyes.

"Thank you for coming," he whispered, and his warm breath tinged her cheek. Then he removed his finger.

"It wasn't for you," she felt obliged to inform him, but the indignation in her voice was gone. "Mary Beth Morgan…invited me."

Russ's mouth quirked just a fraction. "Remind me to thank her."

His grip tightened, and although Taylor was determined to keep a safe, respectable distance from this man, she found herself relaxing in his embrace. He slid his hand up and down the length of her back, sending hunger shooting through her. She eased closer, reveling in the strength she sensed in the rugged, hard contours of his body. She didn't mean to, didn't even want to, but when he tucked her hand between them and rested his face against her hair, she closed her eyes once again. He smelled of rum and spice, and she breathed in deeply, inhaling his scent.

When the song ended, it was Taylor who swallowed a sigh of regret. Dancing like this was a lost art in the city. The last time she'd danced with a man who'd placed his arms around her so tenderly, she'd been with Mark, early in their relationship. She'd almost forgotten how good it was to feel so cherished.

Russ refused to release her; if anything, he pulled her closer. "Let's get out of here for a few minutes."

Taylor groaned inwardly. She couldn't believe how tempted she was to agree. "I…can't. I just got here. People will talk."

"Let them."

"Russ, no." Using her hands for leverage, she pushed herself free. He didn't offer any resistance, but the effort it had cost her to move away left her weak. And furious. How dare he assume she'd go into the parking lot with him—and for what? She'd bet cold hard cash he wasn't planning to discuss cattle breeding techniques with her.

"I want it understood that I'm not going anywhere near that parking lot with you, Russ Palmer."

"Whatever you say." But a smile tugged insolently at his mouth.

The music started again, and they stood facing each other in the middle of the dance floor with couples crowding in around them. Russ didn't take her in his arms, nor did she make a move toward him.

Amusement flickered in his eyes. There was no resisting him, and soon Taylor responded to his smile. He slipped his hands around her waist, drawing her back into the circle of his arms. They made a pretense of dancing but were doing little more than staring at each other and shuffling their feet.

No woman in her right mind would deliberately get involved with an avowed chauvinist like Russ Palmer, yet here she was, a thoroughly modern woman, so attracted to him that she ached to the soles of her feet.

The music came to an end, and his arms relaxed. A careless, handsome grin slashed his mouth. "Enjoy yourself," he whispered. "Dance with whomever you like, but remember this. I'm the one who's taking you home tonight. No one else. Me."

An immediate protest rose in Taylor's throat, but before she could utter a single word, Russ bent forward and set his mouth over hers. She clenched her fists against his gray suit jacket while his lips caressed hers. Taylor could hear the curious voices murmuring around them, and she gave a small cry.

Russ ended the kiss, smiled down on her and whispered, "Remember."

Then he walked off the floor.

Taylor felt like a first-class fool, standing there by herself with half a dozen couples staring at her. When the hushed whispers began, she smiled blandly and all but ran from the dance floor.

Taylor was so mortified that she headed directly for the ladies' room and stayed there a full five minutes, trying to compose herself. If there'd been a sofa, she would have sat down and wept. Wept because she'd been so tempted to let Russ take her outside. Wept because she felt so right in his arms. Wept because she hadn't learned a thing from her disastrous affair with Mark Brooks.

Once she reappeared at the dance, she didn't lack for attention. She waltzed with Cody Franklin, chatted over punch with Les Benjamin, another rancher, and even managed a second two-step with Harry Donovan. She smiled. She laughed. She pretended to be having the time of her life, but underneath everything was a brewing frustration she couldn't escape. Every now and then she'd catch a glimpse of Russ dancing with someone else. Usually someone young and pretty. Someone far more suited to him than she'd ever be. Yet, each time, she felt a stab of jealousy unlike anything she'd ever experienced.

By the time the evening started to wind down, Taylor decided the best way to thwart Russ was to accept someone else's offer to drive her home.

Only no one asked.

Of the dozen or so men she danced with, not a single, solitary one suggested taking her home. Charles and Mary Beth Morgan had already left by the time Taylor realized she had no option except to find Russ.

He was waiting for her outside, standing at the bottom of the Grange steps, looking as arrogant and pleased as could be.

"I want to know what you said to everyone," she demanded, marching down the steps. It was more than a little suspicious that she'd been virtually abandoned without a ride.

Russ's eyes fairly shone with devilment. "Me? What makes you think I said anything?"

"Because I know you, and I want one thing clear

right now. You can take me home, but nothing else. Understand?"

"You insult me, madam!"

"Good. Now, where's Mandy?" Taylor asked.

"She's spending the night with Chris," Russ explained. "However, rest assured, you're perfectly safe with me."

"I'd be safer in a pit of rattlesnakes," she said wryly. "Do you have any idea how humiliating it was when you kissed me on that dance floor and then took off?" Her voice was a low hiss.

"I promise I'll never do it again," he vowed, and led her across the parking lot where he held open the truck door.

This was a newer model than the one she'd ridden in earlier. She paused and glanced inside and was relieved to see it had seat belts. However, the truck stood probably three feet off the ground, and there wasn't any way she'd be able to climb inside without assistance.

"Here," Russ said, "I'll help you up." His hands closed around her waist and he lifted her effortlessly off the ground.

Once she was inside and Russ had joined her, she asked him, "Where do you drive this thing? Through the Rockies?"

Russ chuckled and started the engine. "You'd be surprised the places this truck has been."

"I'll bet," Taylor grumbled.

She didn't say a word during the short drive to her rented house. Russ didn't, either.

He pulled in to her driveway, cut the engine and was out of the cab before she could object. Opening her door,

Russ helped her down. But when her feet were firmly planted on the ground, he didn't release her.

His eyes held hers in the dim light from a nearby streetlamp, and a current of awareness flowed between them. "You were the most beautiful woman there tonight."

"I'm surprised you even noticed." The minute the words escaped, Taylor regretted having spoken. In one short sentence she'd revealed what she'd been doing all evening.

Watching him.

She'd counted the number of women he'd danced with and, worse, envied them the time they'd spent in his arms.

Russ didn't answer her. Not with words, anyway. Instead he pulled her into his arms and kissed her. His mouth was hard, his kiss thorough. When he lifted his head, their panting breaths echoed each other.

"Invite me inside," he whispered, his voice husky.

Taylor felt powerless to do anything other than what he asked. Her hands were shaking as she drew the keys from her purse. Russ took them from her and unlocked the door, pushing it open for her to precede him.

She walked through the living room and to the kitchen, turning on the lights. "I'll...make some coffee."

"No," Russ said, stopping her. His arms anchored her against the wall. "I don't want any coffee and neither do you."

Taylor gazed into his face and recognized his hunger, aware that it was a reflection of her own. Closing her eyes, she leaned against the wall, feeling needy and weak.

"Trust me," Russ whispered. "I know what you're

thinking. We're both crazy. I should stay as far away from you as possible. You don't want to feel these things for me any more than I want to feel them for you. We argue. We fight. But, lady, when we kiss, everything else pales by comparison."

"What we're experiencing is just physical attraction," she whispered as her fingers sank into his thick, dark hair.

"Physical attraction," he repeated, seconds before his mouth came crashing down on hers. Low, animal sounds came from deep within his throat as his mouth twisted and turned over hers.

Braced against the wall, she could feel every hard, rugged inch of him.

Restlessly she moved against him as her hands clenched fistfuls of his hair.

"Russ," she panted, lifting her head. "I...I think we should stop now."

"In a minute." Grasping her by the waist, he dragged her against him and groaned.

Taylor did, too.

He was so hard. She was so soft.

Man to woman.

Cowboy to lady.

They fit together so perfectly.

Drawing in deep, shuddering breaths, Russ buried his face in the curve of her neck. It took him several seconds to regain control of himself.

It took Taylor even longer.

He raised his head and smoothed the hair from her face. "I've changed my mind," he murmured. "I will take that coffee, after all."

Grateful for something to occupy herself, Taylor

moved to the counter where she kept her coffeemaker. While waiting for the aromatic coffee to drip through, she got two mugs and placed them on a tray. She was so absorbed in her task that when she turned around she nearly collided with Russ.

He took the tray from her hands and carried it into the living room. "I think it's time we cleared the air," he said, setting their mugs on the oak coffee table.

"In what way?" Taylor asked, perching on the edge of the sofa cushion.

"Above all else, we've got to be honest with each other."

"Right."

Taylor sipped from her mug, the scalding coffee too hot to savor or appreciate.

"Are you wearing a bra?" he asked unexpectedly.

"What?" She jerked forward, setting her cup back on the tray to avoid spilling hot coffee down her front. It sloshed over the edges of the mug.

Taylor's mouth gaped as she glared at him. "Is *that* the kind of honesty you're interested in?" Unable to sit still, she got up and started pacing, so furious she was tempted to throw him out of her home.

"I'm sorry. Forget I asked. I was holding you and it felt as if you weren't and the question just…slipped out. You're right—that was a stupid question."

He lowered his eyes, and Taylor noted that his ears were red. As red as Harry Donovan's had been when he'd asked her to dance. Russ Palmer embarrassed? The very thought was inconceivable.

Stepping around the low table, Taylor sat back down and reached for her coffee. "As a matter of fact, no."

Russ closed his eyes as though in pain. "You

shouldn't have told me." He took a gulp of coffee, then stood abruptly. "Maybe it'd be best if I left now."

"I thought you wanted to talk. I refuse to answer personal questions like the last one, but I think you're right about us being honest with each other."

Now it was Russ's turn to do the pacing. He stood and stalked across her living room carpet and then back again as if he intended to wear a pattern in it.

"Russ?"

He rammed his fingers through his hair and turned to face her. "If you want honesty, I'll give it to you, Taylor, but I'll guarantee you aren't going to like what I have to say."

She wasn't sure she was up to this. But, on the other hand, she didn't want him to leave, either. "Just say it."

"All right," he said sharply. "Right now, I want you so damn much I can't even think straight." He raked one hand down his face. "Does that shock you?"

"No," she cried softly.

"Well, it should."

Holding the mug so tightly that it burned her palms, Taylor gathered her courage. "Earlier I objected when you called me your lady. The lady part wasn't what offended me. It might be an old-fashioned term, but I *am* a lady. And I'll always be a lady."

Russ frowned. "I know that, Taylor. No one can look at you and not realize the kind of woman you are."

"I have no intention of falling into bed with you, Russ. I wish I understood why we're so attracted to each other, but I don't. I do know we're playing with fire. Unfortunately, if we continue like this, one of us is going to get burned."

Russ closed his eyes and nodded. "You're right, of

course." He inhaled deeply. "Does this mean you want me to leave?"

"No," she said, smiling at her own lack of willpower. "But I think you should, anyway."

Chapter 5

"Mandy, I'm not going near that horse."

"Taylor, please. I want to do something to thank you for all the sewing lessons you've given me."

As far as Taylor was concerned, the chestnut gelding looked as huge as the Trojan horse. He didn't seem all that friendly, either. Her palms were sweating, and her throat felt dry from arguing with the persistent teen.

"Shadow is as gentle as they come," Mandy assured her, stroking the white markings on the horse's face. "You don't have a thing to worry about."

"That's what they said to Custer, too," Taylor muttered under her breath. This whole episode had started out so innocuously. Taylor had spent an hour after school helping Mandy cut out the pattern for a vest. Then, because Russ was busy with an errand in Miles City, Taylor had dropped her off at the ranch. One of the men had been exercising a horse, and Taylor had innocently inquired about the stock. Before she knew how it had happened, Mandy was insisting on teaching her to ride, claiming she couldn't accept sewing lessons from Taylor without giving her something in return.

"Once you climb into the saddle, you'll feel a whole lot better about it," Mandy told her.

"I'm not much of a horse person," Taylor said.

"That doesn't matter. Shadow's gentle. I promise you."

"Another time perhaps," Taylor murmured.

"But today's perfect for riding."

Before Taylor could answer, she saw Russ's truck speeding down the driveway, leaving a trail of dust in its wake. Taylor hadn't seen Russ since the night of the Grange dance, and she hated the way her pulse immediately started to race.

Russ pulled to a stop and leaped out of the truck, but he paused when he saw Taylor's Cabriolet parked near the barn. Setting his hat farther back on his head, he changed his direction and walked toward them.

"Hello, Taylor," he said, bowing his head slightly.

"Russ."

"Maybe you can talk some sense into her." Mandy gestured toward Taylor, looking wistful. "I think she should learn to ride. Here she is giving me all these sewing lessons, and I want to repay her."

"You've already had me over for dinner," Taylor reminded the girl. "Really, horses just aren't my thing. The last time I sat on a horse was on a carousel when I was ten years old."

"If Taylor's afraid…"

"What makes you say that?" Taylor demanded. "I'm

not *afraid* of horses. It's just that I'm unfamiliar with them. I don't think now is the time for me to do more than gain a nodding acquaintance with Shadow here, but I most certainly am not afraid."

"Then prove it," Russ challenged. He patted Shadow on the rump. The gelding returned the greeting with a nicker and a swish of his thick tail.

"I promise you'll enjoy it," Mandy said.

Grumbling under her breath, Taylor took the reins from Mandy's hands. "Why do I have the sinking suspicion I'm going to regret this?"

"You won't," Mandy vowed.

"This kid is much too free with her promises," Taylor told Russ. Lifting her left foot and placing it in the stirrup, Taylor reached for the saddle horn and heaved herself up.

"You might need some help," Mandy said. "Russ, help her."

"She seems to be doing fine without me."

Taylor had hoisted her weight halfway up when she started to lose her grip. Russ was behind her in an instant, supporting her waist. "All right, Annie Oakley, I'll give you a hand."

Swinging her leg over the back of the horse, Taylor held on to the saddle horn as if it were a life preserver and she was lost at sea.

"See?" Mandy cried triumphantly. "There isn't anything to it. Didn't I tell you?"

Russ adjusted the stirrups for her. "You look a little green around the gills. Are you okay?"

"It's…a little higher up here than I imagined. Can I get down now?"

Mandy giggled. "But you haven't gone anyplace yet."

"Isn't *this* enough to prove I'm not afraid? You didn't say anything about actually moving."

"Josh, bring me Magic," Russ instructed the hand who'd saddled Shadow earlier. A large black gelding was led from the barn, and with Josh's assistance Russ saddled and bridled the horse.

"You go ahead and take Taylor out and I'll start dinner," Mandy suggested. "By the time you two get back, everything will be ready."

"Uh… I'm not so sure this is the best time for me to ride," Taylor said, struggling to hide the panic in her voice. "I've got papers that need to be corrected and a couple of loads of wash…and other things."

"It's Friday," Mandy announced over her shoulder as she strolled toward the house. "You can do all that tomorrow."

"Of course," Taylor muttered. "I should've thought of that."

"Don't look so terrified. This is going to be a good experience for you," Russ told her, his expression far more smug than she liked.

He mounted the black gelding, gave instructions to the hands to unload the pickup, then turned to Taylor. "We'll take it nice and easy. You haven't got a thing to worry about."

"If that's the case, why do I feel like I'm about a mile off the ground?"

Russ's returning chuckle warmed her heart. She'd missed him this week—although she'd had to search her soul to even admit that. With Mandy stopping in after school, three days out of five, Taylor had been kept well-informed about Russ's activities. He'd done the ordering on Tuesday and was grumpy most of the night, and Mandy didn't have a clue why. Thursday he was out on the range, looking for strays, and Friday he'd traveled into Miles City for supplies. Taylor had never openly asked about Russ, but she was always pleased when Mandy slipped her small pieces of information.

Russ, riding Magic, set the pace, and once they were past the barn, he pointed out a trail that led toward rolling hills of fresh, green grass. "We'll head this way."

"Do you mind if we go a bit slower?" She swayed back and forth, beginning to feel a little seasick with the motion.

"If we went any slower, we'd be standing still."

"What's wrong with that?" she muttered. "By the way, if it isn't too much to ask, where are you taking me?"

Russ waggled his eyebrows suggestively. "*Now* she asks."

"And what's that supposed to mean?"

"Nothing." But his dark eyes were twinkling—a look Taylor had seen before, once too often.

She pulled back on the reins several minutes later, mildly surprised when Shadow slowed to a stop. "I don't trust you, Russ. Tell me this minute exactly where we're going."

Russ leaned back in the saddle, nonchalantly throwing one leg around the saddle horn and clasping his hands behind his head. He was as at ease in a saddle as he was in his own living room. "No place in particular. You want to stop and rest a minute? There's a valley about a quarter mile from here."

Taylor hated to admit how sore her posterior already felt. And they hadn't even gone very far. If she squinted, she could just make out the back of the red barn in the distance.

"Yes, let's stop and rest," she agreed. "But no funny business."

Theatrically Russ removed his hat and pressed it over his heart with a roguish grin. "Once again you insult me, madam."

Taylor said nothing, unwilling to take part in his performance.

"Mandy says you're helping her sew a vest," Russ said conversationally a few minutes later. He slowed Magic and swung down with a grace Taylor could only envy. It had taken all her strength just to raise herself into the saddle. If Russ hadn't given her a boost, she would've been caught with one foot in the stirrup and the other madly waving in midair—until she crashed to the ground.

"Need any help?"

"I can do it myself," she announced, not the least bit confident. Surely climbing out of the saddle would be less of a strain than getting into it had been. Besides, if Russ lent her a hand, he'd use it as an excuse to kiss her. Not that she'd mind, but for once she'd enjoy having a relaxed conversation without falling into his arms like a love-starved teenager.

Taylor was pleased at how easy dismounting turned out to be. Her legs felt a little shaky, but once her feet were on the ground and she'd walked around a bit, she decided this horseback riding business wasn't as difficult as she'd assumed.

"I don't expect many more warm days like this one," Russ said. He tilted his hat back on his head and stared into the distance. Several cattle were grazing on a hill across from them.

Taylor joined him, and he slipped an arm around her waist as familiarly as if he'd been doing so for years.

"Thank you for everything you're doing for Mandy."

"It's nothing."

"It's a lot. Teaching her to sew. Encouraging her. She comes home high as a kite after she's been with you, chattering a mile a minute." A boyish grin lifted his mouth. "For that matter, I come home happy, too."

Taylor lowered her eyes. "I think her making the drill team is what boosted her spirits more than anything. She could've walked on water the day she learned she'd been chosen."

"Only three freshmen made the squad," Russ said, smiling proudly.

Linking her hands behind her back, Taylor strolled over to a large tree. Leaning against the trunk, she raised one knee and rested her booted foot behind her. "I've enjoyed working with Mandy this week. She reminds me of my sister, Christy, when she was fourteen. Unfortunately I was sixteen at the time and considered Christy a major pest."

"Mandy told me you came from a large family."

"By today's standards, I guess you could say that. I have three older brothers, Paul, Jason and Rich. Paul's the only one who's married, and believe me, the rest of us are eternally grateful to him because he quickly presented my parents with twin sons. Now that Mom and Dad have grandchildren, the rest of us are off the hook, at least for a while."

"You're close to your family, aren't you?"

Taylor nodded. "I can't believe how much I miss

them. They must be feeling the same way because I've heard from them practically every day."

Russ lowered himself to the grass, stretching his legs in front of him and crossing his ankles. "Mandy said something about how your father reminds you of me."

"Is nothing sacred?" she teased. If his sister had been dropping tidbits about him, she'd also done a bang-up job of keeping Russ informed of their conversations. "My dad's a born chauvinist. I don't think he's sure it was a good thing that women were granted the vote."

Russ didn't laugh the way most people would. "I don't mind if women vote. It's holding public office that concerns me."

Taylor shoved away from the tree so fast, she nearly fell. Her mouth worked for several seconds before any words came out. "I can't *believe* you just said that. Why *shouldn't* a woman hold public office?"

"My, my, you're always so touchy."

"Who can blame me when you say something so ludicrous?"

"Think about it, Taylor. A woman is the very heart of a home and family. What kind of wife and mother would she be if she was so deeply involved in politics that she couldn't tend to her family?"

"I'm not hearing this," she muttered.

"Don't you think a woman's place is with her children?"

"What about a father's place?"

"The husband's got to work in order to support the family."

Taylor covered her face with both hands. Even if his opinion was half-meant to be provocative, arguing with him would do no good. She'd tried often enough with her father, but to no avail. The two men were equally out of date in their views, equally stubborn and difficult.

Not knowing what possessed her, she leaped forward, jerked Russ's hat from his head and took off running.

"Taylor?" Russ vaulted to his feet in one smooth movement and chased after her. "What are you doing with my hat? What's gotten into you?"

Walking backward, keeping a safe distance from him, Taylor hid the Stetson behind her. "You're narrow-minded and the second-worst chauvinist I've ever known."

"You stole my hat because of that?"

"Yes. It was the only way I could make you suffer."

Russ advanced toward her, taking small steps. "Give me back the hat, Taylor."

"Forget it." For a good part of her life, Taylor had been playing keep-away with her brothers. She might not be as big as Russ and not nearly as agile, but she was quick.

"Taylor, give me the hat," he said again. His gaze narrowed as he advanced toward her, holding out his hand.

"No way. Women don't have any business holding public office? I can't let something that outrageous pass without making you pay."

Laughter flashed from his eyes as he lunged for her. Taylor let out a playful shriek and darted sharply to the left. Russ missed her by a yard.

Russ turned and was prepared to make another dive toward her when Taylor tossed the black cowboy hat with all her might into the sky. "Catch it if you can!" she shouted, bobbing past him. She was in such a rush that she stumbled and would have crashed face-first onto the grass if Russ hadn't captured her around the waist and brought her against him. The full force of her weight caught him off balance. He twisted so that he took the brunt of the impact, and they toppled onto the ground.

Within a heartbeat, Russ had reversed their positions, pinning her hands above her head. Taylor looked up into the dark warmth of his eyes and smiled. Her breasts were heaving with excitement.

"Who's making whom pay?" Russ demanded. He pressed his mouth to her neck, running the tip of his tongue over the smooth skin of her throat. Sensation wove its way down her spine, and she moaned softly and bucked. "No..."

"You're going to be doing a lot more begging before I'm through with you," Russ whispered. He kissed her then, his lips teasing and taunting hers with soft nibbles, promising but never quite delivering.

Arching her back, she struggled and was immediately released. With her hands free, she buried her fingers in his hair, raised her head and fused her mouth to his. She could feel herself dissolving, melting against him.

Russ kissed her mouth, her eyes, her throat. Taylor felt as if she were on fire, her whole body aflame with need. His hand found her breast, and Taylor sighed as a fresh wave of fiery sensation engulfed her.

"Oh, Russ," she pleaded, not sure what she was asking of him. The physical urge was strong and compelling, but there had to be so much more before she could freely give herself to him. A merging of their hearts. Commitment. Love.

She had no time to voice her concerns. Russ kissed

her, and a swift, acute sensation of hot, urgent desire rose up in her, blocking out everything but her awareness of Russ and her growing need.

She wanted him to continue—and yet...

"Either we stop now or we finish." His breathing was raspy as he slid his hands from her hips to her shoulders. "The choice is yours."

Taylor squeezed her eyes shut. Her throat was tight as she slowly shook her head. She didn't need to think twice; the decision had been made for her the moment she met Russ. He was as much a part of this landscape as the sycamore trees around them. She was as misplaced as a hothouse flower. But beyond that, Russ was a chauvinist. There was no other word for it. After the years of battling with her father, Taylor had no intention of falling in love with a man who shared the same outdated attitudes toward women.

She gave a shake of her head.

Russ exhaled sharply. "That's what I thought." His breath left him in a defeated rush and he stroked her hair. "Were you hurt when we hit the ground like that?"

She shook her head a second time, wishing she could hide her face in her hands and never look at him again. She certainly hadn't intended to let things go this far. One moment she was teasing him, playfully tossing his hat into the air, and the next...

"Are you sure you're all right?"

"Of course." But that was far from the truth. Taking his cue, she moved away from him and sat on the grass.

"Mandy's probably wondering about us," she said, doing her best to keep her voice from trembling as badly as her hands did.

"Don't worry. She won't send out a search party."

To Taylor's way of thinking, it might have been better if Mandy had.

It seemed everyone was looking at Taylor when she rode back into the yard. The ranch hands' curiosity about her was probably due to her precarious seat atop Shadow more than anything. As soon as she was able to stop the horse, she tossed the reins over his head and slid ingloriously from the saddle. Her feet landed with a jarring thud when she connected with the ground.

Mandy came out of the house, waving. "Gee, what took you guys so long?" she called, walking toward them. "I've had dinner ready for ages."

"We stopped and rested for a bit," Russ said, sharing a secret smile with Taylor, who was confident the color in her cheeks spelled out exactly what they'd been doing.

"I thought you were going to be back right away, so I fixed soup and sandwiches for dinner. That's all right, isn't it?"

"Actually, I should be getting back to town," Taylor said, eager to make her escape. Only when she was alone would she be able to analyze what had happened. Of one thing she was sure: there wouldn't be a repeat of this.

All her good intentions to take the time to heal her broken heart properly were like dust particles caught in the wind, blowing every which way. She had no business getting involved with Russ.

"Oh, please, don't go yet." Mandy's face fell at Taylor's announcement.

"I really have to," Taylor insisted. Spending any more of this day with Russ would have been agonizing, reminding her of what she couldn't allow herself to have.

* * *

Taylor hadn't been in her rental house five minutes when she felt the urge to talk to her mother. But it was her father who answered on the third ring.

"Hi, Dad."

"Taylor, sweetheart, how are you?" No matter what his mood, he always sounded gruff.

"Fine."

The pause that followed was brief. "What's wrong?"

Taylor smiled to herself. She'd never been very good at keeping anything from her parents. "What makes you ask?"

"You don't call home very often."

"Dad," she whispered, closing her eyes, "is Mom around? I'm in the mood for a mother-daughter chat."

"Your mother's shopping. Just pretend I'm her and talk."

"I can't do that." She loved him dearly, but they were constantly arguing. Of all the Manning children, Taylor was the one who didn't hesitate to stand up to him. Her bravery had won her the esteem of her siblings.

"Why can't you talk to me? I'm your father, aren't I? You're the one who's always throwing equality of the sexes in my face. So talk."

"But, Dad, this is different."

"Hogwash. I haven't been married to your mother for the past thirty-five years without knowing how she thinks. Tell me what you want and I'll respond just as if I were your mother."

"It's nothing really, but, well…" She decided to jump in with both feet. "What would you say if I told you I met a cowboy I think I might be falling in love with? The problem is, I'm not sure I could even get along with this man. From the moment we met he set my teeth on edge."

"I take it the situation has changed?"

"Not really," she mumbled, knowing she wasn't making much sense. "He still says things that make me so mad I could scream, but then at other times he'll do something so sweet and sincere I want to cry." Her voice shook. "I realize it probably goes back to Mark, and you're going to say I'm on the rebound. Russ and I are as incompatible as any two people could be. I can't even believe I'm so attracted to him." She pulled in a deep breath once she'd finished. There was silence on the other end. "Dad?"

"I'm here."

"Well, say something."

"You want me to say something?" he repeated, but he didn't sound like himself. He paused and cleared his throat. "In this case I think you might be right—talk this over with your mother. She knows about these things."

Taylor laughed softly into the phone and shook her head. For the first time in recent history she'd won an argument with her father.

On Tuesday afternoon, as Taylor walked home, she stopped at the grocery store, then mailed her electric bill payment at the pharmacy. She loved going into Cougar Point's drugstore. Not only could she have a prescription filled, but she could buy just about anything she needed. A tiny branch of the post office operated there, as well a liquor store. In Seattle one-stop shopping generally referred to a large mall, but in Cougar Point it meant going to the pharmacy.

As she carried her groceries home, she noticed that

the leaves were starting to change and wondered how long this pleasant fall weather would continue. Turning off Main Street and onto Oak, she saw Mandy sitting on her front porch.

"Mandy?" The girl's eyes were red and puffy from crying. "Sweetheart, what's wrong?"

Russ's sister leaped to her feet and wiped her eyes. Her chin was tilted at a proud, indignant angle and her mouth trembled. "I'm leaving."

"Leaving?"

"Running away," she explained in a tight voice. "But before I go, I thought I should tell someone so Russ won't send Cody Franklin out looking for me."

Chapter 6

"Come inside," Taylor urged the girl. "I think we should talk about this."

Mandy hedged, keeping her eyes downcast. "I don't really have time."

"It'll just take a few minutes. I promise." Withdrawing the key from her purse, Taylor opened the door, walked inside and deposited her groceries on the kitchen counter.

Mandy followed, clearly anxious to be on her way.

Pulling out a chair, Taylor indicated she should sit down. Then she grabbed them each a can of cold soda as inducement and took the chair opposite Mandy.

"It's Russ," the girl said in a choked whisper. "He's making me quit the drill team."

Taylor struggled to hide her dismay. "Is it your grades?"

"No. I've always been high honor roll. We got our uniforms this afternoon and I tried mine on and Russ happened to come into the house. He saw me and got all bent out of shape, saying the skirt was too short. I tried to tell him the skirts have been the same length for the past hundred years, and that just made him madder."

"I don't think your brother appreciates sarcasm."

"No kidding. He insisted I drop the hem on the skirt five inches. I know I should've been more subtle, but I couldn't help it. I laughed and told him he was being ridiculous."

"I can't imagine that pleased him."

"No," Mandy said, shaking her head. She clutched the can with stiff fingers, but as far as Taylor could see she hadn't taken a sip. "Then he said this wasn't an issue we were going to discuss. He was ordering me, as my legal guardian, to lower the hem of the skirt, and he didn't want any arguments."

"Naturally you refused."

"Naturally. What else could I do?" Mandy yelped. "I'd look totally asinine with a drill team skirt that went to midcalf. I'd be the laughingstock of the entire school district, and all because my bullheaded brother won't listen to reason."

"Is that when he issued the ultimatum?"

"H-how'd you know?"

"I know Russ, or at least someone a whole lot like him. The way I figure it, he suggested that either you lower the hem or you quit the drill team, and then he stalked out of the house."

Mandy blinked, then took a deep swallow of the soda. "That's exactly what happened."

"You've gotten into plenty of arguments with your

brother before without deciding to run away. Why now?"

Mandy's green eyes clouded with tears as she lifted one shoulder in a halfhearted shrug. "Because."

"That doesn't tell me much." Taylor stood and reached for a box of tissues, setting it on the table.

"He doesn't want me around."

"That isn't true," Taylor said. "We were talking about you making the drill team just the other day, and Russ was so proud. He loves you, Mandy. I'm sure of it."

"I'm not. At least not anymore. He's so stubborn."

"Opinionated?"

"That, too, and…" She hesitated, searching for another word.

"Unreasonable?"

Mandy slowly raised her eyes to Taylor. "I didn't realize you knew Russ so well."

"I told you before that my father and I had trouble getting along when I was your age, didn't I?"

Mandy nodded and jerked a tissue from the box, as though admitting that she needed one was a sign of weakness.

"Sometimes I swear my father and your brother were cut from the same cloth. It would be easier to change the course of the Columbia River than to get them to alter their opinions." Raising her feet onto the edge of the chair, Taylor looped her arms around her bent knees. "The family money was limited and my parents couldn't afford to pay for all five of us to go to college. So he decided that educating the boys was more important. He assumed they'd be supporting families, while Christy and I would end up with husbands."

"But you went to college."

"Indeed I did, but I paid for every cent of it myself. It took me eight years to complete my education. I worked summers in Alaska when I could, in addition to nights and weekends during the school year. Once I was a senior, I was able to get on as a dorm mother, and that took care of my room and board."

"But, Taylor, that's not fair!"

"In my father's eyes it was. Granted, if Christy and I had been the only two, I'm sure he would have gladly paid for our education, but Dad was financially strapped paying for the boys."

"Yeah, but your brothers will probably end up getting married, too."

Mandy's logic was closely aligned with Taylor's own. "Yes, but as my father said, they won't be having babies, and it's unlikely they'll have to delay whatever career they choose in order to raise a family."

"Women are entitled to a career if they want one!"

"Of course. But it wasn't only college that my father and I argued over. It started with the usual things, like clothes and makeup and friends, but later we found ourselves at odds over just about everything else."

"W-what about boyfriends? Did your dad find reasons to dislike them all?"

"No. Just one." Now Taylor lowered her eyes. From the moment her father had met Mark, he hadn't liked the up-and-coming financial planner. When Taylor had questioned him about his instant dislike, Eric Manning had given her the most nonsensical reply. Her father had claimed Mark was too smooth. Too smooth! He'd made Mark sound like a used car salesman. Her father had refused to look past the friendly smile and the easy laugh to the talented man beneath. Mark had tried hard to win him over; Taylor gave him credit for that. The more effort he'd put forth, the more she'd loved him. Taylor and her father had argued constantly over Mark.

Then one day she'd learned that everything her father had guessed about Mark was true. She'd gone to him and broken into bitter tears. For the first time he hadn't said I told you so. Instead, he'd held her in his arms and gently patted her head while she wept. She'd heard later from her brothers that their father had wanted to confront Mark and tell him what a bastard he was. It had taken some fast talking on their parts to convince him it was best to leave the situation alone.

"You've had arguments with Russ before," Taylor said again, tearing herself away from the memories of a painful past.

Mandy plucked out another tissue, noisily blew her nose and nodded. "Lots of times, especially lately. He's always finding things to gripe at me about."

"But why run away now?"

"I have my reasons."

Her words were so low that Taylor had to strain to hear. "Where will you go?"

"I have an aunt in New Jersey.... I'm not exactly sure where. She was my mother's half sister, and she sent me a birthday present once before my mom died. I think she might let me live with her."

Taylor didn't bother to point out the numerous holes in Mandy's plan. "Wouldn't it be a good idea to contact her first?" she asked.

"I...was hoping to surprise her."

"You mean show up on her doorstep so she can't say no?"

"Something like that," Mandy admitted.

The phone rang, and standing, Taylor walked over to answer it. Apparently Mandy thought this was a good time to use the bathroom and left the kitchen.

"Hello."

"Taylor, this is Russ. I don't suppose you've heard from Mandy, have you?" He sounded impatient and more than a little worried. "I'm at my wits' end with that girl. I've called practically everyone in town. I've got enough to do without playing hide-and-seek with her."

"She's here."

"We had another one of our fights and—" He stopped abruptly. "She's there? In town? With you?"

"That's what I just said."

"How'd she get there?"

"I assume she either walked or hitchhiked."

"Into town?" He groaned. "Listen, keep her there. I'll be at your place in ten minutes. You can warn her right now, she may be on restriction for the rest of her natural life."

"Russ, there seems to be a lack of communication here."

"You're damn right there is. She can't go running to you every time she needs someone to champion her cause. And while I'm on the subject, I refuse to listen to your arguments regarding this skirt issue. I'm not going to have any sister of mine running around half-naked."

"Mandy didn't ask me to champion her cause," Taylor said, having trouble holding back her own quick temper. "She came to tell me she was running away."

Russ's response was a short, harsh laugh. "We'll see about that," he said, and slammed down the receiver.

Stifling a groan herself, Taylor hung up.

"I should be leaving," Mandy said when she returned to the kitchen.

"What about clothes?"

"I packed a bag and hid it in the bushes outside. I wasn't going to tell you I was running away at first. I only came to thank you for being my friend. I...I think Russ likes you and I hope that you two...well, you know." She smiled bravely, but tears rolled down her face and she smeared them across her cheeks with the back of her hand.

"Money?" Taylor tried next, thinking fast. She had to stall Russ's sister until he arrived, although in his present frame of mind, she wasn't sure he'd help matters any.

"I have enough."

"How much is enough?"

"A couple of hundred dollars. I was saving it for a new saddle, but after I saw the dress you made for the dance I was going to buy a sewing machine. Now I'll need it to get to New Jersey."

"But, Mandy, that won't even pay for a bus ticket."

"I'll...think of something."

"I've got some cash," Taylor said, reaching for her purse. "It's a shame you're leaving. I was asked to be a chaperone when the drill team goes to Reno next month. I was looking forward to seeing you perform."

"You were?" Mandy brightened somewhat. "It's going to be fun. We've been practicing early every morning for this competition, and by next month we should be really good. The larger high schools almost always win, but all the girls who go have such a good time." Some of the excitement left her, and her shoulders sagged. She forced a smile. "At least in Reno you'll be able to use your American Express."

"And order pizza. I would kill for a good pepperoni pizza on a Friday night."

"The bowling alley makes a decent one. You should try it sometime."

"I suppose I will," Taylor said, rummaging through her wallet. "Are you sure you won't change your mind? Mandy, sweetheart, it's a cold, cruel world out there. If you like, you can call your aunt from here and feel her out before you leave Cougar Point."

"I guess maybe I should," Mandy murmured, not looking certain about anything. She hesitated, then turned huge appealing eyes on Taylor. "I was wondering…do you think maybe I could live with you? No, don't answer that," she said quickly. Regretfully. "Russ would never allow it, and, well, it wouldn't work. Forget I asked."

"I'd love it if you did, but, honey, that isn't any solution."

Mandy tucked her chin against her collarbone. "I'll leave in a few minutes, okay?"

"Mandy." Taylor stopped her. She couldn't continue this pretense. "That was Russ on the phone a few minutes ago. He's on his way to talk to you."

The pale green eyes widened with offense. "You told him I was here? How could you, Taylor? I thought you were my friend. I trusted you.…"

"I am your friend. I care about you and can't let you ruin your life because you've had a spat with your brother."

"It's more than that."

"I know. Trust me, I know," Taylor said gently, resisting the urge to pull Mandy into her arms. "What I'd like to suggest is that when your brother arrives you stay in the kitchen, and I'll keep him in the living room and try to talk some sense into him."

"He won't listen," Mandy cried. Tears ran unrestrained down her cheeks, and she clenched her fists at her sides. "It would be best if I just left now."

The sound of Russ's truck screeching to a stop outside the house was a welcome relief, at least to Taylor. "Give me ten minutes alone with him," she said.

"All right," Mandy reluctantly agreed. "But that's all the time I've got." She made it sound as if she had a plane to catch.

Taylor was at the front door before Russ could even knock. What she saw didn't give her any hope that this matter could easily be put to rest. His fury was all too evident; his face was red and his steps were quick and abrupt as he let himself in the house. Taylor practically had to throw herself in front of the kitchen door to keep him in the living room.

"Where is she?"

"Before you talk to Mandy, you and I need to discuss something."

"Not now," he said, looking past her. "I've never raised a hand to that girl, but I'll tell you she's tempting fate. Running away? That's a laugh. And just where does she intend to go?"

"Russ, would you stop shouting and listen to me." Taylor used her best schoolteacher voice and placed her hands threateningly on her hips as if to suggest one more cross word and she'd report him to the principal.

"I have somewhere to go, so you needn't worry," Mandy yelled from the kitchen.

"Sit down," Taylor said, pointing at her sofa. "We've got a problem here that isn't going to be settled by you hollering threats at your sister."

"They're a lot more than threats." Russ continued pacing the floor, occasionally removing his hat long enough to angrily plow his fingers through his hair.

"Mandy didn't come to me about the length of the drill team uniform—"

"It's a damn good thing because I'm not changing my mind. No sister of mine is going to parade around a field in that skimpy little outfit." His frown informed Taylor that he didn't appreciate her interference in what he considered a family affair.

"I'm leaving!" Mandy shouted from the other room.

"Over my dead body," Russ retaliated. "I'll drag you back to the ranch if I have to."

"Then I'll run away tomorrow. You can't force me to live with you."

"She's right, you know," Taylor whispered.

Russ shot her a look hot enough to boil water.

"Listen to what she's really saying," Taylor pleaded.

Russ advanced a step toward the other room. Taylor's hand on his arm stopped him. He glanced down at her and blinked as though he'd almost forgotten that she was there. "This is between me and my sister," he growled.

"Listen to her," Taylor repeated, more forcefully this time. "Hear the doubt and pain in her voice. She doesn't want to leave any more than you want her to go."

"Then why…?"

"Because she's convinced you don't love her and you don't want her living with you anymore."

Russ removed his hat and slapped it against the coffee table. "Of all the foolish…" Suddenly he seemed at a loss for words. "That's the most ridiculous thing I've ever heard."

"Mandy," Taylor called, "come out here and sit down." She gestured toward Russ, motioning for him to do the same. "The only way I can see that'll do any good is for the two of you to clear the air. You need to talk face-to-face instead of hurling insults at each other."

Mandy hesitantly moved into the living room. She sank slowly into a chair and picked up a women's magazine sitting on the arm, absently flipping through the pages.

Russ sat on the other side of the room, looking nonchalant and relaxed. He propped his ankle on one knee and spread his arms across the back of the davenport as if they were discussing the abrupt change in weather rather than the future of his only sister and their relationship.

"Mandy, why do you want to move in with your aunt?" Taylor asked.

"Because my pigheaded brother is so unreasonable."

"You've gotten along with him up until now."

"No, I haven't." Her voice grew smaller and smaller. "Besides, I'm just in the way."

"Russ," Taylor said, twisting around to confront him, "is Mandy in the way?"

"Hell, no, I need her."

"Sure, to cook your meals and wash your clothes. You can hire someone to do that. I bet Mary Lu Randall would do it for free. She's had a crush on you forever."

"You're all the family I've got," Russ countered gruffly.

"I'm nothing but a problem," Mandy said, rubbing the tears from her eyes. "You think I don't notice, but

I do. There isn't a single thing you like about me any-more. You're always complaining. If it isn't my hair, it's my clothes or I'm wearing too much makeup or spend-ing too much time with my friends."

Russ dropped his leg and leaned forward, hands clasped. He studied Mandy, then started to frown. "I'm just trying to do the best job I can to make sure you turn into a responsible adult."

Mandy looked away. Unable to stand still, Taylor crossed the room, sat on the arm of the chair and placed her own on Mandy's thin shoulders.

"I love you, Amanda," Russ said starkly. "Maybe sometimes I don't show it the way I should, but I do. You're as much a part of my life as the Lazy P. I need you, and not to do the cooking and laundry, either."

Mandy sniffled in an effort not to cry, and Taylor reached inside her pocket for a fresh tissue, handing it to the girl.

"I…didn't realize this drill team thing was so impor-tant to you," Russ went on. "I suppose Taylor's going to tell me I should've been more sensitive." Russ paused, shaking his head. "When I saw you all dressed up like that, it made me realize how grown-up you're getting, and I guess I didn't want to face the fact you're going to be a beautiful young woman soon. It kind of scares me. Before long, the boys are going to be swarming around the ranch like ants."

"I-if you really want me to quit the drill team, I will," Mandy offered in a thin, raspy voice.

"No, you can stay on the team. If the other parents are willing to let their daughters prance around a play-ing field in those little outfits, then I'll just have to get used to the idea." Russ stood up and walked across the room, standing in front of his sister. "Friends?"

Mandy nodded, fresh tears streaking her face. She jumped up and moved into Russ's arms, hugging him tight. "I didn't really want to live with Aunt Joyce in New Jersey."

"That's good because the last I heard she retired someplace in Mexico."

"She did? How come you never told me?"

"Maybe because I was afraid you'd think it was an exotic, fun place to be and decide you'd rather live with her. I meant what I said about loving you, Mandy. You're going to have to be more patient with me, I guess, but I promise I'll try harder."

"I...will, too."

Russ slowly shut his eyes as he hugged his sister close.

Taylor felt her own eyes fill with tears. She hadn't expected Russ to be so open about his feelings for Mandy. When he'd first arrived, she'd been convinced everything was going to go from bad to worse. Russ was so proud and so furious, but once he'd stopped to listen to his sister and heard her fears, he'd set the anger aside and revealed a deep, vulnerable part of himself that Taylor had never even suspected was there.

"Say, how about if I treat my two best girls to dinner?" Russ suggested.

"Yeah," Mandy responded. "Pizza?"

"Anything you want," he said, smiling down on his sister. He raised his eyes to Taylor, and they softened perceptibly.

"I...can't," she said, declining the invitation. "Any-

way, this should be a time for the two of you to talk. I'd just be in the way."

"No, you wouldn't. We'd never have been able to do this without you," Mandy insisted. "I really want you to come."

"Another time," Taylor promised. "You two go and have fun."

Russ squeezed Mandy's shoulders. "I don't know about you, but I'm famished. If Taylor wants to turn down an offer for the best pizza in town, there's only one thing we can do—let her suffer."

"It's your loss," Mandy told Taylor on their way out the door.

"Yes, I know," she said, standing behind the screen door. Mandy bounded down the front steps and ran around the side of the house, where she'd apparently hidden her bag of clothes.

While Russ was waiting for his sister to reappear, he turned to Taylor and mouthed the words, "Thank you." Then he touched his fingers to his lips and held his hand out to her. She pressed her open palm against the screen door.

The following evening Taylor sat at the kitchen table with her feet propped on a chair, stirring a bowl of soup. "You're in deep trouble here," she muttered to herself. "If you don't watch it, you're going to fall in love with a cowboy. You're already halfway there. Admit it."

She vigorously stirred her chicken noodle soup until it sloshed over the rim of the bowl. Setting the spoon aside, Taylor leaned her elbows on the table and buried her face in her hands.

The whole purpose of coming to Montana was to

avoid relationships. She hadn't been in town a week when she'd met Russ. And from there everything had quickly gone downhill. From the first time he'd kissed her she'd known she was headed for disaster. But had that stopped her? Oh, no. Not even the cool voice of reason—or the memory of Mark's betrayal—had given her pause. Instead she was walking straight into his arms, knowing full well that nothing could ever come of their relationship. She wouldn't have an affair with him. Marriage was out of the question; Russ would agree with her there. So exactly where was their relationship going?

Nowhere.

"Nowhere," she repeated out loud. "Save yourself some heartache," she told herself, then sat back and wondered if she was wise enough to follow her own advice, immediately doubting that she was. The voice in her heart was so much louder than anything her brain was telling her. She'd been a fool once. Hadn't she learned anything? Apparently not!

The phone rang, startling her. She dropped her legs and stood to answer it, afraid it might be Russ and not knowing what she'd say.

It was.

"Hi," she said, forcing some enthusiasm into her voice. The man had no idea of the turmoil he was causing her.

"I'm calling to thank you for what you did for Mandy and me yesterday."

"It wasn't anything," she said lightly. Her hand tightened around the telephone receiver as she supported herself against the kitchen wall. She hated the way her pulse reacted to the sound of his voice. If he had a voice like other men, it wouldn't affect her so strongly. His was deep and so sexy....

"You were right about me not being aware of her doubt and fear," he went on to say. "I don't know what I did to make her think I don't want her around anymore, but she's totally wrong."

"You were wonderful with her." Taylor meant that. She hadn't expected him to be half as understanding or sensitive to his sister's needs. Perhaps it would be easier to walk away from him if she could continue to view him as a difficult male, but he'd shown her another side of his personality, one so appealing that she found her heart softening toward him.

"I felt bad because I'd overreacted to the whole issue of her drill team uniform," Russ explained. "I'd come into the house, and seeing Mandy dressed in that outfit caught me by surprise. My nerves were on edge, anyway. We'd just found a dead calf, and when I saw Mandy, I took my frustration and anger out on her. She didn't deserve that."

"But you apologized. And taking her out to dinner was nice."

"I wish you'd come along. We both owe you."

"Nonsense. That was your time with Mandy."

Taylor could sense Russ's smile. "I will admit that we did have fun. I'd forgotten what a kick my sister can be. She's a sweet kid, but she's growing up too fast." There was a pause. "Listen, I didn't call you just to talk about Mandy. How about dinner Friday night?"

Taylor closed her eyes. The lure of the invitation was as strong as the pull of the tide. Squaring her shoulders, she shook her head.

"Taylor?"

"I don't think it's a good idea for us to see each other again," she said flatly.

Chapter 7

"What the hell do you mean?" Russ demanded. He didn't know what kind of game Taylor was playing, but he wasn't about to become a participant. If there was a problem, he wanted it out in the open.

"Exactly what I said," she returned, sounding shaky and unsure. "I don't think it's wise for us to continue seeing each other."

"Why not?" He tried to keep his voice even, but dammit, Taylor was irritating him, not that this was anything new.

Russ had never met a woman like Taylor Manning before. She could make him madder than anyone he'd ever known, but when he kissed her, the earth moved, angels sang, and whatever else people said about moments of passion. Russ didn't understand it. No one had ever affected him the way Taylor did.

He'd tried staying away from her. Tried exercising a little more self-control, but five minutes with her and his good intentions went the way of all flesh. He wanted her in his bed, her hair spread out over his pillow. He thought about that a lot, far more than he should. Not for the first time, the image brought with it the stirrings of arousal. How could this teacher—and worse, one from a big city—inspire such hunger in him? It made no sense.

He'd run into a cocktail waitress friend when he'd been in Miles City the week before. It had been an uncomfortable encounter. April had expected him to come home with her for what she called "a little afternoon pleasure." Instead, Russ couldn't get away from her fast enough. Not that he didn't crave being with a woman. But deep down he'd known that the only woman he wanted was Taylor.

That afternoon Russ had seen April for what she was, jaded and cold, and he wanted nothing to do with her. He'd escaped and hurried back to the Lazy P, only to discover Taylor there with his sister. He'd wanted her so badly that day. There was no use lying to himself about it. Even now, almost a week later, when he closed his eyes, he could still smell the fragrance of her perfume. Her mouth had parted beneath his, eager for his kisses. Every touch had hurled his senses into chaos.

"I...don't want there to be any misunderstandings between us," Taylor said, cutting into his thoughts.

Reluctantly Russ pulled himself from his musings. "I don't, either. If you won't have dinner with me, I'd like to know why. That's not such an unreasonable request, is it?"

"I...think the reason should be obvious."

"Tell me, anyway."

Russ felt her hesitation, and when she spoke again, her voice was a little raspy, as if she found it difficult to share her thoughts. "Our personality differences should be more than adequate reason for us to use caution."

She sounded exactly like the schoolteacher she was. "That hasn't stopped us before. Why should it now?" he asked.

"Darn it, Russ Palmer," she cried. "You aren't going to make this easy, are you?"

"All I want is the truth."

Her sigh sang over the wire. "I can't give you anything less than the truth, can I?"

"No," he said softly. "I'll admit we're different. Anyone looking at us could be able to see that. Our opinions on most subjects are completely opposite, but frankly, I'm willing to work around that. I like you, Taylor."

"I know," she whispered dismally. That knowledge seemed to cause her distress rather than celebration.

Russ wasn't pleased, but he refused to make an issue of it. "There are plenty of girls in Cougar Point who'd be mighty pleased if I invited them out to dinner," he added, thinking that might set her back some, help her realize she had competition.

"Ask them out then," she said tartly.

"I don't want to. The only woman who interests me is you."

"That's the problem," she mumbled, and it sounded like she was close to tears.

The thought of Taylor crying did something funny to Russ's stomach. His protective urges ran deep when it came to this woman. "Taylor, maybe I should drive into town and we can talk face-to-face."

"No," she returned abruptly. "That would only make

this more difficult." She paused, and Russ had to restrain the yearning to put the phone aside and go to her
immediately.

"Is this about what happened the other day?" he
asked. "I know our kissing went further than it should
have, but that wasn't intentional. If you want an apology…"

"No, that's not it. Oh, Russ, don't you see?"

He didn't. "Tell me."

"I like you too much. We both know where this is
going to lead—one of these days we're going to end up
in love and in bed together."

That didn't sound too tragic to Russ. He'd been
dreaming about it for weeks. "So?"

"So?" she shouted, and her voice vibrated with anger.
"I'm not interested in a permanent relationship with
you. You're a wonderful man—and you'll make some
woman a terrific husband. But not me."

He let a moment of tense silence pass before he com-
mented. "If you'll recall, the invitation was for dinner.
All I was asking for was a simple meal together. I'm
not looking for a lifetime commitment."

"You're doing your best to make this difficult, which
is all too typical. I will not have an affair with you, and
that's exactly where our relationship is headed. People
are already talking, especially after the Grange dance.
And then we went horseback riding and… Before I
know it, you're going to be telling me how to vote and
insisting a woman's place is in the home." She paused
only long enough to inhale a quick breath. "I'm sorry…
I really am, but I don't think we should have anything
to do with each other. Please understand."

Before Russ could say another word, the line was

disconnected. He held the receiver in his hand for several minutes in disbelief. His first response was anger. He didn't know what Taylor was muttering about. Her words about voting and a woman's place were utterly nonsensical.

He had every right to be upset with her; no one had ever hung up on him before. Instead he felt a tingling satisfaction. Slowly, hardly aware that it was happening, Russ felt a smile creep over his face.

Mandy strolled past him just then. "Hey, what's so funny?"

"Taylor," he said, grinning hard. "She likes me."

Russ was riding the range, looking for strays, when he saw his lifelong friend come barreling toward him in a battered pickup. Removing his hat, Russ wiped his forearm across his brow. He'd been in the saddle since morning, and he was wearier than he could remember being in a long while. He hadn't been sleeping well; Taylor was constantly on his mind, and he still hadn't figured out what to do about her. If anything. He'd delayed confronting her, thinking it was best to give her time. But he was growing anxious. In the past couple of days Russ had faced a few truths about the two of them.

"Cody, good to see you," Russ greeted him, dismounting from Magic. "Problems?"

"None to speak of," Cody said, opening the cab door and getting out.

"You didn't come looking for me to discuss the weather."

Cody wasn't wearing his sheriff deputy's uniform, which was unusual. Instead, he had on jeans and a thick sweater. He was about the same height as Russ, but he kept his dark hair trimmed short.

"It's been nice the past week or so, hasn't it?" Cody said, gesturing toward the cloudless blue sky. He tucked his fingertips into the hip pocket of his Levi's and walked to the front of the truck. Leaning his back against the grille, he raised one foot and rested it on the bumper.

For early October the weather had been unseasonably warm. They'd experienced several Indian summer days, and while Russ appreciated the respite before winter hit, he knew better than to take anything about Montana weather for granted.

"What's up?" he asked. "It isn't like you to beat around the bush."

Cody nodded, looking slightly chagrined. "I came to talk to you about the new schoolteacher."

"What about her?" Russ asked, tensing. He moved over to the truck and put his foot on the bumper, meeting Cody's eyes.

The deputy glanced away, but not before Russ saw the troubled look on his face.

"We've been friends a lot of years, and the last thing I want is for a woman to come between us."

"I take it you want to ask Taylor out?"

Cody nodded. "But only if you have no objection. Word is the two of you aren't seeing each other anymore."

"Who told you that?" Russ demanded, fighting to repress the surge of instant jealousy that tightened around his chest. He'd resisted the temptation to rush into town and talk some sense into Taylor, assuming she'd have second thoughts by now. Apparently that wasn't the case. Truth be known, Russ had been doing some thinking about their situation. They were both mature adults and they weren't going to leap into something that would be wrong for them. Okay, so they were strongly attracted—that much was a given—and not seeing each other wasn't going to change the situation, not one bit.

It came as a shock for Russ to admit he was falling in love with Taylor. There wasn't any use in fighting it—hell, he didn't even want to. Nor was he going to pretend he didn't care about her.

"Mary Beth Morgan said something to me this morning," Cody continued. "Mary Beth said she and Taylor were having coffee in the faculty lounge and she inquired about the two of you. Evidently Taylor told her you'd decided not to see each other again."

"Taylor came right out and said that?"

"I don't know her exact words. Hey, I'm repeating what someone else repeated to me. How close it is to the truth, I wouldn't know. That's why I'm here."

The mental image of Cody holding Taylor in his arms brought a sudden flash of rage so strong that for a moment Russ couldn't breathe. Shoving away from the truck, he returned to Magic, reached for the reins and leaped onto the gelding's back.

"Russ?" Cody asked, frowning.

"Go ahead and ask her out."

Taylor couldn't remember Friday nights being so lonely before moving to Cougar Point. It seemed she'd always had something to do, someplace to go. But that wasn't the case anymore. Her entertainment options were limited. The town sported one old-time theater.

One screen. One movie. The feature film for the week was a comedy Taylor had seen six months earlier in Seattle. By now it was probably available on video in most parts of the country.

There had been an offer for dinner from Cody Franklin, which had been a surprise, but she'd turned him down. In retrospect she wished she hadn't been so quick to refuse him. He was certainly pleasant. They'd met at the dance, and she'd found him reserved, and perhaps a little remote.

If she was looking for some way to kill time, she could sew, but Taylor simply wasn't in the mood. After a long week in the classroom, she was more interested in doing something relaxing.

Well, she could always read, she supposed. Locating a promising romance, she cuddled up in the armchair and wrapped an afghan around her legs. She hadn't finished the first chapter when her eyes started to drift closed. Struggling to keep them open, she concentrated on the text. After the third yawn, she gave up, set the open book over the arm of the chair and decided to rest for a few minutes.

The next thing she knew someone was pounding at her front door.

Taylor tossed aside the afghan and stumbled across the room, disoriented and confused. "W-who is it?" she asked. The door didn't have a peephole; most folks in town didn't even bother to lock their front doors.

"Russ Palmer," came the gruff reply.

Taylor quickly twisted the lock and opened the door. "What are you doing here?" she insisted. It took all her willpower not to throw her arms around him.

Now that Russ was standing in the middle of her

living room, he didn't look all that pleased about being there.

The wall clock chimed, and Taylor absently counted ten strikes. It was ten! She'd been "resting" for nearly two hours. Good grief, she'd been reduced to falling asleep at eight o'clock on a Friday night.

"Russ?" she prodded. He was frowning, and she had no idea why. "Is something wrong?"

"No." He gave her a silly, lopsided grin. "Everything's wonderful. You're wonderful. I'm wonderful. The whole world's wonderful."

"Russ?" She squinted up at him. "You've been drinking."

He pointed his index finger toward the ceiling. "Only a little."

She steered him toward the sofa and sat him down. "How much is a little?"

"A couple of beers with a bunch of guys." His brows drew together as he considered his words. "Or was that a couple of guys and a bunch of beers? I don't remember anymore."

"That's what I thought," she murmured. He'd obviously downed more than two beers! "I'll make you some coffee."

"Don't go," he said, reaching out and clasping her around the waist. "I'm not drunk, just a little tipsy. I had this sudden urge to visit my lady, and now that I'm here, I want to hold you."

He effortlessly brought her into his lap. Her hands were on his shoulders. "I thought we agreed this sort of thing had to stop," she whispered.

His mouth found the open V of her shirt, and he

kissed her there, gliding his tongue over her warm skin, creating sensations that were even warmer.

"We weren't going to see each other anymore, remember?" she tried again. Her nails dug into the hard muscles of his shoulders as she exhaled slowly.

"I've been thinking about that," Russ said between nibbling kisses that slid along the line of her jaw. "I haven't thought of anything else all week."

"Russ, please stop," she whimpered.

To her surprise, he did as she asked. Her hands were in his hair, and she reluctantly withdrew them. "You shouldn't be driving."

"I know. I left the truck at Billy's and walked over here. Only I didn't realize where I was headed until I arrived on your doorstep."

Billy's was one of the town's three taverns—the most popular, according to what Taylor had heard. During the summer months, they brought in a band every third Friday, and apparently every adult in town showed up.

"You shouldn't have come," she whispered. Then why was she so glad he had? Taylor didn't want to analyze the answer to that, afraid of what she'd discover.

"You're positively right," Russ concurred. "I have no business being here. Go ahead and kick me out. I wouldn't blame you if you did. Fact is, you probably should."

"If you promise to behave yourself, I'll put on a pot of coffee." She squirmed off his lap and moved into the kitchen. She'd just poured cold water into the automatic drip machine when Russ stole up behind her. He slipped his arms around her waist and buried his face in the curve of her neck.

"Russ...you promised."

"No, I didn't."

"Then...you should leave."

He dropped his arms, walked over to the chair, turned it around and straddled it. He was grinning, obviously pleased. "Cody told me," he announced.

Taylor busied herself bringing down two mugs from the cupboard and setting them on the counter. Apparently there were no secrets in this town. Taylor regretted not accepting Cody Franklin's dinner invitation. She certainly wished she had now.

"You turned him down. Why?" His dark eyes held hers with unwavering curiosity, demanding a reply.

"I...don't think that's any of your business."

He shrugged, his look indifferent. "I'd like to think it *is* my business."

"You don't own me." She pressed her hands into the counter behind her.

He grinned. "Not for lack of trying." He held out his arms to her, beseeching her to walk over. "We've got a good thing going, and I can't understand why you want to throw it away." His eyes continued to hold hers, but he was no longer smiling. "The first time I met you, I recognized trouble. That didn't stop me, and it didn't stop you, either, did it?"

She lowered her gaze rather than answer. When she raised her head, she discovered Russ standing directly in front of her.

"Did it?" he repeated. He grabbed her around the waist, and with one swift movement set her on top of the counter.

She stared at him, wondering about his mood. "Russ?"

He slanted his mouth over hers, kissing her long and

hard, and when he'd finished, she was panting. "Did it?" he asked a third time.

He reached for her shoulders again, intent on another kiss—and more.

"Russ, you're drunk." From somewhere she found the strength to stop him, although it felt like the most difficult task of her life.

Ever so slowly he tilted back his head. His grin was sultry and teasing. "I'm not that drunk."

"You shouldn't have come here."

"Yes, I know." His hands were in her hair. He couldn't seem to leave it alone. Every time they were together, he ran his fingers through it. Carefully he removed the combs, then arranged it over her shoulder, smoothing it with his callused fingertips. Then his hands framed her face and he kissed her once more.

Unable to resist him, she parted her lips in welcome, and they clung to each other.

When he finally dragged his mouth from hers, he smiled at her. "Go ahead and give me that coffee, and then you can drive me home."

Without question, Taylor did as he asked. They drank their coffee in silence, and its sobering effect hit her immediately. After all her intentions to stay away from him, she'd been giddy with happiness when he'd arrived. It hadn't mattered that he'd been drinking. It hadn't mattered that he took liberties with her. All that mattered was seeing him again. Taylor had never thought of herself as a weak person, but that was how Russ made her feel. Spineless and indecisive.

Russ fell asleep on the drive out to the ranch. Taylor was glad to see that the back porch light was on when she pulled in to the yard. She parked the car and hurried around to the passenger side.

"Russ," she said, shaking him by the shoulders. "Wake up."

His eyes opened slowly, and when he recognized her, he grinned, his gaze warm and loving. "Taylor."

"You're home."

His arms circled her waist. "Yes, I know."

Taylor managed to break free. "Come on, let's go inside, and for heaven's sake, could you be a little less noisy? I don't want anyone to know I brought you here."

"Why not?" He inclined his head as if the answer demanded serious concentration.

"There's enough talk about us as it is. The last thing I need is for someone to report seeing my car parked at your house late on a Friday night."

"Don't worry. No one can see the house from the road."

"Just get inside, would you?" She was losing her patience with him. Despite the coffee, his actions were slower than before. He moved with the deliberateness of inebriation, taking unhurried wobbly steps toward the house.

The back door was unlocked, and Russ slammed it shut with his foot. The sound ricocheted through the kitchen like a blast from a shotgun, startling Taylor.

"Shh," Russ said loudly, pressing his finger over his lips. "You'll wake Mandy."

Taylor wished the teenager *would* wake up and come to help her. Russ was increasingly difficult to handle.

"You need to go to bed," she said and prepared to leave.

"I'll never make it there without you." His smile

was roguish and naughty, and he staggered a few steps as though that was proof enough. "I need you, Taylor. No telling what might happen to me if I'm left to my own devices."

"I'm willing to chance that."

"I'm not." With his arm around her waist, he led her toward the stairs. He stumbled forward, bringing Taylor with him. She had no choice but to follow. She didn't know if it was an act or not, but he really did seem to need her assistance.

They were two steps up the stairs when Russ sagged against the wall and sighed heavily. "Have I ever told you I think you're beautiful?"

"I believe the word was wonderful," she muttered, using her shoulder to urge him forward.

"You're both. A man could drown in eyes that blue and not even care."

"Russ," she said in a whisper, "let's get you upstairs."

"In bed?" He arched his brows suggestively.

"Just get upstairs. Please."

"You're so eager for my body, you can hardly wait, can you?" he asked, then chuckled softly, seeming to find himself exceptionally amusing. He leaned forward enough to kiss the side of her neck. "I'll try to make it worth your while."

Taylor was breathless by the time they reached the top of the stairs. "Which room is yours?" she asked.

Russ turned all the way around before raising his arm and directing her to the bedroom at the end of the hall. "There," he said enthusiastically, pointing straight ahead as if he'd discovered uncharted land.

With her arm firmly around his middle, Taylor led him to the room. The hall was dark, lit only by the light of the moon visible through an uncurtained window. She opened the door, and together the two of them staggered forward, landing on the bed with a force that drove the oxygen from her lungs.

Russ released a deep sigh and rolled onto his back, positioning Taylor above him. His unrelenting dark eyes stared up at her.

"I...should be going."

"Not yet," he whispered. "Kiss me good-night first."

"Russ, no." She tried to move, but his hands were on her hips, holding her fast.

"All I'm asking for is one little kiss. So when I wake up in the morning I'll remember you were here and that'll make me feel good."

She rolled her eyes. "The only thing you're going to feel in the morning is a world-class headache."

"If you won't kiss me, then you leave me with no option but to kiss you."

He began to kiss her lips, tiny nibbling kisses that promised so much more than they delivered. Then he changed tactics, drugging her with prolonged kisses that chased away all grounds for complaint.

For some reason he stopped. Suddenly. He threw back his head and dragged in several deep breaths.

"Does this prove anything?" he asked urgently.

"That...that I should have left you to your own devices. You didn't need my help."

"I did. I do. I always will."

She shook her head, but Russ ignored that.

"In case you haven't figured it out yet," he informed her, "you belong in my bed, and that's exactly where you're going to end up."

With what remained of her shredded dignity, Taylor

pushed herself free. She bolted off the bed and paced the room. As she did, Russ sat up on the bed, leaning against the bunched pillows, looking smug and arrogant. "You're so beautiful."

It was all Taylor could do not to throw her hands in the air and scream. "This doesn't change a thing," she insisted. "Not a thing."

His answering grin was filled with cocky reassurance. "Wanna bet?"

Chapter 8

"Hi, Taylor," Mandy said as she stepped into Taylor's classroom early the following week.

"Howdy."

Mandy grinned. "You're beginning to sound like a country girl."

That gave Taylor cause to sit back and take notice. "I am?"

Mandy nodded. "Russ told me just the other day that he's going to make a country girl out of you yet." Mandy walked over to the front row of desks and sat on the edge of one as she spoke.

At the mention of Russ, Taylor began to fiddle with the pencils on her desk.

"Do…you remember the day I was thinking about running away?" Mandy asked, and her voice lowered.

"Of course," Taylor said.

"I asked you what your father thought about the boys you dated, and you told me he'd generally approved of your boyfriends." She pressed her books close to her chest, and Taylor noted how tense her hands were. "There was…a reason I asked about that. You see, there's this boy in school—he's a junior and his name is Eddie and…well, he's really nice and my family knows his family and we've known each other almost all our lives and—"

"You like Eddie?"

Mandy's responding nod was fervent. "A whole lot, and I think he likes me, too. We've only talked in the hall a couple of times, but this morning when I was putting my books in my locker, he walked up and we started talking…not about anything in particular, at least not at first, then all of a sudden he asked if I wanted to go to the movies with him Saturday night."

"I see." Taylor did understand her dilemma. All too well. Mandy was only fourteen, and Russ would surely consider a high school freshman too young to date. In fact, Taylor agreed with him, but she'd been fourteen once herself and attracted to a boy who'd liked her. He'd been older, too, and had asked her to a party, which her father had adamantly opposed her attending. The memory of the argument that had followed remained painfully vivid in her mind.

"I really, really want to go to the movies with Eddie, but I'm afraid Russ will get upset with me for even asking. I mean, he's been trying hard to listen to my point of view, but dating is something that's never come up before and…well, I have a feeling we aren't going to be able to talk about me having a boyfriend without…

an argument." She sighed heavily. "What should I do, Taylor?"

Taylor wished she had an easy answer. "I really don't know."

"Will you talk to him for me?"

"Absolutely not."

"Oh, please! You don't know how much this would mean to me. Don't you remember what it's like to be fourteen and have a boy like you?"

That was the problem; Taylor *did* remember. "When I was your age, a sixteen-year-old boy invited me to a party. My father made it sound as if he wanted to drag me into an opium den. More than anything in the world, I wanted to go to that party."

"Did you?"

Taylor shook her head sadly. "I was too young to date."

Mandy's shoulders sagged with defeat. "It's only a movie, and I don't understand why it would be so bad if Eddie and I went to a show together."

Crossing her arms, Taylor started to pace her classroom, her thoughts spinning. "What about a compromise?"

"H-how do you mean?"

"What if Russ were to drop you off at the theater, you paid your own way and then you sat next to Eddie? With Russ's approval, of course."

Mandy looked more perplexed than relieved. "Eddie could buy me popcorn, though, couldn't he?"

"Sure. It wouldn't be like a real date, but you'd still be at the movies with Eddie."

Mandy's hold on her schoolbooks relaxed. "Do you think Russ would go for it?"

"He's a reasonable man." Taylor couldn't believe she was actually saying this, but in some instances it was true, and he was trying hard with his sister. "I'm sure he'd at least take it into consideration."

Mandy nodded, but her lips were still pinched. "Will you talk to him about it?"

"Me?" Taylor returned spiritedly. "You've got to be joking!"

"I'm not. Russ listens to you. You may not think so but I know he does. It's because of you that I'm allowed to wear makeup and buy my own clothes. Russ and I are trying hard to get along, but I'm afraid this thing with Eddie will ruin everything. Oh, Taylor, please. I'll do anything you want. Cook your meals, do your laundry…all year, anything. *Please.*"

"Russ will listen to you."

"Maybe," Mandy agreed reluctantly, "but this is too important to mess up. I told Eddie I'd have to talk it over with my brother, and he said I should let him know tomorrow. I'm afraid if I put him off he'll ask some other girl, and I'd die if he did."

Against her better judgment, Taylor felt herself weakening. She hadn't seen Russ since Friday night when she'd dropped him off at the house, taken him up the stairs and put him to bed. That whole episode was best forgotten as far as Taylor was concerned.

"Please," Mandy coaxed once more.

"All right," Taylor muttered. When she was growing up, she'd been able to go to her mother, who'd smooth things over with her father. Mandy didn't have anyone to run interference for her. Taylor didn't really mind—although she worried that Russ would use this opportunity to press her with a few arguments of his own, ones that had nothing to do with his sister.

Russ had been having a bad day from the time he'd woken up that morning. The minute he'd stepped out of the house he'd encountered one problem after another, the latest being a calf standing two feet deep in mud. After an hour of fruitless effort, Russ had lost his patience and accepted the fact that he was going to need help. He'd contacted a couple of his hands by walkie-talkie and was waiting for them to arrive.

Every calf was valuable, but this one, trapped and growing weaker, had been marked for his breeding herd. Like most of the ranchers in Cougar Point, Russ kept two herds. One for breeding purposes, which he used to produce bulls that he often sold for a handsome profit. Bull calves that didn't meet his expectations were turned into steers and raised for beef. His second herd was strictly grade cattle, sold off at the end of the season.

This particular calf had been the product of his highest quality bull and his best cow. Russ had great expectations for him and sure didn't want to lose him to a mud hole.

Russ checked the sun and wondered how much longer he'd have to wait. He'd sent his two best hands out to mend fences, a tedious but not thankless task.

There was still a lot of work left to complete before winter set in, and he didn't have time to waste. Miles of fence to inspect and mend, which was no small chore. If the fences weren't secure, Russ would soon be dealing with the elk that come down from the mountains in winter. If elk could get through his fence, they'd eat his oats and hay. No rancher could afford to feed elk, and a good fence was the best protection he had.

If Russ had to choose his favorite time of year, it would be autumn. The sun was still warm, but the air was crisp, and morning frost warned of encroaching winter. When he drove his cattle into the feed ground, it was like a homecoming, a culmination of the year's efforts.

The calf mewled, reminding Russ of his predicament.

"I know, fellow," Russ muttered. "I've tried everything I can think of. I'm afraid you're stuck here until one of the other men swings by and lends me a hand."

No sooner had the words escaped his mouth than he saw a truck heading slowly in his direction. He frowned, wondering who'd be coming out this way, knowing all his men were on horseback. Maybe there'd been trouble at the house.

After the day he'd been having, Russ didn't look forward to dealing with any more problems. As the blue ranch truck approached, Russ realized it was Taylor at the wheel.

He walked out of the mud and stood with his hands on his hips, waiting for her. He hadn't seen her since the night she'd driven him home. The truth was, he didn't feel proud of the way he'd finagled her into his bedroom. Yes, he'd had too much to drink, but he hadn't been nearly as drunk as he'd led her to believe.

"Hello," Taylor said as she climbed awkwardly out of the cab. She was dressed in jeans, but they were several inches too short and a tad too small. The sweater looked suspiciously like one of Mandy's.

Russ pulled off his gloves. "What brings you out

here?" He didn't mean to sound unfriendly, but he was frustrated, tired and hungry. Despite that, he was damn glad to see her.

She didn't answer him right away, but instead focused her attention on the calf, which mewled pitifully. "Mandy suggested I drive out so I could talk to you," she muttered, then pointed at the mud hole. "That calf's stuck."

"No kidding."

"There's no need to be sarcastic with me," she announced primly. As she stood there, he couldn't help noticing just how tight those jeans were.

"Aren't you going to do something?" she demanded.

Undressing her occurred to him.... Russ brought his musings to an abrupt halt. "Do something about what?" he asked.

"That cow. She needs help."

"She's a he, and I'm well aware of the fact."

"Then *help him*," Taylor ordered, gesturing toward the calf as though she suspected Russ was simply ignoring the problem.

"I've spent the past hour helping him."

"Well, you certainly didn't do a very good job of it."

He raised his eyebrows. "Do you think you can do any better?"

She looked startled for a moment, then said, "I bet I could."

"Here we go again." He took off his hat long enough to slap it against his thigh and remove the dust. "Because you're a woman, an independent, competent woman, you're convinced you can handle this problem, while I, a chauvinist and a drunk, am incapable of even assessing the situation."

"I...I didn't exactly say that."

"But it's what you implied."

"Fine," she agreed. "I'll admit I can't see why you aren't helping that poor animal."

"I guess I just needed you. Go to it, lady."

"All right, I will." Cautiously she approached the edge of the mud hole. She planted her boots just outside the dark slime and leaned forward slightly. In a low voice she started carrying on a soothing, one-sided conversation with the calf as if she could reason him out of his plight.

"You're going to have to do a lot more than talk to him," Russ couldn't resist telling her. He walked over to the truck, crossed his arms and leaned against the side. Already he could feel his sour mood lifting. Just watching Taylor deal with this would be more entertainment than he'd enjoyed in a long while.

"I'm taking a few minutes to reassure him," Taylor returned from between clenched teeth. "The poor thing's frightened half out of his wits."

"Sweet-talkin' him is bound to help."

"I'm sure it will," she said, giving him a surly look.

"Works wonders with me, too," Russ had to tell her, although he couldn't keep the humor out of his voice. "However, it's my belief that actions speak louder than words. When you're finished with the calf, would you care to demonstrate your concern for me?"

"No."

Russ chuckled softly. "That's what I thought."

Taylor cast him a furious glance before walking around the edges of the mud-caked hole. The calf continued to mewl, not that Russ could blame him. The fellow had gotten himself into one heck of a quandary.

"It appears he's completely trapped," Taylor announced in formal tones.

It had taken Russ all of three seconds to come to that conclusion.

"Can't you put a rope around his neck and pull him out?" She motioned toward Russ's gelding. "You could loop one end around the calf and the other around the saddle horn and have Magic walk backward. I saw it done that way in a TV rerun. Trigger, I think it was Trigger, saved Roy Rogers from certain death in quicksand doing exactly that."

"It won't work."

Taylor gave an indignant shrug of her shoulders. "Why won't it? If it worked for Roy Rogers, it should work for this poor little guy."

"With a rope around his neck, he'd probably strangle before we budged him more than a few inches."

"Oh." She gnawed on her lower lip. "I hadn't thought of that."

Russ hated to admit how much he was enjoying this. She'd outsmarted him once before with that flat tire business, but Taylor was on his turf now, and Russ was in control. "I don't suppose you'd care to make a wager on this?"

"No more bets."

"What's the matter? Are you afraid you'll lose?"

Taylor firmly shook her head. "I'm just not interested, thanks."

"How about this? If you get the calf out, I'll come willingly to your bed. If you don't, then you'll come willingly to mine."

"Does everything boil down to *that* with you?"

"*That,* my sweet lady, is exactly what we both want."

"You're impossible."

"If you were honest with yourself, you'd admit I'm right."

Her mouth was pinched so tightly that her lips were pale. "You're disgusting."

"That isn't what you said the other night," Russ murmured.

"If you don't mind, I'd prefer it if we didn't talk about Friday night."

"As you wish," he said with a grin.

Taylor frowned, studying the calf. "Couldn't we prod him out?"

"*We?* It was my understanding that you could do this all on your own."

"All right," she flared, "if you won't help me, then I'll do it myself." She took two tentative steps into the thick, sticky mud and wrinkled her nose as she moved warily toward the distressed calf. "For being such a great rancher, you certainly seem to be taking this rather casually," she accused him, glancing over her shoulder. Her arms were stretched out at her sides as though she was balancing on a tightrope.

Russ shrugged. "Why should I be concerned when you're doing such a bang-up job?"

Taylor took two more small steps, her face wrinkled with displeasure.

"You're doing just great," Russ called out to her. "In another week or so you'll have reached the calf."

"I never realized how sarcastic you were before now," she muttered.

"Just trying to be of service. Are you sure you're not willing to stake something on the outcome of this?"

"I'm more than sure," she said. "I'm absolutely, totally positive."

"That's a shame."

She glared at him. "It seems you've forgotten that this calf belongs to you. The only reason I'm doing anything is because I find your attitude extremely callous."

"Extremely," Russ echoed, and laughed outright. He tried to disguise it behind a cough, but the irate look she shot him told him he hadn't succeeded.

The sound of pounding hooves caught his attention, and Russ turned to see two of his men galloping toward him.

"Who's coming?" Taylor demanded. She twisted around to glance over her shoulder and somehow lost her balance. Her arms flailed as a look of terror came over her. "Russ…"

Russ leaped forward, but it was too late. He heard her shriek just as she tumbled, hands first into the thick slime. For a shocked second he did nothing. Then, God forgive him, he couldn't help it, he started laughing. He laughed so hard, his stomach hurt and he clutched it with both arms.

A long string of unladylike words blistered the afternoon air when he waded into the mud. Taylor was sitting upright, her knees raised, holding out her hands while the gunk oozed slowly between her fingers. At least the upper portion of her body had been spared.

"Get away from me you…you—" She apparently couldn't think of anything nasty enough to call him. "This is all your fault." Taking a fistful of black mud, she hurled it at him with all her strength, using such force that she nearly toppled backward with the effort.

The mud flew past Russ, missing him by several feet.

"Here, let me help you," he said, wiping tears of mirth from the corners of his eyes.

"Stop laughing," she shouted. "Stop right this second! Do you understand me?"

Russ couldn't do it. He'd never seen anything funnier in his life. He honestly tried to stop, but he simply couldn't.

Taylor was so furious that despite several attempts she couldn't pull herself upright. Finally, Russ moved behind her and, gripping her under the arms, heaved her upward.

The second they were out of the mud, Taylor whirled around, talking so fast and so furiously that he couldn't make out more than a few words. From those he recognized, he figured he was better off not knowing what she had to say.

Russ's two hands, Slim and Roy, stood by, and when Russ met their eyes, he saw that they were doing an admirable job of containing their own amusement. Unfortunately Russ wasn't nearly as diplomatic.

"You two can handle this?" he said, nodding toward the calf.

"No problem," Slim said.

"Taylor didn't think she'd have a problem, either," Russ said, and started laughing all over again.

Both Slim and Roy were chuckling despite their best efforts not to. They climbed down from their horses and leaned against the side of the truck, turning away so Taylor couldn't see them. It wasn't until then that Russ noticed she was missing. He discovered her walking in the direction of the house, which by his best estimate was a good three miles north. Her backside was caked with mud, and her arms were swinging at her sides.

"Looks like you got woman problems," Roy said, glancing at Taylor.

"Looks that way to me, too," Slim said, reaching for his kerchief and wiping his eyes. "I'd be thinking about what Abe Lincoln said if I were you."

"And what's that?" Russ wanted to know.

"Hell hath no fury like a woman scorned."

"That wasn't Abe Lincoln," Roy muttered. "That was Johnny Carson."

Whoever said it obviously knew women a whole lot better than Russ did. The way he figured it, if he ever wanted Taylor to ever speak to him again, he was going to have to do some fast talking of his own.

Taylor had never been angrier in her life. That mud was the most disgusting thing she'd ever seen, and having it on her clothes and skin was more horrible than she even wanted to contemplate. She was cold and wet, and all Russ had done was laugh.

He'd laughed as if she was some slapstick comedian sent to amuse him with her antics. To add to her humiliation she couldn't find the key to the stupid truck. She'd thought she'd left it in the ignition. One thing she did know: she wasn't going to stand around and listen to those men make fun of her.

The least Russ could've done was tell her he was sorry! But he hadn't. Oh, no! He'd roared so loud she swore she'd hear the echo for all eternity.

The sound of the pickup coming toward her did nothing to quell her fury. She didn't so much as turn and look at him when Russ slowed the truck to a crawl beside her.

"Want a ride?"

"No." She continued, increasing her pace. She was already winded, but she'd keel over and die before she'd let Russ know that.

"In case you're wondering, we're about three miles from the ranch house."

She whirled around. "What makes you think I'm going there?"

He shrugged. "Would it help if I said I was sorry?"

"No." Her voice cracked, and her shoulders started to shake while she tried to suppress the tears. Her effort was for naught, and they ran down her face, hot against her skin. Forgetting about the thick mud caked on her hands, she tried to wipe off the tears and in the process nearly blinded herself. The sobs came in earnest then, and her whole body shook with them.

She heard Russ leap out of the pickup, and before she could protest, he was wiping the mud from her face, using a handkerchief. She only hoped it was clean, and once she realized how preposterous that was, she cried harder.

"I hate you," she sobbed, and her shoulders heaved with her vehemence. "I hate Montana. I hate everything about this horrible place. I want to go home."

Russ's arms came around her, but before she could push him away, he'd picked her up and carried her to the truck.

"I...can't sit in there," she wailed. "I'll ruin the upholstery."

Russ proceeded to inform her how little he cared about the interior of his truck. He set her inside the cab, with her feet hanging out the door, then reached into the back and grabbed a blanket and placed that around her shoulders.

"You're cold," was all he said.

"I'm not cold. I'm perfectly—" She would've finished what she was going to say, but her teeth had started to chatter.

Russ brushed the hair from her face, his fingers lingering at her temple. "I am sorry."

"Just be quiet. I'm in no mood for an apology."

Russ moved her legs inside, then closed the door. The blast of heat coming from the heater felt like a warm breeze straight from paradise, and tucking the blanket more securely around her, Taylor hunched forward. She didn't want to know where this tattered old blanket had been.

Russ hurried around the front of the truck and climbed in beside her. "Hold on," he said. "I'll have you at the house in two minutes flat."

"Where did you find the truck key?" she asked grudgingly.

"I always carry one on my key chain."

"What about the poor little calf?"

"Don't worry. The guys'll get him out. And they'll bring Magic back for me."

If Taylor had thought the ride from town the day they'd met had been rough, it was a Sunday School picnic compared to the crazy way Russ drove across the pasture.

Mandy must have heard them coming, because she was standing on the back porch steps when Russ pulled in to the yard and screeched to a halt. He turned off the engine and vaulted out of the cab.

Taylor couldn't seem to get her body to move. Russ opened the door and effortlessly lifted her into his arms.

"What happened?" Mandy cried, racing toward them.

"Taylor fell in the mud. She's about to freeze to death."

"I…I most certainly am not going to freeze," she countered. "All I need is a warm bath and my own clothes."

"Right on both counts," Russ said, bounding up the back steps with her in his arms. He paused at the top and drew in a deep breath. "How much do you weigh, anyhow?"

"Oh," Taylor cried, squirming in his arms, struggling to make him release her.

Her efforts were in vain as Mandy held open the door and Russ carried her through the kitchen and down a narrow hallway to the bathroom.

"How'd it happen?" Mandy asked, running after them.

Russ's eyes met Taylor's. "You don't want to know the answer to that," Taylor informed the teenager.

"I'll tell you later," Russ mouthed. When they reached the bathroom, Mandy opened the door wider so Russ could haul Taylor inside.

"Boil some water and get the whiskey bottle from the top cupboard," he instructed.

Mandy nodded and dashed back to the kitchen.

"Put me down," Taylor insisted. If it wasn't for this egotistical, stubborn, *perverse* man, she wouldn't be in this humiliating position in the first place.

Russ surprised her by doing as she asked. Gently he set her feet on the tile floor, then leaned over the tub to adjust the knobs, starting the flow of warm water.

For the first time Taylor had an opportunity to survey the damage. She looked down at her legs and gasped at the thick, black coating. A glance in the mirror was her second mistake.

Her lower lip trembled and she sniffled, attempting to hold back the tears.

"You're going to be just fine in a few minutes," Russ said in an apparent effort to comfort her.

"I'm not fine," Taylor moaned, catching her reflection in the mirror again. "I look like the Creature from the Black Lagoon!"

Chapter 9

"Taylor!" Russ shouted from the other side of the bathroom door, "close the shower curtain. I'm coming in."

Resting her head against the back of the tub until the warm soothing water covered her shoulders, Taylor turned a disinterested glance toward the door. She felt sleepy and lethargic. "Go away," she called lazily, then proceeded to yawn, covering her mouth with the back of her hand.

"If you don't want to close the curtain, it's fine with me. Actually, I'd be grateful if you didn't."

The doorknob started to turn and, muttering at the intrusion, Taylor reached for the plastic curtain and jerked it closed.

"Damn," Russ said from the other side, not bothering to hide his disappointment. "I was hoping you'd be more stubborn than this."

"Why are you here?" she demanded.

"I live here, remember?"

"I mean in the bathroom! You have no business walking in on me like this." Actually Taylor should have been out of the bathtub long ago, but the water was so warm and relaxing, and it felt good just to sit there and and soak.

"I'm taking these clothes out so Mandy can put them in the washing machine," he said, and his voice faded as he went down the hall.

All too soon he was back. "Stick out your arm."

"Why?"

"You'll find out."

Taylor exhaled sharply, her hold on her temper precarious. "May I remind you that I'm stark naked behind this curtain."

"Trust me, lady, I know that. It's playing hell with my imagination. Now stick out your arm before I'm forced to pull back this shower curtain."

Grinding her teeth, Taylor did as he asked, knowing full well he'd follow through with his threat given the least provocation. Almost immediately a hot mug was pressed into her palm. She brought it behind the curtain and was immediately struck by the scent of whiskey and honey mixed with hot water. "What's this for?"

"It'll help warm you."

"I wasn't really that chilled." Actually she'd been far too angry to experience anything more than minimal discomfort.

"If you want the truth," Russ said in low, seductive tones, "I was hoping the drink would help take the edge off your anger."

"It's going to take a whole lot more than a hot toddy to do that."

"That's what I thought," he muttered. "I've left a couple of Mandy's things here for you to change into when you've finished. There's no hurry, so take all the time you want."

"Are you leaving now?" she asked impatiently.

"Yes, but I'll be waiting for you."

"I figured you would be," she grumbled.

Taylor soaked another ten minutes until the water started to turn cool, then she reluctantly pulled the plug and climbed out of the tub.

A thick pale blue flannel robe that zipped up the front was draped over the edge of the sink, along with a pair of fuzzy pink slippers. After Taylor had finished drying, she slipped into those, conscious that she wore nothing underneath.

Russ was sitting at the kitchen table. "Where's Mandy?" she asked, doing her best to sound casual and composed, as if she often walked around a man's home in nothing more than a borrowed robe.

"She's on the phone, talking to Travis Wells's boy."

This must be the famous Eddie who'd caused Taylor so much grief. Not knowing what she should say or do, she walked over to the counter and filled her empty mug with coffee. She'd just replaced the pot when Russ's hands settled on her shoulders. He turned her around and gazed into her eyes.

"I shouldn't have laughed." His voice was husky, his expression regretful.

She lifted one shoulder in a delicate shrug. "I don't think you could've helped it—laughing was a natural reaction. I must have looked ridiculous."

"Do you forgive me?"

She nodded. Her sojourn in the bath had washed away more than the mud; it had obliterated her anger. She acknowledged that she hadn't been completely guiltless in this fiasco, either. "You weren't really to blame. I did it to myself with my stubborn pride. You're the rancher here, not me. I was a fool to think I could free that poor calf when you couldn't. I brought the whole thing on myself, but you were handy and I lashed out at you."

Russ lifted her chin with his index finger. "Did you mean what you said about hating Montana?"

Taylor didn't remember saying that, although she'd muttered plenty about Russ and his stupid cows and everything else she could think of.

"Not any more than I meant what I said about everything else."

"Good." Russ obviously took that as a positive answer. He raised his finger and traced it slowly over her cheek to her lips. His touch was unhurried and tender as if he longed to ease every moment of distress he'd caused her, intentionally or otherwise. His eyes didn't waver from hers, and when he leaned forward to kiss her, there wasn't a single doubt in Taylor's mind that this was exactly what she wanted.

His mouth settled over hers, and she sighed softly in hopeless welcome. His kisses, as always, were devastatingly sensual. Taylor felt so mellow, so warm.

"I could get drunk on you," Russ murmured in awe.

"It must be the whiskey," she whispered back.

He shook his head. "I didn't have any." His hands were in her hair, his lips at her throat, and the delicious, delirious feelings flooded her.

Sliding her hands over the open V of his shirt, she wound her arms around his strong neck. He leaned her against the counter and pressed himself against her, creating a whole new kaleidoscope of delectable sensations. Taylor let her head fall back as he continued to kiss her. He was so close she could feel the snap of his jeans. He was power. Masculine strength. Heat. She sensed in him a hunger she'd never known in any man. A hunger and need. One only she could fill.

Then, when she least expected it, Russ stilled his body and his hands and roughly dragged his mouth from hers. Not more than a second had passed when…

"Oops…oh, sorry," Mandy said as she walked into the kitchen. "I bet you guys want me to come back later. Right? Hey, no problem." She backed out of the kitchen, hands raised.

Russ's arms closed protectively around Taylor, but she broke free and managed a smile, then deftly turned toward the teenager. "There's no reason for you to leave."

"Yes, there is," Russ said. "Taylor and I have to talk."

"No, we don't," she countered sharply. "We've finished…talking."

Russ threw her a challenging glance that suggested otherwise, and Taylor, who rarely blushed, did so profusely.

"We haven't even started *talking*," Russ whispered for her ears alone. Taylor wasn't going to argue with him, at least not in front of his sister.

Mandy stared down at the linoleum floor and traced the octagonal pattern with the toe of her tennis shoe. "You've already talked to Russ?" she asked, darting a quick glance at Taylor. Her soft green eyes were imploring.

"Not yet," Taylor said pointedly.

"Disappear for a while, Mandy," Russ urged, turning back to Taylor.

"No," Taylor said forcefully. The minute the girl was out of the room, the same thing would happen that always did whenever they were alone together. One kiss and they'd burst spontaneously into a passion hot enough to sear Taylor's senses for days afterward.

"No?" Mandy echoed, clearly confused.

"I haven't talked to Russ yet, but I will now."

The fourteen-year-old brightened and nodded eagerly. She pointed toward the living room. "I'll just wait in there."

"What's going on here?" Russ demanded once Mandy was out of the room.

"Nothing."

"And pigs fly."

"Sit down," she coaxed, offering him a shy smile. She got a second mug and filled it with coffee, then carried it to the round oak table where Russ was waiting for her. His arm slipped around her waist, and she braced her hands against his shoulders.

"You're supposed to talk to me?" he asked.

She nodded.

"This has to do with Mandy?"

Once more Taylor nodded.

Russ frowned. "That was why you drove out to see me earlier, wasn't it?"

"Yes," she answered honestly. He kept his arms securely around her waist, but he didn't look pleased. Taylor felt the least she could do was explain. "Mandy came to talk to me after school, and she asked me to approach you about…something."

"She isn't comfortable coming to me herself?" Russ muttered, looking offended. "I've been trying as hard as I can to listen to her. I can't be any fairer than I've already been. What does she want now? To get an apartment in town on her own?"

"Don't be silly," Taylor answered, riffling his hair, seeking some way to reassure him. "Mandy knows you're trying to be patient with her, and she's trying, too. Only this was something special, something she felt awkward talking to you about, so she came to me. Don't be offended, Russ. That wasn't her intention and it isn't mine."

He nodded, but his frown remained. From the first, Taylor hadn't been sure she was doing the right thing by approaching Russ on Mandy's behalf. She'd only wanted to help, but regretted her part in this now. Look where it had led her! Two feet deep in mud.

Positioning herself on his lap, she rested her arms over his shoulders, her wrists dangling. "You're right," she said, and kissed him long and leisurely by way of apology.

His eyes were still closed when she'd finished, his breathing labored.

"Mandy," Taylor called, embarrassed by how noticeably her voice trembled.

The teenager raced into the kitchen so fast she nearly skidded across the polished floor. "Well?" she asked expectantly. "What did he say?" She seemed a little startled to see Taylor sitting on her brother's lap, but didn't mention it at all.

"I haven't said anything yet," Russ growled. "I want

to know what's going on here. First of all, Taylor drives out to talk to me, and from what I can tell she's wearing your clothes."

"I couldn't very well send her out there in the dress she was wearing at school. I'm certainly glad I insisted she put on something of mine, otherwise look what would've happened!" Mandy declared.

"What's that got to do with this?"

"You were supposed to be back early today, remember?" Mandy reminded him pointedly. "You said something about driving over to Bill Shepherd's this afternoon—"

"Oh, damn," Russ muttered, "I forgot."

"Don't worry. He phoned while you were out with Taylor, and I said you'd probably run into some trouble. He's going to call you back tonight."

Russ nodded. "Go on."

"Well, anyway, I thought it might even be better if Taylor talked to you when I wasn't around, so I suggested she take the truck and—"

"How'd you know where I was?" Russ asked his sister, clearly confused.

"I heard you speaking to Slim this morning about checking the south fence lines. I just headed Taylor in that direction. I knew she'd find you sooner or later."

Russ's gaze shot to Taylor. "She found me all right. Now tell me what you were going to talk to me about." The tone of Russ's voice suggested he was fast losing patience.

"Mandy, I'm holding him down, so you do the talking," Taylor said, smiling at Russ.

"You ask him, Taylor. Oh, please…" the girl begged.

"Nope, you're on your own, kiddo."

"Will the two of you stop playing games and tell me what's going on here?"

"Okay," Mandy said, elevating her shoulders as she released a deep breath. She pushed up the sleeves of her sweater, not looking at her brother, and launched into her request. "You know Travis Wells, don't you?" She didn't give Russ time to respond. "His son Eddie goes to school with me."

"Eddie's older than you."

"He's sixteen," Mandy returned quickly. "Actually he's only twenty-two months and five days older than I am. If he'd been born in October and I'd been born in August we might even have been in the same class together, so there's really not that big a difference in our ages." She paused as though waiting for Russ to comment or agree.

"All right," he said after an uncomfortable moment.

Mandy looked at Taylor pleadingly, silently asking her to explain the rest. Taylor shook her head.

"Eddie's been talking to me lately…in the halls and sometimes at lunch. Yesterday he sat with me on the bus." This was clearly of monumental significance. "Eddie was the one who encouraged me to try out for the drill team, and when I made it, he said he knew I would."

"That was him on the phone earlier, wasn't it?"

A happy grin touched the girl's mouth. "Yes—he wanted to know if I'd talked to you yet."

"About what?" Russ asked, then stiffened. His eyes narrowed. "You're not going out with that young man, Amanda, and that's the end of it. Fourteen is too young to date, and I don't care what Taylor says!"

If she hadn't been sitting on his lap, Taylor was sure

Russ would have jumped to his feet. Framing his face with her hands, she stroked the rigid muscles of his jaw. "There's no need to yell. As it happens, I agree with you."

"You do?"

"Don't look so shocked."

"Then why were you coming to talk to me about it? Because I'll tell you right now, I'm not changing my mind."

"I'm not, either," she said softly, "so relax."

"Mandy?" Russ turned to his sister, his frown threatening.

"Well…as you've already guessed, Eddie asked me out on a date. Actually he just wanted me to go to the movies with him."

"No way," Russ said without so much as a pause.

Mandy's teeth bit her trembling bottom lip. "I thought you'd feel that way. That's the reason I went to Taylor, but she said she agreed with you that fourteen's too young to date. But while we were talking she came up with a…compromise. That is, if you'll agree."

"I said no," Russ returned resolutely.

Taylor felt she should explain. "When I was fourteen, my father—"

"You're from the city," he said in a way that denigrated anyone who lived in a town with a population over five hundred. "Folks from the country think differently. I don't expect you to understand."

His harsh words were like a slap in the face to Taylor. She blinked back the sharp pain, astonished that he would offend her so easily.

"Russ," Mandy whispered, "that was a terrible thing to say."

"What? That Taylor's from the city? It's true."

"You're right, of course." She slipped off his lap and looked at Mandy. "Are my clothes in your room?"

The girl nodded. "I hung them in my closet."

Drawing in a deep breath, Taylor looked at Russ. "I apologize. I should never have involved myself in something that wasn't my affair. I went against my better judgment and I was wrong. Now, if you'll excuse me, I'll change clothes and get out of here." The way she felt at the moment, she never intended to come back. What Russ had said was true; he was only repeating what she'd been saying to him from the first. They were fooling themselves if they believed there was any future in their relationship.

Mandy's bedroom was on the main floor, next to the bathroom. Taylor shut the door and walked over to sit on the bed. Her hands were trembling, and she felt close to tears. Raised voices came from the kitchen, but Taylor couldn't make out the words and had no intention of even trying. If anything, she was regretful that she'd become yet another source of discord between brother and sister.

Taylor was dressing when someone tapped politely on the door. "I'll just be a minute," she said, forcing a cheerful note into her voice.

Slipping the dress over her head, Taylor walked barefoot across the room and opened the door. Mandy came inside, her face red and stained with tears. Sobbing, she threw both arms around Taylor's waist.

"I'm sorry," she whispered. "I'm really sorry…it was so selfish of me to involve you in this. Look what happened. First you fell in that terrible mud—"

"But, remember, I was wearing your clothes."

"I don't care about that." She lifted her head to wipe the tears from her face. "You could take all my clothes and put them in a mud hole if you wanted."

"If you don't mind, I'd prefer to avoid any and all mud holes from now on."

Mandy's responding chuckle sounded more like another sob. "Russ should never have said what he did."

"But it's true," Taylor said lightly, pretending to dismiss the entire incident.

"Maybe so, but it was the way he said it—as if you're not to be trusted or something. You're the best thing that's ever happened to my brother—and to me. All the kids in school are crazy about you and…and for Russ to say what he did was an insult."

"Don't be so hard on him. You can take the girl out of the city, but you can't take the city out of the girl," she joked.

"He'll be sorry in a little bit," Mandy assured her. "He always is. He's the only man I know who slits his own throat with his tongue."

"There's no need for him to apologize," Taylor said, hugging the teenager close. She broke away, slipped on her shoes and reached for her jacket. She draped her purse over her shoulder. "Chin up, kiddo. Everything's going to work out for the best."

Mandy bobbed her head several times.

Russ wasn't around when Taylor walked through the kitchen and out the back door. For that she was grateful. She opened her car door, but didn't get inside. Instead she found herself studying the house and the outbuildings that comprised the Lazy P, giving it a final look. Sadness settled over her and she exhaled slowly.

This was her farewell to Russ and to his ranch.

* * *

If the day Taylor fell in the mud hole had been full of problems, Russ decided, the ensuing ones were just as impossible. Only now the difficulties he faced were of his own making.

Taylor had been on his mind for the past three days. Not that thinking about her constantly was anything new, but now, every time he did, all he could see were her big blue eyes meeting his, trying so hard to disguise the pain his words had inflicted. He'd been angry with Mandy for going to Taylor, and angry with Taylor for listening.

Unfortunately Russ didn't have time to make the necessary amends. Not yet, anyway. Slim and Roy had set up cow camp in the foothills, and Russ and two of his other hands were joining them. They were running cattle, branding the calves born on the range, vaccinating and dehorning them. It would be necessary to trim hoofs, too; otherwise the snow, which was sure to arrive sometime soon, would clump in their feet.

There'd been snow in the mountains overnight, and there was nothing to say the first snowfall of the season couldn't happen any day. With so much to do, he didn't have time for anything but work. The cattle buyers would show up right after that, and Russ would be occupied with them, wheeling and dealing to get the best price he could for his beef.

He'd contact Taylor later and apologize.

When Russ returned to the house, it was after seven and he was exhausted. Mandy was sitting at the kitchen table, doing her homework.

"Any calls?" he asked hopefully. Maybe Taylor had finally decided to forgive him, although he doubted it.

"None."

Russ frowned. That woman was too stubborn for her own good—or his.

"Dinner's in the oven," Mandy said, not looking at him. She closed her book and inserted pages into her binder.

Russ took the plate from the oven with a pot holder, then set it on the table. "I've been thinking over what you suggested about this thing with Eddie," he said while he took a glass from the cupboard and poured himself some milk.

Mandy's eyes rose to search his. "It wouldn't be like a real date. I'd be paying for my own ticket and all Eddie and I would be doing is sitting together. It'd be just as if we'd accidentally met there. If Eddie wants, I'd let him buy me some popcorn—but only if you think it would be all right."

"I'd drop you off and pick you up at the theater?"

"Right."

Russ pulled out a chair and sat down. "This is a sensible compromise," he said as he spread the paper napkin across his lap. "This idea shows maturity and insight on your part, and I'm proud of you for coming up with it."

"I didn't."

Russ finished his first bite and studied his sister, who was standing across the table, her hand resting on the back of the chair. "Taylor's the one who suggested it first. She tried to explain it to you…. Actually, we both did, but you wouldn't listen."

The bite of chicken-fried steak stuck halfway down Russ's throat, and he had to swallow hard before he could speak normally. "Taylor came up with the idea?"

"I think her parents were the ones who thought of it because she was telling me that's what they did with her and her sister when they were fourteen and boys began asking them out."

"I see."

"Just think, Russ," Mandy murmured sarcastically. "Taylor's parents are from the big city, and they managed to come up with this all on their own. Naw, on second thought, I bet someone from the country suggested it."

Normally Russ wouldn't have tolerated his sister talking to him in that tone of voice. The kid sure knew all the right buttons to push. But this time Russ didn't react as he usually did. The pressure that settled on his chest made it difficult to concentrate on anything else.

His appetite gone, Russ pushed his plate away, propped his elbows on the table and stared straight ahead.

He'd done it now. Taylor would never speak to him again. Unless...

Another lonely Friday night, Taylor mused as she sat at the kitchen table with paper and pen. She owed everyone letters, and it wasn't as though she had anything pressing to do.

She leaned back in the chair and reread the long letter from Christy, chuckling over her youngest sibling's warmth and wit.

Someone knocked at the door and, laying aside the letter, Taylor went to answer it. A smiling Mandy stood on the other side.

"Mandy? Is everything all right?"

"It's perfect. Well, almost…" she said, beaming. She seemed in a hurry and glanced over her shoulder.

Taylor's gaze followed hers, and she noticed Russ's truck parked alongside the curb. He was sitting in the cab.

"Russ said I could meet Eddie at the movies and sit with him under one condition, and I'm afraid that involves you."

Taylor couldn't have heard Mandy correctly. "I beg your pardon?"

"Russ seems to feel that Eddie and I are going to need a couple of chaperones."

"That's ridiculous."

"No, it isn't," Mandy insisted much too cheerfully to suit Taylor. "At least I don't mind if you guys sit on the other side of the theater from Eddie and me."

"You guys?"

"You and Russ. He said I can only do this if you agree to sit with him during the movie so he doesn't look like a jerk being there all by himself."

"You can tell your brother for me—"

"Taylor," Mandy cut in, leaning forward to whisper as if there was a chance Russ might overhear. "This is the *only* way Russ could think of to get you to talk to him again. He's really sorry for how he acted and the things he said."

"Sending you to do his apologizing for him isn't going to work," Taylor said matter-of-factly. "Neither is this little game of blackmail."

Mandy thought about it for a moment, then nodded. "You know what? You're absolutely right!" Placing her hands on her hips, she whirled around to face the street. *"Russ!"* she yelled at the top of her lungs.

Russ leaned across the cab of the pickup and rolled down the window.

"If you want to apologize to Taylor, you're going to have to do it yourself!" Mandy shouted. Taylor was certain half the neighbors could hear. Her worst fears were confirmed when she saw the lady across the street pulling aside her drape and peeking out.

"*And* Taylor says she refuses to be blackmailed."

Taylor was mortified when the doors to several more homes opened and a couple of men stepped onto their porches to investigate the source of all the shouting.

"What are you going to do about it?" Mandy yelled.

By this time Russ had climbed out of the truck. He was wearing the same gray suit jacket with the suede yoke he'd had on the night of the Grange dance.

"Hey, Palmer, what's going on with the schoolteacher?" one of Taylor's neighbors heckled.

Two or three others came off their porches and onto the sidewalk. A low murmur followed Russ's progress toward Taylor.

"Hey, Russ, apologize, would you?"

"Yeah," another chimed in. "Then we can have some peace and quiet around here."

Russ paid no attention. When he reached the end of the walk, he looked straight at Taylor, then leaped up the steps. "You want a formal apology?" he asked. "Fine, I'll give you one, but after that we're going to the movies."

Chapter 10

"I'm not going to the movies with you, Russ Palmer. That's all there is to it," Taylor said, and gently closed the door. She turned the lock just to be on the safe side and went back to the kitchen where she'd started a letter to her sister.

A few minutes later, she heard the faint strains of a guitar and someone singing, badly off key. Good grief, it sounded like...Russ. Russ singing?

Deciding the only thing she could do was ignore him, Taylor returned to her letter-writing project.

Apparently Russ wasn't going to be easily foiled, and when she didn't immediately appear, he countered by singing and playing louder. His determination was evident in each word of his ridiculously maudlin song. He was completely untalented as a singer, and his guitar-playing abilities weren't anything to brag about, either.

Covering her ears, Taylor slid as low as she could in her chair. The man's nerve was colossal. If she'd learned anything during her time in Cougar Point, it was that cowboys didn't lack arrogance. To assume that she'd be willing to forget everything simply because he serenaded her was downright comical.

It was then that the phone rang. Taylor answered it on the second ring, grinning at Russ's impertinence, despite her irritation.

"For heaven's sake," her neighbor shouted over the line, "do something, will you? His singing is making my dog howl."

No sooner had Taylor replaced the phone than it rang again. "My china's starting to rattle. Would you please kiss and make up before my crystal cracks?" Taylor recognized the voice of Mrs. Fergason, the lady from across the street.

Grinding her teeth with frustration, Taylor tore across the living room and yanked open the door. "Stop!"

Russ took one look at her and grinned broadly. He lowered the guitar, obviously delighted with himself. "I see you've come to your senses."

"Either stop singing or I'm calling the police. You're disturbing my peace and that of my neighbors. Now leave."

Russ blinked, apparently convinced he'd misunderstood her. "I wish I could, but I owe you an apology and I won't feel right until I clear the air."

"Okay, you've apologized. Now will you kindly go?"

He rubbed his hand down his jaw. "I can't do that."

"Why not?" Taylor jerked back her head hard enough

to give herself whiplash. "I don't believe it. Why are you doing this?"

"Because I'm falling in love with you."

A lump immediately formed in Taylor's throat. This was the last thing she'd wanted. Living in Cougar Point was supposed to give her a chance to heal from one disastrous relationship, not involve her in another.

"Russ," Mandy called, leaning out the window of the truck, "hurry or we'll be late for the movie."

"Are you going or not?" Mrs. Fergason shouted. "Decide, will you? *Jeopardy*'s about to start, and I don't want to miss Alex Trebek."

Taylor was still too stunned to react. "Don't love me, Russ. Please don't love me."

"I'm sorry, but it's too late. I knew the minute you went headfirst into that mud hole that we were meant for each other. Now, are you going to ruin Mandy's big night with your stubbornness, or are you going to the movie with me?"

If she'd had her wits about her Taylor would never have agreed to this blatant form of blackmail, but Russ had taken all the wind from the sails of her righteousness. Before she realized exactly how she'd gotten there, she was inside the Cougar Point Theater, sitting in the back row with Russ, munching on hot buttered popcorn.

"We've got to talk," she whispered as the opening credits started. She'd seen the movie months earlier, and although she'd enjoyed it, she wasn't eager to see it a second time—especially now, after Russ's shocking declaration.

His large callused hand reached for hers, closing around her fingers. "We can talk later."

How she managed to sit through the entire film, Taylor didn't know. Her mind was in a chaotic whirl. All too soon the closing credits were rolling and the house lights came up. The theater began to empty.

Mandy dashed down the aisle, the famous Eddie at her side. "Would it be all right if we went over to the bowling alley? Chris's mom and dad offered to buy everyone nachos. Lots of other kids are going."

"How long will you be?" Russ asked.

Mandy looked at Eddie. "An hour," the boy said firmly, perhaps expecting Russ to argue with him. He was over six feet tall and as lean as a telephone pole, yet Mandy gazed at him as if he were a Hollywood heartthrob.

"All right," Russ said, apparently surprising them both. "I'll pick you up in exactly one hour."

"Thanks," Mandy said, and impulsively kissed his cheek.

"That gives us forty-five minutes to settle our differences," Russ said, smiling over at Taylor, his eyes filled with silent messages.

By now Taylor felt more than a little disoriented. It was as if her entire world resembled the flickering frames in a silent movie. Everything had a strange, staccato feeling, and nothing seemed real.

"Where are we going?" she asked when Russ opened the truck door for her.

"Back to your place. Unless you object."

Russ had ignored every one of her objections from the moment they'd met, and there was no reason to assume he was going to change at this stage.

When Russ parked his truck, Taylor half expected her neighbors to file out of their homes and line the sidewalk, offering advice. But all the excitement earlier in the evening had apparently tired everyone out. It was only nine, and already most of the houses were completely dark.

"I'll make us some coffee," Taylor said, finding her voice. She unlocked the door, but before she could flip on the living room lights, Russ gently turned her around and pulled her into his arms.

He closed the front door with his foot and pressed her against the wall. Their eyes adjusted to the dark, and met. "You're so beautiful," he whispered reverently. He lifted his hands to her hair, weaving the thick strands through his fingers. Taylor felt powerless to stop him. She closed her eyes and savored the moment. Savored the exquisite sensations Russ evoked within her.

"Please don't fall in love with me," she pleaded, remembering the reason for this discussion. "Don't love me."

"I can't help myself," he whispered, kissing the taut line of her jaw. "Trust me, Taylor, I wasn't all that happy about it myself. You belong in the city."

"Exactly," she said, breathing deeply. It never seemed to fail: Russ would hold her and she'd dissolve in his arms. Her breathing became labored, and her heart went on a rampage. She tried to convince herself that they were simply dealing with an abundance of hormones, but no matter how many times she told herself that, it didn't matter.

Russ *couldn't* love her. He just couldn't. Because then Taylor would be forced to examine her own feelings for him. She'd be compelled to face what she intuitively knew would be better left unnamed.

"You're a West Coast liberal feminist."

"You're a small-town Montana redneck."

"I know," he agreed, continuing to kiss her jaw, his mouth wandering down the side of her neck.

Listing their differences didn't seem to affect their reactions to each other. Russ raised his head and traced his thumb across her lower lip. It was all Taylor could do not to moan. No man had ever incited such burning need.

Taylor took Russ's finger between her teeth and slowly drew it into her mouth, sucking lightly. He closed his eyes and smiled, then sighed from deep within his chest.

With his hands cupping her face, he kissed her, and it was incredibly sweet, incredibly sexy. Every time Russ took her into his arms, he eliminated all the disparities between them, took everything in their lives and reduced it to the simple fact that they were man and woman.

She gripped his wrists and held on tightly. "Russ, no more...please." With a strength she didn't realize she had, Taylor broke off the kiss.

"I've just begun," he warned.

His lips remained so close to hers that she inhaled his moist, warm breath.

"Why does everything come down to this?" she murmured. Her knees were slightly bent as she struggled to hold on to what little strength she still possessed.

"I don't know," he answered honestly. "I can't seem to keep my hands off you." As though to prove his point, he trailed a row of kisses across the curve of her shoulder.

"Russ..."

"Not here... I know." His voice was so husky Taylor

barely recognized it. Without any difficulty, he lifted her into his arms.

"What are you doing?" she demanded.

"Carrying you into the bedroom."

"No," she whispered, close to tears.

"Rhett Butler carried Scarlett—I can't do any less for you. I thought all women, even you feminist types, went for this romantic stuff."

"We can't do this.... Russ, listen to me. If we make love, we're both going to regret it later." She was nearly frantic, desperate to talk some sense into him. Talk some sense into herself. All the while, Russ was walking along the hallway to her bedroom.

Her weight must have gotten to be too much for him, because he paused and leaned heavily against the wall. Before she could argue, insist that he put her down, his mouth sought hers, his lips sliding back and forth over hers with mute urgency. Whatever objection Taylor was about to raise died the instant his mouth took hers. She entwined her arms around his neck and boldly kissed him back.

"I thought that would shut you up," he murmured triumphantly as he shifted her weight in his arms and carried her directly into the bedroom.

There was ample time to protest, ample time to demand that he stop, but the words, so perfectly formed in her mind, were never spoken. Instead she leaned her head against his shoulder and sighed heavily. She couldn't fight them both.

Russ placed her on the bed. Taylor closed her eyes, hating this weakness in her. At the same moment, savoring it. "I can't believe we're doing this."

"I can," he said. "I haven't stopped thinking about it

since the day we met. I haven't been able to stop thinking about *you*," Russ murmured, "day and night, night and day."

She smiled softly up at him and slipped her arms around his neck. "You've been on my mind, too."

"I'm glad to hear it. But it's more than that," he continued between kisses. "I can't seem to rid myself of this need for you. I want to make love to you more than I've wanted anything in my life."

Taylor felt his moist breath against her cheek and sighed audibly as he began kissing her again, creating magical sensations. Scorching need.

Her arms and legs felt as if they were liquid, without strength. Russ continued to hold her, to rain kisses over her face. Then he nuzzled her neck. Taylor tried to immerse herself in his tenderness, but as hard as she tried, she couldn't seem to block out the fact that their lovemaking would only lead to pain. It had been months since she'd seen Mark, and she was still suffering. How could she do this to herself a second time when she was all too aware of the emotional aftermath?

She'd tried so hard to fight her attraction to Russ. Yet here she was, inviting even more pain, more doubts, more questions. She wasn't the type of woman who leaped into bed with a man just because it felt good.

"Russ...no more," she pleaded, pushing with all her strength against the very shoulders she'd been caressing only moments earlier. "Stop...oh, please, we have to stop."

He went still, and slowly raised his eyes. They were darker than she'd ever seen them. Hotter than she'd ever seen them, but not with anger.

"You don't mean that." Lovingly, tenderly, he ran his

hands over her face and paused when he discovered the moisture on her cheeks.

"You're crying."

Taylor hadn't realized it herself until he'd caressed her face. His eyes questioned hers, filled with apprehension, misgivings. "What's wrong?"

She placed the tips of her fingers on his cheek. "I can't make love with you…. I can't."

"Why not?" His voice was little more than a whisper, and gruff with anxiety. "I love you, Taylor." As if to prove it, he kissed her again, but even more gently this time.

Twisting her head away, Taylor buried her face in the curve of his neck, dragging in deep gulps of air as Russ held her close.

"I don't want you to love me," she sobbed. "If we continue like this, it'll only cause problems—not just for me, but for you, too."

"Not necessarily."

How confident he sounded, how secure, when she was neither.

"I've been in love before…and it hurts too much." She raised her head and swallowed a sob, then wiped the tears from her face. "His name was Mark—and he's the reason I moved to Montana. I had to get away…and heal…. Instead, I met you."

The sobs came in earnest then. Huge heaving sobs that humiliated and humbled her. She wasn't crying for Mark; she was over him. Yet the tears fell and the pain gushed forth in an absolution she hadn't expected. Pain she'd incarcerated behind a wall of smiles, and then lugged across three states.

Russ obviously didn't know what to think. He stroked

her hair, but he didn't say anything, and she knew her timing couldn't have been worse. Bringing up the subject of Mark now, tonight, was insane, but she'd had to stop Russ. Stop them both. She'd had to do *something*.

Still sobbing, she rolled off the bed. Finding her footing, she gestured in his direction, miming an apology and at the same time pleading with him to go. She needed to be alone.

"I'm not leaving you."

Unable to find the strength to go on standing, Taylor lowered herself to the edge of the bed. "Do you always have to argue with me? Just for once couldn't you do what I want?"

"No." He eased himself behind her and wrapped his arms around her shoulders, holding her carefully. "I love you," he told her again.

"Please don't."

"The choice was taken from me long ago."

"No…don't even say it. I can't bear it if you love me—I can't deal with it now. Please, try to understand."

His arms tightened slightly, pulling her back against him. "I wish it wasn't so, for your sake, but my heart decided otherwise. I can't change the way I feel."

"I refuse to love you! Do you understand?" Taylor cried. "Look at us! We're a pair of fools. It won't work, so why should we put each other through this? It doesn't make sense! Oh, Russ, please, won't you just leave me alone?"

"Loving you makes sense. We make sense. I love you, Taylor. Nothing will change that."

"Don't tell me that. I refuse to love you," she repeated. "Do you understand? Nothing has changed. Nothing!"

"It doesn't matter."

If Russ had been angry or unreasonable, it would've helped her. Instead he was gentle. Loving. Concerned.

While she was angry. Angrier than she'd ever been.

"Leave me alone. Go!" She pointed to the door in case he wasn't convinced that she meant what she said. "Stay away from me. I don't want to get involved with you."

Russ studied her for several nerve-racking minutes, then sighed and stalked out of the room.

The whole house went quiet, and it reminded her of the hush before a storm. Russ had left; he'd done exactly what she'd asked. She should be glad. Instead, the ache inside her increased a hundredfold and the emptiness widened.

Clutching her stomach, Taylor sobbed while she sat on the bed and rocked. Back and forth. Side to side. She wept because of one man she no longer loved. She wept for another she was afraid of loving too much.

She lost track of time. Five minutes could have been fifty-five; she had no way of telling.

A noise in her kitchen alerted her to the fact that she wasn't alone. Curious, she righted her clothes, wiped her face with a corner of the sheet and walked out of the bedroom.

Russ was sitting in the kitchen, his feet balanced on a chair, ankles crossed. He was drinking a cup of coffee. Apparently he'd made it himself.

"You didn't leave?"

"Not yet."

"What about Mandy?"

"I called the bowling alley and told her to kill another

hour." Dropping his legs, he stood and poured Taylor a mug, then set it down for her. "Feeling any better?"

Embarrassed, she looked away and nodded. She would rather he'd left when she'd asked, but that would have created other problems. Eventually she'd need to explain, and the sooner the better. "I'm…sorry. I shouldn't have yelled at you."

"Do you want to talk about it?"

"Not really, but…" She shrugged, then pulled out a chair, sat down and reached for the coffee. Cradling the mug, she warmed her hands with it.

"I suppose I should've suspected something," Russ said after a moment. "Someone like you wouldn't accept a teaching position in this part of the country without a reason. You didn't come to Montana out of a burning desire to learn about life in the backwoods of America."

Her gaze continued to avoid his, but she did manage a weak smile.

"So you were in love with Mark. Tell me what happened."

She sighed. "How much do you want to know?"

"Everything. Start at the beginning, the day you met him, and work through to the day you moved to Cougar Point. Tell me everything—don't hold back a single detail."

Taylor closed her eyes. He wouldn't be satisfied with anything less than the truth, the whole truth. He wanted names, places, dates, details. Gory, painful details. The man was wasted on a cattle ranch, she thought wryly; he should've been working for the Internal Revenue Service. Or the FBI.

"I can't," she whispered as the ache in her heart increased with the memories. "I'm sorry, Russ. If I talked to anyone about Mark, it would be you, but he's behind me now and I'm not about to dredge up all that pain."

"You wouldn't be dredging it up," he told her. "You've been carrying it with you like a heavy suitcase all the way to Cougar Point. Get rid of it, Taylor."

"You think it's that easy?" she responded tartly. "You're suggesting I casually take what little remains of my pride and my dignity and lay it out on the table for you to examine. I can't do it."

The heat in the kitchen felt stifling all of a sudden. Taylor stood abruptly and started pacing. "I wanted to get away—that's understandable, isn't it? I read everything I could find about Montana, and the idea of living here for a year or so appealed to me. I thought... I hoped I could use these months to recharge my emotions, to mend."

"It hasn't worked, has it?"

She hung her head. "No."

"Do you know why?"

"Of course I know why!" she cried. "Meeting you has messed up everything. I wasn't in town a week and you were harassing me. Goading me. I'd be a thousand times better off if we'd never met. Now here you are, talking about loving me, and I'm so afraid I can't think straight anymore."

"Are you looking for an apology?"

"Yes," she cried, then reconsidered and slowly shook her head. "No."

"That's what I thought."

She reached for her coffee, downed a sip and set the mug back on the table. The hot liquid burned her lips and seared its way down the back of her throat. "I met Mark while I was student-teaching." She folded her arms around her waist and resumed pacing. "Between working and school I didn't have a lot of time for relationships. For the first four years of my college education, I might as well have been living in a convent."

"Why was Mark different?"

"I...don't know. I've asked myself the same question a hundred times. He was incredibly good-looking."

"Better-looking than me?" Russ challenged.

"Oh, Russ, honestly, I don't know. It isn't as if I have a barometer to gauge the level of cute."

"Okay, go on."

"There isn't much more to tell you," she said, gesturing with her hands. "We became...involved, and after a couple of months Mark brought up the idea of us living together."

Russ frowned. "I see."

Taylor was sure he didn't; nevertheless she continued. "I loved him. I truly loved him, but I couldn't seem to bring myself to move in with him. My parents are very traditional, and I'd never come face-to-face with something that contradicted my upbringing to such an extent."

"Mark wanted you to be his 'significant other'?"

"Yes. He wasn't ruling out the idea of marriage, but he wasn't willing to make a commitment to me, either, at least not then."

"Did you agree to this?"

It took Taylor a long moment to answer, and when she did, her voice was low and husky. "No. I needed time to think over the decision, and Mark agreed it was a good idea. He suggested we not see each other for a week."

"So what did you decide?"

Russ's question seemed to echo through the room. "Yes… I reached an intelligent, well-thought-out decision, but it didn't take me a week. In fact, five days was all the time I required. Having made my choice, I planned to contact Mark. I'd missed him so much that I went over to his apartment the following evening after work…." The floor seemed to buckle, and she reached out and grabbed the back of a chair. "Except that Mark wasn't alone—he was making love with a girl from the office." The pain, the humiliation of that moment, was as sharp now as it had been several months earlier. "Correction," she said in a breathy whisper. "In his words, he was 'screwing' the girl from the office. But when he was with me, he was making love."

Russ stood and walked over to her side, then drew her into his arms.

Clenching her hands in tight fists, Taylor resisted his comfort. The burning tears returned. Her breath seemed to catch in her throat and released itself with a moan. "You don't understand," she sobbed. "You don't know…no one does. No one ever asked."

"I do," Russ whispered, brushing the tendrils from her face. "You'd decided to move in with him, hadn't you?"

Sobbing and nearly hysterical, Taylor nodded.

Chapter 11

Every part of Russ longed to comfort Taylor. He wasn't immune to pain himself. His mother had run off and abandoned him when he was still a child. He'd been unable to understand what had driven her away, unable to understand why she hadn't taken him with her. Then, several years later, his father met and married Betty. Mandy was born and Russ was just beginning to feel secure and happy when Betty died. His father had buried himself in his grief and followed not long afterward. Russ had been left to deal with his own anguish, plus that of his young sister, who was equally lost and miserable.

Emotional pain, Russ had learned during the next few years, was a school of higher learning, a place beyond the instruction of ordinary teachers. It was where heaven sagged and earth reached up, leaving a man to find meaning, reconciliation and peace all on his own.

Taylor sobbed softly, holding him close. Russ shut his eyes. The ache he felt for this woman cut clear through his heart. Taylor had loved another man, loved him still. Someone who didn't deserve her, someone who didn't appreciate the kind of woman she was. The overwhelming need to protect her consumed him.

Lifting her head, Taylor brushed the confusion of hair from her face. "I think you should go now," she said in a voice thick with tears.

"No," he answered, his hands busy stroking her back. He couldn't leave her. Not now. Not like this.

"Please, Russ, I want to be alone. I need to be alone."

"You'll never be alone again," he promised her.

Her head drooped, and her long hair fell forward. "You don't understand, do you? I can't... I *won't* become involved with you. I'm here to teach, and at the end of my contract I'm leaving. And when I do, I don't want there to be any regrets."

"There won't be. I promise you." Russ tried to reassure her, but when he bent to kiss her, she broke away from him and skittered over to the other side of the kitchen, as if that distance would keep her safe.

"It would be so easy to let myself fall in love with you," she whispered. "So easy..."

Witnessing her pain was nearly Russ's undoing. He moved toward her, but for every step he advanced, she retreated two. He hesitated. "All I want to do is love you."

"No," she said firmly, holding out her arm as if that should stop him. Russ found little humor in her pathetic attempt. *He* wasn't the one who'd cheated on her. He wasn't the one who'd abused her love and her trust. And he damn well refused to be punished for the sins of another.

"Taylor, listen to me."

"No," she said with surprising strength. "There isn't anyone to blame but me. From the moment you and I met I realized we were in trouble, and we've both behaved like fools ever since. Me more than you. I've said it once, and apparently you didn't believe me, so I'm saying it again. I don't *want* to become involved with you."

"You're already involved."

"I'm not—not yet, anyway. Please, don't make this any more difficult than it already is. I'm not asking you this time. I'm telling you. If you care about me, if you have any feelings toward me whatsoever, you'll forget you ever knew me, forget we ever met."

Her words seemed to encircle his heart and then tighten like barbed wire. If he cared for her? He was crazy in love with her! His breath felt frozen in his chest.

"Am I supposed to forget I held you and kissed you, too?"

She nodded wildly. "Yes!"

Russ rubbed the back of his neck while he contemplated her words. "I don't think I can forget."

"You've got to," she said, and her shoulders heaved with each pleading syllable. "You have to."

Walking out on her then would have been like taking a branding iron and burning his own flesh. Despite everything she'd claimed, and asked for, Russ walked to her side, took her by the shoulders and pulled her against him. She fought him as though he was the one responsible for hurting her so terribly. As if he was the one who'd betrayed her.

Her fists beat against him, but he felt no pain. None. Nothing could hurt him as much as her words.

Gripping her by the wrists, he pinned her hands behind her back. She glared up at him, her eyes spitting fire. "Why do you have to make this so difficult? Why?"

"Because I don't give up easily. I never have." He raised his hand and glided his fingertips over the soft contours of her face. He traced her stern, unyielding mouth, and with his hand at the small of her back, pressed her forward until her body was perfectly molded to his. Then he buried his face in her sweet-smelling hair and inhaled deeply.

"Russ," she pleaded, bending her head to one side, "don't do this."

He answered by sliding his mouth over hers. His hand freed her wrists as he held her against him. The fight had gone out of her, and her arms crept up his chest, pausing at his shoulders, her nails digging hard into his muscles. But Russ still felt no pain.

A moment later, she pulled away from him, looking into his eyes. "Do I have to walk out on my contract, pack my bags and leave town to convince you I mean it?" she asked. "Is that what it's going to take?"

"If you want me out of your life, just say so," Russ said, shoving his hands in his pockets.

"What do you think I've been trying to do for the past weeks? Stay away from me, Russ! I've got to get my head straightened out. I'm not ready to fall in love again, not with you, not with anyone. I can't deal with this—with you—right now. I may not be able to for a long time."

"All right," he said gruffly. "I get the message. Loud and clear." He stalked out of the kitchen, paused long enough in the living room to reach for his hat and then he was gone.

But as he closed the door, he heard Taylor's sobs. He forced himself to walk away from her, but he hesitated on the porch and sagged against the pillar. Regret and pain worked through him before he was able to move.

Once more he had to find meaning, reconciliation and peace in the aftermath of pain.

"Cody Franklin just pulled into the yard," Mandy told Russ as though that was earth-shattering news.

Russ grumbled something in reply, and his muscles tensed involuntarily. If Cody was stopping by to talk, Russ knew what—who—the subject was bound to be.

Taylor.

"I don't understand you," Mandy said, clearly at the end of her wits. "Why don't you just call Taylor and put an end to this nonsense? You've been walking around like a wounded bear all week."

"When I need your advice, I'll ask for it," Russ bit out, and stood up so fast, he nearly toppled the kitchen chair. "Stay out of it, Amanda. This is between me and Taylor."

"She obviously isn't doing any better. She called in sick twice this week."

"How many times are you going to tell me that?" Russ muttered. "It doesn't change the situation. She doesn't want anything to do with me. If and when she does, she'll contact me. Until then it's as if we never met."

"Oh, that's real smart," Mandy said, her fists digging into her hips. "You're so miserable, it's like having a thundercloud hanging over our lives. You love Taylor and she loves you, so what's the problem?"

"If Taylor feels anything for me, which I sincerely doubt, she'll let *me* know. Until then I have nothing to say to her." It gnawed at him to admit it, but the truth was the truth, no matter how many different ways he chose to examine it. Taylor had claimed she wanted nothing to do with him often enough for him to believe her. He had no other choice.

"Save me from stubborn men," Mandy groaned, as she headed for the door, pulling it open for Russ's friend.

"Howdy, Amanda," Cody Franklin said as he walked into the kitchen. He removed his cap and tucked it under his arm. He was dressed in his uniform—green shirt and coat and tan slacks. His gunbelt rode low on his hips.

"Hello, Cody." Mandy craned her neck toward Russ. "I hope you've come to talk some sense into my bull-headed brother."

Cody seemed uneasy. "I'll try."

Mandy left the two of them alone, a fact for which Russ was grateful. He didn't need a letter of introduction to deduce the reason for his friend's latest visit. One look at Cody confirmed what Russ had already guessed. The deputy had stopped by as a courtesy before going out with Taylor himself.

"So you intend to ask her for a date?" Russ forestalled the exchange of chitchat that would eventually lead to the subject of Taylor.

Cody's eyes just managed to avoid Russ's.

"Frankly, Cody, you don't need my permission. Taylor is her own woman, and if she wants to date you that's her business, not mine."

Having said as much, Russ should have felt relieved, but he didn't. He'd been in a rotten mood from the moment he'd left Taylor's nearly a week before, and Cody's coming by unannounced hadn't improved his disposition any.

Cody must have sensed his mood, because he gave Russ a wide berth. He walked over to the cupboard, brought down a mug and poured himself coffee before he turned to face Russ.

"Sit down," Russ snarled. "I'm not going to bite your head off."

Cody grinned at that, and it occurred to Russ that Cougar Point's deputy sheriff wasn't bad-looking. Handsome enough to stir any woman's fickle heart. Plenty of women were interested in him, but he took his duties so seriously that no romantic relationship lasted more than a couple of months. Cody Franklin didn't smile very often, and Russ thought he knew why.

The two men went back a long way, and Russ didn't want their friendship to end because of one stubborn woman. "You're planning on asking Taylor out, aren't you?" he demanded when Cody didn't immediately respond.

Cody joined Russ at the table. "Actually, I wasn't going to do anything of the kind. I asked her once already, and she turned me down. I figured she wasn't interested, so I was willing to leave it at that."

"Then why are you here?"

"Because she phoned the other day and asked *me* to dinner Friday night." He paused to rub the side of his jaw. "I don't mind telling you, I was taken aback by that. I've never had a woman ask me for a date."

"What did you tell her?"

Cody looked uncomfortable. "I said I needed some time to think it over."

"So Taylor's the one who called you?" Russ was surprised his voice sounded so normal.

"I've never had a woman approach me like this," Cody went on to say a second time. "I'm not sure I like it, either. It puts me in one hell of a position." He twisted the mug around in his hands, as though he couldn't locate the handle. "From what she said, I assume she intends to pay, too. I've never had a woman pay for my meal yet, and I'm not about to start now."

"Don't blame you for that," Russ felt obliged to say, although he couldn't help being slightly amused. He didn't need a script to realize what Taylor was doing. She'd asked Cody Franklin to dinner to prove something to herself and possibly to him.

"You've got feelings for her, haven't you?" Cody asked, eyeing him suspiciously.

"You could say that," Russ confirmed, understating his emotions by a country mile. He had feelings, all right, but he wasn't willing to discuss them with his friend.

Cody grinned, revealing even white teeth. Crow's-feet crinkled at the corners of his eyes. "So, what do you want me to say to her?"

"That you'll be happy to let her buy you dinner."

Cody hesitated before taking a sip of his coffee. "You don't mean that," he finally said.

"Yes, I do. In fact, I've never been more serious in my life."

"But—"

"Taylor Manning doesn't want anything to do with me."

"And you believe her?"

Russ shrugged. "The way I see it, I don't have any choice. If she wants to go out with you, fine. That's her decision."

Cody shook his head. "I can't believe I heard you right."

"You did. Trust me, dealing with this woman isn't easy."

Cody set his half-finished coffee on the table and stood. "Okay, but I have the feeling you're going to regret this."

Cody Franklin was as nice a man as Taylor had ever met. And a gentleman to boot. He arrived promptly at seven, dressed in a suit and tie. He really was handsome. Considerate. And Taylor was badly in need of some tender loving care. She'd just spent the most miserable week of her life, and an evening with a man who didn't pose the slightest emotional threat was exactly what she needed to pull herself out of this slump. At least that was what she kept telling herself.

"I hope I'm not too early," Cody said, stepping inside and glancing around. Apparently he approved of what he saw, because he gave her a smile.

"No, this is perfect." She reached for her coat, but Cody took it from her hands and held it for her so she could slip it on. With a murmured thanks, she picked up her purse.

"Before we leave," he began, then cleared his throat, "there's something I'd like understood. If we go to dinner, I pay the tab."

"But I invited you," Taylor reminded him, somewhat surprised at the vehemence with which he spoke.

"I pay or we don't go."

Taylor couldn't see any point in arguing. She'd encountered enough stubborn male pride with Russ to know it wasn't going to do her any good. "If you insist."

"I do."

Once that was resolved, they managed to carry on a pleasant conversation while Cody drove to the restaurant. He'd chosen Larry's Place, the one halfway decent eating establishment in town. Taylor hadn't eaten there before, but she'd heard the food was good—and the company was exemplary. For the first time in a week she found herself smiling and talkative.

The hostess escorted them to a table, and they were handed menus. It took Taylor only a moment to decide. Her appetite had been nonexistent for days, and she was determined to enjoy this evening no matter what.

"Hello, Cody. Taylor."

Russ's voice came at her like a blast of cold air. She drew in a deep breath before turning toward the man who'd dominated her thoughts all week. "Hello, Russ," she said coolly.

"Russ," Cody said, standing. The two exchanged handshakes. "Good to see you again, Mary Lu."

"Have you met Taylor Manning?" Russ asked his date. His hand was casually draped over the other woman's shoulder as he smiled down on her. "Taylor's the new schoolteacher."

"Pleased to meet you," Mary Lu said, and she actually sounded as if she was.

Taylor smiled and nodded. The woman didn't reveal a single shred of jealousy, she mused darkly. Surely by now everyone in town knew there was something going on between her and Russ. The least the other woman could do was look a little anxious. But then, why should she? Mary Lu was the one with Russ. Taylor was with Cody Franklin.

Cody reclaimed his seat. "Would you two care to join us?"

Taylor's heart shot upward and seemed to lodge in her throat. Seeing Russ accompanied by another woman was painful enough without having to make polite conversation with them for the rest of the evening.

"Another time," Russ said. His thoughts apparently reflected her own.

Taylor was so grateful, she nearly leaped from her chair to thank him with a kiss. It wasn't until he'd left the table that she realized how tense she was. Smiling in Cody's direction, she forced herself to relax. Elbows on the table, she leaned toward her date. "So how long have you been in law enforcement?"

"Since I graduated from college," he answered, but his concentration wasn't on her. Instead, his gaze followed Russ and Mary Lu to the other side of the restaurant.

His frown disturbed her. "Is something wrong?" she asked.

"I don't know yet."

Taylor sighed. This whole evening was a mistake.

She'd phoned and asked Cody to dinner for two reasons. The first and foremost was simply because she was lonely, and the thought of spending another weekend alone was more than she could bear. The second was to prove that... She was no longer sure what she'd hoped to accomplish.

Cody sipped his water. "You're in love with him, aren't you?"

This man certainly didn't pull any punches. The least he could've done was lead into the subject of Russ Palmer with a little more tact. Taylor considered pretending she didn't know what he was talking about, but that would've been ridiculous.

She lowered her gaze to the tablecloth. "I don't know if I love him or not."

"What's there to know? I saw the look in your eyes just now. Russ walked in with Mary Lu, and I swear you nearly keeled over."

"You're wrong. I was mildly surprised, that's all."

"It doesn't bother you that he's with Mary Lu?"

She managed a casual shrug. "Not really. I wasn't expecting to see him. If I reacted, which I don't think I did, it was due to that and that alone."

"So what are you going to do about it?"

"Do about what?"

"The way you feel for Russ."

"I'm not going to do anything." She didn't need time to make that decision; it had been made weeks earlier. All the arguments she'd put forth, time and again, crowded her mind. All the reasons a relationship with him couldn't work... Yet she couldn't turn her eyes away from Russ, couldn't stop gazing at him with an emotional hunger that left her trembling.

"He loves you, too," Cody whispered. He reached across the table and took hold of her hand. "I don't know what drove you two apart, but I'm here to tell you right now, it's eating him alive." His smile was gentle, concerned. "It seems to be having the same effect on you."

"It's not that simple," she whispered.

A long moment passed before Cody spoke again. "Nothing worthwhile ever is."

"Taylor, do you realize what time it is?" her sister, Christy, groaned after she answered the phone on the fifth ring.

"I'm sorry… I should've checked," Taylor said, feeling utterly foolish and completely miserable.

Christy yawned loudly. "It's three in the morning! Why are you phoning at this hour? Are you all right? You're not in trouble, are you?"

If only Christy knew! "I…was calling to see if you were going to be free next weekend."

"Are you flying home? Oh, Taylor, it would be so good to see you. I can't believe how much I miss you. Paul, Jason and Rich, too. Mom and Dad don't say much, but know they feel the same way."

"No, but I'll be in Reno, and I thought that, well… I was hoping I could talk you into joining me. There are a bunch of cheap flights out of Sea-Tac and I thought maybe you could meet me in Nevada."

Christy slowly released her breath. "I can't. I'm really sorry, but I can't possibly swing it at this late date. What will you be doing in Reno?"

"Nothing much. The drill team is competing there, and I volunteered to be a chaperone—but apparently the team will be busy for two days and I'm going to have a lot of time to kill. I thought it would be fun if we got together."

"All right, Taylor," Christy said after a moment. "What's wrong? And don't try to tell me *nothing*. The last time you called me at three in the morning was when... I'm sure you remember."

"This doesn't have anything to do with Mark."

"Thank God for that." Her voice lowered slightly with concern. "What's wrong, then?"

Taylor reached for a tissue and blew her nose loudly. "I...think I'm in love."

Christy groaned again. "You've got to be kidding. Who?"

"His name is Russ Palmer and he owns a cattle ranch."

"I was afraid of that. I read your last letter to Mom and Dad and it was full of that cowboy! It was Russ this and Mandy that. Taylor, get control of yourself. You don't want to spend the rest of your life on a ranch out in the wilds of Montana, do you?"

"Of course not!" Taylor sobbed. "The last thing I intended to do was fall in love—especially with someone who thinks just like Dad."

"Your cowboy believes women shouldn't have the right to vote?" Christy asked, aghast.

Taylor started to laugh even while she was crying. "He said he doesn't care if we vote. It's females holding public office that bothers him." She paused. "He knows how much I hate it when he says stuff like that. He does it to get a rise out of me and it works every time."

She could hear Christy taking a deep breath and imagined her mentally counting to ten. "Listen, Taylor, you're my sister and my dearest friend. What you feel isn't love. It's a natural and common emotion following the breakup of any romance."

"That's what I thought...at first."

"You were right. For most of your life your judgment was totally sound. Nothing's changed all that much. So you made a mistake with Mark. So what? But when you come out of a long-term relationship, there's an emptiness and the normal reaction is to immediately find someone to fill it."

"I don't think that applies in this case," Taylor argued. In the beginning she'd assumed the same thing, but not anymore. This ache she felt went deeper than anything she'd ever experienced.

"You've spent the past six weeks in a town where no one even accepts American Express," Christy reminded her. "Taylor, this thing with the cowboy is all due to what happened with Mark. You're away from your family. You're lonely and vulnerable, and it's only natural to find yourself attracted to another man. I know I would be if the situations were reversed."

"You would?"

"Of course," Christy said smoothly and with conviction. "Just hold on for another week, and once you're in Reno, where there are real stores and real people, you can reevaluate your feelings. I'm sure being there will help clear your mind."

"Do you honestly think so?"

"I know so," Christy said without the least qualm. "Now take two aspirin, go to bed and call me next week when you get back from Reno. Ten to one, you're going to feel a lot different than you do tonight."

"Okay," Taylor said. After a few more minutes she replaced the receiver, convinced her sister was right.

* * *

The next week flew past, the days blending as Taylor threw herself into her job. Friday afternoon, her suitcase packed, she headed for the school bus and the twenty girls who comprised the Cougar Point High School Drill Team.

The first girl she saw was Mandy, who flew across the yard and hugged Taylor close. "I'm so glad you're going with us."

"Me, too," Taylor said, meaning it.

Mandy reached for Taylor's suitcase, setting it beside the others. "Everyone's here except the driver." She paused and rolled her eyes. "But then he's always late."

The girls gathered around Taylor, and soon they were chatting away like old friends. Taylor knew many of the team members as well as their coach.

"Everyone ready?" a male voice called out.

Taylor recognized it immediately as Russ's. She swallowed and turned toward him, frowning. "What are you doing here?" she demanded.

He tossed one suitcase into the compartment on the side of the bus and then another. "The same thing as you," he said without the least animosity. "You're a chaperone, and I happen to be driving the bus."

Chapter 12

It wasn't the twenty boisterous, exuberant high school girls who were driving Russ crazy. They sang, they cheered and they shouted as he drove the school bus across three states.

No, it wasn't the girls—it was Taylor. Taylor, who laughed and sang. Taylor, who joked and teased as if she hadn't a care in the world.

Each and every one of those girls adored her. The problem was, so did Russ.

Other than their brief exchange before they'd boarded the bus, she hadn't said more than a handful of words to him. True, there hadn't been a lot of opportunity. They'd stopped in Billings for something to eat and she'd sat in a booth surrounded by teenagers. Russ had eaten with Carol Fischer, the drill team coach, and another of the chaperones. Carol and he had exchanged a few pleasantries, but the entire time they were eating, Russ had found his gaze drawn again and again to the table next to his where Taylor was seated.

He would've liked nothing better than to get Taylor alone for a few hours. Then, and only then, would he have the chance to talk some sense into that stubborn head of hers.

Okay, she'd gone and fallen in love with the wrong man. Everyone made an error in judgment at some point, but that was in the past and Russ was very much part of the present. Although he told himself this a hundred different times and in as many different ways, the thought of Taylor aching, wanting, crying over another man felt like a knife slicing deep into his heart. It hurt so much that for a moment he couldn't breathe normally. Hell, he hadn't been breathing normally from the second he'd stumbled upon Taylor in the five-and-dime last September.

The long, lonely miles sped past. The girls gave up singing even before they left Montana. Around midnight the only one on the bus who wasn't sleeping was Russ.

"Do you want some coffee?"

Taylor's soft voice behind him sounded like an angel's, Russ thought gratefully.

"Russ?"

"Please." He waited to speak until she'd poured him some from the thermos she carried and he'd sipped it, appreciating the way it revived him. "I figured everyone was asleep."

"They are."

"What's keeping you awake?" He'd love it if she admitted he'd been in her thoughts for two desolate weeks and that she couldn't let another hour pass, or even another second, without telling him how she felt.

"I never could sleep in a moving vehicle."

"Oh," he said, trying to disguise his disappointment. He should know by now that Taylor wasn't going to fulfill his fantasies by saying all the things he longed to hear.

"How have you been?"

They'd barely said a word to each other in two weeks, he mused darkly, frowning, and she was asking about his health!

Briefly he wondered what she'd say if he told her he wasn't sleeping well, his mood was sour and he couldn't sit down to a single meal without suffering indigestion afterward. All these ailments he attributed entirely to her stubbornness.

"I'm fine," he said instead. "How about you?"

"Fine, just fine."

"Now we've got that settled, what else would you like to talk about? The weather seems a safe enough subject, doesn't it?"

"I...I think I'll go back and check on the girls."

"You do that," he muttered, then immediately wanted to kick himself for being such an idiot. At least Taylor had been willing to talk to him, which was a lot better than the strained silence that had existed between them up to this point.

It wasn't until midafternoon the following day that they pulled into the congested streets of Reno. The girls were leaning out the windows, shouting at tourists, while Carol and the other adults attempted to calm their rampant enthusiasm.

Carol and Russ had traded off driving, but like Taylor, Russ didn't sleep well in a moving vehicle. He leaned back, shoved his hat low over his face and did a fair job of pretending, but he hadn't slept a wink in over twenty-four hours.

When Russ pulled in to the parking garage at Circus Circus, the hotel where they were booked, he heaved a giant sigh of relief. He was exhausted, mentally and physically. With the help of two bellboys, he unloaded the ton of luggage the girls had found indispensable for this short trip. While he was busy with that, Carol and the other chaperones, accompanied by the entire drill team, checked in. As soon as he was finished, Carol handed him his room key and suggested he get some sleep.

Russ didn't need to be told twice. He practically fell asleep in the elevator on the way up to his floor. Taylor and several of the girls rode with him, and just before he entered his room, Russ saw that she'd been assigned one on the same floor.

Some of his tiredness vanished when he discovered that Taylor would be sleeping down the hall from him. Not bothering to unpack his bag he tossed his hat onto the small table and collapsed on top of the bed. Bunching up the pillow, he closed his eyes and savored the quiet, the peace. It wasn't until sleep began to overtake his mind that he realized he had two whole days in which to convince Taylor she loved him.

Taylor couldn't remember a time when she'd been more exhausted. Other than brief stops, the bus had spent nearly twenty hours on the road, and she hadn't gotten more than a catnap the entire distance. Carol, bless her heart, had insisted Taylor go upstairs to bed while she and the assistant coach managed the girls. Taylor didn't offer a single argument.

From the moment they pulled in to the hotel, the girls' schedule was packed. In less than two hours they were meeting several other out-of-state teams, who would also be competing the following day, for a social. Then, first thing the next morning, Carol would be driving the drill team to a local high school and they'd be there the entire day until their performance, which was scheduled late that evening. After a good night's sleep, they'd be back on the road again, heading home to Montana.

Yawning, Taylor ran a tub of hot bathwater and soaked in it, struggling to stay awake. When she got out, she crawled between clean, crisp sheets, already half-asleep.

There was noise and confusion around her for part of the time, since her room adjoined one with teenagers, but she hardly noticed. She woke at eight the next morning, just in time to see the team off and wish them well.

"You're coming to watch us, aren't you?" Mandy pleaded.

"Wild horses couldn't keep me away," Taylor promised.

"Do you think Russ will want to come?"

Taylor nodded. "I'm sure of it."

Beaming, Mandy hugged Taylor and then rushed to join her teammates.

Once the Cougar Point High School Drill Team had departed the hotel, Taylor wandered downstairs to the casino, where most of the gambling took place. Bells jingled incessantly and smoke rose like a sacrificial offering to the unpredictable gods of chance and good for-

tune. Row upon row of slot machines lined the brightest, reddest carpeting Taylor had ever seen.

She'd never gambled much, but the excitement that crackled through the room lured her toward the slot machines.

Trading her hard-earned cash for several rolls of nickels, she grabbed a plastic container and picked out a one-armed bandit at the end of a long row of identical machines.

"A fool and her money are soon parted," she muttered, seating herself on a stool.

She inserted three nickels and gingerly pulled down on the handle. Oranges, plums and cherries whirled past in a blur, then came to an abrupt halt.

Nothing.

She tried again and again and was rewarded by several minor wins. Two nickels here, ten there.

Someone slid onto the stool next to hers, and when she glanced over, a ready smile on her lips, her eyes clashed with Russ's. He looked well-rested and so devastatingly handsome that her breath jammed in her throat. The lazy grin he gave her was more potent than any of the free drinks she could have ordered.

"How are you doing?" he asked.

"Fine…good, really good." She plopped three more coins into the appropriate slot and pulled the lever with enough energy to dismantle the machine.

"How much have you won?"

She looked down at the small pile of nickels.

"Actually, I think I'm out a couple of bucks."

He grinned. "I'm down about the same. I don't suppose I could talk you into having some breakfast with me? You wouldn't consider that a breach of protocol, would you?"

"I... That would be fine." Taylor didn't know how a grown woman, a college graduate and teaching professional, could be so flustered around one man. The way her heart was jitterbugging inside her chest, anyone might assume Russ had asked her to join him in bed instead of in a restaurant.

Neither of them appeared to have much to say until they'd been seated by the hostess and handed menus.

Russ chose quickly and set his aside. "So how did your dinner with Cody Franklin go last weekend?"

"Cody's a wonderful man," she answered, glancing over her menu. Their eyes met briefly and she quickly switched her gaze back to the list of breakfast entrées.

"So you plan on seeing him again?" Russ demanded. Then he shook his head. "I'm sorry. I didn't have any right to ask you that. Whom you choose to date is your business."

Actually, she'd decided against dating Cody again, but not because she hadn't enjoyed his company. He'd been polite and gentlemanly all evening. After they'd left the restaurant, she'd invited him in for coffee and he'd accepted, but to her dismay their entire conversation then, as it had through most of dinner, centered on Russ. Cody hadn't kissed her good-night, nor had he asked her out again. Why should he? Taylor mused. She'd spent the evening with one man, while longing to be with another.

The waitress came by for their order and filled their coffee cups. Taylor took a sip of hers, and decided if Russ could question her, she should feel free to inquire about his own evening out. She carefully returned her cup to the saucer. "How was your dinner with Mary Lu Randall?"

"Great," Russ answered. "She's a lovely woman. Interesting, fun to be with, thoughtful…"

Taylor's throat constricted painfully as she nodded. Everything Russ said was true. Mary Lu Randall was known as a generous, unassuming woman.

"I won't be seeing her again, though," Russ muttered, drinking his coffee.

Despite everything she'd hoped to prove to this man, Taylor sighed with relief. "You won't? Why not?"

Russ set his coffee cup down hard enough to attract attention, and several heads turned in their direction. Russ glanced apologetically at those around him.

"Why?" he asked in a heated whisper. "Do you honestly need me to explain the reason I won't be dating Mary Lu again?" He threw his head back and glared at the ceiling. "Because I'm in love with you is *why*. In addition, you've ruined me for just about any other woman I might happen to meet."

"I've ruined you?" she echoed vehemently. She leaned toward him, managing to keep her voice low enough not to attract further attention.

The waitress delivered their meals, and Russ dug into his fried eggs as though he hadn't eaten in a week. He'd eaten both eggs before Taylor had finished spreading jelly across her toast, which she did with jagged, awkward movements.

"I would've thought Mary Lu was perfect for you," she said, unwilling to let the subject drop. "She's sweet and gentle and *deferential,* and we both know how important that is to a man of your persuasion."

"I used to think that was what I wanted until I met

you." He stabbed his fork into his fried potatoes. "I'll be damned if you didn't ruin me for decent women."

"Ruined you for decent women?" Taylor cried, not caring whose attention she drew.

"That's right. *You.* This is all your fault. No woman ever challenged me and dared me the way you do, and I'm having one heck of a hard time adjusting. Compared to you, every other woman has the appeal of watered-down soup." He jammed his index finger against the top of the table before continuing. "Mary Lu's one of the nicest women in Cougar Point, and any man she married would consider himself lucky."

"But it won't be you," Taylor stated, hating the way her heart gladdened at that.

"How can it be when I'm crazy about you?"

The irritation drained out of Taylor as quickly as it had risen. She set her slice of toast aside and dropped her eyes, suddenly close to tears. "I wish you wouldn't say that."

"Why? Because you don't like hearing it? Fine, I won't say it again, but that isn't going to change a thing. If you want to put us both through this hell, then go ahead. There's nothing I can do to stop you. But I love you, Taylor, and like I said, that's not going to change."

"But I don't *want* you to love me."

"Don't you think I know that? Trust me, lady, if I had any choice in the matter, you'd be the last woman I'd fall in love with. Do you honestly believe I need this aggravation in my life? If so, guess again."

"There's no need to be angry."

Russ pushed his near-empty plate aside and downed the last of his coffee in a single gulp, apparently doing his best to ignore her.

"Thank you for breakfast," Taylor said, pushing her own plate aside after a moment. She'd only managed a few bites of egg. The toast she'd so carefully spread with jelly remained untouched.

"You're welcome." Leaning back in his chair, Russ rubbed a hand over his eyes. When he dropped his hand, it was clear that he was forcing himself to put their disagreement behind him. He smiled. "What are your plans for today?"

"The first thing I'm going to do is shop. There's a fingernail hardener with epoxy that I need to find," she said, glancing down at her carefully groomed nails. "Not a single store in Cougar Point carries it."

"Don't they use epoxy in glue?" Russ frowned as he stared down at her hands. "If you want to go putting that stuff on your pretty nails, far be it from me to stop you."

"Thank you," she said graciously, resisting the urge to roll her eyes. "After that, I thought, since I was in town, I'd pick up a few other things for the sheer joy of using my American Express card."

Russ chuckled. "Would you mind if I tagged along?"

"Of course not," she said promptly. She didn't mind. In fact—perversely—the prospect delighted her.

Over the past few weeks and all the disagreements, Taylor had forgotten what pleasant company Russ could be. He was good-natured and patient to a fault as she dragged him from one store to the next. He was more than tolerant while she tried on a series of dresses, and after she chose one, he went with her to the shoe department and helped her pick out a comfortable pair of heels.

Taylor tried to return the favor and help him choose new work shirts. Russ seemed to be of the opinion that if he found one shirt that suited him, he might as well buy five exactly like it. Taylor made a concerted effort to convince him otherwise.

"Where would you like to go for lunch?" Russ asked four hours later. His arms were loaded with a large number of bags and packages as he led the way down the street.

"Since you asked," Taylor said, smiling up at him, "I'm dying for a good pepperoni pizza, only—"

"Only what?"

"Only my favorite pizza chain doesn't have inside seating."

Russ looked at her as if she were deranged. "How do they do business then?"

"It's take-out and delivery only."

"All right," he said, mulling over this information. "Then I suggest we go back to the hotel. You can drop off the packages in your room while I phone and order a large pepperoni pizza."

Taylor agreed without realizing what she'd done until it was too late. After returning to her room, she piled her shopping on the double bed, then sat on the edge while she considered this latest development. She'd agreed to join Russ in his room. In the middle of the day. With no one else around.

Walking into the bathroom, she ran a brush through her hair. She toyed with the idea of finding an excuse, phoning Russ's room and canceling the whole thing. The hotel was filled with restaurants. The food was good and so reasonably priced it was a shame to order out.

Taylor slumped against the bathroom sink and closed her eyes dejectedly. Who was she kidding? Certainly not herself. She was in love with Russ and had been for weeks. They had no business falling in love, but it had happened, and instead of fighting it she should be grateful. Her attitude should be one of thanksgiving that she'd come across a man as fundamentally honest as Russ. There was no comparison to Mark, none whatsoever.

Five minutes later, she knocked on Russ's door. He let her in but had obviously been having second thoughts of his own. He marched to the other side of the room as though he feared she was carrying some dangerous virus.

"I phoned that pizza place and ordered," he said, apparently trying to sound casual. He tucked his hands into his pockets as if he suddenly didn't know what to do with them. "They said they'd be here in thirty minutes or less." He checked his watch. "That gives them nearly twenty-five minutes."

"Good," Taylor said, walking farther into the room. His was almost identical to her own. One queen-size bed, a dresser, one small table and two chairs.

"Make yourself at home," he said, pulling over a chair. Then he walked around the bed, averting his eyes.

"That was quite a morning we had, wasn't it?" he asked, rubbing his palms together. Heaving a sigh, he whirled around and faced her. "Listen, Taylor, this isn't going to work. If you want to have your pizza, fine, but I've got to get out of here."

"You don't have to leave," she said as she sauntered across the room, making sure her hips swayed just a fraction more than normal. When she turned to look at Russ, she was well rewarded for the little extra she'd put into her walk. His jaw was tight, and the edges of his mouth had whitened. His hands were knotted into fists at his sides.

"I...don't think you understand," Russ said faintly.

She moved close so that she was almost directly in front of him. Standing on her toes, she raised her arms and slid them around his neck, then molded her body against his.

Russ held himself completely rigid. Then he brought up his hands and closed them around her wrists, ready to pull her away from him. For some reason he hesitated. His gaze was hot and questioning when it locked with hers. "Just what kind of game are you playing?"

"The seductress. How am I doing?"

His gaze narrowed, and she noted that his breathing had become ragged. "Good. Too good."

He gazed down on her, his look a mixture of doubt and wonder. "Do you love me?" he asked.

She found herself lost, the words confusing her before they even reached her lips. Before she could tell him everything, before she could explain what was in her heart, Russ sighed and hauled her back in his arms.

His hands were in her hair, and his mouth was seeking hers. "It doesn't matter," he whispered brokenly. "I love you enough for both of us. It doesn't matter," he said again, just before his hungry lips claimed hers.

The passion between them was explosive. Tears clouded her eyes and fell down her face without restraint. But these were tears of joy, tears of thanksgiving and discovery, surging from deep within.

"I love you, I love you," she chanted silently as she felt the tremors that went through Russ. He pulled her against him and held on as if he'd jerked her from the jaws of death and feared losing her a second time.

For the longest moment he didn't move.

"Russ?" she whispered. "What's wrong?"

The merest hint of a smile turned up the corners of his mouth. He leaned forward and with infinite care he brushed the hair from her brow. His callused, work-roughened hands had begun to shake.

"Russ?" she repeated, growing alarmed. Her hands framed his face, and he dragged one palm across his cheek to his lips and kissed the inside of her hand.

"I need to explain something first," he whispered, and the words seemed to be pulled from the farthest reaches of his soul. "If we make love now, there'll be no turning back."

Taylor blinked. She heard the desperation in his voice and read the havoc in his handsome face.

Her own mind was reeling, her thoughts jumbled. Had she been able to speak, her words would have made no sense.

Russ lowered his mouth to hers, but his kiss was featherlight. "Look at me," he whispered. "I want you so much I'm shaking like a newborn calf. All these weeks I've dreamed of this moment, of making you mine, and when the time arrives, I discover... I can't."

Not according to the evidence pressing against her thigh. Taylor didn't know a delicate, or even indelicate, way of mentioning the fact.

"I know your career is important to you, and it should be. You worked too hard for your education to give it up now," he said.

"That's r-right," Taylor returned, puzzled.

Holding her hand in his own, Russ whispered, "And another thing..."

"There's more?"

"Lots more," he said, grinning down at her. His mouth brushed hers in a lazy, affectionate kiss. "I know you haven't come to appreciate Cougar Point yet, but that's all right. I promise you will in time. There's something about standing outside on a crisp autumn night and seeing the moonlight through the branches. Or hearing the crunch of snow under your boots in winter. In spring it's newborn animals, the smell of the earth and the rush of wind as it blows over the treetops. Those are the things I love most."

Taylor frowned in confusion. Her hands went back to his face and she studied him, seeking some meaning to his words. "Why are you telling me all this?"

"Because I want you to love my home as much as I do. I want you to love the country. Cougar Point will never rival Seattle. It won't even rival Reno, but it's a good place to live, a good place to raise a family."

Taylor had no argument with that. None. From the first, she'd seen how strong the sense of family was in this small community. "In the beginning I was so lost. Moving to Montana was like visiting a foreign country. Time seemed to have been turned back thirty years."

"What about ranch life?"

Again she wasn't sure what he was asking. "In many ways it's beautiful. I never thought I could say that and mean it. At first all I saw was the harshness of the land, and how unforgiving it could be. I saw how hard you and the others work. How busy you are. I learned a little about the problems and wondered why anyone would bother when ranching's such a demanding way of life."

"And now?"

"Now...there's still a great deal I don't understand about your kind of life, and I probably never will, but I see the contentment of knowing you've worked hard." She hesitated, surprised at how well-formed her thoughts actually were since she'd never voiced them before. "I moved to Cougar Point looking for one thing and found something else entirely. In the past few weeks I've learned what's important in life and what isn't."

Russ smiled and rewarded her with a lengthy kiss. "Now that we've got that subject all cleared up, I want you to know that I consider babies a woman's business...."

Bracing her hands against his chest, Taylor lifted her head. "What are you talking about? Honestly, Russ, I have no idea where this conversation is going."

His mouth dropped open. "You don't?"

She shook her head.

"Good grief, I thought you knew all along. I'm asking you to marry me."

Chapter 13

"Marriage!" Taylor said, stunned. "You're joking."

"Trust me, a man doesn't joke about something like this."

All at once Taylor's knees didn't feel as if they would support her anymore, and she slumped onto the bed. Breathless and light-headed. She held her hand over her heart in an effort to calm its erratic beating, but that didn't seem to help.

"Taylor, what's wrong?" Russ knelt in front of her and took both her hands in his own. "You look like you're about to faint."

"Don't be ridiculous."

"What's wrong?"

She pointed at his door. "When I walked into this room, I wasn't thinking about getting married. Not for a second."

"Do you mean to say you came here after my body? Well, and the pizza, of course," he added with a laugh.

"Your body? Don't go all righteous on me," she muttered. "You've been after mine for weeks."

"I've reconsidered," Russ said with infuriating calm. "I want more than an occasional tumble with you. A whole lot more."

"Isn't marriage carrying this a little too far?"

"No. Is it so wrong to want to wake up with you at my side?"

"You shouldn't hit a woman with this kind of talk. I'm not prepared for it." She pulled her hands from his and waved them dramatically. "Out of the blue he starts talking about marriage."

Russ ignored her outburst and sat beside her on the bed. "When I come into the house after a hard day's work, it's you I want to find."

Taylor's gaze narrowed. "I suppose it's me you want cooking your dinner and laundering your clothes!"

"Yes," he said matter-of-factly. "Because I'll have spent the past twelve or more hours building a good life for us. But if washing a load of clothes bothers you so much, I'll bring someone in. I'm not marrying you for your domestic talents."

He was serious. "Russ," she whispered, running her hands down his face, "marriage isn't something we should discuss now. Let's talk about it later...much, much later." Leaning forward, she slanted her mouth over his. Russ resisted her at first but quickly surrendered. His response was gratifying.

He wrapped his arms around her, and his returning kiss was urgent, charged with unleashed passion. As their kissing intensified, Russ eased her onto the bed and positioned himself above her.

"Taylor…" He lifted his head and groaned. He looked like a man who didn't know what to do, a man trapped in one world, seeking entrance to another. His eyes were shut.

Taylor had no answers to give him. All she knew was that she was tired of fighting this feeling, tired of living a life filled with denial. She hadn't meant to fall in love with Russ Palmer, but she had. Her fingers tangled in his hair as she directed his lips back to hers.

She yearned for more of him. He kissed her again, and she felt it in every part of her body, from the crown of her head to the soles of her feet.

When she least expected it, he started kissing her in a fierce and raging storm of his own, and then without warning, he moved away from her.

With shaking hands, Taylor said, "Russ?" She kissed him lightly. "Why did you stop?"

"I already told you. If we're going to make love, even once, there's no turning back. I've got to have more from you than your body…. I want you for my wife."

"Does it have to be all or nothing?"

"Yes," he said forcefully.

"But why talk about marriage now?" she asked gently. "Isn't that something we could consider later?"

"No…it'll be too late to think about it afterward," he said fervently. "If we're going to make love, there's got to be a commitment between us."

"But, Russ…" She wasn't sure why she was fighting him so hard; the reasons had escaped her. She'd already admitted she loved him, and if she'd gone that far, then accepting responsibility for their feelings was the next logical step. Only she felt as if she'd just learned to walk and Russ was signing her up for a marathon.

Russ took her by the shoulders. "I realize things are done differently in the city. Men and women change partners as often as they do their sheets. I've read about 'swinging singles' and 'hooking up.'"

"That's not true," Taylor argued. "At least not for me. There's only been one other man in my life, and it was the biggest mistake I've ever made."

"Then don't repeat it. I'm offering you what Mark never would have, because I don't want anything less. When we make love, there won't be any doubt in your mind about my commitment to you. It's complete and total. When I told you I loved you, that wasn't a momentary thing based on physical attraction or a case of overactive hormones. It's something that's been growing from the first moment we met. It's not going to change or go away. I love you, and it's the first time I've ever said that to a woman and truly meant it."

A lump formed in Taylor's throat, and tears brimmed in her eyes. "But we're so different...."

"Of course we are," Russ said, tucking both her hands between his. "That's the crazy part in all this. At first I thought those differences would doom any chance of a lasting relationship between us. I figured we didn't have any business joining our lives together when our views are so far apart. Then I realized that being with you, fighting with you, has brought balance into my life. You've shown me and taught me things I needed to know. There's a lot I still disagree with, but we can face those issues when they arise. Basically I'm coming around to your way of thinking."

That was news to Taylor. He still seemed as obstinate

as ever in several areas. But then again, he'd allowed
Mandy to wear makeup and he'd changed his opinion
about the drill team uniform and even agreed to her
compromise on the dating issue. There'd been other
changes, too. Subtle ones. When she argued with him
now, Russ listened and weighed her argument, which
was something she'd never gotten her father to do. Her
mother had always lent a willing ear, but never her father.

"I can see the changes in you, too," Russ continued. "Remember how you felt when you first moved
to Cougar Point? As I recall, you said it was the farthest corner of the known world. Yet just a moment ago
you were telling me you've come to appreciate some of
the qualities of small-town living. True, no merchant
in town accepts American Express, but who knows?
And if you really get a craving to use that card, Billings isn't all that far."

"It's three and a half hours," she muttered, resisting
the urge to laugh. She was actually considering this
crazy proposal of his! What he said about Mark had
hit home. The months apart had given her perspective.
Russ was right; Mark would never have married her.

"Billings is only three hours, and that isn't far," he
explained eagerly. "If you like, we'll make a regular
weekend trip of it and spend our days shopping and
our nights making love. I'm willing to compromise. If
doing housework offends you—"

"That's not it!"

"Then what is?"

For the life of her, Taylor couldn't think of a single
argument that made sense. She stuck with one that was
tried and true. "It's the idea of a woman working for a

wage and then being expected to do everything else at home, too. If a wife works outside the home, her husband should do his share of the housework and rearing the children."

"I agree," Russ murmured, although it looked as if he'd had to swallow a watermelon to say so. "But that's also why I feel a mother's place is in the home."

"Oh, please, let's not get into that again."

"Right," Russ said emphatically. "We could inadvertently start another war, and the last thing I want to do is fight with you. I love you, Taylor. Heaven help me, but it's true."

She raised her hand and caressed the side of his face. "I love you, too."

Russ pressed his own hand over hers and sighed deeply. "I knew you did. I couldn't believe anything else because it hurt too damn much. I swear to you, Taylor, I've never been a jealous man, but when you were having dinner with Cody Franklin last weekend, it took every ounce of restraint I possess not to march across that restaurant, pick you up and carry you out of there."

Taylor smiled and leaned forward until their foreheads touched. Her lips brushed his. "I'm not much for the green-eyed monster myself, but Mary Lu Randall should consider herself a lucky woman. I felt like tearing her hair out."

"Does this mean you'll marry me?"

Taylor closed her eyes and waited for a list of sound, rational arguments to convince her otherwise. To her surprise there were none. "Yes...."

With a triumphant shout loud enough to crack the windows, Russ bolted to his feet, taking her with him.

With his arm at her waist, he whirled her around until Taylor, laughing, begged him to stop.

Instead, he lifted her higher and higher until she supported her hands on his shoulders and threw back her head.

The knock on the door caught them both by surprise. Taylor's eyes found Russ's. She didn't even want to imagine who was on the other side.

"Who is it?" Russ demanded, carefully lowering her to the floor.

"Pizza delivery."

Taylor hurriedly arranged her clothes and paused to smile when she heard that. She'd completely forgotten about the pizza.

Russ paid for their meal and brought the cardboard box and a stack of napkins inside. The scent of pepperoni and melting cheese filled the room.

Taking the box from Russ, Taylor placed it on the table and immediately opened it, inhaling deeply. She was grateful for the napkins the delivery boy had included, and pulled a slice free for Russ. Next she helped herself, savoring the first delicious bite.

"Taylor," Russ groaned, sitting in the chair across from her, "we're having the most important discussion of our lives. How can you eat at a time like this?"

"The pizza is hot *now*," she said, and gobbled down two extra bites, in case he convinced her to put it aside.

"I suppose we're going to have to figure out how to get your pizza fix, too, aren't we?"

She nodded. "At least once a month, please." She closed her eyes. "Oh, my goodness, I'd forgotten how wonderful a pizza can taste. Russ, I'm sorry, but I can't marry you unless we arrange to have a decent pepperoni pizza every few weeks."

"The bowling alley—"

"Makes a great breakfast, but someone has to let those people know that good pizza is made fresh and doesn't come out of the freezer."

Russ jammed his fingers through his hair. "I'll do what I can. Anything else?"

"When are we going to announce the engagement? Christmas time?"

Russ stood abruptly and started pacing. He didn't look at her and seemed to be composing his thoughts.

"Russ?"

He turned to face her. "Taylor, I want us to get married this afternoon. I know you're entitled to a big wedding with the fancy dress and the dinner and dancing and everything else, but dammit all, we could be married within the hour if you'd agree."

The pizza that had seemed so important a few minutes before was forgotten. "You want us to get married *now*? *Today*?"

"We're in Reno, aren't we? What else do folks do in this town?"

She shrugged, and when she started to speak, her voice sounded as though she'd suddenly been struck with laryngitis. "I understand gambling is a big interest."

"Okay," Russ said, rubbing the side of his jaw, clearly calling upon all his powers of self-control. "Rushing you wouldn't be fair. I've been thinking for weeks about us getting married, but for you it's coming out of the blue. If you want to wait until Christmas, then fine. I can accept that. I don't like it, and I don't know how I'm going to keep my hands off you till then, but I'll try."

"You know what they say: marry in haste, repent at leisure," she felt obliged to remind him.

"Right," he returned with a complete and total lack of conviction. "When we look back on our wedding day, I don't want there to be any regrets. None."

"I certainly wouldn't want you to have any, either."

"The best thing to do is take this nice and slow," he said, raising both hands. "You're a teacher, so you tend to be methodical, and although you've seen evidence to the contrary, I'm not normally one to act on impulse, either."

"I don't think you heard me correctly," Taylor murmured, because he really had misunderstood her. "I thought we'd *announce* our engagement this Christmas."

Russ whirled around and stared at her, looking even more disgruntled. "Are you saying you'd like to be a traditional June bride?"

"School will be out, and it makes sense, doesn't it? But then, I'm not really much of a traditionalist."

He grinned at that and bent to kiss her. "You're more of one than you realize, otherwise you wouldn't have had any qualms about moving in with Mark." Once more he knelt in front of her. "I plan to do everything right for you, Taylor. Set whatever date you want for the wedding."

His eyes were filled with such intensity that Taylor saw herself mesmerized by the love she saw there. "I don't know…" she whispered, feeling overwhelmed by his willingness to commit his life to her. "We're both in Reno now. We're in love, but there are problems…."

"Nothing we can't settle," he suggested with an eagerness that brought a smile to her lips.

Closing her eyes, Taylor leaned forward and slipped her arms around Russ's neck. "Are you *sure* you want to marry me? You haven't met a single member of my family, and my father's opinionated enough to test the patience of a saint."

"It's not your family I'm marrying—it's you." He drew her hand to his mouth and kissed her knuckles. "As for whether I'm sure about marrying you, I've never felt more confident of anything in my life."

Despite everything, Taylor felt equally certain. "Now that you mention it, today does have appeal, doesn't it?"

"Yesterday had appeal, too, as does tomorrow and all the rest of my tomorrows."

"Oh, Russ, sometimes you say the most beautiful things."

"I do?" He seemed completely surprised by that. "I wasn't trying." With his hands at the small of her back, he drew her forward until she was perched on the very edge of the chair. "I love you, Taylor, and I'm going to love you all the days of my life." His mouth captured hers, and he worshiped her in a single kiss.

When he pulled away, Taylor felt like clay in his arms, her will shaped and molded by his. "I'll wear my new dress."

"One more question," he whispered close to her ear. "Are you on birth control?"

Her eyes flew open. "No. Are you?"

He jerked his head back and stared at her, open-mouthed. Then his face relaxed into a lazy smile. "I'm beginning to know you, Taylor Manning, soon to be

Taylor Palmer. You're telling me birth control isn't just a woman's responsibility."

She rewarded him with a long, slow, leisurely kiss.

"I'll stop at the drugstore," he murmured when she'd finished.

"No," she whispered between nibbling kisses. "I don't want you to."

"But you might get pregnant."

"Yes, I know." She found his earlobe and sucked it gently. "I'd like it if I did. What about you?"

"I'd like it, too.... Taylor," he moaned, "stop now while I've still got my sanity."

She pressed her breasts against him, loving the feel, savoring the sensations the action aroused.

"Taylor," Russ groaned once more. "Stop...please."

"In a moment."

"Now." He clasped her around the waist and stepped back.

He stood, clutching the back of the chair. "I'll go find us a preacher," he said, and his voice was shaking. "Can you be ready in an hour?"

Taylor stood in the foyer of the wedding chapel, holding a bouquet of small pink rosebuds. The minister who'd married her pointed out the line on the wedding certificate where she was supposed to sign. Taylor did so with a flair, then smiled at her husband and handed him the pen. Russ in turn gave the pen to the receptionist and clerk who'd served as their witnesses.

Russ hurriedly signed the document, and when he'd finished, he shook the minister's hand and guided Taylor out of the chapel.

"I don't think I've ever seen you more beautiful,"

he said, sliding his hand around her waist and drawing her close. His eyes shone with a light that had been
transmitted straight from his heart, a message of joy.

"I don't think I've ever seen you more handsome,"
Taylor told him.

His eyes didn't stray from her. "What would you like
to do next? Have dinner? See a show?"

Taylor chuckled. "You've got to be kidding. You
know what I want because it's the same thing you want.
Besides, we've only got a few hours."

"A few hours. Why?"

"Because," she said, leaning forward to press her
mouth over his, "the drill team is scheduled to perform at eight, and Mandy would never forgive us if we
weren't there for her big moment."

Russ grumbled something under his breath and
quickened his pace, leading her back to the hotel.

"You seem to be mighty eager, Mr. Palmer," she said
as they entered into the hotel elevator.

"Move your hips like that one more time and I'll
show you how eager I can be."

"And I'd let you."

Russ reached for her then, dragging her against him.
His mouth took hers, and he gave her a glimpse of the
pleasure that awaited her. The elevator had stopped at
their floor, and the doors had glided open before either
of them was aware of it.

As soon as they stepped into the long, carpeted hallway, Russ lifted her in his arms. "You didn't get the big
fancy wedding, with the bridesmaids and orange blos-
soms and the organ music, but there are some traditions
I can and will provide."

However, opening the door with Taylor in his arms

proved to be awkward, and after a frustrating moment, Russ tossed her over his shoulder like a bag of grain.

"Russ," Taylor cried, "put me down this minute."

"Be patient," he said, crouching down in an effort to insert the key into the lock. Apparently he was having trouble, because it was taking him forever.

A middle-aged couple strolled past and, mortified, Taylor covered her face with both hands.

"Dear," the woman whispered to Taylor, "do you need help?"

"Not really," she answered. "Just don't ever let your daughters grow up to marry cowboys."

"You're recently married?" the woman asked as if that was the most romantic thing she'd ever heard. "Did you hear that, John? They just got married."

The door finally opened, and Russ walked inside with Taylor still dangling over his shoulder. "We've been married for all of about fifteen minutes," Russ told the couple. "Now, if you'll excuse us, we're going to have our honeymoon." With that he shut the door.

"Russ Palmer, put me down," she ordered him again.

"With pleasure."

He walked to the bed and released her. Taylor went flying backward, a cry hovering on her lips. Chuckling, Russ lowered himself over her.

"Was that really necessary?" she asked, feigning indignation.

"If I wanted to get you inside this room, it was. And trust me, I wanted you in this room."

A smile twitched at the edges of Taylor's mouth.

"Oh, Taylor," Russ groaned, "I'm so crazy about you." He set his long fingers in her hair and pulled up her head to receive his kiss. His mouth was hard over her own, hard with passion and with need.

"Oh, sweet Taylor," he murmured as he tore his mouth free and nestled his face in the delicate curve of her neck. He kissed her there, his lips hot and moist. His hands were gentle as he helped her stand and slip out of her dress. It fell to the floor in a pool of silk and lace. He picked it up and set it aside.

Their mouths met once more in another kiss, a kiss that promised passion about to be assuaged—and a love that would last through all the seasons of their lives.

An hour later, just before they left for the drill team performance, Taylor used the phone in Russ's room to call her family.

Russ stood behind her, his hands caressing her shoulders. Without her ever having said a word, Russ seemed to know how difficult this discussion would be for her.

"Mom?" she said excitedly when her mother answered. "If Dad's home, get him on the other phone. I've got some important news."

Taylor heard her mother's hurried call. Within a minute, Eric Manning was on an extension.

"Taylor," her father's voice boomed over the long-distance line, "what is it? Is anything wrong? Listen, I've been reading between the lines in your letters, and I'm worried about you and this cowpoke. Christy said you called and talked to her, but she never told us exactly why. Just said you were having trouble with that cowboy."

"Dad...stop a minute, will you?"

"Now you listen to me. If he gives you any more

problems, I want you to let me know because your brothers and I will deal with him."

"Eric," her mother interrupted, "Taylor called because she has some news."

It took Taylor a tense moment to compose herself.

"Mom and Dad," she said after swallowing hard, "congratulations are in order.... I was married today." A second of stunned silence followed her announcement. "I'm afraid I married that cowboy." She handed the receiver to Russ.

Chapter 14

Russ took the telephone receiver, worried about the way she was frowning, wondering what her parents had said. It looked as if she wanted to advise him, but there wasn't time.

"Hello," Russ said. "I'm Russ Palmer."

"What the hell have you done?" a loud male voice shouted at him.

Russ moved the phone away from his ear. "I married your daughter," Russ explained, doing his best to keep his tone even and controlled. He didn't much take to being yelled at, but he could understand Eric Manning's feelings.

"Taylor's just broken off one relationship, and the last thing she should do is get involved in another, especially with—"

"A cowboy," Russ finished for him. Taylor was sitting on the edge of the bed, her hands clasped tightly in her lap, her blue eyes staring up at him.

"That girl of mine should have her head examined. She doesn't understand what she's done and—"

A soft, feminine voice interrupted the tirade. "Eric, dear, all this shouting isn't going to settle anything. They're already married. Didn't you hear Taylor tell you that?"

"And we intend to stay married," Russ added, in case there was any doubt in the older man's mind.

"It's too soon," Taylor's father continued, his voice less menacing. "Surely you realize she married you on the rebound. You may be a perfectly fine young man, but my daughter—"

"Is twenty-six and old enough to know her own mind."

"She's always been a hothead. No doubt her sister told her I was dead set against her having anything to do with you."

"I can understand your concern," Russ said, now that his anger had worn off. "You don't know me from Adam."

"What about your family?" Eric thundered anew. "What do they have to say about this?"

"The only family I have is a younger half sister. We haven't told her yet, but Mandy will be delighted."

"You don't have any family?" Eric shouted. "How are you supposed to know what's right? By the way, how old are you?"

"Thirty-five."

"Thirty-five! You're nine years older than Taylor— that's too much."

"Now, Eric," Elizabeth Manning broke in. "You're

Dear Reader,

Your opinions are important to us. So if you'll participate in our fast and free "One Minute" Survey, **YOU** can pick up to four wonderful books that **WE** pay for!

As a leading publisher of women's fiction, we'd love to hear from you. That's why we promise to reward you for completing our survey.

IMPORTANT: Please complete the survey and return it. We'll send your Free Books and Free Mystery Gifts right away. **And we pay for shipping and handling too!** ← *We pay for EVERYTHING!*

Try **Essential Suspense** featuring spine-tingling suspense and psychological thrillers with many written by today's best-selling authors.

Try **Essential Romance** featuring compelling romance stories with many written by today's best-selling authors.

Or TRY BOTH!

Thank you again for participating in our "One Minute" Survey. It really takes just a minute (or less) to complete the survey… and your free books and gifts will be well worth it!

Sincerely,

Pam Powers

Pam Powers
for Reader Service

being ridiculous. If you recall, you're seven years older than I am. Russ, you'll have to excuse my husband's temper. It's just that he loves Taylor and is terribly proud of her, except he has trouble letting her know that."

"You don't need to go telling *him* that."

"Russ is family, dear."

"Not if I have anything to say about it."

"Frankly, Mr. Manning," Russ said firmly, "you don't. The deed is done. Signed, sealed and delivered."

"We'll see about that."

"Stop it now, the pair of you. Eric, either you be civil to Taylor's husband or you can get off the phone. I won't have you speaking to him that way." Her words were followed by the click of a telephone receiver.

Russ waited a moment to compose himself. Taylor had mentioned the type of man her father was more than once, but butting heads with him had been even more of a challenge than Russ had anticipated.

"Mrs. Manning, believe me, I can understand your concern, and I can't say I blame you. But I want you to know I love Taylor, and I have every intention of being a good husband."

"I'm sure you do. Please forgive my husband. Personally I think he was disappointed that he didn't get to walk Taylor down the aisle. Only one of our sons is married, and I think Eric was looking forward to taking part in a wedding for one of his daughters."

"I'm sorry to have cheated him out of that."

"Don't worry about it. There's always Christy, and we expect she'll be engaged to an attorney friend of hers soon. Now, before you think the worst of us, I want to offer you a hearty welcome to the family, such as it is."

"Thank you," Russ said, and smiled reassuringly at Taylor, who was looking more anxious by the minute.

"Would you mind putting Taylor back on the line?"

"Of course not." Russ's eyes found Taylor's as he held the receiver out to her. "Your mother wants to talk to you."

"Was it bad?" she whispered, sounding guilty when there was no reason for it.

"No, I think your father and I will get along just fine."

"The two of you are quite a bit alike."

Russ figured it was probably a good thing that he'd first been introduced to Taylor's father over the phone. Had they met in person it was entirely possible that they would have swung at each other.

Taylor took the phone and relaxed visibly as she started talking to her mother. Russ was relieved to see her good spirits return. This was their day, the one he'd been thinking about for weeks, and he didn't want anything or anyone to ruin it.

The problem, Russ decided an hour later, was that he'd reckoned without Mandy, his cantankerous younger sister.

"You did *what?*" the teenager shrieked in outrage.

"We got married," Taylor explained softly, holding out her ring finger, adorned with a simple gold band, as proof. He could tell that she was equally surprised by his sister's response. "I thought you'd be pleased."

"You did it without even talking to me?" Mandy cried. She stood with her hands on her hips as though she were the adult and they were recalcitrant children. "I can't believe the two of you." She whirled around and confronted Carol Fischer. "Did you hear what they just did?" Mandy demanded.

Carol had trouble containing a grin. "Yes, I did," she said, and stepped forward to hug Taylor. "Congratulations."

"You didn't so much as consult me," Mandy reminded him, her eyes narrowing. "Can you imagine how I feel? I'm your sister, and I should've been in on this! Good grief, you wouldn't have even *met* Taylor if it hadn't been for me!"

"Do you mind our getting married so terribly much?" Taylor asked softly.

"Of course I don't mind. Marrying you is the smartest thing Russ has done in his whole sorry life. It's just that..." She paused, and tears clouded her pretty green eyes. "I would like to have been there. You couldn't have waited until after the drill team performance?"

"Yes, we could have. We should have," Russ agreed, stepping closer to his sister. "I'm sorry if we offended you. That wasn't our intention."

"We were so lost in each other that we forgot everyone else," Taylor said.

"I can't believe it. When we left this morning, you were barely talking to each other, and the next thing I know, you're married. I just don't understand it."

Taylor placed her arm around Mandy's shoulders. "I've been in love with your brother from the first, but I was fighting it because...well, because I didn't think I'd fit into his life. Then we started talking and I realized I couldn't even remember why I was fighting him so hard when I love him so much. This probably doesn't make a lot of sense to you, and I'm sorry."

Mandy lifted one shoulder in a halfhearted shrug.

"In a way it does make sense. I just wish you'd waited a little longer. I would've liked to throw rice or birdseed or something."

"We were just thinking about going out for a wedding dinner. We'd like it if you came."

With her arms folded, Mandy cocked her head to one side. "Are you sure I wouldn't be intruding?"

"More than sure," Russ told her. "I'm going to order a bottle of champagne and you can have a virgin daiquiri if you want. It isn't every day a brother can share his wedding dinner with his sister, and we have a lot to celebrate, don't we? In fact, Taylor's and my wedding day wouldn't be complete if you weren't here to share part of it with us."

"You're just saying that," Mandy said with a regal tilt to her chin. "However, I'm going to let you get away with it because I really am pleased." She dropped her arms and threw herself against Russ with such force that he nearly toppled backward. "Hey," she cried, wiping tears from her cheeks with the back of her hand, "did you see how great the team did? Aren't we fabulous?" She didn't wait for a response, but reached for Taylor, slipping an arm around her waist and the other around Russ. "Now listen," she said, serious once more. "A wedding is one thing, but if you're going to start having babies, I want to be consulted. Understand?"

Three weeks later, early on a Saturday morning, Taylor nestled close to her husband under a layer of quilts, seeking his warmth. When she'd first arrived in Montana, Russ had warned her about the winters, but nothing could have prepared her for the bitter cold that had descended upon them in the past ten days.

Russ stirred, rolled over and pulled her into his arms. Taylor smiled contentedly as she repositioned herself so that her head rested on his shoulder. She settled her hands over his chest. Married life certainly seemed to agree with him—and she knew it agreed with her. From the moment they'd said their vows in Reno, Russ had been a devoted and loving husband, with the accent on the word *loving*. He couldn't seem to get enough of her, which was fine with Taylor, since she couldn't get enough of him, either.

With Mandy living with them, it sometimes became embarrassing. More than once after their wedding, Russ had insisted he was exhausted and dragged Taylor upstairs practically before they'd finished clearing the dinner dishes. Mandy loved to tease Russ about his sudden need for extra sleep since he'd returned from Reno.

At one point Taylor had felt it was necessary to talk to Russ's sister. Her fear was that Mandy would feel excluded, and that was the last thing Taylor wanted.

"Are you kidding?" Mandy had said, exchanging a smile with Taylor. "I think getting married is the best thing that's happened to Russ. He should've done it years ago. He's too mellow to fight with me anymore. Keep him happy, okay? Because when he's happy, I'm happy."

Keeping Russ happy made Taylor feel delirious with satisfaction herself. Every now and then they clashed over some issue, but that was to be expected. Both seemed willing, however, to listen to the other's point of view.

"Good morning," Russ whispered. His hand found her breast, and she sighed at the instant surge of pleasure.

"They seem fuller," he whispered.

"I know what you're thinking," she said, snuggling closer. "But it's much too soon to make that kind of assumption."

"Taylor," Russ groaned, kissing her hungrily. "We haven't used any kind of protection. Not once. Have you...you know, started yet?"

"Not yet, but I'm often a few days late."

Russ smoothed the hair about her face. "You know the problem, don't you?"

"The problem is you and your sexy ways," she muttered.

"You've never complained before."

"I'm not complaining now. I'm just telling you."

"Actually, the problem I'm talking about is your parents. They'll be here next week for Thanksgiving, and you don't want to have to tell them you're pregnant."

"My father will assume the worst."

"Let him. We know the truth."

"My father's always been ridiculously protective of us girls, and if he even suspects I was pregnant before we were married, he's going to raise the roof."

"Do you think I care?" Tenderly he rested his hand on her abdomen, and the smile that came to his face was filled with an abundance of pride. "I bet this baby's a boy."

"What a terrible, chauvinistic thing to say."

"I can't help it. Every time I think about you having my son I get all warm. I still have trouble believing we're really married. It seems like a dream."

"We could very well have a girl. In fact, I'd be pleased if we did."

"So you're willing to admit you might be expecting."

Taylor was expecting, all right, but not the way Russ

meant. She was waiting for trouble, and the minute her parents arrived there was bound to be plenty of it. Not once since she'd phoned to tell her mom and dad that she and Russ were married had Taylor spoken to her father. Her mother had phoned about the possibility of visiting for Thanksgiving, and Taylor had readily agreed. But she knew the real reason for this visit, and that was so her father could confront Russ about their rushed marriage. Several times in the past three weeks Taylor had tried to prepare Russ for the meeting, but he seemed to let everything she said roll off him. Either he really wasn't concerned or he was living in a world of his own. After doing battle with her father for most of her life, Taylor was nervous. Seldom did she back down from Eric Manning, but this was different. She wanted her family to love and appreciate Russ the way she did.

It wasn't that her father was such a monster, but he tended to be opinionated and hotheaded, especially when it came to his daughters. After Taylor had broken up with Mark, her father had taken pains to introduce her to a handful of eligible young men. All of them were professionals. Taylor didn't doubt for a moment that her father would consider Russ an inappropriate husband for her.

"And for another thing," she said stiffly, reminding him of the ridiculous statement he'd made when they were discussing marriage, "babies are *not* just a woman's business."

"Oh? And what am I supposed to do?"

"Plenty!"

"Come on, Taylor, be sensible. There's not a lot I can do with a baby. They're too…tiny."

"You can change a diaper."

"You've got to be joking."

She rolled away from him and buried her face in the pillow, embarrassed by the tears that sprang to her eyes. Even if she was pregnant, it would be months before the baby was born, and there was plenty of time to deal with the issue of Russ's role as a parent.

"Taylor?" Russ asked softly, his hand on her shoulder. "Are you crying?"

She refused to admit it. "Of course not."

"I've been doing a little reading on pregnancy and birth, and I understand that tears are perfectly normal. Women become highly emotional during this time."

"I suppose you're going to be quoting facts and statistics to me for the next eight months," she said, then immediately regretted her waspish tone. Turning back to Russ, she sobbed and threw her arms around his neck. "I'm sorry... I didn't mean that. It's just that I'm worried about you meeting Dad."

Russ gently kissed the tip of her nose. "There isn't going to be a problem, sweetheart. I promise you."

"You can't say that—you don't know my dad."

"I won't let there be a problem. We have one very important thing in common. We both love you. Two men of similar persuasion are going to get along famously. So stop borrowing trouble, all right?"

She nodded. "Okay, but I don't think we should say anything about the possibility of me being pregnant until after Christmas. Agreed?"

"If that's the way you want to handle it." He eased her more fully into his arms. "But I'm afraid I might inadvertently give it away. I'm so happy about it I have trouble not shouting every time I think about us having a son."

"Or daughter."

"I still think it's a boy."

"Whichever it is, I'd better tell Mandy. Otherwise we'll be subjected to her wrath—just like after the wedding. Weren't we given specific instructions to clear the idea of having kids with her first?"

"I already told her."

"Russ?" Taylor levered herself up on one elbow.

"I hadn't intended to, but we were sitting at the table one afternoon and apparently I was wearing a silly grin and—"

"It was probably more of a satisfied smirk," Taylor interrupted. Then she said, "Go on."

"Anyway, I was sitting there minding my own business and she wanted to know what I found so funny. Of course, I said I didn't find anything funny, and before I knew it, I was telling her about the book I'd picked up at the library about pregnancy and birth and how I thought you were going to have a baby. She was delighted. By the way, I told her the baby's probably a boy."

"Russ, you don't know that!"

"Somehow I do. Deep in my heart I feel he's a boy. Do you think your father will settle down if we promise to give the baby some family name of yours?"

"We've got to get him accustomed to the fact that we're married first. That might take some time." She made a wry face. "You know, like approaching a wild animal slowly…"

"Right," Russ grumbled. "I forgot." He reached for her and pulled her close. "If you're looking for ways to tame *this* wild beast, I might be able to offer a few suggestions." He wiggled his eyebrows provocatively.

Giggling, Taylor encircled his neck with her arms. "I tamed you a long time ago."

"That you did," he whispered as his mouth sought hers. "That you did."

The Wednesday before Thanksgiving Eric and Elizabeth Manning pulled their thirty-foot RV into the yard of the Lazy P.

Since school had been dismissed at noon, Taylor was home. The instant she recognized the vehicle, she called out to Russ, threw open the back door and flew down the steps, hardly taking time to button her coat. Russ followed directly behind her.

Standing by the door, Russ felt Eric Manning's eyes on him. The two men quickly sized each other up, and Russ descended the steps. He waited until Taylor had welcomed each of her parents before he placed his arm protectively around her shoulders.

If her parents didn't immediately guess she was pregnant, he'd be surprised. Taylor positively glowed—just like they said in the books. And he felt no less happy himself. Only rarely had he been this content. This *complete*. Taylor had filled all the dark, lonely corners of his life.

He hadn't been joking when he told her he felt all warm whenever he thought about the child growing inside her. At odd moments of the day he'd think about his wife and how much he loved her, and he'd actually feel weak with emotion. Some nights he'd lie awake and cherish these peaceful moments with Taylor sleeping at his side. She'd been sleeping a lot more lately. The books had told him she'd be extra-tired. He would prefer it if she'd quit work, but the one time he'd suggested it, she'd almost bitten his head off. Moodiness. That was something else the books had addressed. Russ decided he'd let Taylor decide when and if she should stop teaching. She knew her own limits.

"Mom and Dad," Taylor said, slipping her arm around Russ's waist, "this is my husband, Russ Palmer. You'll meet his sister, Mandy, this evening."

Russ stepped forward and extended his hand to Taylor's father. The older man muttered something unintelligible, and the two exchanged hearty handshakes.

"Come inside," Russ invited, ushering everyone into the warmth of the kitchen. He took their coats and hung them in the hall closet while Taylor settled her parents in the living room.

There had been lots of small changes in the house since she'd moved in. She had a natural flair for decorating and had rearranged the furniture and done other things that gave the living room a fresh, comfortable feel.

"Would you like some coffee?" she asked.

"No, thanks. We just had some, honey," her mother said.

Elizabeth Manning was an older version of her daughter. They both had the same intense blue eyes and long, thick dark hair. Eric Manning was as big as a lumberjack, tall and muscular, intimidating in appearance. It was important to Russ to win over this man. Important for Taylor. She'd fought with her father for most of her life. She'd often gone against his will, but she loved him, and his approval meant a great deal to her.

"Eric," Elizabeth Manning said softly, looking at her husband.

The older man cleared his throat. "Before I say anything more to get myself in hot water, I want to apologize for the way I behaved when we last spoke. It's just that finding out my daughter had married without a word to either of her parents came as a surprise."

"I understand," Russ said, "and I don't blame you. If my daughter had done that, I don't think I would've behaved any differently."

The two men shared a meaningful look.

"There's something you should both know," Taylor said, sitting on the arm of Russ's chair. She gave him a small smile, her eyes wide. "I'm pregnant. Now, Daddy, before you assume the worst," she added in a rush, "this baby was conceived in love with a wedding band on my finger. I swear to you it's the truth."

Russ stared up at his wife in shock. For days she'd been schooling him on the importance of keeping their secret until the Christmas holidays. Again and again she'd insisted the worst thing they could do was announce her pregnancy the moment her parents rolled into the Lazy P. Then, with barely a second's notice, Taylor had spilled it all.

"Oh, Taylor, that's absolutely wonderful." Her mother was clearly delighted. One look told Russ that wasn't the case with her father.

"Daddy?" Taylor turned expectantly to her father. She took Russ's hand and held it tightly. "I love him, Dad, more than I ever dreamed it was possible to love a man."

"He's good to you?"

"Damn right I'm good to her," Russ muttered. He wasn't sure what was going on between father and daughter, but he resented being left out of the conversation.

"That true?" Eric asked, tilting his head toward Russ. "Yes, Dad."

Eric opened his arms to her, and Taylor flew across the room, to be wrapped in a bear hug by her robust father. The older man's gaze found Russ's. "She's more trouble than a barrel of monkeys. Opinionated and strong-willed, and has been from the day she was born. I suggest you keep her barefoot and pregnant."

"Daddy!" Taylor tore herself away from her father, hands on her hips. "What century are you living in?"

"The same one I am," Russ said, and chuckled boisterously when Taylor whirled around to glare at him.

The two men smiled at each other. Taylor understood what Russ was doing but couldn't help reacting anyway.

"If the two of you think you can run my life, I want you to know right now that—"

She wasn't allowed to finish. Russ gently turned her around, draped her over his arm and kissed her soundly.

"I can see our daughter married the right man," Russ heard Eric Manning inform his wife. "The right man indeed."

* * * * *

Visit the Author Profile page
at Harlequin.com for more titles.

SMALL-TOWN NANNY

Lee Tobin McClain

To the real Bob Eakin.
Thank you for your service.

"For I know the plans I have for you," declares the
Lord, "plans to prosper you and not to harm you,
plans to give you hope and a future."
—*Jeremiah* 29:11

Chapter 1

Sam Hinton was about to conclude one of the biggest business deals of his career. And get home in time to read his five-year-old daughter her bedtime story.

He'd finally gotten the hang of being a single dad who happened to run a multimillion-dollar business.

Feeling almost relaxed for the first time since his wife's death two years ago, Sam surveyed the only up-scale restaurant in his small hometown of Rescue River, Ohio, with satisfaction. He'd helped finance this place just to have an appropriate spot to bring important clients, and it was bustling. He recognized his former high school science teacher coming through the door. There was town matriarch Miss Minnie Falcon calling for her check in her stern, Sunday-school-teacher voice. At a table by the window, one of the local farmers laughed

with his teenage kids at what looked to be a graduation dinner.

And who was that new, petite, dark-haired waitress?
Was it his sister's friend Susan Hayashi?

Sam tore his eyes away from the pretty server and
checked his watch, wondering how long a visit to the
men's room could take his client. The guy must be either
checking with his board of directors or playing some
kind of game with Sam—seeming to back off, hoping
to drag down the price of the agricultural property he
was buying just a little bit more before he signed on the
dotted line. Fine. Sam would give a little if it made his
client's inner tightwad happy.

Crash!

"Leave her alone! Hands off!" The waitress he'd noticed, his sister's friend Susan, left the tray and food
where she'd dropped them and stormed across the dining room toward his client.

Who stood leering beside another, very young-
looking, waitress. "Whoa, hel-lo, baby!" his client said
to Susan as she approached. "Don't get jealous. I'm man
enough for both of you ladies!"

"Back *off*!"

Sam shoved out of his chair and headed toward the
altercation. Around him, people were murmuring with
concern or interest.

"It's okay, Susan," the teenage waitress was saying
to his sister's friend. "He d-d-didn't really hurt me."

Stepping protectively in front of the round-faced
teenager, Susan pointed a delicate finger at his client.
"You apologize to her," she ordered, poking the much
larger, much older businessman in the chest with each
word. She wore the same dark skirt and white blouse as

all the other waitstaff, but her almond-shaped eyes and high cheekbones made her stand out almost as much as her stiff posture and flaring nostrils. Three or four gold hoops quivered in each ear.

"Keep your hands off me." Sam's client sneered down at Susan. "Where's the owner of this place? I don't have to put up with anything from a…" He lowered his voice, but whatever he said made the color rise in Susan's face.

Sam clapped a hand on his client's shoulder. He hadn't pegged the guy as this much of a troublemaker, but then, he barely knew him. "Come on. Leave the ladies alone."

The other man glanced at Sam and changed his tone. "Aw, hey, I was just trying to have a good time." He gave Susan another dirty look. "Some girls can't take a joke."

"Some jokes aren't funny, mister." She glared at him, two high spots of color staining her cheeks pink.

The restaurant manager rushed up behind them. "We can work this out. Mr. Hinton, I do apologize. You girls…" He clapped his hands at the two waitresses. "My office. Now."

"I'm so sorry, I didn't mean to cause trouble!" Crying, the teenage waitress hurried toward the office at the back of the restaurant.

Susan touched the manager's arm. "Don't get mad at Tawny. I'm the one who got in Prince Charming's face." She jerked her head sideways toward Sam's client.

The restaurant manager frowned and ushered Susan to his office.

Sam's client shrugged and gave Sam a conspiratorial grin as he turned toward their table. "Ready to get back to business?"

"No," Sam said, frowning after the restaurant manager and Susan. "We're done here."

"What?" His client's voice rose to a squeak.

"I'll see you to your car. I want you out of Rescue River."

Ten minutes later, after he'd banished his would-be client, settled the bill and fixed things with the restaurant manager, Sam strode out to the parking lot.

There was Susan, standing beside an ancient, rusty subcompact, staring across the moonlit fields that circled the town of Rescue River. He'd only met her a couple of times; unfortunately, he worked too much to get to know his sister's friends.

"Hey, Susan," he called as he approached. "I got you your job back."

She half turned and arched an eyebrow. "Oh, you did, did you? Thanks, but no, thanks."

"Really?" He stopped a few yards away from her. Although he hadn't expected gratitude, exactly, the complete dismissal surprised him.

"Really." She crossed her arms and leaned back against her car. "I don't need favors from anyone."

"It's not a favor, it's just...fairness."

"It's a favor, and I don't want it. You think I can go back in there and earn tips after the scene I just made?"

"You probably could." Not only was she attractive, but she appeared to be very competent, if a little on the touchy side. "Rescue River doesn't take kindly to men being jerks. Most of the people in that room were squarely on your side."

"Wait a minute." Her eyes narrowed as she studied him. "Now I get it. You're part owner of the place."

"I'm a silent partner, yes." He cocked his head to one side, wondering where this was going.

"You're trying to avoid a sexual harassment lawsuit, aren't you?"

His jaw dropped. "Really? You think that's why…" He trailed off, rubbed the heavy stubble on his chin, and thought of his daughter, waiting for him at home. "Look, if you don't want the job back, that's fine. And if you think you have a harassment case, go for it."

"Don't worry. It wasn't me your buddy was groping, and I'm not the lawsuit type." She sighed. "Probably not the waitress type either, like Max said when he was firing me."

Sam felt one side of his mouth quirk up in a smile as he recognized the truth of that statement. He found Susan to be extremely cute, with her long, silky hair, slender figure and vaguely Asian features, but she definitely wasn't the eager-to-please type.

Wasn't *his* type, not that it mattered. He preferred soft-spoken women, domestic ladies who wore makeup and perfume and knew how to nurture a man. Archaic, but there it was.

Just then, the teenage waitress came rushing out through the kitchen door. "Susan, you didn't have to do that! Max said he fired you. I'm sorry!"

"No big deal." She shrugged again, the movement a little stiff.

"But I thought you needed the money to send your brother to that special camp—"

"It's fine." Susan's voice wobbled the tiniest bit, or

was he imagining it? "Just, well, don't let guys do that kind of stuff to you."

"I know, I know, but I didn't want to get in trouble. Especially with Mr. Hinton on the premises…" The girl trailed off, realizing for the first time that Sam stood to one side, listening to every word. "Oh, I didn't know you were there! Don't be mad at her, Mr. Hinton. She was just trying to help me!"

Susan patted her on the shoulder. "Go back inside and remember, just step on a guy's foot—hard—if he tries anything. You can always claim it was an accident."

"That's a great idea! You're totally awesome!" The younger woman gave Susan a quick hug and then trotted back into the restaurant.

Susan let her elbows drop to the hood of her car and rested her chin in her hands. "Was I ever that young?"

"Don't talk like you're ancient. What are you, twenty-five, twenty-six?" Susan was relatively new in town, and if memory served, she was a teacher at the elementary school. Apparently waitressing on the side. Sam assumed she was about his sister Daisy's age, since they'd fast become thick as thieves.

"Good guess, *Mr.* Hinton. You didn't even need your bifocals to figure that out. I'm twenty-five."

Okay, at thirty-seven he *was* a lot older than she was, but her jibe stung. Maybe because he knew very well that he wasn't getting any younger and that he needed to get cracking on his next major life goal.

Which would involve someone a lot softer and gentler than Susan Hayashi. "Listen," he said, "I'm sorry about what happened. You should know that guy who caused the trouble is headed back toward the east coast even as we speak. And he's not my friend, by the way. Just a client. Former client, now."

She arched a delicate brow. "My knight in shining armor, are you?"

What was there to say to a woman who misinterpreted his every move? He shook his head, reached out to pat her shoulder, then decided it wasn't a good idea and pulled his hand back. If he touched her, she might report him. Or throw a punch.

Definitely a woman to steer clear of.

There didn't seem to be any sweetness in her. So it surprised Sam when, as he bid her goodnight, he caught a whiff of honeysuckle perfume.

The next day, even though she wanted to pull the covers over her head and cry, Susan forced herself to climb out of bed early. She'd committed to spend her Saturday morning helping at the church's food pantry, and honestly, even that might not have gotten her out of bed, but she knew her best friend, Daisy, was going to be there.

"Come on," Daisy said when Susan dragged herself down the steps and into the church basement, "we're doing produce. Hey, did you really get fired last night?"

Embarrassment heated Susan's face as she followed her friend to an out-of-the-way corner where bins of spinach and lettuce donated by local farmers stood ready to be divided into smaller bunches. "Yeah. How'd you hear?"

"That sweet little Tawny Thompson spread it all over town, how you rescued her from some creepy businessman. What were you thinking?"

"He practically had his hand up her skirt! What was I supposed to do?"

"I don't know, tell the manager? Honestly, I would've done the same thing, but I'm not in your position. You needed that job!"

"I know." Susan blew out a sigh as she studied the wooden crates of leafy greens. Her hopes of funding the summer respite her mom needed so desperately had flown out the window last night. "Waitressing at a nice restaurant like Chez La Ferme is definitely the best money I can make, but I get so mad at guys like that. I thought Max would back me up, not fire me."

"Can you even send your brother to camp now?"

"Probably not. I shouldn't have told him he could go, but when I landed this waitressing job and found out it could be full-time as soon as school lets out for the summer, I thought I had the fee easy. I had a payment plan, everything. Now..." She focused on lettuce bunches so Daisy wouldn't see the tears in her eyes.

"What are you going to do?"

"I don't know. And to top it off, I might have to move home for the summer." Even saying it made her heart sink. She loved Rescue River and had all kinds of plans for her summer here.

"Why? You're always talking about how you and your mom..."

"Don't get along? Yeah." She sighed, wishing it wasn't so, wishing she had a storybook family like so many of the Midwestern ones she saw around her these days. "I love Mom, but she and I are like oil and water. If I go back, honestly, it'll stress her out more. I just want—*wanted*—her to have a summer to garden and antique shop with her friends, maybe even go on a few dates, without worrying about Donny."

An older couple wandered over. "You guys okay? Need any help?"

"We've got it." Daisy waved them away and carried a load of bagged lettuce to a sorting table. "So you had a good plan. But you couldn't help what happened."

"I could have been more...refined about it." A couple of tears overflowed, and Susan took off her plastic gloves to dig in her pocket for a tissue. "When am I ever going to learn to control my temper?" She blew her nose.

Daisy put an arm around her. "When you turn into a whole different person. You know, God made you the way you are, and He has a plan for you. Something will work out." She paused. "Why would you move back home, anyway? What's wrong with your room at Lacey's?"

"Lacey's got renovation fever." Susan pulled on a fresh pair of plastic gloves. "Remember, she gave me my room cheap because she knew I'd have to move when she started fixing up the place. So now her brother—you know Buck, right?—well, he's dried out and ready to help, and summer's the best time for them to get going." She gauged the right amount of lettuce for a family of four, put it in a plastic bag and twist-tied it. "And I don't have money for a deposit on a new place. I'll need to save up."

"You can stay with me. You know that."

"You're sweet." Susan side-hugged her friend. "And you live in a tiny place with two dogs and a cat. You have exactly zero room, except in that big heart of yours."

Daisy pried open another crate, this one full of kale leaves. "We just have to pray about it."

"Well, pray fast, because Lacey asked if I could be out next week. And even if I can land a job at another restaurant in Rescue River—which I doubt, with the non-recommendation Max is giving me—I won't be making anything like the tips I could bring in at Chez Le Ferme." She sighed as she dumped out the last of the kale leaves and stowed the wooden crate under the table. "I'm such an idiot."

"I've got it!" Daisy snapped her fingers, a smile lighting her plump face. "I know exactly what you can do for the summer!"

"What?" Susan eyed her friend dubiously and then went back to bagging kale. Daisy was wonderful, but she tended to get overexcited when she had a new idea.

"You know my brother Sam, right? He was at the Easter service at church, and at Troy and Angelica's wedding."

"I remember. In fact, he was at the restaurant last night. He...actually said he could get me my job back, but I turned him down." Susan felt her face flush as she thought of their conversation. She'd still been heated about the encounter with that jerk of a businessman, and she hadn't had her guard up around Daisy's brother, as she had the previous couple of times they'd met. She had the distinct feeling she'd been rude to him, but truthfully, he'd disconcerted her with his dominant-guy effort to make all her problems go away.

He was a handsome man, no doubt of that. Tall and broad-shouldered, an all-American quarterback type with a square jaw and close-cropped dark hair.

But he was one of those super traditional guys, she

could just tell. In fact, he reminded her of her father, who thought women belonged in the home, not the workplace. Dad had wanted his wife to stay home, and Mom had, and look where it had gotten her. To make matters worse, her father had expected Susan to do the same, sending her to college only for her MRS degree, which she obviously hadn't gotten. Which she had no interest in getting, not now, not ever. She was a career woman with a distinct calling to teach kids, especially those with special needs. Susan wasn't one of those people who heard clear instructions from God every week or two, but in the case of her life's work, she'd gotten the message loud and clear.

Daisy waved her hand impatiently. "You don't want that job back. I have a better idea. Did I tell you how Sam hired a college girl to take care of Mindy over the summer?"

"What?" Susan pulled herself back to the present, rubbed the back of her plastic-gloved hand over her forehead and tried to focus on what Daisy was saying.

"Sam texted me this morning, all frantic. That girl he hired to be Mindy's summer nanny just let him know late last night that she can't do it. She got some internship in DC or something. Now Sam's hunting for someone to take her place. You'd be perfect!"

Susan laughed in disbelief. "I'd be a disaster! I'm a terrible cook, and...what do nannies even do, anyway?" She had some impression of them as paid housewives, and that was the last thing she wanted to be.

"You're great with kids! You're a teacher. Do you know Mindy?"

Susan nodded. "Cute kid, but sort of notorious for playground fights. I've bailed her out a few times."

"She can be a bit of a terror. Losing her mom was hard, and then Sam hasn't been able to keep a babysitter or nanny..."

"And why would that be?" Susan knew the answer without even asking. You could tell from spending two minutes with Sam that he was a demanding guy.

"He works a lot of hours and he expects a lot. Not so much around the house, he has a cleaning service, but he's very particular about how Mindy is taken care of. And then with Mindy being temperamental and, um, *spirited*, it's not been easy for the people Sam has hired. But you'd be absolutely perfect!"

"Daisy, think." Susan raised a brow at her friend. "I just got fired for being too mouthy and for not putting up with baloney from chauvinistic guys. And you think this would be perfect how?"

Daisy looked crestfallen for a minute, and then her face brightened. "The thing is, deep inside, Sam would rather have someone who stands up to him than someone who's a marshmallow. Just look how well he gets along with me!"

Susan chuckled and lifted another crate to the table. "You're his little sister. He has to put up with you."

"Sam's nuts about me because I don't let him get away with his caveman attitude. You wouldn't, either. But that's not the point."

"Okay, what's the point?" Susan couldn't help feeling a tiny flicker of hope about this whole idea—it would be so incredible to be able to send Donny to camp, not to disappoint him and her mother yet again—but she tamped it down. There was no way this would work from either end, hers or Sam's.

"The point is," Daisy said excitedly, "you're certified in special education. That's absolutely amazing! There's no way Sam could say you don't know what you're doing!"

"Uh-huh." Susan felt that flicker again.

"He'll pay a lot. And the thing is, you can live in! You'll have the summer to save up for a deposit on a new place."

Susan drew in a breath as the image of her mother and autistic brother flickered again in her mind. "But Daisy," she said gently, "Sam doesn't like me. When we talked last night, I could tell."

One of the food pantry workers came over. "Everything okay here, ladies?"

"Oh, sure, of course! We just got to talking! Sorry!"

For a few minutes, they focused on their produce, efficiently filling bags with kale and then more leaf lettuce, pushing a cartload of bundles over to the distribution tables, coming back to bag up sugar snap peas and radishes someone had dumped in a heap on their table.

Working with the produce felt soothing to Susan. She'd grown up urban and gotten most of her vegetables at the store, but she remembered occasional Saturday trips to the farmers market with her mother, Donny in tow.

Her mother had tried so hard to please her dad, who, with his Japanese ancestry, liked eggplant and cucumbers and napa cabbage. She and her mom had watched cooking videos together, and her mom had studied cookbooks and learned to be a fabulous Japanese chef. Susan's mouth watered just thinking about daikon salad and salt-pickled cabbage and broccoli stir-fry.

But had it worked? Had her dad been happy? Not really. He'd always had some kind of criticism, and her mother would sneak off and cry and try to do better, and it was never good enough. And as she and Donny had grown up, they hadn't been enough either, and Susan knew her mother had blamed herself. Having given birth to a rebellious daughter and a son with autism, she felt she'd failed as a woman.

Her mom's perpetual guilt had ended up making Susan feel guilty, too, and as a hormonal teenager, she'd taken those bad feelings out on her mother. And then Dad had left them, and the sense of failure had been complete.

Susan shook off the uncomfortable reminder of her own inadequacy and looked around. Where was Daisy?

Just then, her friend stood up from rummaging in her purse, cell phone in hand. "I'm calling Sam and telling him to give you an interview."

"No!" Panic overwhelmed Susan. "Don't do it!" She dropped the bundle of broccoli she was holding and headed toward Daisy. There was no way she could interview with a man who reminded her so much of her father.

"You can't stop me!" Daisy teased, and then, probably seeing the alarm on Susan's face, put her phone behind her and held out a hand. "Honey, God works in mysterious ways, but I am totally sensing this is a God thing. Just let me do it. Just do an interview and see what he says, see how you guys get along."

Susan felt her life escaping from her control. "I don't—"

"You don't have to take the job. Just do the interview."

"But what if—"

"Please? I'm your friend. I have no vested interest

in how this turns out. Well, except for keeping you in town."

"I..." Susan felt her will to resist fading. There was a lot that was good about the whole idea, right? And so what if it was uncomfortable for her? If her mom and Donny could be happy, she'd be doing her duty, just as her dad had asked her to do before he'd left. *You have to take care of them, Suzie,* her dad had said in his heavily accented English.

"I'm setting something up for this afternoon. If not sooner." Daisy turned back to the phone and Susan felt a sense of doom settling over her.

That afternoon, Susan climbed out of her car in front of Sam's modern-day mansion on the edge of Rescue River, grabbed her portfolio and headed up the sidewalk, all the while arguing with God. "Daisy says You'll make a way where there is no way, but what if I don't like Your way? And I can say for sure that Sam Hinton isn't going to like *my* way, so this is a waste of time I could be—"

The double front doors swung open. She caught a glimpse of a high-ceilinged entryway, a mahogany table full of framed photos and a spectacular, sparkling chandelier, but it was Sam Hinton who commanded her attention. He stood watching her approach, wearing a sleeves-rolled-up white dress shirt and jeans, arms crossed, legs apart.

Talk about a man and his castle. And those arms! Was he a bodybuilder in his spare time or what?

"Thanks for coming." He extended one massive hand to her.

She reached out and shook it, ignoring the slight

breathlessness she felt. This was Sam, Daisy's super-traditional businessman of a brother, not America's next male model. "No problem. Daisy thought it would be a good idea."

"Yes. She had me squeeze you in, but you should know that I'm interviewing several other candidates today."

"No problem." Was God going to let her off this easy?

"It seems like a lot of people are interested in the job, probably because I'm paying well for a summer position." He ushered her in.

"How well?"

He threw a figure over his shoulder as he led her into an oak-lined office in the front of the house, and Susan's jaw dropped.

Twice as much as she'd ever hoped to make waitressing. She could send Donny to camp and her mom to the spa. Maybe even pay for another graduate course.

Okay, God—and Daisy—You were right. It's the perfect job for me.

He gestured her into the seat in front of his broad oak desk, and Susan felt a pang of nostalgia. Her dad had done the exact same thing when he wanted to talk to her about some infraction of his rules. Only his desk had just been an old door on a couple of sawhorses in the basement. How he would have loved a home office like this one.

"I don't know if you've met Mindy, but she has some…limitations." His jaw jutted out as if he was daring her to make a comment.

"If you think of them that way." The words were out before she could weigh the wisdom of saying them, and she shouldn't have, but come on! The child was missing a hand, not a heart or a set of lungs.

Sam's eyebrows shot up. "I think I know my child better than you do. Have you even met Mindy?"

Rats, rats, rats. Would she ever learn to shut her big mouth? "I teach at Mindy's school, so I've been the recess and lunchroom monitor during her kindergarten year. I know about her hand. But of course, you know her better, you're her father."

Sam was eyeing her with a level glare.

"We have a sign up at school that reads, 'Argue for your limitations, and sure enough, they're yours.' I think it's Richard Bach. I just meant…it's an automatic response." *Stop talking, Susan.* God might have a nice plan for her, but she was perfectly capable of ruining nice plans. She'd done it all her life. She fumbled in her portfolio. "Here's my résumé."

He took it, glanced over it. Then looked more closely. "You've done coursework on physical disabilities? Graduate coursework?"

"Yeah. I'm working on my master's in special ed. Bit by bit."

"Why not go back full-time? At least summers? Why are you looking to work instead?"

"Quite frankly, I have a mother and brother to help support." *Hello, Mr. Rich Guy, everyone's not rolling in money like you are.*

"Doesn't the district pay for your extra schooling?"

"Six credits per year, which is two classes. I've used mine up."

He was studying her closely, as if she was a bug pinned on the wall. Or as if she was a woman he was interested in, but she was absolutely certain that couldn't be. "I see." He nodded. "Well, I'm not sure this would be the job for you anyway. I go out in the evenings pretty often."

"Really?" She opened her mouth to say more and then clamped it closed. *Shut up, you want this job.*

"I know, being young and adventurous, you must go out a lot yourself."

"Don't make assumptions. That's not what I was thinking." She looked away from him, annoyed.

"What were you thinking?"

"Do you really want to know?"

"Try me."

"I was thinking: you work super long hours, right? And you go out in the evenings. So...when do you spend time with your daughter?"

Sam stared at Susan as her question hung in the air between them. "When do I...? Look. If you've already decided I'm a terrible parent, this isn't going to work."

Truthfully, her words uncovered the guilt that consumed him as an overworked single dad. He hated how much time he had to spend away from Mindy. Half the time, he hated dating, too, but he'd promised Marie that he'd remarry so that Mindy wouldn't be raised without a mother in the home. Probably, she'd made him promise because she knew how much he worked and feared that Mindy would be raised by babysitters if he didn't remarry.

Well, he'd changed and was trying to change more, but he'd made a promise—not just about remarrying, but about what type of mom Mindy needed, actually—and he intended to keep it. Which didn't mean this snippy schoolteacher had the right to condemn him.

"Look, I'm sorry. It's not my place to judge and I don't know your situation. Ask Daisy, I'm way too outspoken and it always gets me into trouble." Her face was contrite and her apology sounded sincere. "The thing is, I know kids and I'm good with them. If you're struggling, either with her disability or with…other issues, I could help. Build up her self-esteem, encourage her independence." Those pretty, almond-shaped brown eyes looked a little bit shiny, as if she was holding back tears. "Don't turn me down just because I'm mouthy, if you think I'd be a help to Mindy."

She was right. And he was a marshmallow around women who looked sad, especially seriously cute ones like Susan. "It's okay."

And it *was* okay. He recognized already that his burst of anger had more to do with his own guilty feelings than with her comment. But that didn't mean he had to hire her.

The doorbell chimed, making them both jump. "That's probably my next interview. I'm sorry." He stood. "Here's your résumé back."

"It's all right, you can keep it. In case you change your mind." She stood and grabbed her elegant black portfolio. Come to think of it, all of her was elegant, from her close-fitting black trousers to her white shirt and vest to her long black hair with a trendy-looking stripe of red in it, neatly clipped back.

Just for a minute, he wondered what that hair would look like flowing free.

Sam forced that thought away as he came around his desk to Susan's side. She looked neat and professional, but as soon as she opened her mouth, it became apparent that she was quite a character. Sam shook his head as he ushered her through the entryway. Why Daisy had thought he and Susan could work together was beyond him.

Thinking about her interview, he couldn't help grinning. What job applicant questioned and insulted the potential boss? You didn't see that in the business world. He was used to people kowtowing to him, begging for a job. Susan could take a few lessons in decorum, but he had to admit he enjoyed her spunk.

The doorbell chimed again just as they reached it, so he was in the awkward position of having two job applicants pass each other in the doorway. The new one, a curvaceous blonde in a flowered dress, stood smiling, a plate of plastic-wrap-covered cookies in her hands.

"Hi, are you Mr. Hinton? Thank you so much for agreeing to interview me. I would just absolutely love to have this job! What a great house!"

"Come on in." He gestured the new applicant into the entryway. "Susan, I'll be in touch."

"I hope so," she murmured as she brushed past him and out the door. "But I'm not holding my breath."

Chapter 2

The next Thursday afternoon, Sam arrived at the turn-off to his brother Troy's farm with a sense of relief. His sister was right; he needed to take a break from interviewing nannies during the day and working late into the night to make up for it. But he was desperate; Mindy's last day of school had been Tuesday, and without a regular child care provider, he'd had to stay home or use babysitters who weren't necessarily up to par.

Mindy bounced in her booster seat. "There's the sign! Look, it says *D-O-G*, dog! But what else does it say, Daddy?"

He slowed to read the sign aloud: "A Dog's Last Chance: No-Cage Canine Rescue."

"Cuz Uncle Troy and Aunt Angelica and Xavier rescue dogs. Right?"

"That's right, sugar sprite." And he hoped they could

rescue him, too. Or not rescue—they had too much going on for that—but at least give him ideas about getting a good child care provider for Mindy for the summer.

"There they are, there they are! And look, there's baby Emmie!"

Sure enough, his brother and sister-in-law stood outside the fenced kennel area. He parked, let Mindy out of the car and then paused to survey the scene.

Troy was reaching out for the baby, all of two weeks old, so that his wife could kneel down to greet Mindy with a huge hug.

The tableau they presented battered Sam's heart. He wanted this. He wanted a wife who would look up at him with that same loving, admiring expression Angelica gave Troy. Wanted a woman who'd embrace Mindy, literally and figuratively. Seeing how it thrilled Mindy, he even thought he wouldn't mind having another baby, a little brother or sister for them both to love.

This was what he and Marie had wanted, what they would have had, if God hadn't seen fit to grab it away from them.

He pushed the bitterness aside and strode up to the happy family. "How's Emmie? She sleeping well?"

Troy and Angelica looked at each other and laughed. "Not a chance. We're up practically all night, every night," Troy said, and then Sam noticed the dark circles under his brother's eyes. Running a veterinary practice and a rescue while heading a family had to be exhausting, but though he looked tired, there was a deep happiness in Troy's eyes that hadn't been there before.

That was the power of love. Troy and Angelica had married less than a year ago and instantly conceived a baby, at least partly in response to Angelica's son Xavier's desire for a little sister. They'd even gotten the gender right.

Sam renewed his determination: With or without God's help, he was going to find this for himself and Mindy. He didn't need the Lord to solve his problems for him. He could do it on his own.

"Where's Xavier, Uncle Troy?"

Troy chuckled. "It's Kennel Kids day. Where do you think?"

For the first time, Sam noticed the cluster of boys on the far edge of the fenced area. It was the ragtag group of potential hoodlums that Troy mentored through giving them responsibilities at the kennel. Amazing that his brother, busy as he was, had time to work with kids in need. Or made time, truth be known, and Sam's conscience smote him. He ought to give more back to the community, but he felt as if he was barely holding his own life together these days. "Who's monitoring the boys? Is that Daisy?"

"Can I go play, Daddy?" Mindy begged.

"No."

"Why not?"

"It's not safe, honey."

"But Xavier's over there."

"Xavier's a boy, honey. And…" He broke off, seeing the knowing glance Troy and Angelica exchanged. Okay, so he was overprotective, but those boys were playing rough and Mindy, with her missing hand, had one less means of defense.

And one more reason to get teased, in the sometimes-cruel world of school-aged kids.

Mindy's face reddened and she drew in a breath, obviously about to have a major meltdown.

Sam squatted down beside her, touching her shoulder, willing her to stay calm. He was so tired after another late night working, and he wasn't that great about dealing with Mindy's frequent storms. Didn't know if there even was a good way to deal with them.

"Hey!" Angelica got a little bit in Mindy's face, startling her out of her intended shriek. "I know! Why don't you and your daddy go ask Xavier to take you down to the barn? He can show you the newest puppies. You can stay outside the fence," she added, rolling her eyes a little at Sam.

"Okay! C'mon, Daddy!"

Thank you, he mouthed to Angelica, bemused by the way a little girl's mood could change in a second.

"Not sure if you'll be thanking me in a minute," she said with a chuckle.

She must mean his ongoing battle with Mindy, the one where Angelica and Troy were staunchly on Mindy's side. "We're not getting a puppy!" he mouthed over his shoulder to Angelica, keeping his voice low so he wouldn't reawaken Mindy's interest in the issue.

But as he and Mindy approached the group at the other end of the fenced enclosure, Sam wondered if Angelica might have been talking with Daisy…and if her joke about him not thanking her might have meant something entirely different.

Because *she* was there.

Susan, the firebrand waitress and job candidate he hadn't been able to get out of his mind for the past four days.

Who was she to tell him he wasn't raising his daughter right?

And what on earth was she doing here?

The answer, apparently, was that she was working with the kids, because she was squatting down beside one of the smaller boys, probably seven or eight years old. From the boy's awkward movements, Troy guessed he had some kind of muscular disorder.

And Susan was helping him to pet a pit bull's face.

Sam shook his head. Of course she was. The woman obviously had no common sense, no safety consciousness, no awareness of what was age-appropriate. If that kid's parents could see what she was doing... Of course, given the nature of Kennel Kids, the boy might not have involved parents. Still, Troy or Angelica ought to rein Susan in.

At that moment, she lifted her head and saw him. Her mouth dropped open, and then her eyes narrowed as if she was reading his mind.

"Xavier!" Mindy's joyous shout was a welcome distraction. "C'mere! C'mere!"

Susan called out to Daisy, who was, he now realized, standing guard over the overall group. Daisy came and knelt beside the boy Susan had been helping, and Susan exchanged a few heated words with her, then rose effortlessly to her feet. She followed Xavier, who was running toward the fence to see Mindy.

A knee-high black-and-white puppy bounded over on enormous, clumsy feet, barking. The kids immediately started playing with it, Mindy poking her fingers through the fence to touch its nose and Xavier jumping and rolling with the puppy on the inside of the enclosure. Which left Sam to watch Susan's approach.

She wore cutoff shorts and a red shirt, hair up in a long ponytail. She looked young and innocent, especially since she'd removed her multiple earrings. "Didn't expect to see you here," he said, hoping his voice didn't betray his strange agitation.

"The feeling's mutual, and when I get the chance, I'm going to strangle your sister." She knelt down, and Xavier, along with the black-and-white dog, fell into her lap, pushing her backward.

Daisy. Oh. Susan's being here was Daisy's doing. "I never could control that girl. She always does exactly what she wants."

She flashed a smile. "And she always means well."

He watched Susan struggle out from under the dog, laughing when it licked her face. Then she handed Xavier a ball from her shorts pocket and he threw it for the dog to fetch.

"What's Daisy doing?" Sam asked. "Is she pushing us together on purpose?" If his sister was playing matchmaker, she was doing a poor job of it. She had to know Susan wasn't his type, even though the thought of going out with Susan sounded the tiniest bit appealing, probably just for the chance to argue with her.

"She wants you to give me your nanny job, which you and I both know is ridiculous."

Oh, the *job*. Heat rose to the back of Sam's neck as he realized he'd misinterpreted his sister's actions as dating-type matchmaking. And, yes, it was ridiculous from his own point of view to hire someone as mouthy and inappropriate as Susan, but why did *she* find the idea ridiculous?

"Hi, Miss Hayashi," Mindy said, looking up at Susan with a shy smile.

"Hi, Mindy." Susan's voice went rich and warm as honey when she looked down at his daughter. "Want to come in and play with the dogs?"

"No, she can't come in!" The words practically exploded out of Sam's mouth.

"Oh." Susan looked surprised, and Mindy opened her mouth to object.

"She can't…" He nodded down at her. "It's not safe."

Xavier provided an unexpected escape route. "You're too little to come in here," he explained. "But I can take you to the barn and show you our new tiny puppies. There's eight of them, and they're all gray 'cept for one spotted one, and their eyes are shut like this!" He squeezed his eyes tightly shut, them immediately opened them, grinning.

"I want to see them!" Mindy jumped to her feet, hugged Sam's leg and gazed up at him. "Please, Daddy?"

Love for his daughter overwhelmed him. "Okay, if you have an adult with you."

Xavier ran a few yards down to the gate, and with an assist from Susan, got it open. "Come on, Dad will help us," he said, and the two children rushed off toward the barn.

Leaving Sam and Susan standing with a fence between them. "You shouldn't have invited Mindy to come in without my permission," he informed her.

"Right. You're right. I just… Who knew you were *that* overprotective? She's not made of glass, but you're going to have her thinking she is."

"I think we've already established that you don't have the right to judge."

"Yeah, but that was when I was trying to get the

job with you. Now, I'm just a…well, an acquaintance. Which means I can state my opinion, right?"

"She's an acquaintance with a double certification in elementary and special ed," his sister, Daisy, said, coming from behind to put a hand on Susan's shoulder. "Sam, when are you going to realize you're way too cautious with that child? Marie was even worse. You're going to have Mindy afraid of her own shadow."

"That day is a long way off," Sam said, frowning at the idea that Marie had been anything but the perfect mother. Did everyone think he was too overprotective? Was he? Was he hurting Mindy?

"Um, think I'll go help get the kids ready to go home." Susan walked off, shoulders squared and back straight.

Daisy glared up at Sam. "What's your problem, anyway? Susan said her interview with you didn't go well."

"Did she tell you she couldn't stop questioning my abilities as a father? I hardly think that's what I want in a summer nanny."

"Come on, let's walk up to the house," Daisy said, coming out through the gate and putting an arm around him. "Sam, everyone knows you're the best dad around. You stepped in when Marie got sick and you haven't taken a break since. If you're a tiny bit controlling, well, who can blame you? Mindy's not had an easy road."

"You're using your social worker voice, and I'm sensing a 'but' in there." He put his own arm around his little sister. She definitely drove him crazy, but he didn't question her wisdom. Daisy was the intuitive, people-smart one in the family, and Sam and his brother had learned early on to respect that.

"The thing is, you're looking for a clone of your dead

wife. In a nanny and in a partner. What if you opened your mind to a different kind of influence on Mindy?"

"What do you mean, in a partner?" He'd kept his deathbed promise to Marie a secret, so how did Daisy know he was looking for a new mom for Mindy?

Daisy laughed. "I've seen the women you date. They're all chubby and blonde and worshipful. It's not rocket science to figure out that you're trying to find a replica of Marie."

The words stung with their truth. "Is that so bad? Marie was wonderful. We were happy." He'd never been like Daisy and Troy, adventurous and fun-loving; he'd always been the conventional older brother, wanting a standard, solid, traditional family life, and Marie had understood that. She'd wanted the same thing, and they'd been building it. Building a beautiful life that had been cut short.

"Oh, Sam." Daisy rubbed a hand up and down his back. "It's understandable. It was a horrible loss for you and Mindy. For all of us, really. I loved Marie, too."

Reassured, Sam could focus on the rest of what Daisy had said. "You think I need to be worshipped?"

"I think you're uncomfortable when women question your views, but c'mon, Sam. You're Mensa-level smart, you're practically a billionaire and you've built Hinton Enterprises into the most successful corporation in Rescue River, if not all of Ohio. It's not like you need reassurance about your masculinity. Why don't you try dating women who pose a little bit of a challenge?"

"I get plenty of challenge from my family, primarily you." He squeezed her shoulders, trying not to get defensive about her words. "My immediate problem is finding a nanny, not a girlfriend. And someone like

Susan has values too different from mine. She'd have Mindy taming pit bulls and playing with hoodlums."

"She'd let Mindy out of the glass bubble you've put her in!" Daisy spun away to glare at him. "Look, she's the one with coursework in special ed, not you. She's not going to put your daughter at risk. She'd be great for Mindy, even if she does make you a little uncomfortable. And you did kind of contribute indirectly to her getting fired from her waitressing job."

A hard lump of guilt settled in his stomach. He didn't want to be the cause of someone losing their livelihood. He'd always prided himself on finding ways to keep from laying off employees, even in this tough economy.

She raised her eyebrows. "Think about it, bro. Are you man enough to handle a nanny like Susan, if it would be the best thing for Mindy?"

Susan sat at the kitchen table with Angelica and the new baby while Daisy warmed up the side dishes she'd brought and ordered her brothers outside to grill burgers.

"Do you want to hold her?" Angelica asked, looking down at the dark-haired baby as if she'd rather do anything than let her go.

"Me?" Susan squeaked. "No, thanks. I mean, she's beautiful, but I'm a disaster with babies. At a minimum, I always make them cry."

Of course, Sam came back into the kitchen in time to hear that remark. She seemed to have a genius for *not* impressing him.

"I used to feel that way, too," Daisy said, "but I'm great with little Emmie. Here, you can stir this while

I hold her." She put down her spoon and confidently scooped the baby out of Angelica's arms.

Susan walked over to the stove and looked doubtfully at the pan of something white and creamy. "You want me to help cook? Really?"

"Oh, never mind, I forgot. Sam, stir the white sauce for a minute, would you?"

"You don't cook?" he asked Susan as he took over at the stove, competently stirring with one hand while he reached for a pepper grinder with the other.

In for a penny, in for a pound. "Nope. Not domestic."

"You'll learn," Angelica said, stretching and twisting her back. "When you find someone you want to cook for."

"Not happening. I'm the single type."

"She is," Daisy laughed. "She won't even date. But we're going to change all that."

"No, we're not." Susan sat back down at the table.

"Yes, we are. The group at church has big plans for you."

"*My* singles group? Who would run it if I somehow got involved with a guy?" Susan pulled her legs up and wrapped her arms around them, taking in the large, comfortable kitchen with appreciation. Old woodwork and gingham curtains blended with the latest appliances, and there was even a couch in the corner. Perfect.

She enjoyed Daisy and enjoyed being here with her family because she'd never had anything like this. Her family had been small and a little bit isolated, and while Donny was great in his way, you couldn't joke around with him.

She watched Sam stir the sauce, taste it, season it some more. This was another side of the impatient businessman. Really, was there anything the man wasn't good at?

He probably saw her as a bumbling incompetent. She couldn't succeed at waitressing, at cooking, at holding a baby. He thought she'd be bad for his daughter, that much had been obvious.

Too bad, because she needed the money, and Mindy was adorable. Kids were never the problem; it was the adults who always did her in.

Suddenly, the door burst open and Xavier rushed through, followed closely by Mindy. "Give it back. Give it back!" she was yelling as she grabbed at something in his hands.

"No, Mindy, it's mine!"

Mindy stopped, saw all the adults staring at her, and threw herself to the floor, holding her breath, legs kicking.

Sam dropped the spoon with a clatter and went to her side. "Mindy, Mindy honey, it's okay."

The child ignored him, lost in her own rapidly escalating emotional reaction.

"Mindy!" He scolded her. "Sit up right now." He tried to urge her into an upright position, but she went as rigid as a board, her ear-splitting screams making everyone cringe.

Sam was focused on her with love and concern, but at this point that wasn't enough. Susan knew that interfering wasn't wise, but for better or worse, she had a gift. She understood special-needs kids, and she had a hunch she could calm Mindy down.

She sank to her knees beside the pair. "Shhhh," she whispered ever so softly into Mindy's ear. "Shhhh."

Gently, she slid closer in behind the little girl and raised her eyebrows at Sam, tacitly asking permission.

He shrugged, giving it.

She wrapped her arms around Mindy from behind, whispering soothing sounds into her ear, sounds without words. Sounds that always soothed Donny, actually. She rubbed one hand up and down Mindy's arm, gently coaxing her to be calm. While she wasn't a strict proponent of holding therapy, she knew that sometimes physical contact worked when nothing else could reach a kid.

"Leave me 'lone!" Mindy cried with a little further struggle, but Susan just kept up her gentle hold and her wordless sounds, and Mindy slowly relaxed.

"He has a picture frame that says…" She drew in a gasping breath. "It says, Mom. *M-O-M*, Mom. I want it!"

Sam went pale, and Susan's heart ached with sympathy for the pair. Losing a parent was about the worst thing that could happen to a kid. And losing a wife was horrible, but it had to be even more painful to watch your child suffer and not know how to help.

To his credit, Sam regrouped quickly. "Honey, you can't take Xavier's picture frame. But we can get you one, okay?"

"It might even be fun to make one yourself," Susan suggested, paying attention to the way the child's body relaxed at the sound of her father's reassuring words. "Then it would be even more special. Do you have lots of pictures of your mom?"

"Yes, 'cause I'm afraid I'll forget her and then she'll never come back."

Perfectly normal for a five-year-old to think her dead

mother would come back. But ouch. Poor Mindy, poor Sam. She hugged the child a little tighter.

"Hon, Mommy's not coming back, remember? She's with Jesus." Sam's tone changed enough on the last couple of words that Susan guessed he might have his doubts about that. Doubts he wasn't conveying to Mindy, of course.

"But if I'm really good…"

"No, sweetie." Sam's face looked gray with sadness. "Mommy can't come back to this world, but we'll see her in heaven."

"I don't like that!" Mindy's voice rose to a roar. "I. Don't. Like. That!"

"None of us do, honey." Daisy squatted before her, patting the sobbing child's arm, her forehead wrinkling. "I don't know what to do when she's like this," she said quietly to Susan.

"Mommy!" Mindy wailed over and over. "I'll be good," she added in a gulp.

Sam and Daisy looked helplessly at each other over Mindy's head.

"It's not your fault. You're a good, good girl. Mommy loved you." Susan kept her arms wrapped tightly around Mindy and rocked, whispering and humming a wordless song. Every so often Mindy would tense up again, and Susan whispered the soothing words. "Not your fault. Mommy loved you, and Daddy loves you."

She knew the words were true, even though she hadn't known Sam and his wife as a family. And she knew that Mindy needed to hear it, over and over again.

She was glad to be here. Glad she had enough distance to help Sam with what was a very tough situation.

Very slowly, Mindy started to relax again. Daisy shot Susan a smile and moved away to check the stove.

"Shhh, shhh," Susan whispered, still holding her, still rocking. Losing a piece of her heart to this sweet, angry, hurting child.

Finally, Mindy went limp, and Susan very carefully slid her over to Sam. Took a deep breath, and tried to emerge from her personal, very emotional reaction and get back to the professional. "Does she usually fall asleep after a meltdown?"

Sam nodded. "Wears herself out, poor kid." He stroked her hair, whispering the same kind of sounds Susan had made, and Mindy's eyes closed.

"She'll need something to eat and drink soon, maybe some chocolate milk, something like that," Susan said quietly after a couple of minutes. "Protein and carbs."

"Thank you for calming her down," he said, his voice quiet, too. "That was much shorter than she usually goes."

"No problem, it's kind of my job. Did she have tantrums before you lost your wife?"

Sam nodded. "She's always been volatile. We thought it was because of her hand."

Susan reached out and stroked Mindy's blond hair, listening to the welcome sound of the child's sleep-breathing. "Having a disability can be frustrating. Or she could have some other sensitivities. Some kids are just more reactive."

"Did you learn how to be a child-whisperer in your special ed training?"

Susan chuckled. "Some, but mostly, you learn it when you have a brother with autism. Donny—that's my little brother—used to have twenty tantrums per day. It was too much for my mom, so I helped take care of him."

Sam's head lifted. "Where's Donny now?"

"Home with Mom in California," she said. "He's eighteen, and…" She broke off. He was eighteen, and still expecting to be going to a camp focused on his beloved birds and woodland animals, because she hadn't had the heart to call and tell him she'd screwed up and there wasn't any money. "He's still a handful, that's for sure, but he's also a joy."

Mindy burrowed against her father's chest, whimpering a little.

"How long has it been since you lost your wife?" Susan asked quietly.

"Two years, and Mindy does fine a lot of the time. And then we have this." He nodded down at her.

"Grief is funny that way." Susan searched her mind for her coursework on it. "From what I've read, she might re-grieve at each developmental stage. If she was pre-operational when your wife died, she didn't fully understand it. Could be that now, she's starting to take in the permanence of the loss."

"I just want to fix it." Sam's voice was grim. "She doesn't deserve this pain."

"No one deserves it, but it happens." She put a hand over Sam's. "I'm sorry for your loss. And sorry this is so hard on Mindy, too. You're doing a good job."

"Coming from you, that means something," he said with a faint grin.

Their eyes caught for a second too long.

Then Angelica and Daisy came bustling back into the room—when had they left, anyway?—followed by

Xavier. How long had she, Sam and Mindy been sitting in the middle of the kitchen floor?

"Hey, the potatoes are done," Daisy said, expertly pouring the contents of one pan into another. She leaned over and called out through the open window. "Troy, how about those burgers?"

"They're ready." Troy came in with a plate stacked high with hamburgers, plus a few hot dogs on the side.

Sam moved to the couch at the side of the kitchen, cuddling a half-asleep Mindy, while the rest of them hustled to get food on the table. Susan folded napkins and carried dishes and generally felt a part of things, which was nice. She hadn't felt this comfortable in a long time. Being around Mindy, she felt as if she was in her element. This was her craft. What she was good at.

Again, she couldn't help comparing this evening to those she'd spent with her own family. The tension between her mom and dad, the challenges Donny presented, made family dinners stressful, and as often as not, the kids had eaten separately from the adults, watching TV. Susan could see the appeal of this lifestyle, living near your siblings, getting to know their kids. Cousins growing up together.

This was what she'd want for her own kid.

And where on earth had that thought come from? She totally didn't want kids! And she didn't want a husband. She was a career girl, and that was that.

So why did she feel so strangely at home here?

Chapter 3

A while after dinner, Sam came back into the kitchen after settling Mindy and Xavier in the den with a movie.

The room felt empty. "Where's Susan?"

"She left." Daisy looked up from her phone. "Said something about packing."

"She's going on a trip?" That figured. She seemed like a world traveler, much too sophisticated to spend her free summer in their small town. Applying for the job as Mindy's nanny had probably been just a whim.

Then again, she'd mentioned needing to help support her mother and brother...

And why he was so interested in figuring out her motives and whereabouts, he didn't have a clue.

"No..." Daisy was back to texting, barely paying attention. "She's gotta move back home for the summer."

"Move?"

"Yeah, to California."

"What? Why?"

Daisy was too engrossed in her phone to answer, and following a sudden urge, Sam turned and walked out into the warm evening. He caught up to Susan just as she opened her car door. "Weren't you even going to say goodbye?"

"Did I hurt your feelings?" she asked lightly, turning back to him, looking up.

She was so beautiful it made him lose his breath. So he just stared down at her.

It must be the way she'd helped Mindy that had changed her in his eyes, softened her sharp edges, made her not just cute but deeply appealing.

And he obviously needed to get on with his dating project, because he was having a serious overreaction to Susan. "Daisy said you're leaving town."

She wrinkled her nose. "Yeah, in a few days. Got to go back to California for the summer."

"You're not driving that, are you?" Lightly, he kicked the tire of her rusty subcompact.

"No! I'm taking the Mercedes." She chuckled, a deep, husky sound at odds with her petite frame. "Of course I'm driving this, Sam. It's my car."

"It's not safe."

She just raised her eyebrows at him. As if to ask what right he had to make such a comment. And it was a good question: What right *did* he have?

The moonlight spilled down on them and the sky was a black velvet canopy sprinkled with millions of diamond stars. He cleared his throat. "Does this mean you don't want the job?"

"Does this mean I'm still in the running?" There was a slightly breathy sound to her voice.

They were standing close together.

"You are," he said slowly. "I liked… No. I was amazed at how you were able to calm Mindy." He couldn't stop looking at her.

She stepped backward and gave an awkward smile. "Years of experience with my brother. And the coursework. All the grief stuff. You could call a local college, find someone with similar qualifications."

"I doubt that. I'd like to hire you."

"We don't get along. I wouldn't be good at this. I mean, nannying? Living in? Seriously, ask anyone, I'm not cut out for family life."

He cocked his head to one side, wondering suddenly about her past. "Oh?"

She waved her hand rapidly. "I was engaged once. It…didn't work out."

He nodded, inexplicably relieved. "Maybe you should come work for me on a trial basis, then."

"A…trial basis?" That breathy sound again.

"Yes, since you're not cut out for family life. It's a live-in job, after all."

"I do need a place to stay," she said, "but no. That wouldn't look right, would it? Me living in your house."

Her eyes were wide and suddenly, Sam felt an urge to protect her. "Of course, I wouldn't want to compromise your reputation. We have a mother-in-law's suite over the garage. It has a separate entrance and plenty of privacy."

"Really? You're offering me the job? Because remember, I can't cook."

"You can learn."

"Maybe, maybe not. I... What made you change your mind? I thought you didn't like me." She was nibbling on her lower lip, and right now she looked miles from the confident, brash waitress who'd stood up to a businessman in front of a restaurant full of people.

He smiled down at her. "My sister. My brother. And the way you handled Mindy."

"But she's probably not going to have another trauma reaction for a long time. Whereas cooking's every day. You really don't want to hire me."

"Why are you trying to talk me out of it?" Her resistance was lighting a fire in him, making him feel as if he had to have her, and only her, for Mindy's nanny. "I do want to. The sooner the better. When could you start?"

"Well..." She was starting to cave, and triumph surged through him. "My room is going to be remodeled out from under me starting this weekend."

"Great," he said, leaning in to close the deal. "I'll have a truck sent round tomorrow. You can start setting up your apartment over the garage."

"You're sure?"

"I'm sure."

"Paying what you told me before?"

He flashed a wide smile. "Of course."

She paused, her nose wrinkling. Looked up at the stars. Then a happy expression broke out on her face. "Thank you!" she said, and gave him a quick, firm handshake.

Her smile and her touch sent a shot of joy through his entire body. He hadn't felt anything like that before, ever. Not even when Marie was alive.

Guilt overwhelmed him and he took a step back. "Remember, it's just a trial," he said.

What had he gotten himself into?

Of course, everyone and his brother was in downtown Rescue River the next Saturday morning to comment on the moving truck in front of Susan's boarding house. The truck carrying Susan to her absolute doom, if the scuttlebutt was to be believed.

"So you're the next victim," said Miss Minnie Falcon, who'd hurried over from the Senior Towers, pushing her wheeled walker, to watch the moving activities. "Sam Hinton eats babysitters for lunch!"

"It's just on a trial basis," Susan said, pausing in front of the guesthouse's front porch. "If I don't like the job, I can leave at any time. Don't you want to sit down, Miss Minnie?"

"Oh, no, I'd rather stand," the gray-haired woman said, her eyes bright. "Don't want to miss anything!"

"Okay, if you're sure." That was small-town life: your activities were like reality TV to your neighbors, and truthfully, Susan found it sweet. At least everyone knew who you were and watched out for you.

"I'm going to miss you so much," her landlady, Lacey, said as she helped Susan carry her sole box of fragile items down the rickety porch steps. "I'm really sorry about making you move. It's just that Buck seems to be serious about staying sober, and he's looking to make money, and of course, he's willing to work on this place for cheap because he's my brother."

"It's fine. You've got to remodel while you can," Susan soothed her. "And we'll still hang out, right?" She'd enjoyed her year at Lacey's guesthouse, right in the heart of her adopted town. She wouldn't have minded staying. But sometimes, she felt silly being twenty-five years old and having to use someone else's kitchen if she wanted to make herself a snack.

"Of course we'll hang out. I'll miss you!"

"I know, me, too." She and Lacey had gotten close during a number of late-night talks. Susan had comforted Lacey through a heartbreaking miscarriage, and they'd cried and prayed together.

"And it's not just me. The cats will miss you!" Lacey said. "You have to come back and visit all the time."

As if to prove her words, an ancient gray cat tangled himself around Susan's ankle and then, when she grabbed the bannister to keep from tripping, offered up a mournful yowl.

Susan reached down to rub the old tomcat's head. "You and Mrs. Whiskers take care of yourselves. I'll bring you a treat when I come back, promise."

They went outside and loaded the box of breakables into the front seat of Susan's car, only to be accosted by Gramps Camden, another resident of the Senior Towers. "Old Sam Hinton caught himself a live one!" he said. "Now you listen here. Those Hintons are trouble. Just because my granddaughter married one—and Troy is the best of the bunch—that doesn't mean they're a good family. I was cheated by that schemer's dad and now, his corporation won't let up on me about selling my farm. You be careful in his house. Lock your door!"

"I will." She'd gotten to know Gramps through the schools, where he now served as a volunteer.

"He wasn't good enough for that wife of his," Gramps continued.

"Marie was pretty nearly perfect," agreed Miss Minnie Falcon.

From what Susan already knew about Sam, she figured any woman who married him would have to be. And yet, for all his millionaire arrogance, he obviously adored his little daughter. And a man who loved a child that much couldn't be all bad. Could he?

"Is that all your stuff, ma'am?" the college-age guy, who'd apparently come with the truck, asked respectfully.

Gramps waved and headed back to the Towers with Miss Minnie.

"Yes, that's it," Susan said. "What do I owe you?"

"Nothing. Mr. Hinton took care of it."

"Let me grab my purse. I want to at least give you a tip for being so careful."

The young man waved his hand. "Mr. Hinton took care of that, too. He said we weren't to take a penny from you."

"Is that so," Susan said, torn between gratitude and irritation.

"Money's one thing Sam Hinton doesn't lack." The voice belonged to Buck Armstrong, Lacey's brother. He put a large potted plant into the back of her car, tilting it sideways so it would fit. The young veteran had haunted eyes and a bad reputation, but whenever Susan had run into him visiting his sister, he'd been nothing but a gentleman. "You all set?"

"I hope so. I'm hearing horror stories about my new boss, is all." And they were spooking her. As the time came to leave her friendly guesthouse in the heart of Rescue River, she felt more and more nervous.

Buck nodded, his eyes darkening. "Sam didn't use to be quite so...driven. Losing a wife is hard on a guy."

Sympathy twisted Susan's heart. Buck knew what he was talking about; he'd lost not only his wife, but their baby as well. That was what had pushed him toward drinking too much, according to Lacey.

"You giving this gal a hard time?" The voice belonged to Rescue River's tall, dark-skinned police chief. He clapped Buck on the shoulder in a friendly way, but his eyes were watchful. Chief Dion Coleman had probably had a number of encounters with Buck that weren't so friendly.

"He's trying to tell me Sam Hinton is really a nice guy, since I'm going to work for him," Susan explained.

Dion let out a hearty laugh. "You're going to work for Sam? Doing what?"

"Summer nanny for Mindy."

"Is that right? My, my." Dion shook his head, still chuckling. "I tell you what, I think Mr. Sam Hinton might have finally met his match."

"What's that supposed to mean?" Susan asked, indignant.

"Nothing, nothing." He clapped Buck's shoulder again. "Come on, man, I'll buy you a cup of coffee if you've got half an hour to spare. Got something to run by you."

Buck was about to get gently evangelized, if Susan knew Dion. He headed up a men's prayer group at their church and was unstoppable in his efforts to get the hurting men of Rescue River on the right path. According to Daisy, he'd done wonders with her brother Troy.

As Buck and Dion headed toward the Chatterbox Café, Lacey came out to hug her goodbye. "You'll be fine. This is going to be an adventure!" She lowered her voice. "At least, let's hope so."

An odd, uncomfortable chill tickled Susan's spine as she climbed into her car and headed to her new job, her new life.

Chapter 4

Sam paced back and forth in the driveway, checking his watch periodically. Where was she?

Small beach shoes clacked along the walkway from the back deck, and he turned around just in time to catch Mindy in his arms. He lifted her and gave her a loud kiss on the cheek, making her giggle.

And then she struggled down. "Daddy, Miss Lou Ann says I can play in the pool if it's okay with you. Can I?"

Lou Ann Miller, who'd worked for his family back in the day and had helped to raise Sam, Troy and Daisy, followed her young charge out into the driveway. "She's very excited. It would be a nice way for her to cool off." She winked at him. "Nice for you if she'd burn off some extra energy, too."

Sam hesitated. Lou Ann was an amazing woman,

but she was in her upper seventies. "If she stays in the shallow end," he decided. "And Mindy, you listen to Miss Lou Ann."

"Of course she will," Lou Ann said. "Run and change into your suit, sweetie." As soon as Mindy disappeared inside, Lou Ann put a hand on her hip and raised an eyebrow at Sam. "I was the county synchronized swimming champion eight years running," she said. "And I still swim every morning. I can get Mindy out of any trouble she might get into."

"Of course!" Sam felt himself reddening and reminded himself not to stereotype.

He just wanted to keep Mindy safe and get her home environment as close to what Marie had made as was humanly possible. Get things at home back to running like a well-organized company, one he could lead with confidence and authority.

The moving truck chugged around the corner and up to the house, and Sam rubbed his hands together. Here was one step…he hoped. If Susan worked out.

He gestured them toward the easiest unloading point and helped open the back of the truck as Susan pulled up in her old subcompact, its slightly-too-dark exhaust and more-than-slightly-too-loud engine announcing that the car was on its last legs. He'd have to do something about that.

As the college boys he'd hired started moving her few possessions out, she approached. Her clothes were relaxed—a loose gauzy shirt, flip-flops and cutoff shorts revealing long, slender, golden-bronzed legs—but her face looked pinched with stress. "Hey," she said, following his glance back to her car. "Don't worry, I'll pull it behind the garage as soon as the truck's out of the way."

"I didn't say—"

"You didn't have to." She grabbed a box off the truck and headed up the stairs.

He helped the guys unload a heavy, overstuffed chair and then followed them up the stairs with an armload of boxes.

There was Susan, staring around the apartment, hands on hips.

"What's wrong?" he asked. "Is it suitable? Too small? We can work something out—"

"It's fine," she said, patting his arm. "It's beautiful. I'm just trying to decide where to put things."

"Good." There was something about Susan that seemed a little volatile, as if she might morph into a butterfly and disappear. "Well, you need to put the desk in that corner," he said, gesturing the movers to the part of the living room that was alcoved off, "and the arm-chair over there."

"Wait. Put the desk under the window. I like to look out while I work."

The young guys looked at him, tacitly asking his permission.

Susan raised her eyebrows, looking from the movers to Sam. There was another moment of silence.

"Of course, of course! Whatever the lady wants." But when they got the desk, a crooked and ill-finished thing, into the light under the window, he frowned. "I might have an extra desk you can use, if you like."

"I'm fine with that one."

He understood pride, but he hated to see a teacher with such a ratty desk. "Really?"

"Yes." She waited while the young movers went down to get another load, then spun on him. "Don't you have something else to do, other than comment about my stuff?"

"I'm sorry." He was controlling and he knew it, but it was with the goal of making other people's lives better. "I just thought… Are you sure you wouldn't rather have something less…lopsided? The money's not a problem."

She walked to the desk and ran a hand over it, smiling when one finger encountered a dipped spot. "My brother made it for me at his vocational school," she explained. "It was his graduation project, and he kept it a secret. When he gave it to me, it was about the best moment of my life."

"Oh." Sam felt like a heel. "So he's a woodworker?"

She shook her head. "No, not really. He's still finding his way, but the fact that he pushed past the frustration and made something so big, mostly by himself… and that he did it for me…it means a lot, that's all." She cleared her throat and got very busy flicking dust off an immaculate built-in shelf as the college boys came in with another load.

Obviously her brother was important to her. And obviously, Sam needed to pay attention to something other than just the monetary value of things.

He didn't have any family furniture, heirloom or sentimental or otherwise. For one thing, his dad still had most of their old stuff out at the family estate. For another, Marie had liked everything new, and he'd enjoyed providing it for her.

As the movers carried the last load into the bedroom, Susan looked up at him, then rose gracefully to her feet.

"I was going to spend a little time getting settled. But is there something I can do for you and Mindy first?"

"Do you need help unpacking?"

One corner of her mouth quirked up, and he got the uncomfortable feeling she was laughing at him. "No, Sam," she said, her voice almost…gentle. "I've moved probably five or six times since college. I'm pretty good at it."

Of course she had, and the fact that she looked so young—and had a vulnerable side—didn't mean he had to take care of her. She was an employee with a job to do. "I'll be in the house," he said abruptly. "Come in as soon as you're set up, and we'll discuss your duties."

As he left, he saw one of the college boys give Susan a sympathetic glance.

What was that all about? He just wanted to have things settled as soon as possible. Was that so wrong?

Okay, maybe he was pushing her a little bit, but that was what you did with new employees: you let them know how things were going to be, what the rules were. This was, for all intents and purposes, an orientation, and he wanted to make sure to do things right.

But he guessed he didn't need to rearrange her furniture. And given her reaction to the desk suggestion, she probably wouldn't welcome his getting his car dealer to find her a better car, either.

No, Susan seemed independent. Which was great, but also worrisome. He wondered how well she would fit in with his plan for a traditional, family-oriented summer for Mindy. What changes would she want to make?

He walked by the pool and saw with relief that Mindy

was happily occupied with her inflatable shark in the shallow end.

Lou Ann Miller sat at the table in the shade. He did a double take. Was that a magazine she was reading? He opened his mouth to remind her that Mindy needed close attention. When Marie had brought Mindy out to the pool, before she'd gotten too sick to do it, she'd been right there in the water with her.

But the moment Mindy ventured away from the edge of the pool, Lou Ann pushed herself to her feet and walked over to stand nearby.

"See what I can do!" Mindy crowed as she swam a little, her stroke awkward. She had an adaptive flotation device for her arm, but she didn't like to use it.

"Try kicking more with your feet, honey," Lou Ann said. "If you get tired, you can flip over to your back."

"Show me how?"

"Sure." Lou Ann shrugged out of her terrycloth cover-up, tossed it back toward the table and walked down the steps into the water, barely touching the railing. She wore a violet tank suit and her short hair didn't seem to require a swim cap.

Glad he hadn't interfered and satisfied with Lou Ann's abilities as a caregiver and swim instructor, Sam strode toward the house. He hoped Susan wouldn't take long to get settled and come down. The sooner they established her duties, the sooner things could go back to normal.

He'd just finished a sandwich when there was a tap on the back door.

"You ready for me?" Susan asked, poking her head

inside. "Am I supposed to knock or just come in? I really don't know how to be a nanny."

"Just come in." If he needed privacy, there was the whole upstairs. "I'm ready. Let me give you a quick tour so you know where things are."

"Great." She was looking around the kitchen. "Is this where you spend most of your time?"

He nodded. "It's a mess. Sorry. My cleaning people come on Mondays."

"You call this a mess?" She laughed. "I can barely tell you have a kid."

"Mindy's pretty neat. Me, I have to restrain my inner slob. Plus, Lou Ann Miller's been helping me until I find...well, until I found you. She's a whiz at cooking and cleaning."

"Why didn't you just hire her?" Susan asked as he led her into the living room.

"She doesn't want a permanent job. Says she's too old, though I don't see much evidence of her slowing down. This is where we...where I...well, where we used to entertain a lot." The room had been Marie's pride and joy, but Sam and Mindy didn't use it much, and he realized that, without a party full of people in it, the place looked like a museum.

Susan didn't comment on the living room nor the dining room with its polished cherry table and Queen Anne chairs. He swept her past the closed-off sunroom, of course. When they got to Mindy's playroom, Susan perked up. "This is nice!"

She walked over to inspect the play kitchen and peeked into the dollhouse. "What wonderful toys," she said almost wistfully. She looked at the easel and smiled approvingly at the train set. "Good, you're not being sexist. I see you got her some cars, too."

"Those are partly for my sake," he admitted. "I go nuts after too many games with dolls."

"Me, too." She walked over to perch on the window seat, crossing her arms as she surveyed the playroom. "It's a big place for one little girl."

A familiar ache squeezed Sam's chest. "We were going to fill it up with kids." He stared out the window and down the green lawn. "But plans don't always work out."

When he looked back at her, she was watching him with a thoughtful expression on her face. "That must be hard to deal with."

He acknowledged the sympathy with a nod. "We're managing."

"Do you ever think of moving?"

"No!" In truth, he had. He'd longed to move, but it wouldn't be fair to Marie's memory. She'd wanted him to continue on as they'd begun, to create the life they'd imagined together for Mindy. "We're fine here," he said firmly.

She arched one delicate brow. "Well, okay then." She stood up, looked around and gave a decisive nod. "I know a lot of kids, so we'll work on filling up the playroom and pool with them this summer. This place is crying out for noise and fun."

"Vetted by me," he warned. "I don't want a lot of kids I don't know coming over."

"You want to approve every playdate?"

"For now, yes."

She pressed her lips together, obviously trying not

to smile, but a dimple showed on her face. A very cute dimple.

"Hey, look. I'm a control freak, especially where Mindy is concerned."

"No kidding." She raised her eyebrows in mock surprise. "It's okay, Sam. We'll figure out a way to manage this. But Mindy does need friends around this summer. She needs to work on her social skills."

"There's nothing wrong—"

She cocked her head to one side and tucked her chin and looked at him.

"Her social skills are okay." He frowned at Susan's pointed silence. "Aren't they?"

"It's not a big problem," Susan said. "But she's very sensitive about her disability and her mother, or lack of one. I've broken up several playground brawls. The best way to work on it is to give her lots of free-play experience with other kids." She squatted down beside the bookshelves that lined one side of the room. "And there are books that can help. But these—" She ran a delicate finger along the spines of the books. "These are books for toddlers, Sam. She can read better than this."

Her criticism stung, but he nodded. "Her mother was the big book-buyer. That's why I'm glad you're here, Susan. I can see that you have an expertise the other candidates didn't have. I want to do right by Mindy."

"Weekly trips to the library. Fern can help us pick out some good books, including ones about social skills."

"Sure." He led the way back through the kitchen. "Now, I don't expect you to cook for us—"

"That's good," she interrupted. "Remember, I'm a disaster in the kitchen."

"I'm sure you can figure out how to make breakfast

and lunch. I'll do dinner, or order it in. But I do want you to eat dinner with us most nights."

"What?" She froze, staring at him.

"It's better for Mindy," he explained. "All kinds of studies show the importance of family dinners. I'd like to have you be a part of that."

She looked a little trapped. "I'm not your family, I'm a hired—"

"Five days per week," he bargained. "You can have a couple of nights off."

Through the open kitchen window, he could hear Lou Ann and Mindy laughing together in the backyard. He leaned back against the granite counter and watched an array of expressions cross Susan's face.

Was he being unfair, demanding too much of her? He'd looked over lists of nanny duties online, and while having a sitter eat with the family wasn't common, he'd seen a few examples of it being done. He was paying her well, much better than the average.

"You have to eat," he reminded her. "It's free food."

She chuckled, a throaty sound that made all his senses spring to life. "We'll give it a try."

He pushed his advantage. "And Sunday dinner is the most important meal of all, so I'd appreciate your being there. I think we agreed that you'd work Sunday afternoons and take a weekday afternoon off, correct?"

"You mean, like, tomorrow?"

He nodded. Best to start out as you meant to go on. "Yes. Definitely tomorrow."

"We'll give it a try," she repeated doubtfully. "But I'm not... Well. We'll see."

Score one for him. But her resistance proved this wasn't going to be as easy as he'd hoped.

* * *

The next day, Susan stood at the kitchen counter scooping deli salads into bowls. Even though she'd turned down Sam's offer of an apron to protect her church clothes—which, hello, consisted of a faded denim skirt with a lime-green tee and sneakers, hardly designer duds that needed special care—she still felt uncomfortable and out of place. She was used to grabbing a bagel with friends or fixing herself a peanut butter sandwich after church. Fixing a family lunch in a big, fancy kitchen was way out of her comfort zone.

Since she attended the same church as Sam and Mindy, it had made sense to all go together. Uncomfortable with the intimacy of that, she'd made a beeline for her singles group friends once they'd gotten there, but she hadn't had a choice about a ride home, which had included a stop at the grocery store for supplies.

It was all too, too domestic. And Sam had been entirely too appealing during the grocery story visit, brawny arms straining his golf shirt, thoughtfully discussing salad options with the deli clerk, whose name he remembered and whose children he asked about.

And since Sunday dinner was, quote, the most important meal of the week, here she was helping to cook it, or at least dish it up. Though she didn't see the point of setting the table and putting deli food into serving dishes when all Mindy wanted was to play in the pool.

Through the window, she studied Sam and Mindy, side by side on the deck while Sam grilled chicken. He was talking seriously to her, explaining the knobs on the gas grill and putting out a restrictive arm when she came too close.

Sam. What a character. He might be the head of an

empire, able to boss around his employees and make each day go according to plan, but he wasn't going to be able to control everything that happened in his own home. Not with a kid. Kids were never predictable.

And he couldn't control her, either. She had to maintain some sense of independence or the cage door would shut on her, just as it had almost done with her former fiancé. Encouraged by her father, they'd gotten engaged too quickly, before they knew each other well. Once Frank had found out what she was really like, he hadn't wanted her. And she'd been guiltily, giddily happy to get free.

She wasn't the marrying kind. And this stint in a housewifely role was temporary, just long enough to help her family financially.

From the front of the house, she heard a female voice. "Yoo-hoo! Surprise!"

Susan spun toward the sound, accidentally flinging a spoonful of macaroni salad on the floor in the process. "In here," she called. Then she grabbed a paper towel to clean up the dabs of macaroni scattered across the floor.

"Who are *you*?" asked a voice above her.

"It must be some of the hired help, Mama," said a male voice.

Susan paused in her wiping and looked up to see a yacht-club-looking, silver-haired couple. She gave the floor a last swipe, rinsed her hands and then turned to face them as she dried her hands on the dishtowel. "Hi, I'm Susan. Mindy's summer nanny. Who are you?" She softened the question with a smile.

"I didn't know he was hiring someone," the woman said, frowning. "He should have asked me. I know several nice young women who could have helped out."

"Now, Mama, maybe there's a reason he wanted to do things his own way." The man looked meaningfully at Susan. "We're Mindy's grandparents," he explained. "We like to pop in when we can on Sundays."

"That macaroni salad is from Shop Giant?" the woman asked, picking up the container and studying it. Then she walked over to the refrigerator, opened it and scanned the contents.

Susan took a breath. There was no reason to feel defensive of this kitchen; it wasn't hers. "Yes, Sam picked it up on the way home from church."

"Oh, men." The woman waved a perfectly manicured hand. "They never know what to get, and with Sam so busy... Are you in charge of the cooking? Because I'd recommend Denise's Deli in town, if you don't have time to make homemade."

Susan's stomach knotted and she flashed back to her mom trying to please her dad with her culinary skills. It was a role Susan had vowed to avoid, so why was she feeling as if she needed to make an excuse for not having labored over doing all the chopping and boiling herself? For a family that, after all, wasn't her own?

The door from the deck burst open. "Grandma! Grandpa!" Mindy shrieked. She flung herself at the man.

He bent to pick her up. "Oh, missy, you're getting too heavy for an old man!"

Sam followed with a plate of grilled chicken breasts. "Hey, Ralph, Helen. I thought you two might stop by."

He had? Why hadn't he warned her?

"We can slide a couple of extra places in at the table. Susan, would you mind..."

"Consider it done," she said drily, adding just one

place setting. And then, as soon as both grandparents were occupied with Mindy's excited explanation of the grilling process, she grabbed Sam's arm and pulled him into the playroom that adjoined the kitchen. "Look, since it's a family meal, I'm just going to leave you to it," she said. "Everything's ready to go here, and I've got a new thriller from the library that's calling my name."

"You have to eat," he said, frowning. "I'd like it if you'd stay."

"They seem a little...overwhelming," she admitted. "I'd feel more comfortable if—"

"Come on, Miss Susan, you forgot to make a place for Grandma! I got the extra placemats."

"Just stay for dinner," Sam said as Mindy tugged at her hand. "Then you can take off all afternoon."

"But—"

"I'm paying you to be here."

Clenching her teeth, Susan helped Mindy add another place setting to the table.

They all stood around it, and Sam said a prayer, and then they took their seats. Susan busied herself for a couple of minutes with bringing over food and fetching drinks, but then that was done and Sam urged her to sit down.

"Oh," the grandma, Helen, said, "are you eating with the family?"

Susan raised an eyebrow at Sam. "Not my idea."

"Susan's agreed to eat with us. Mindy needs a female role model."

"Oh, right," the older woman said. "At least until..." She gave Sam a meaningful look.

"Right," he said.

So was something in the works, then? Was Yacht

Club Grandma cooking up a girlfriend for Sam? That would be ideal, Susan told herself as she helped cut Mindy's chicken breast. It would take her off the hot seat and out of a role she obviously wasn't suited for.

Amidst the clanking silverware and clinking glasses, there was a noticeable absence of small talk. Finally, the awkward silence was broken by Mindy's grandfather. "What *are* you?" he asked Susan.

"Hey, now, Ralph…" Sam started, a flush crossing his face.

Susan drew in her breath and let it out in a sigh. "It's fine," she said to Sam. She'd been answering that question all her life, but the questions had gotten a little more frequent since she'd moved from California to the Midwest.

Mindy looked alertly from one adult to the next, sensing the tension.

"I meant no offense," Ralph said, lifting both hands, palms up. "I'm just curious. You look a little…" He broke off, as if he was trying to think of the word.

As a person who blurted out the wrong thing herself fairly often, Susan thought it best to cut off his speculation. "I'm half-Japanese."

The older man snapped his fingers. "I thought so! You look a little bit Mexican, but I was guessing Oriental. Your mom's Japanese?"

Yes, he was a blurter. But that was so much more comfortable than his wife's sputtering disapproval. She smiled at him. "Nope. We don't fit the stereotype. It's my dad who's Japanese."

"Your English sounds just fine," the older man said reassuringly.

"I hope so!" Susan said, chuckling. "I was born in California."

Helen made a strangled sound in her throat, whether regarding California, Japan or her husband's line of questioning, Susan wasn't sure.

"California," Mindy broke in, "that's where earth-quakes are, and Hollywood."

"You're right!" Susan smiled at Mindy. Hooray for kids, who could break through adult tension with their innocent remarks. She took a bite of macaroni salad. Not bad. She'd definitely choose Shop Giant's brand over anything she could make herself.

"Mommy was from Ohio, like me," Mindy informed Susan. "You're sitting just where she used to sit."

Everyone froze.

Wow. Susan's stomach twisted. She hadn't meant to intrude, hadn't wanted to take anyone's place. Should she apologize? Offer to move? Ignore the remark? Sud-denly, the food tasted as dry as ashes in her mouth.

"Mindy," Sam said, taking the child's hand in his own, "honey, saying that might make our guest feel uncomfortable."

He was right, it did…but that wasn't something Mindy should have to worry about. Just like that, Su-san's own discomfort melted away as her training clicked in. Stifling a child's natural comments about a loss was a way to push grief underground, causing all sorts of psychological issues. "That's probably kind of sad for everybody," Susan said quickly. "Did your mom like to cook out?"

Mindy looked uncertainly at her father. "I think… she liked to lie down the best."

Susan's throat constricted. Mindy had only been four

when her mom died. She couldn't remember much of what had happened when she was younger, of course.

Couldn't remember her mother as a healthy woman.

"Oh, no, Marie *loved* cooking of all kinds." Helen's eyes filled with tears. "You just don't remember, honey, because she was sick."

Ralph was staring down at his plate.

This wonderful family meal was turning into an outright disaster. The grief of parents who'd lost their beloved daughter was *way* beyond Susan's ability to soothe. She met Sam's gaze across the table. *Do something*, she tried to telegraph with her eyes.

Sam cleared his throat and brushed a hand over Mindy's hair. "I remember how Mom loved to make cookies with you," he said. "At Christmastime, you two would get all set up with icing and sprinkles and colored sugar. Mom let you decorate the cookies however you wanted."

Susan breathed out a sigh of relief and smiled encouragingly at Sam. He was doing exactly the right thing. "That sounds like fun!"

"Did I do a good job?" Mindy asked.

Sam chuckled, a slightly forced sound. "There was usually more frosting and decoration than cookie. You were little. But Mom loved the cookies you decorated and always made me take a picture."

"I remember those pictures!" Mindy said. "Can we look at them later?"

"Of course, honey." Sam leaned closer to put an arm around Mindy and give her a side hug, and Susan's heart melted a little.

"That reminds me, I want to take some pictures today," Ralph said, "maybe out by the pool."

The conversation got more general, then, and the awkwardness passed.

Later, Susan insisted on doing the dishes so that the family could gather out by the pool. But after a couple minutes, Helen came back in. "I didn't want you to put things away in the wrong place," she said.

"Oh...thanks." That was a backhanded offer of help if Susan had ever heard one.

"Marie always had this kitchen organized so perfectly, but every time I come it's more messed up."

Susan's hands tightened on the platter she was washing. "I'm sure it's hard for Sam to manage the house along with his business."

"It's not Sam's job to manage." The remark sounded pointed.

Susan lifted her eyebrows at the woman, wondering where this was going. "If not Sam's, then whose?"

"Well, I just hope you're not thinking it's *your* job."

"Of course not!" Susan burst out. Where did Helen get off, coming over and criticizing the help? She wasn't Susan's boss!

She glanced over at the older woman and noticed that her eyes were shiny with tears, and everything started to make sense. Helen didn't want the kitchen arrangements to change, because she was trying to preserve her daughter's memory. But inevitably, things would get moved around, and sentimental treasures misplaced. Life had to go on, but for a grieving mother, every change must feel like losing another piece of her daughter. "Look, I'm sorry," she said, drying her hands and walking over to give the woman she barely knew a clumsy little pat on the arm. "It's a loss I can't even imagine."

"It's just hard to see another woman in her place," Helen said in a wobbly voice.

"I'm not trying to take her place," Susan said, feeling her way. "No one can do that, but especially not me. I'm just here for the summer."

"You're just not the kind of woman Sam and Mindy need."

Susan blew out a breath and plunked the platter down on the counter. Grief was one thing, but outright rudeness was another. "Did you…did you want to talk, or would you rather be alone?"

"Alone," Helen croaked out, dabbing at her eyes with a tissue.

"Sure. You go ahead and put stuff away wherever you want. I've got some reading to do." Half-guiltily, she fled the kitchen and made her way to her apartment via the front door, the better to avoid Sam and Mindy and Ralph.

Helen was right. Susan *wasn't* the kind of woman Sam and Mindy needed. But why that truth felt so hurtful, she didn't have a clue.

Chapter 5

Sam pulled into his driveway the next Friday after-noon, right after lunchtime. It would be good to get out of this monkey suit and work the rest of the rainy afternoon at home. He had a little planning to do on the summer picnic he put on for his employees, but it was all fairly low-key; Mindy could interrupt without bothering him.

And he had to admit to himself that seeing Susan was part of what had drawn him home. Not really see-ing her, he told himself, but rather, seeing how she was interacting with Mindy.

He'd been so busy the past week, catching up on all the work he'd put off during the no-nanny period, that he hadn't spent a lot of time at home. Mindy seemed happy and Susan had said things were going well. He knew they'd visited the library and gone to the park with a couple of other kids. One day, Mindy had had her friend Mercedes over to play.

Sam was feeling pleased with the solution he'd come up with for Mindy's summer. She seemed to be thriving under the supervision of an active and engaged nanny.

Susan herself seemed guarded, but he had to assume she'd get more comfortable as the summer went on. That Sunday dinner with Ralph and Helen had been awkward, but that was because they hadn't understood that Susan was only a temporary fixture in the home. Next time would surely be better.

When he got inside, the sound of a busy, humming household met his ears, confirming his satisfaction with the arrangements he'd made for Mindy. He stopped in the kitchen to look at the mail, and the sound of voices drifted his way.

He heard his nephew, Xavier, explaining the finer points of Chutes and Ladders to Mindy. That meant Xavier's little sister, Baby Emmie, must be here, too, but he didn't hear baby fussing or cooing; apparently she was sleeping or content.

The low, steady murmur of women's voices let him know that his sister-in-law and Susan were both in the room with the kids.

"I know I can talk them into it," Susan was saying doubtfully. "The payment will just be a week late, maybe ten days. It's tips versus wages, that's all. I expected to have a little more money by now."

"Troy and I could probably loan you the—"

"No! Thanks, but I'll be fine."

Angelica made some sound as if she was comforting a baby, which she probably was. "What's your mom going to do with your brother away?"

"Enjoy her freedom. And I'm hoping I can send her a plane ticket later in the summer."

"That's so nice she's coming to visit you!"

"Oh, she's not visiting me," Susan said, sounding alarmed. "I want her to be able to go to New York to see some shows, or to a nice spa. Coming to see me would be nothing but stress."

"I doubt that. You're her daughter! Or…are things bad between you?"

Sam took a step closer and leaned on the counter, eavesdropping unabashedly. Mindy and Xavier argued a little in the background. Sam could smell the remains of a mac-and-cheese lunch. He saw the telltale blue-and-white boxes in the trash and shook his head, a grin crossing his face. Susan hadn't claimed to be a cook.

"I'm…a bit of a disappointment to her."

"I'm sure—"

"Don't feel bad, it doesn't bother me anymore. I know she's really just upset about her own life. She had a vision for me to do a better job than she did, to be a perfect wife who made her husband happy, but I'm not falling into line."

"Well, considering that you don't have a husband at all—"

"Exactly." They both laughed.

There was a little more murmuring and the sound of a baby fussing, then some quiet shuffling.

Sam felt bad about eavesdropping, knew he should say hello to let them know he was here, but if Angelica was feeding the baby, he didn't want to intrude. Quietly, he grabbed a fork and the pan of leftover mac and cheese and picked at it, thinking about what Susan had said.

Wages versus tips. Of course, she'd been expecting to make speedy cash as a waitress. He needed to bump her paycheck forward rather than waiting the customary two weeks to pay her.

"You should just ask Sam to advance you the money," Angelica advised as if she was channeling his thoughts.

"No way! That wouldn't be right. This is a job, and you don't ask for special favors in a job."

Sam got himself a glass of water, making some noise about it, to warn everyone of his presence.

"Daddy!" Mindy called, and ran to him.

"Hey, sugar sprite. Having fun?" He swung her up into his arms, feeling that odd mixture of joy and concern that was fatherhood for him.

"Yeah! Xavier is here!"

"Go back and play with him," he said, putting her down. "I'm going to change my clothes, and then I'll want to talk to Susan a couple of minutes."

He'd move her payday up, no matter whether she protested or not. And as he trotted up the stairs, an idea came to him: he'd send her mother a go-anywhere ticket. It was a benefit of his airline program and frequent flyer miles; it wouldn't even cost him anything. And it would help out proud, independent Susan.

Which, for whatever reason, was something he very much wanted to do.

"No!" she said twenty minutes later. "I'm sorry you overheard that, but I don't need any special favors."

"It's not a favor, it's just a change in pay date." He for sure wasn't going to tell her about the ticket he'd just told his assistant to send to her mother. That would go over about as well as rat poison.

"Why are you doing this?"

"To help you out," he said patiently.

"I don't need your help!" She banged open the dishwasher and started loading dishes in. Thankfully, they were plastic ones; the china wouldn't have survived her violent treatment.

He cocked his head to one side. "I thought someone was hassling you about a late payment. If that's not the case…"

"Oh, it's true, but I can talk some sense into them. Probably."

"What's the problem? The car?" Maybe now was the time to offer her the services of his car dealer.

"No!" She scanned the now-empty counter and slammed the dishwasher shut. "My car is paid for. It's… it's my brother."

"What's wrong?"

"His camp. The last installment for this special camp I want to send him to, it's due Monday. It's why I'm working this summer. He'll just love it, and he needs the extra stimulation. And my mom needs the break." She let out an unconscious sigh, and Sam felt the strangest urge to put an arm around her.

She was a little thing to be bearing the burden for an entire family, but she didn't complain; she just accepted the responsibility. Exactly what he would have done in the same situation. Admiration rose in him, along with a strange little click of connection. Maybe he and Susan weren't as different as he'd initially thought.

"Will your first paycheck cover the payment?" he asked her.

"Just about exactly."

"Then give me the number and I'll have the money wired today."

Relief warred with resistance in her dark eyes. "But it's not fair—"

"Look," he said, "it's nothing I haven't done for other people who work for me. I take care of my employees. Go get the information."

She drew in a breath and let it out in a sigh. "All right. Thank you, Sam."

The wheels were turning in his brain now. "In fact..." he said slowly.

"What?" she asked warily.

"Do you want to earn some extra money this summer?"

She laughed, a short sound without humor. "Always. I need to send some money to my mom. And I'd love to pay for an extra course toward my master's."

"And maybe buy a new car?" he needled.

"Sam!" She put her hands on her hips. "I know my car isn't pretty, but it runs fine."

"It runs loud. And smoky."

"It's fine." She turned away. "If you're through insulting my stuff, I'd better go help Angelica with the kids."

"She's fine. Wait a minute. Listen to my proposal."

The corner of her mouth quirked upward as she spun back around. "What proposal is that?"

Their eyes met, and held, and something electric zinged between them.

The breeze through the window lifted a strand of her hair, but even as she brushed it back, she still stared at him. He could see the pulse in her neck.

His own pulse was hammering, too.

Wow.

They both looked away at the same time. "So what are you thinking of?" she asked in a businesslike voice, grabbing a sponge to wipe down the already-clean counter.

He cleared his throat and leaned forward, resting his elbows on the kitchen island. "I'm having my annual summer picnic for my employees, and the woman who usually plans it for me is out on maternity leave. How are you at party planning?"

She laughed. "I'm a whiz with the elementary set, but I've never planned an adult party in my life."

He should definitely get someone else, then. "You could get Daisy to help," he heard himself saying. "And it's a family picnic, so we always try to make it fun for the kids. I'd pay you what I normally pay Trixi, the one on maternity leave. She gets overtime for the extra work."

"Really?" She frowned, bit her lip.

"Of course," he said, watching her, "you'd have to work pretty closely with me."

There was a beat of silence. Then: "I'm already working way too closely with you."

"What?"

She clapped her hand over her mouth. "Oh, wow, did I say that out loud?"

"Susan." He sat down on one of the bar stools to be more at her level. She was so petite. "I hope I'm not making you uncomfortable in some way. That's the last thing I intend."

"No!" She was blushing furiously. "No, it's not that, it's just… I don't know." She turned away, staring out the window.

He came over to stand behind her, a safe couple of feet away. "I know this is pretty close quarters for two strangers. But I want you to know that I'm very pleased with your work, Susan. I think we can stop thinking of the nanny job as a trial run. I'd like for you to stay all summer."

She gripped the counter without looking at him.

"I haven't seen Mindy so happy since…well, since she was a baby and her mom was healthy."

She half looked back over her shoulder. "Really?"

The plaintive sound of her voice was so at odds with her feisty personality that he felt a strange compulsion to touch her shoulder, to run a hand over that silky hair, offering comfort.

The super-independent, super-confident teacher evidently had some vulnerabilities of her own. It almost seemed as if she hadn't received much praise, although he couldn't imagine why, when she seemed to be so good at everything she did.

Well, everything except cooking.

And why was his hand still moving toward her hair?

Just in time, he pulled it back. That wouldn't do at all.

He was getting a little too interested in Susan. She was too young, too independent, totally wrong for him in the long term, even though she was turning out to be an amazing summer nanny. He needed to get on with his program of finding Mindy a real, permanent mom. And he needed to do it soon.

He'd make sure to get back on the dating circuit right away. There were a couple of women he'd seen once and then left hanging. He'd give them a call. His secretary, who was of necessity a little too involved in his life, had a niece she wanted to fix him up with, and Mindy's

Sunday school teacher had handed him her phone number along with Mindy's half-completed craft last week.

He just needed to get himself motivated to do it. He'd been too busy. But now that Susan was in place—Susan, who was completely inappropriate for him—he'd jump back into pursuing that all-important goal.

He forced himself to take a step backward. "If you're interested in the extra job, I'd appreciate having you do it. It would be easy, because you're here in the house anyway. But if you're not comfortable with it, by all means back off and I'll find someone else."

She studied him, quizzical eyes on his face, head cocked to one side. "I can give it a try," she said slowly.

And Sam tried to ignore the sudden happiness surging through him.

"When will we get to the lake, Daddy?"

Sam glanced back at Mindy, bouncing in her car seat, and smiled as he steered into the parking lot by Keystone Lake. "Hang on a minute or two, and we'll be here and out of the car."

As Mindy squealed her excitement, Sam felt tension relax out of his shoulders. Now things were falling into place.

He pulled into his old parking spot, surveying the soothing, tree-surrounded lawn with satisfaction. He'd grown up with Saturday trips to the lake, and he and Marie had brought Mindy here most summer weekends when she was small. He'd meant to continue the tradition, but it had fallen by the wayside...until now.

They'd play on the blanket, and have a nice picnic, and spend family time together. The only thing missing was the woman beside him. But Susan had agreed to

work today in exchange for a weekday off next week.
She'd fill the role temporarily, until he could get on his
larger goal of finding a new mom for Mindy.

"It's a little cold for swimming," Susan said as she
helped Mindy undo the buckles. "But there's a lot to do
at the lake aside from swimming."

Sam's arms were loaded down with the picnic basket,
blankets and a couple of lawn chairs, but looking around
the stuff, he could see Mindy's lower lip sticking out.

"I want to swim!" his daughter said.

Susan nodded comfortably. "Okay. You can. I'm not
going in that lake until the sun comes out, but I'll watch
you."

Sam came around to the side of the car where Susan
was bent over, gathering an armload of beach toys. "She
can't go in the lake. It's too cold."

Mindy had already taken off for the water.

Susan pressed the beach toys into his already over-
loaded arms. "She'll figure that out for herself!" she
called over her shoulder as she raced after Mindy.
"Relax, Sam!"

Sam gritted his teeth, dumped the gear on a picnic
table and hustled after them.

Mindy was already up to her knees in the water. She
looked back toward the shore, her expression defiant.

He opened his mouth, but Susan's hand on his arm
stopped him. "It's called natural consequences," she
said. "If she goes in, she'll get cold and come out
quickly. No harm, no foul. And she learns something."

"But she'll catch a cold!"

Susan shrugged. "I actually think colds come from
viruses, but whatever. A cold never hurt anyone."

"For a nanny, you're not very protective."

"For a successful entrepreneur, you're not much of a risk taker."

They glared at each other for a minute.

"Come in, Daddy!" Mindy called.

"No way!" He looked at his shivering daughter and took a step forward.

"Then I'll come out," Mindy decided, and splashed her way to the shoreline.

Susan gave him an I-told-you-so grin. "What are you waiting for, Dad? Get her a towel. She's freezing!"

As Sam jogged off toward the beach bags, he couldn't help smiling. A trip to the lake with Susan was never going to be dull.

After Mindy was toweled off and building a sandcastle under Susan's supervision, Sam set up the colorful beach tent they'd always used to protect Mindy's tender skin. Then he rummaged for the tablecloth, but it was nowhere in sight.

Nor was the picnic. Had Susan forgotten to pack it?

Don't be controlling, he reminded himself. Maybe she thought packing food for a Saturday beach trip was beyond her regular duties. They could always call Daisy and ask her to bring something, or as a last resort, could get something from the junk food stand at the other end of the beach.

Noticing that several children had gathered around Susan and Mindy, he strolled down to see what was going on. The little group had already created a somewhat complicated castle with the help of Mindy's multiple beach buckets and molds.

Mindy held a bucket with her half arm and shoved sand in with her whole one, attracting the attention of the two visiting boys.

"How come you only have one hand?" one of the boys asked Mindy.

"This is how I was born," she answered simply.

"That's weird," the child said.

Color rose on the back of Mindy's neck, and Sam opened his mouth to yell at the kid, and then closed it again. He was learning from Susan that he needed to wait and watch sometimes, rather than intervening, but when someone made a comment about his kid, it was hard. Natural consequences and learning better social skills were all well and good, but insults, not so much.

He looked at Susan to find her watching the kids with a slightly twisted mouth.

"Yeah, it's really weird," said the other boy, and they both started to laugh.

"That's enough!" Susan stepped toward them and squatted down, a protective hand on Mindy's shoulder.

"It's bullying," Mindy said. "Right, Miss Hayashi?" She'd automatically reverted to Susan's professional name, maybe because bullying was something they talked about in school.

"Very good, Mindy. You're right." Susan turned a steely glare on the two young offenders. "And bullies can't play. Goodbye, boys."

"Aw, I didn't want to play with her anyway," said one of the boys. He jumped up and ran toward the water.

"I didn't mean to be a bully," the other boy said, looking stricken. "I'm sorry."

Susan looked at Mindy. "What do you think? Can he still play, or would you rather he goes away?"

Mindy considered. "He said he was sorry."

"Yes, he did."

"He can play," Mindy decided.

"Thanks!" And the two of them were back to building a castle as if nothing had happened, while the other boy kicked stones on the beach, alone.

Susan stood and backed a little bit away, keeping her eyes on the scene as another little girl joined the group. She ended up right next to Sam.

"You did a good job handling that," he said to her, sotto voce. "I want to strangle anyone who teases my kid."

"Believe me, I felt the same way." She smiled up at him.

There was that little click of awareness between them again. She looked away first, her cheeks turning pink.

He needed to nip that attraction in the bud. He needed to start dating, before he did something silly like let Susan know that he found her…interesting.

As he was casting about in his mind for a new subject, Mindy looked up at them. "I'm hungry," she announced.

"Well, I think we forgot a picnic," he said tactfully.

"No, I brought stuff," Susan said. "Come on over, we'll have lunch."

"I'm hungry, too," said the little girl who'd just joined in the group.

"Me, too!" The little boy stood up and brushed sand off his hands onto his swim trunks.

"Tell you what, go ask your mom or dad if you can share our lunch," Susan said easily.

"Do we have enough?" Sam hadn't seen evidence of *any* food, so the thought of sharing was puzzling.

"Oh, sure," she said as the children ran toward their separate families. "It'll be fine."

He didn't see how, but he followed Susan and Mindy, curious to see what she came up with.

From the bottom of the bag of beach toys, she tugged a loaf of whole wheat bread, a tub of peanut butter and a squeeze bottle of grape jelly. "Voila," she said as the other two kids approached. "Let's play 'make your own sandwich!'"

"Yay!" cheered the kids.

Sam frowned at the splintery picnic table, thinking of the neat checkered tablecloth Marie had always brought to the lake. "It's not very clean."

She was digging again in the toy bag and didn't hear him. "Hey, Sam, grab me one of those beach towels, could you? Oh, there we go." Triumphantly, she produced a small stack of paper cups.

He handed a towel to her and she spread it over the table. "Everybody, take a cup. We'll wash hands and then get water from the drinking fountain." She looked at Sam. "Coming?"

"So lunch is…peanut butter sandwiches and water?"

She seemed genuinely puzzled. "You were expecting caviar?"

"No, but maybe… Never mind." He didn't elaborate on checkered tablecloths and homemade chicken salad and cut up melon in a special blue bowl, but for a second, his whole chest hurt with missing his wife.

Mindy was tugging at his hand. "Come on, Daddy, I'm hungry!"

The next fifteen minutes were a blur of helping a bunch of primary-school-aged kids make messy PB&J sandwiches and chatting with the parents who came over to check everything out. Both families, it turned out, knew Susan from the school, and showed respect for her and interest in her summer plans.

Finally the kids headed back to the water with one of the other families, and he and Susan collapsed down onto the picnic bench. Susan cut the sandwich she'd managed to make for herself and offered him half.

To his surprise, it actually tasted good.

"What I wouldn't give for a cup of coffee," she admitted.

"I could buy you one at the refreshment stand, since you provided the lunch," he offered.

"Well, technically you provided it. But if you'll buy me a coffee I'll follow you anywhere."

"Anywhere?" he asked lightly as they stood up together.

"Maybe." She had the cutest way of wrinkling her nose.

And he needed to watch it, or he'd be getting those romantic feelings for her again. He pulled himself together, checked one last time on Mindy, and then led the way to the concession area.

They were halfway across the grassy lawn when a young guy tossed a ball straight at Susan.

Sam stepped forward, ready to slug the guy, but Susan had already caught the ball and tossed it back, laughing. "Hey, Hunter," she said. "What's going on? Enjoying the summer off?"

The twentysomething guy rose to his feet, shirtless and in surf-style jammer shorts, and pushed his sunglasses to the top of his head. "I'd be better if you'd join the teachers' volleyball league," he said. "Every Wednesday. It's fun."

"Oh, well, I don't think so, but thanks."

"What are you doing for fun this summer?" the guy asked. Focused on Susan, he was completely ignoring Sam.

Sam restrained the urge to move closer and put a protective arm around Susan. No way could she be interested in this guy, right? He was much too young and silly.

He's Susan's age, his inner critic reminded him.

"I'm at the lake! That's fun, right?" She gestured toward a couple of people who'd headed down toward the water. "Your friends are leaving you. You'd better catch up."

"Hey, good to see you. I'll give you a call." He jogged off.

Susan rolled her eyes. "And I'll block your number," she muttered.

Relief washed over him. "You don't like him?"

She shook her head. "He's fine, but he just won't take no for an answer."

Curious now, Sam fell into step beside her. "That must be a problem, guys hitting on you."

She laughed. "No, not usually, but Hunter is fairly new in town. He doesn't know my reputation."

"What's your reputation?"

"I'm known as a cold fish." She kicked at a rock with a small, neat bare foot, toenails painted pale blue. "Or, sometimes, too mouthy and assertive. I don't get asked out a lot."

"That surprises me," Sam said, tearing his eyes away from those delicate feet. "Does it bother you?"

She shook her head. "Not really," she said. "I'm not looking for love. I'm one of those people who's meant to be single, I think."

Sam knew with everything in him that this warm, funny, kid-loving woman was meant to be a mother. And a wife. "That surprises me, too."

"Why?" she asked.

"Well, because you're...cute. And a lot of fun."

"Thanks," she said drily. "I didn't know you cared."

He lifted his hands. "I didn't mean I cared like *that*..." He felt heat rising up his neck.

She studied him sideways. "It's okay, Sam. I really have no expectations in that area. I'm not angling for a date with Rescue River's richest bachelor."

She seemed to be telling the truth, and to his surprise, he found that refreshing. A lot of the women he dated did have expectations. They liked him for his big house and his money and his CEO position. Not so much for who he was inside.

"So tell me about *your* love life," she said, seeming to read his mind. "Since I don't have one."

"Not much to tell on my side, either," he said.

She made a small sound of disagreement in her throat. "Daisy says you date women just like your wife."

He felt his face redden. "Daisy has a few too many opinions."

She chuckled. "I know what you mean. And there's nothing wrong with having a type. What was Marie like?"

He smiled, remembering, for once, with enjoyment rather than pain. "Beautiful, though she always worried about her weight. Loved being a mother more than anything else."

"I'm sure Mindy was a joy to her."

"That she was." He thought some more. "Marie

was…a perfectionist. Wanted her home and her flowers and her family to be just picture-perfect."

She nodded. "How did she deal with Mindy's disability, then?"

He frowned, thinking. "She didn't want to highlight it, but she loved Mindy just as she was."

"That's good," Susan said. "Sounds like the two of you were…in sync. Perfect, loving parents."

"We were." They'd reached the food stand, and he ordered them both coffees. "We were in sync, that is. Perfect, of course not. Nobody is."

"Some people try harder at it," she said as she stirred an inordinate amount of sugar into her coffee.

She was making him think: about his history, his relationship with Marie, his views on how life should be lived. In the past year of dating, no other woman had really got him to examine his life.

He wasn't sure if he loved it or hated it. Yet another thing to think about, but not today. "What about you?" he asked. "You seem driven in the career area of your life. Wouldn't you say you try to be perfect there?"

She shook her head. "I'm in elementary and special ed. Aiming for perfection doesn't work for us."

He eyed her narrowly. "Excellence?"

"As a teacher, I try. In my personal life…I pretty much ruled that out a long time ago."

"That's cryptic." He paused, giving her space to respond, but for whatever reason, she didn't.

They strolled together back toward the picnic table. "Mindy's having fun," Sam said, pointing to her as she splashed in the lake with her new friends. "Thanks for making this happen."

"I didn't. It was your idea."

"I know, but…for whatever reason, I don't tend to do stuff like this alone with Mindy."

"Why don't you?"

"It just doesn't seem…right. Not without Marie."

"It doesn't seem perfect?"

"I guess not."

They strolled together more slowly. "Somehow," she said, "I don't think it was just Marie who was the perfectionist. But I'll do my best to keep things together for you guys this summer, until the right woman comes along."

Chapter 6

Back at the house, after a quick dinner of beefaroni stirred up by Sam, they watched an hour of TV. All sprawled together on the sectional sofa, Sam on one side of Mindy and Susan on the other.

Like a family. Too much so. Susan was hyperaware of Sam's warm arm, curved around Mindy but brushing against her. Of the smell of his skin, some brisk manly bodywash or deodorant he used. Of the carefree way he threw back his head and laughed at the cartoon antics on the TV screen. She liked seeing this carefree, boyish side of him. He didn't relax enough.

And wherever that wifely thought had come from, it needed to go right back there.

As the show ended, Mindy slumped to her side, asleep.

"Poor kiddo, she's exhausted," Susan said, stroking Mindy's soft hair.

Sam slid his arms underneath her. "I'll carry her upstairs. C'mon, Mindy. Time for bed."

"Miss…Susan…come," Mindy ordered sleepily.

"Do you mind?" Sam asked.

Did she mind playing the mother role, hanging out with this sweet father and daughter and falling for them more each day? "No problem," she said, and followed Sam up the stairs.

While Sam helped Mindy get ready, Susan looked around the big bedroom, really paying attention to its décor for the first time. With a Noah's Ark theme, it had a hand-painted border, and the bed was shaped like an ark. Ruffly curtains portrayed cheery pairs of animals, and a mobile dangled above the bed. It was a gorgeous room…for a three-year-old.

It made sense that Sam hadn't redecorated; that had to be the last thing on his mind, and the room was fine. But noticing all the things in this house that had frozen, at the point where a loving mother had gotten too ill to update them, made sadness push at Susan's chest.

Once Mindy was in her pajamas with teeth brushed, she was awake enough to want to talk. "That boy today was a bully," she said seriously. "Wasn't he, Miss Susan?"

Susan nodded. "He was. Did he hurt your feelings?"

"Yes. I don't like the way my arm is." Mindy held it up to look at it critically. "I wish I had two hands like other kids."

Susan glanced up in time to see pain flash across Sam's face. It must be hard to see your child suffering. And it didn't look as if Sam knew what to say.

But suddenly, Susan remembered how her own mother had talked to her about looking different. "You know," she said, "when I was a little girl, I wished I had round eyes instead of Japanese ones," she said.

"Your eyes aren't round," Mindy agreed, "but they're pretty."

"Thank you! But I still wished I looked like my mom. Even my brother came out looking more white, with round eyes. But I got my dad's Japanese look. For a while, I really hated it."

Mindy nodded, trying to understand. "What did you do?"

Susan laughed. "I did eye exercises every night, hoping I could make my eyes round. But of course, I couldn't."

"Sometimes I pull on my arm," Mindy confided, "so maybe it will grow longer."

"Mindy!" Sam sounded horrified. "That won't work, and it could hurt you."

Mindy's lip pouted out. "It *could* work."

"My eye exercises never did," Susan said. "But my mom bought me a poster for my room. It said, 'Be Your Own Kind of Beautiful.' There were pink butterflies on it." She smiled, remembering how happy the special attention from her mom had made her.

"I like butterflies. Can I have a poster like that?"

Susan raised her eyebrows at Sam, pretty sure that he'd order one before midnight struck.

"Of course you can, sweetie," he said.

"What really helped the most," Susan said, "was knowing God made me the way He did for a reason. My mom kept telling me I was part of His plan."

"God made everyone," Mindy agreed doubtfully.

"That's right." Susan patted Mindy's arm. "Also, getting some more friends who looked like me helped a lot, too. I could see I wasn't alone, or strange."

"Nobody else has a short arm," Mindy said.

"Oh, yes, they do. In fact, when we go to the library next week, we'll see if Miss Fern can order us some books about kids with limb differences."

Mindy's eyes were closing. "'Kay," she said. "Can you sing for me, Miss Susan?"

Sing? Susan couldn't restrain a chuckle. "Oh, honey, you don't want me to sing. Maybe Daddy could sing for you."

"Mommy and Daddy...used to sing...together."

Susan drew in a breath and let it out in a sigh and looked at Sam. So much grief in this house. So much healing to do. So many ways she'd never live up to the perfect Marie, not even as a summer nanny. "Go for it, Dad," she said.

Sam cleared his throat, his face closed. "We'll sing tomorrow, sweetheart."

Susan thought to flick on the little music player beside the bed, and some lullabies, meant for a younger child, poured out.

A quiet moment later, Mindy was asleep.

With a glance at each other, Sam and Susan rose at the same moment and tiptoed from the room. As they walked quietly down the stairs, she glanced up at him. "Sorry I can't sing."

"You bring other strengths," he said. "That really helped, what you said to her about wanting to be different from how you are."

"She should definitely meet other kids with limb differences." Susan felt relieved as they eased into a more businesslike topic. "I'll do a little research tomorrow, see what's out there. Angelica said something about a camp for kids with special needs."

"Great. But hey," he said, putting a hand on her shoulder, "did you really want your eyes to be different, or was that just for Mindy's benefit?"

"I wanted it. Every little girl wants to look like her mommy."

His grip tightened on her shoulder, and he turned her toward him. One hand cupped the side of her face, and his thumb touched the corner of her eye with a gentle caress. "I, for one, think your eyes are beautiful just as they are."

Susan went still, but inside, her heart was pounding out of control. She stared up at him, unable to speak.

He smiled, his own eyes crinkling. "Thanks for today."

"It was good to be with you and Mindy."

They were frozen there, in a moment that seemed to last forever, looking at each other. Lullabies sounded quietly from upstairs, and Susan breathed in the soap-and-aftershave scent that was Sam. She tipped her head a little to feel more of the hand that still rested on her cheek.

And then the front door opened, letting in the most unwelcome sound in the world. "Hey, yoo-hoo!"

It was Helen. Susan stepped back guiltily. Sam let his hand drop.

And they came down the steps double time, but not before Mindy's grandmother had appeared at the landing and seen them, her husband close behind her.

And not before Susan caught sight of the giant portrait of Sam, Mindy and the perfect Marie, directly at the bottom of the stairs.

"Just let me know what it costs," Sam said, and Susan looked at him, puzzled.

"That camp for special-needs kids," he explained.

"Oh!" Susan nodded. "You're fine with her going?"

"Sure, fine," he said, trotting the rest of the way down the stairs, obviously having no idea of what he'd just agreed to.

"Mindy isn't special needs." Helen eyed them suspiciously. "What's been going on?"

Way too much, Susan wanted to say as she followed Sam. Too much emotion for a little family that wasn't hers and never would be. A family that had a perfect woman always in the background.

She was starting to see that she might be able to fit into a family, that she might have something to offer, despite her lack of domestic skills. Part of that was Sam's appreciation for what she offered to a child like Mindy.

But she wasn't what he wanted. He wanted another Marie.

And he wasn't what she wanted, either, she reminded herself. She didn't want a businessman like her dad and her ex-fiancé, who would have overly high expectations and just throw money at any problem that arose.

"Sam," Helen said, "we stopped over to invite you to the Fourth of July picnic next week at the country club. There's someone I want you to meet." Her voice was rich with innuendo, and she was practically waggling her eyebrows at Sam.

"Mindy and I always go," Sam said, looking uncomfortable. "Surely you didn't come here just to invite me to that?"

"Oh, my, no. Come on, sit down." Helen led the way to the kitchen and pulled a sheaf of papers out of her large purse. Susan, feeling unwelcome but unsure of what to do, followed along behind them.

"There's all this paperwork for the Little Miss Rescue River Pageant. It's got to be filled out this week. I thought I could help you get Mindy signed up." She held up a brochure portraying a little girl dressed in a super-fancy evening dress.

"A beauty pageant?" Susan couldn't keep the derisive squeak out of her voice.

But Helen didn't seem to notice. "Yes, it's so much fun. I'm on the planning committee, and we've been busy setting up a wonderful show." Her voice was animated, her eyes lively.

"Oh, it's a big to-do," Ralph contributed.

Susan looked at Sam. Was he on board with this?

Thankfully, he was shaking his head. "It's a great event, but I'm not sure Mindy's ready…" He trailed off and sat down at the counter.

"But she's about to turn six, which is the lower age limit. I'm so happy that she can finally join in the fun!" Helen's voice was determinedly peppy, as if she was getting ready to run right over Sam.

And Sam, the big tough businessman, looked about to cave.

Susan jumped in. "I don't think that would be good for Mindy."

All eyes turned her way.

"Why on earth not?" Helen glared at her.

Could the woman really have no clue? "Beauty pageants force little girls to dress in age-inappropriate clothes and focus only on their appearance. There's research that shows they foster eating disorders and an unhealthy dependence on external validation."

"You could use a little more focus on *your* appearance," Helen said, eyeing Susan's cutoffs and T-shirt with disdain.

Ouch! Susan clamped her mouth shut to avoid saying something she couldn't take back, and surprising, unwelcome tears pushed at her eyes. Her self-image had improved since the days when she'd hated the way she looked, but it still wasn't perfect.

"Hey, hey now." Sam held up a hand. "Susan, Mindy and I dressed for a day at the lake, and we look it. Nothing wrong with that."

Helen muttered something that might have been "Sorry."

Susan made a little sound in her throat that might pass for "okay." But it wasn't. She didn't like Helen one bit.

"Let's keep the focus on Mindy," Sam went on. "I just worry, Helen, that with her hand—"

"She could carry something to cover it if she wanted, or wear gloves," Helen said. "You know what a mix the pageant is. Everything from casual and relaxed to hairpieces and fake teeth."

"Exactly! It's a huge fake thing." Susan thought of the little girl sleeping upstairs, pulling on her hand to try to make it look like other children's. "It's an outdated ritual, and it would be bad for Mindy. Have you ever watched *Tiny Tot Beauty*?"

"Susan, it's not that kind of thing." Sam looked distinctly uncomfortable.

She understood. It was hard for him to stand up to Mindy's overbearing grandmother. But she herself had no such qualms. "Have you seen what pageant people are like? What can those parents be thinking, pushing their little kids into that high-glamour lifestyle? I mean, I'm sure this small-town pageant isn't as bad as the big pageants you see on reality TV, but it's a step in the wrong direction."

The room was silent around her.

"Right?" she said, looking at Sam.

"Susan," he said quietly, "Marie was in pageants."

"Yep," Ralph said, nodding. "Those big ones. There wasn't reality TV back in those days, but I've watched the shows. They pretty much tell it like it was for us."

"Oh." Oops. Susan blew out her breath, her face heating.

Helen didn't say anything. Not in words, anyway, but her glare said it all.

Without meaning to, Susan had shot daggers at the woman they all loved so much. The woman Sam had adored and still did. The mother little Mindy aspired to look like and never would. Never would even see again.

They were all looking at her.

When would she ever learn to shut her mouth? "I'm sorry. I'm sure I...don't know everything about pageants. In fact, I probably know a lot less than anyone else in this room, so..." She trailed off into the silence.

The doorbell provided a welcome distraction. "Let me get that," she said.

"She certainly makes herself at home in your house," Susan heard Helen say as she left the room.

"Got some opinions, too," Ralph said.

As she hurried to the door, Susan's face felt as if it was on fire.

She opened it to a welcome sight: Daisy.

"Hey girl, I knocked on your apartment door and when I didn't find you, I figured you must be over here." She squinted at Susan. "Looks like you could use some girl talk."

"More than you know. Let me grab my stuff." She hurried into the kitchen for her beach bag, cell phone and keys as Daisy chatted with Helen.

Five minutes later they were drinking sodas in Susan's tiny living room. "How's it going?" Daisy asked. "You surviving the dragon lady?"

"She didn't like me before," Susan said, "but after tonight, she hates me." She told Daisy about the beauty pageant fiasco. "So if there was any hope of our getting along, not that it really matters, it went out the window tonight."

"She thinks you're after Sam," Daisy said, nodding shrewdly.

"What? Why would she think that?" Even as she spoke, Susan felt her face flush, remembering that moment on the stairs.

If Helen hadn't come, would he have kissed her?

Would she have let him?

Daisy eyed her suspiciously. "What's going on?"

Susan shook her head. Daisy was her best friend, but no way was she going to share the occasional moments of strange attraction between her and Daisy's big brother.

Instead, she turned the topic back to the pageant Helen wanted Mindy to enter.

Daisy rolled her eyes. "I'm with you. Pageants are pretty ridiculous most of the time. But the Rescue River one isn't so bad."

Susan couldn't restrain her curiosity. "Was Marie really a pageant kid? Like on *Tiny Tot Beauty?*"

"Yep. She was way into it, through middle school at least. I'm sure there are some pictures around." Daisy cocked her head to one side, thinking. "In fact, Helen might have been in some pageants, too, back in the day."

Susan groaned. "So it's a family tradition, and I interfered with it with all my big California ideas. Sam's probably getting ready to fire me right now."

Daisy laughed. "Sam can take it. In fact, I think you're good for him. He looks more relaxed than usual. Even seems to have a bit of a tan."

"We were at the lake today," Susan explained, and told her about their day.

Daisy crossed her arms and studied Susan, her expression curious. "Sounds pretty cozy. How do you feel about Sam, anyway?"

"He's a good employer, and we're getting along better than I expected."

"Are you sure that's all there is to it? I mean, Sam's incredibly handsome, and has a great big heart, and he's also the richest man in town. Any chance of you falling for him?"

"No!" Susan held up a hand to stop Daisy's protest. "I don't date, remember? I'm committed to staying single so I can focus on my career. Plus," she added, "if I were going to go out with someone, it wouldn't be one of those classic business types. I like quirky, creative guys, and Sam's anything but."

"Does your dad's treatment of your family have to affect you forever?" Daisy asked bluntly.

"My dad's... What do you mean?" She didn't like

the way Daisy was looking at her, as if she was a social work client. A troubled one.

"Our childhoods have an impact," Daisy lectured, in full counselor mode. "You think Sam is too much like your dad, but he's not only a businessman. He's a brother and a dad. And he's very lonely."

"He misses his wife, I can tell that." Susan frowned. "Even if I *were* interested—and I'm not—it would be crazy to get involved with a family still grieving such a big loss. They'd rip my heart out."

Daisy looked thoughtful. "I know Sam seems obsessed with Marie, but appearances can be deceptive. He's trying to keep her memory alive for Mindy, and he's been too busy surviving to build them a new life. But I can see him changing, letting go."

Susan walked over to the kitchen and snagged the jumbo bag of spicy tortilla chips. "Don't you think they need some counseling?" she asked as she replenished the bowl on the coffee table.

"They've had it. Do you think I would've let them muddle through without help? But it's a process." Daisy grabbed a chip and munched it, thoughtfully, then spoke again. "And you have to remember that Jesus can heal. He can heal Sam and Mindy of what they lost when Marie died. And He can heal you from the way your father treated you."

Susan leaned her head back on the couch and stared up at the ceiling fan. She wanted to believe it. She wished for Daisy's faith. But it was a stretch right now. "I'm afraid to change," she admitted. "I've been committed to being a single schoolteacher for so long. I've felt like that's God's will for me."

"His will might be bigger than you can imagine right

now. Maybe it involves getting married, having kids of your own *and* being a schoolteacher. Ever think of that?"

Susan *had* thought of it lately. Specifically in connection to Sam and Mindy. But the whole idea felt risky and dangerous and scary. "It's out of my comfort zone. What with my family and all."

"God kinda specializes in out-of-our-comfort-zone."

Susan thought about that. God had called her to work with special-needs kids—in the classroom, or so she'd thought. But she knew she was doing good for Mindy right now. Taking this job with Sam had been a risk, but she could see that it was paying off. At least for Mindy, which was the important thing.

"And," Daisy continued, frowning, "it might be time for Sam to take down a few pictures from the Marie gallery. I'll talk to him about it." She grabbed Susan's hand. "But you need to work on healing, too. You're not limited to your past. With God's help, you can have a bright future and you can have love."

"But I don't want—"

"Just think about it."

Night was falling, turning the summer sky to pinks and purples, sending a cool breeze fragrant with honeysuckle through the open window.

Susan heard a car door slam outside. Hopefully, that was Helen and Ralph, leaving.

"Promise me you'll think and pray about healing, okay? Not just so you can work something out with Sam, although that would be totally cool. But no matter what happens with him, I want to see you be happy and whole."

Susan hugged her friend. "Thanks for caring about

me. I know Jesus can heal. I know it in my head. But I'm not quite there with believing it in my heart."

After that emotional night, Susan and Sam steered a little clear of each other, seemingly by mutual agreement. When Susan had a question about the company picnic she was planning, she mostly texted Sam and he responded with brief, impersonal instructions.

She did notice that Sam quietly took down some of the Marie pictures, replacing them with drawings Mindy had made, which he'd had beautifully framed, and more recent photographs of him and Mindy. The change, Susan was sure, was Daisy's doing; she must have had that talk with Sam.

He'd also spent a couple of evenings helping Mindy create a photo album of her mother and her, which Mindy had proudly showed Susan each morning after Sam went to work.

Susan was surprised and impressed. Sam definitely had a stubborn, bossy side, but he also was able to listen to his sister's wisdom and follow it, and his thoughtfulness with his daughter, his intelligent care of her, made him all the more appealing.

She found herself watching him sometimes, in a silly, romantic way that wasn't doing her heart any good at all.

She just needed to keep reminding herself that her goal wasn't to swoon over her boss's softer side. It was to fix her own family's problems while staying independent. She wasn't the marrying kind, and in a tempting situation like this, she had to keep that well in mind.

Sam had brushed aside her apologies about her awkward words to his in-laws, saying everything was fine.

But it wasn't, Susan could tell. He'd been distant, and she felt bad about it. Who was she to judge how others lived their lives? Maybe there was some redeeming value in pageants she didn't understand. And in any case, it wasn't her business. She was just the nanny.

She and Mindy were finger-painting late one afternoon when her phone buzzed. She washed her hands and looked at the text message. From Sam, and her heart jumped.

Did you get my message before?

Susan looked and started to sweat.

Hate to ask but could you fix something easy for dinner? Job candidate here with wife and two active boys. Would like to invite them home. Nothing special, no stress. ETA 5 p.m.

No stress. Ha! She checked the message again. Yes, it did say they'd arrive at 5.

It was 4:15.

She drew in a breath and sat up straighter. Here was her chance to impress Sam with her domestic abilities and make up for being such a screw-up the other night.

No problem, she texted back. She'd disappointed him then, but she wouldn't do it again. She could get it done.

"Come on, Mindy," she said. "We have work to do."

When Sam arrived home promptly at 4:55, he had a little trepidation as he held the car door for Emily, his job candidate's wife.

"Wow, that's a big house!" cried one of the couple's twin boys. They were cute, freckle-faced redheads with energy to burn, probably a couple years older than Mindy.

"How many kids do you have?" the other twin asked.

"One, and she should be inside. Come on in."

Just then, Susan came around the side of the house. She wore neat shorts and a... Was that a golf shirt? He'd never have guessed she owned anything so plain and ordinary.

She didn't look like herself, quite; she looked... almost traditional. A thought crossed his mind: had she dressed that way for him?

Surely she wouldn't do that, but the very notion of it tugged at his heart. If she'd tried to look conservative for him, it was a totally endearing effort.

And she should probably remove some of her multiple earrings to complete the effect.

"Come around back," she said. "Everything's ready."

"I can get the drinks," Sam said, relief washing over him at her gracious greeting. Times like this, he really needed a wife, and Susan was acting like a good stand-in. He wanted to bring Bill in as CEO of his agricultural real estate division, which would free Sam up to focus on the land management side of the business—and to spend a little less time at the office. But Bill and Emily were city people, used to sophisticated living, so he was going to have to sell them hard on the virtues of Rescue River.

On the back deck, overlooking the pool, the table was set with a red checkered tablecloth and there were baskets of potato chips and dip. Retro, casual, but that was okay. He'd only let Susan know today.

Burgers were on the grill, smelling great, and through the open kitchen window, peppy jazz played. Nice.

Mindy came out, carefully carrying a bowl of baby carrots. A glass bowl, but Sam restrained himself from helping her. She was adept with her hand and half arm, and he was learning, from Susan, to let her do as much as possible on her own. He introduced her to the boys and the adults and she greeted everyone politely and turned away. "'Scuse me, I gotta bring the dip."

Susan emerged with a bin of assorted soft drinks on ice, and since everyone seemed to enjoy choosing their own, he didn't even complain about the fact that they were drinking from cans. It was a barbecue, he told himself. Relax.

Susan looked extremely cute. She'd tied a barbecue apron over her shorts and shirt and was concentrating on the burgers. "Hey, I think these are done already," she said, and they all sat down.

Dinner was happening a little too quickly, and he wanted to suggest that everyone needed to enjoy their sodas and relax a bit before eating.

"Yay, I'm starving!" cried one of the boys.

"Me, too!" yelled his brother.

Their mother smiled, so Sam let it go.

It was make-your-own-burgers—again, a little too casual for his tastes, but the family seemed fine with it. Susan ducked back into the kitchen and emerged with a casserole dish which, when she opened it, contained macaroni and cheese that looked suspiciously like the kind from a box. He arched an eyebrow at her.

"Mac and cheese!" the boys shouted.

"I really appreciate your arranging this to be so kid-friendly," the job candidate, Bill, said to Susan.

She chuckled, a throaty sound that tickled Sam's nerve endings. "Casual and kid-friendly, that's my specialty," she said with an apologetic smile to Sam.

Sam offered up a quick prayer and then they all dug in.

Sam took a giant bite of hamburger. His teeth hit something hard and he tasted ice.

Quickly he put the burger down. "I don't think these are done. Better get them back on the grill," he said.

Susan's face flamed. "Oh, no, I'm sorry. They came right out of the freezer, but I thought, with the grill so hot…"

Bill grinned. "Mistake of a novice griller," he said.

"I don't like hamburgers," announced one of the boys. "I like hot dogs better."

"Me, too!" Mindy said.

"We do have some," Susan said hesitantly. "I'm sorry, Sam."

Sam slapped a mosquito and noticed Mindy and the quieter little boy were doing the same. "Couldn't you find the bug torches?" he asked Susan.

"I…never heard of bug torches," she said regretfully. "Look. I'll grab the hot dogs, and we'll put the burgers back on the grill. You guys go hunt down the bug torches because I, for one, am getting eaten alive."

Everyone got up from the table and went to their respective stations. Sam was shaking his head. If there had ever been a worse attempt at impressing a prospective employee, he didn't know what it was.

"Sorry," she whispered as she brushed past him. And

even amidst his annoyance, he felt a rush of sympathy and patted her shoulder.

"Can I come in and help?" asked Emily, a very quiet woman.

Susan shrugged resignedly. "If you want. It's a huge mess inside."

"We'll come, too!" the ginger-haired twins said and rushed inside.

As they walked to the garage, Bill clapped him on the back. "Ask me sometime to tell you about my major disaster of a client dinner," he said.

When they got the torches lit, everyone was still in the house, and the sound of the boys' yelling rang through the open windows. With some trepidation, Sam pushed in, followed by his client. And stopped and stared.

The entire kitchen table was covered with paint pots and paper, and the two visiting boys were having a heyday with it. The mother, who seemed to lack discipline or authority, was scolding ineffectually, and the boys were ignoring her.

"Those are *my* finger paints," Mindy said, looking ready to blow.

Susan was arm-deep in the refrigerator. "I know there are some hot dogs in here somewhere," she was saying.

What a disaster!

The doorbell rang. "Mindy, could you or your daddy get that?" Susan called, obviously glad to have found Mindy a distraction.

Sam started to follow Mindy, but when he saw who'd arrived, he went back to the kitchen to give himself time to take a deep breath.

He needed it.

His daughter came in a moment later with Sam's father, who'd started Hinton Enterprises as a small agricultural real estate firm fifty years ago. "It's Grandpa!" she announced.

Sam felt a rush of the inadequacy he'd grown up with. His father was hard to please and, since he'd met Bill earlier in the day, he knew this dinner should be impressive. Sam was making a mess of things.

"Boys!" Bill scolded, frowning at his own wife.

"What on earth is going on?" Mr. Hinton asked.

Sam blew out a breath, looked around and realized he was going to have to take charge.

But there was a touch on his arm, one that tingled. Susan. "Sorry," she mouthed to him.

And then she proceeded to take charge herself. "Boys!" she said in a firm, quiet voice accompanied by a hand-clap. "Finger paints are for after dinner. Mindy, please show your new friends how to wash their hands at the kitchen sink."

"Marie never would have allowed that," Mr. Hinton said in a voice that was meant to be quiet but wasn't.

Sam saw a muscle twitch in Susan's face. She was no dummy. She knew she was being compared.

She drew in a breath. "Mr. Hinton, here." She put two packages of hot dogs into his hands. "You're in charge of grilling these. Sam." She handed him two packages of buns. "Take these outside, along with your clients. Socialize. Do your thing."

She turned to the children, who stood quietly watching her, obviously recognizing that teacher voice. In fact, Sam thought, even his father seemed to recognize that voice. "Kids, you can play outside with Mindy's toys until dinner. After you eat your hot dogs..." She tapped a finger on her lips. "I think we've got some of Xavier's clothes here. You can put on swimsuits or shorts, and finger-paint for a bit, and then jump in the pool to clean up. If that's okay with Mom?" She looked questioningly at Emily.

"Of course. Thank you."

"Yay!" cried the boys, and all three kids rushed outside.

So the men bonded over how to re-cook half-frozen, half-burnt burgers with ketchup already on them, and they grilled up a bunch of hot dogs. The kids played while Susan talked with Emily, who gradually became more animated. Dinner was eaten half at the table and half by the pool, and Sam's father actually stayed to eat three of the hot dogs he'd cooked and then to sit on a chaise lounge by the pool, watching the kids play.

The sun peeked through the clouds on its way toward the horizon, turning the sky rosy and sending beams of golden light that, as a kid, he'd always thought seemed to come directly from God. Salted caramel ice cream topped with chocolate syrup from a squirt bottle made a fine dessert, to his surprise. As the evening grew chilly, Susan brought out a heap of old sweatshirts from the front closet, and everyone put them on and stayed outside, talking and laughing.

Gradually, Sam relaxed. It wasn't exactly orthodox, but the prospective employee's family seemed to be having a good time.

When darkness fell and the kids climbed out of the pool, shivering, Susan wrapped them in towels and took all of them inside to dress, accompanied by the mother.

"I tell you what," Bill said as he and Sam stood on

the front porch. "When I saw this big house, I thought, oh, man, too rich for our blood. We like to keep it simple. But this has been great." He pumped Sam's hand as his wife and tired children came out onto the porch. "I've made my decision. I like this town and this lifestyle. If you still want me after the way my kids have behaved, I'd like to come work for Hinton Enterprises."

Fifteen minutes later, Sam stood with his father, watching the family drive away. "That's the wackiest business dinner I ever witnessed," Mr. Hinton said, clapping Sam on the shoulder. "But whatever works, son." He gave Sam a squinty-eyed glare. "You're not thinking about marrying that Japanese girl, are you?"

"Her name's Susan," Sam said. "And no. Nothing like that. I have other plans for that side of my life."

His father nodded. "Best to get moving on them. That little girl of yours isn't getting any younger. Seems to me she needs some brothers and sisters to play with."

"Yes, sir, I'm aware of that." He knew the clock was ticking. And every minute he spent noticing the appeal of an unconventional schoolteacher with a knack for causing disasters, even if they did usually turn out just fine, was a minute he wasn't finding the proper sort of mother for his daughter.

Was a minute he spent *not* fulfilling his promise to Marie.

The next Friday, July Fourth, Susan helped Mindy dress in her new red, white and blue shorts and shirt to go to the country club picnic. The day had dawned bright and hot, perfect weather for a picnic.

She was *not* looking forward to this.

She didn't need to spend the time with Sam, who'd

been surprisingly kind about her disastrous efforts to cook dinner for his job candidate's family. He hadn't had a lot to say over the past few days, but she sensed that his attitude toward her had softened.

Which made him even more appealing. But she had to guard her heart. She didn't need to fall for a guy who wanted something altogether different in a woman. She wasn't going to put herself through that again.

"I'm bored," Mindy announced.

There was still an hour until it was time to leave, so Susan took her charge downstairs and looked around for something to occupy her. They'd spent enough time in the playroom, and the formal living room had too many breakables to be a good play area.

"Let's check our seedlings," she suggested, and they went to the kitchen window. To Mindy's delight, tiny, bent plants were appearing in the soil they'd put in an egg carton.

"They're not very green," Mindy said, poking at one with her finger.

"They need more light. Let's find another window to put them in."

They each took an egg carton and wandered around the mansion's downstairs, looking for the perfect spot. It occurred to Susan that she'd never been inside the sunroom. Even though she'd seen it from outside, the blinds had always been drawn. "Come on, Mindy," she said. "Let's try in here."

Mindy emerged from the formal dining room, saw Susan's hand on the doorknob of the sunroom. "No!" she shrieked, dropping her egg carton. "Don't go in there!"

Susan spun back toward the little girl, less concerned

with the dirt and seedlings now soiling the cream-colored carpet than about Mindy's frantic expression. "Hey," she said, putting down her egg carton and kneeling in front of Mindy. "What's wrong?"

"Don't go in there, don't go in there," the child said anxiously, her eyes round.

"Okay, I won't," Susan promised. "But why?"

Mindy's face reddened and her eyes filled with tears. "I don't like that room."

"Okay, okay. Shh." She pulled Mindy into her arms and hugged her until some of the tension left her body. "Come on, we'd better save our plants."

Mindy looked down, only now realizing that she'd dropped her egg-carton planter. "Oh, no, they're gonna be broken."

"I think we can save them," Susan said. "And I have a good idea about how. Come on, you can help."

Forty-five minutes later, the little plants were replanted in some old cartoon character mugs Susan had discovered in the back of a cupboard. The mess was cleaned up, though Susan was going to have to tell the cleaning service to give that area of the rug a little extra attention. And Mindy was calm again, paging quietly through a library book about plants.

As for Susan, she had to get ready. In a weak moment, she'd agreed to go to the club herself, at Daisy and Sam's insistence, so she put on her own faded "Proud to be an American" T-shirt to pair with her standard denim capris and sandals. She pulled her hair up into a ponytail and added a little mascara and blush, and at Mindy's insistence, tied a red, white and blue ribbon into her hair.

But as Sam backed the car out of the driveway, Susan

couldn't help looking toward the sunroom that was visible from the side of the house.

Why was the door always closed? Why was Mindy afraid of the sunroom?

When they reached the country club, Mindy tugged Susan along, chattering a mile a minute, while Sam gathered blankets and lawn chairs for the fireworks later. "C'mon, Miss Susan! We all sit at one big long table. The grown-ups on one end and the kids on the other."

Susan decided instantly on her strategy. "Can I sit with the kids?"

Mindy slowed down a minute to consider. "I guess you could," she said doubtfully. "Xavier likes you, and he's the biggest cousin, so he's kind of the boss."

Susan smiled at the thought of a soon-to-be-second-grader running the show. She adored Xavier, had been his first-grade teacher last year, had helped him catch up and cheered him on in his struggle with leukemia, a struggle he'd now won.

"And there's gonna be Mercedes!"

"I know! She's great." Susan was so happy for Fern and Carlo, Mercedes's foster mother and biological father, who'd fallen in love during a snowstorm over the winter and who were planning to get married soon.

"Put your stuff down here," Mindy ordered, gesturing to the promised long table on one side of the busy dining area, "and then we can go play. Look, there's Mercy!"

Susan waved at Fern, who was sitting at the table chatting with Angelica, Xavier's mom. Behind her, she heard Sam's deep voice, greeting people.

She glanced back to see that he'd paused to talk to a

group of men clad in golf shirts. The preppy crowd. Of course. "I'll keep an eye on the kids," she said to Fern and Angelica, and followed the small pack of cousins before either woman could protest.

Staying with the kids would keep her from spending too much time with handsome Sam.

She watched them jump through the inflatables and play in the ball pit, all under Xavier's leadership. When he'd gotten them all onto a little train that circled the club's giant field, she sat down on a long bench under a tree to wait for the train's return.

A slight breeze rustled the leaves overhead, cooling Susan's heated face. From the bandstand, patriotic songs rang out over the chatter of families. The aroma of roasting corn and hot dogs tickled her nose, reminding her of holidays in the park in her California hometown.

Self-pity nudged at her. Holidays were meant to be experienced with family, and a lot of people here in Rescue River had a whole long tableful of relatives.

She missed her mom and brother, Aunt Sakura and Uncle Ren, and her cousins, Missy and Cameron and Ryan. They hadn't gathered often, but when they did, they'd always had a good time.

Now Uncle Ren had passed away and her cousins were scattered all over the country. She bit her lip and forced herself to concentrate on the buzz of a nearby bee, the beauty of Queen Ann's lace blooming beside the bench, the sight of Miss Lou Ann Miller carrying a tray of decorated cupcakes to the church's booth.

And of course, she wasn't alone long. No one ever was in Rescue River. There was a tap on her shoulder, and Gramps Camden, her buddy from the Senior Towers, sat down heavily beside her on the bench. With him was a weathered-looking man whom she'd occasionally seen around town but didn't know.

And that, too, never lasted long in Rescue River.

"Bob, meet Susan Hayashi. Susan, Bob Eakin. World War II Gliderman."

The thin old man held out a hand and gave her a surprisingly strong handshake. "And present-day librarian," he added with a wink. "Don't ever stop working. That's what'll kill you."

Since the man had to be in his nineties, if he'd fought in World War II, he must know what he was talking about. Susan shook his hand with both of her own. "I'm glad to meet you."

"He runs the library at the Towers," Gramps explained. "Don't worry, he was in Europe in the war, so he's not gonna have any problem with your people."

Susan smiled at the elderly man. "Thank you for your service, and I don't just mean that as a cliché," she said. "One of my great-grandfathers fought for Japan, but another was in an internment camp and eventually fought for the United States."

"Oh, in the 442nd?" His eyes lit up. "I was just reading about them. My buddy Fern brought me a new book about the various regiments."

"I can't believe you know about that! I'd love to borrow it sometime," she said. "I like history, but I don't know much about that period."

"Shame what we did to Japanese Americans back then," Mr. Eakin said. "We've learned better since. Is Rescue River treating you well?"

Susan nodded, her feeling of loneliness gone. "You're nice to ask. It's a great town. I love it here."

Gramps Camden studied her approvingly. "You fit

right in. But how's your summer job with that Sam Hinton? Is he being fair to you?"

"I'm doing my best, Mr. Camden," came a deep voice behind them.

Susan spun around at the sound of it, her heart rate accelerating.

"Don't creep up on people, Hinton," Gramps complained. "We're having a nice conversation. You just leave well enough alone."

Sam ignored the older man. "Brought you some appetizers," he said to Susan. "I didn't mean for you to get stuck watching the kids all day. Come on back and sit with the family."

Gramps snorted. "She doesn't want to listen to your dad give her the third degree, and I don't blame her."

Susan looked at Sam with alarm as she accepted the plate. "Is your dad going to give me the third degree? Why?"

"Because he's like his son," Gramps jumped in, "a millionaire with no consideration for the common folk."

Susan looked up at Sam in time to notice the hurt expression that flickered briefly across his face. Now that she knew Sam better, she understood how unfair Gramps's accusations were. Sam treated his workers well and bent over backward to contribute to the town's well-being. "Sam's not as much of a Scrooge as I expected," she told Gramps, softening her words with a smile. "Maybe your information is a little bit out of date."

"The lady's right," Bob Eakin said, elbowing Gramps Camden. "Leave the man alone. He's done his share for Rescue River, just like we all try to do."

The kids' train returned then, and they all trooped back to the table.

Susan's plan of sitting with the children didn't hold water, though, because Helen was there and adamant about her own position as Mindy's grandmother. "I'll help her if she needs it," she insisted, sliding into the seat beside Mindy.

So Susan had to sit with the other adults. Which turned out to be okay. She stuffed herself with hamburgers and corn on the cob and potato salad, and laughed with Daisy and Angelica, and generally had a good time.

Mr. Hinton stopped by the table but demurred from eating with them. "I've got my eye on Camden. He's sitting a little too close to Lou Ann Miller, and I'd better make sure he doesn't bother her."

Daisy, Fern and Angelica exchanged glances. "Does Lou Ann have a preference for one or the other?" Daisy asked Angelica in a low voice.

"She's doing just fine on her own," Fern said. "I think she likes being single."

"Exactly," Angelica said, salting a second ear of corn. "I don't think she's wanting them to court her, but she can hardly say no if they put their plates down beside hers."

"Age cannot wither her, nor custom stale her infinite variety," quoted Fern's fiancé, Carlo, with a wink at Fern. "William Shakespeare, *Antony and Cleopatra*."

"He was in *one* play at Rescue River High School," Angelica said, rolling her eyes at her brother, "but he uses it every chance he can get. Makes him seem literary."

"I love it when you quote Shakespeare at me," Fern

said, leaning her head on her husband-to-be's shoulder with an exaggerated lash-flutter.

Susan swallowed a huge bite of potato salad and waved her fork at the table of elders. "When I lived near the Senior Towers, I witnessed more drama than you see at a middle school. I wouldn't be surprised if those two came to blows over Lou Ann."

"That's for sure," Fern said with a quiet laugh. "When I go there for book group or to replenish the library cart, things can get pretty lively. Even Bob Eakin has his lady friends, and he's over ninety."

Sam was there, on the other side of Daisy, and it seemed to Susan that he watched her thoughtfully. At one point, as Angelica was apologizing for Gramps Camden's crotchety attitudes, he broke in. "I'm sorry you had to deal with all of that," he said. "I hope the older guys treated you okay."

"Mr. Eakin's going to lend me a book about Japanese who fought for the US in World War II," Susan said. "It's no problem, Sam. I always got along with older relatives."

"Maybe so, but watch out for Mr. Hinton, Senior," Angelica said in a low voice, grinning. "He's a tough nut to crack."

Another remark about Sam's dad. Hmm. After his appearance at the disastrous dinner she'd tried to cook, she wasn't looking forward to seeing him again. Although, she reminded herself, it didn't really matter what he thought. She was just a summer nanny.

Still, right at this moment, Susan felt welcomed and affirmed, almost as if she was a part of the family. Which was strange…but nice.

As they all talked about how full they were—and

made trips to the buffet for seconds—a tall, curvaceous
redhead walked hesitantly toward the table, her four
subdued kids following, all looking to be under the
age of eight.

Susan's teacher radar went up immediately. Why
weren't the kids looking happy in the presence of cot-
ton candy and inflatables and face painters? Why the
tension and caution?

Helen jumped up to greet the woman. "Fiona! Come
on, right here. I have a seat for you, and we can squeeze
in your little ones at this end of the table. Have you
eaten?"

As she settled the woman beside Sam, Helen was
practically glowing with excitement, and it all came
clear to Susan.

Helen had an agenda to set Sam up with a replace-
ment Marie. And here she was.

On Susan's other side, Daisy filled in the facts.
"Fiona Farmingham. Just moved to Rescue River to escape all the gossip. Her celebrity husband just died, and
it turns out he had a whole other family down in Texas."

Susan looked at the woman with sympathy. "Do the
kids know?"

"Oh, yeah, they couldn't help but hear about it. Apparently, they got teased pretty bad. Fiona is Marie's
distant cousin, so she knows the town. She's hoping
Rescue River will be a fresh start."

"Looks like they need one."

But as sympathetic as she felt, she couldn't help feeling jealous as Sam and Fiona talked, egged on by Helen.
Even after the rest of them had stood up, Sam and Fiona
talked on.

Helen came over to share her triumph with Susan

and Daisy. "They're hitting it off, I think," she said in a confiding voice. "Look what lovely manners she has. And she was a stay-at-home mom, and she knows just how to keep a big house nice. She was kind of Marie's role model in that."

"You doing some matchmaking, Helen?" Daisy asked bluntly.

"Sam needs a wife, and Mindy needs a mother. It should have been Marie, but since it can't...well. I hope he'll find a woman who's as like her as possible." Helen's eyes shone with unshed tears.

Susan stuffed down the feelings of hurt and inadequacy prompted by Helen's words. This was good. This was what she wanted: to keep a distance from Sam, which his serious dating of another woman would do. This would be good for Mindy, providing a mother figure and ready-made siblings.

"She's built like a model," Daisy complained in Susan's other ear. "And look, she's just picking at her food. It's hard to like a woman like that."

But Fiona soon excused herself from Sam and came over to talk to them. "Are you guys the moms of these kids?" she asked, her voice throaty and surprisingly deep. "Because I'm fairly desperate for mom friends. I had to leave a lot of people behind when I moved, and I don't know a soul here except for Helen. Well, and I've met Mindy a time or two."

Fern, who was unfailingly kind and accepting, started chatting with Fiona about her daughter, who was the same age as Fern's daughter, Mercedes. Angelica joined in the conversation, and Susan had to admit: the woman was lovely. When she squatted down to see what the kids were doing, she greeted Mindy happily with a hug, reminding the little girl that they'd met before. Soon, she'd engaged all the kids in conversation, introducing her own, encouraging the kids to play together.

As Fiona sat back down with Sam, now surrounded by her children and Mindy, Susan ground her teeth and gave herself a firm talking to.

This was right; this was what everyone, herself included, wanted. Fiona was good with Mindy and was the type of woman Sam needed, way more than Susan herself was.

She swallowed the giant lump in her throat.

She needed to leave them to it.

She excused herself from the others. She was left out anyway. Daisy had gone to see Dion and everyone else was talking. She pulled out her phone and shot Sam a text: Not feeling well, found a way home. There. That sounded breezy.

Then she slipped away and out the side door of the country club.

She'd achieved her goal of staying independent, she told herself as she started walking the two miles toward Sam's house. And it was just her own stupidity that had her feeling teary and blue about it. She'd get over it. She was meant to be alone. This was how it was to be, and it was just going to have to be good enough.

Chapter 7

After Susan left the table, Sam tried to focus on Fiona, new in town and someone his mother-in-law wanted him to get to know better. "She's perfect for you and Mindy, Sam," Helen had whispered as Fiona approached the table. "I know, four kids is a lot, but you have the resources. And she's happy to stay at home. Wouldn't that be wonderful for Mindy?"

The hard sell had made him feel resistant, but Fiona was a genuinely nice woman. They chatted easily about the small liberal arts college they'd both attended, although in different years, about how Rescue River was a great place to raise a family, about people they knew in common, since Fiona was related to Marie.

There was something shuttered in her eyes, some distance, some pain. Still, she was pretty, with her long, wavy red hair, tall as a model but with pleasant curves. Obviously smart.

Sam's attention strayed, wondering where Susan had gone. He scanned the crowd down by the band's tent, where the sounds of pop music emerged alongside patriotic favorites. Checked the food area, where the fragrance of barbecue and burned sugar lingered.

No Susan, though.

"Look," Fiona said, "I get the sense that Helen is trying to push us together, but don't feel obligated to stick around and talk. I'm not in the market for a relationship. I'm just trying to straighten out my life after my husband's death."

He snapped back to focus on her. "I'm sorry for your loss. I faced that and I'm dealing with it, but it's not easy when you had a great relationship and high hopes for the future."

She stared off across the field where people were starting to stake out spots to watch fireworks. Craned her neck, perhaps to see her kids, who were over at the face-painting station with Mindy, under Daisy's supervision. Then she turned back to him. "Be glad if yours was a clean break, Sam," she said, her voice surprisingly intense. "Not everyone has that. In a way, it's harder if the loss was…complicated."

He cocked his head to one side, looking at her and wondering about her story.

One of her children ran to her, a girl of seven or eight, and whispered something in her ear. The two talked in low tones while Sam thought about what she had said.

Thinking about Marie.

It had, in fact, been a clean break. He'd never had any reason to doubt her faithfulness or her love. They'd been genuinely happy together. And right up to the end, her faith had been strong, had guided him even, kept him on a positive path.

It was only after her death that he'd strayed away, mentally, from his faith. Had gotten angry with God about what He'd taken away, not just from Sam himself, but from a little girl who'd sobbed for days as if her heart was breaking—which it surely was—about the loss of her loving mama.

But Mindy had only positive memories of her mother. She'd been well-cared for, and even though the loss had been terribly, terribly hard on her, she hadn't ever questioned her mother's love. She had more moments of joy than pain, these days. Nothing like the skulking, furtive demeanor of the mysterious Fiona's kids.

Marie had been everything a mother should be.

And maybe, just maybe, rather than exclusively feeling bitter about losing her, he should feel grateful to have had a faithful, loving wife.

Fiona's daughter ran off, and she turned to meet his bemused eyes.

"Are you doing okay?" he asked, feeling awkward. "Do you need someone to talk to?"

She waved a hand. "Don't worry about me. I have a strong faith and an appointment with the pastor here. I'll be fine. We'll be fine." Her face broke into a genuinely beautiful smile. "God's good even when times are hard."

"That's…true." And he wasn't just saying it. Maybe it was time for a change. Maybe he needed to not only get to church each week, but get right with God. "You've made me think," he said to Fiona. "I appreciate that."

"Sure, Sam. Nice talking to you."

The obvious ending of their conversation turned on

a light bulb for him: his "find Mindy a mom" campaign was going to be harder than he thought. Because right here in front of him was a perfect woman. Exactly what he would have wanted, had he filled out an order form.

And he had zero interest in her, romantically.

She pushed back her chair, holding out a hand to briskly shake his, and he could tell she felt the same way about him, so there was no guilt. There might even be a friendship, one of these days; they seemed to have some things in common. "Your kids are welcome to swim in my pool anytime," he said. "Mindy would love the company."

"Thanks, that's nice of you." She smiled at him, but her mind was clearly elsewhere. Her eyes held pain and secrets, and Sam resolved to get Daisy on the case.

He walked around for a while, enjoying the companionship of old friends, watching the kids run around in small packs, relishing another piece of pie. But something was missing: he couldn't find Susan. Mindy was still with Daisy, who hadn't seen Susan in a while.

Finally he thought to text Susan, but when he pulled out his phone and looked at it, he saw her message.

He frowned. She'd gone home? How, when she'd ridden over with him?

Sam asked around to see whether anyone had noticed her leaving. "I think she walked," a teenager told him offhandedly.

Walked home? That was close to three miles, mostly on deserted country roads, and darkness was falling. Not good.

He shot her a text: Where are you?

She didn't answer.

He turned to find his mother-in-law at his elbow. "How did you like Fiona?" she asked.

"Can you watch over Mindy tonight and make sure she gets home?"

"Of course!" A wide smile spread over her face. "You liked her, then? Are you taking her home?"

Had she lost her mind? Sam shook his head distractedly. "Fiona is lovely, and we have nothing going on romantically. She seems to need a friend, so if you're wanting to help her out, that's probably the direction to go. Introduce her to some of the local women, something like that."

"But if you're not going to take Fiona home," she asked unhappily, "then why are you leaving?"

"Susan walked home, and I need to check on her."

Helen put a hand on her hip, her forehead wrinkling. "Now, why would anyone do something like that? That's just strange."

He ignored the judgment. "I'll see you when you get home with Mindy," he said, turning toward the parking lot.

"But you'll miss the fireworks!" Helen sounded truly distressed. "That woman is a terrible influence on you. She's not even patriotic!"

"Later, Helen," he called over his shoulder.

After catching Mindy long enough to explain that she was to leave with her grandparents—which appeared to be fine with her, she was having such a good time with all the kids to play with—Sam got in his truck and started driving, thinking about what Helen had said.

Susan *was* different. She was independent and outspoken and didn't always say the proper thing.

But as for patriotism... Sam thought of her interactions with the older veterans and chuckled. She'd had those guys eating from the palm of her hand. She was every bit a proud American, as evidenced by the words on her obviously well-worn T-shirt.

He drove slowly along the country road, windows open. A gentle breeze brought the smells of hay and fresh-plowed soil that had always been part of his homeland experience. Crickets chirped, their music rising and falling, accompanied by a throaty chorus of frogs as he passed a small farm pond.

The sky was darkening, and up ahead, he saw the moon rise in a perfect circle, like a large round coin in the sky.

Even with the moonlight, it was still too dark. Too dark for a young woman to be out alone, a woman unfamiliar with the roads. Could Susan have gotten lost? Could something bad have happened to her?

As he arrived at Main Street in downtown Rescue River, concern grew in his heart. Where was she? Had something happened? He'd been studying the dark road the whole way and hadn't seen her, but could she have fallen into a ditch or been abducted?

Finally he spotted a petite form just sinking onto a bench, a couple of buildings down from the Chatterbox Café. Susan.

She was taking off her sandals and studying one foot, and when he stopped the truck in front of her, she looked up.

She wasn't as classically beautiful as Fiona. Her hair was coming out of its neat ponytail, and her shoulders slumped a little.

He'd never been so glad to see anyone in his life.

He jumped out of the truck and strode over to her. "What were you thinking, walking home?"

She squinted up at him. "Umm…I was tired?"

"You walked two miles on rough country roads. Of course you're tired." He sat down beside her and gestured toward the foot she'd been examining. "What happened?"

"Blister," she said. "I'll live."

He sighed and shook his head. "Wait here a minute."

He trotted over to his truck, fumbled in the glove box and returned with the small first-aid kit he always carried. "Let me see that."

"Why am I not surprised that you have a first-aid kit?" she asked, but she let him take her foot on his lap.

The skin had broken and the blister was a large, angry red. He opened an antibiotic wipe and cleansed it carefully, scolding himself internally for enjoying the opportunity to touch her delicate foot.

"Ow!" She winced when the medicine touched the broken skin.

"Sorry." He patted her ankle. "Now we'll bandage you up."

He rubbed antibiotic ointment over the hurt spot and pressed on a bandage. "There," he said. He kept a loose grip on her foot, strangely reluctant to let it go.

Without the daytime bustle, Main Street felt peaceful. The streetlights had come on. Overhead were leafy trees, and beyond them, stars were starting to blink in the graying sky.

Down the street, the lights of the Chatterbox Café clicked off.

Susan looked at him with eyes wide and vulnerable

above a forced-looking smile. "Didn't you want to stay and talk with the wife Helen picked out for you?"

He felt one side of his mouth quirk up. "Was it that obvious?"

"Kinda. She seemed really nice."

"Yes, she is." He squeezed her foot a little tighter. "And no, I didn't want to stay. Not when I realized you were missing."

"I'm sorry."

"Hey." He touched her chin. "I wanted to come find you."

"How come?"

The question hung in the air between them. He looked at her lips.

Which parted a little, very prettily, and then Susan pulled her foot off his lap and twisted it around her other leg, looking nervous. "Sam…"

He brushed back a strand of hair that had tumbled down her forehead. Her skin felt soft as a baby's.

He breathed in, and leaned forward, and pressed his lips to hers.

Susan's heart pounded faster than a rock-and-roll drumbeat as Sam kissed her. Just a light brush of the lips took her breath away.

She lifted her hands, not sure whether she meant to stop him or urge him on, and her hands encountered the rough stubble on his cheek. Intrigued, she stroked his face, getting to know the planes and angles she'd been studying, without intending to, for days.

What did this mean? And why, oh why, did it have to feel so good? She drew in a sharp breath, almost a gasp, because he hadn't moved away. His handsome face was still an inch from hers, and this felt like every forbidden dream she'd ever had, coming true.

"Close your eyes," he said in his bossy way that, right now, didn't bother her in the least.

And he leaned closer and pressed his lips to hers again, just a little harder.

Susan's heart seemed to expand in her chest, reaching out toward his. Everything she'd admired about him, everything she'd been drawn to, seemed alive in the air around them.

There was a booming sound, a bunch of crackling pops, and she jerked back as Sam lifted his head. At the same time, they both realized what it was.

"Fireworks!" Sam exclaimed, a grin crossing his face. "How appropriate." He studied her tenderly. "Was that okay?"

Was it okay that he'd rocked her world? Was it okay that his lightest touch made her feel as if she was in love with him? "When I kissed my boss, I felt fireworks," she joked awkwardly to cover the tension she felt.

He looked stricken as the fireworks continued to create a display above their heads, green and red and gold. "Oh, Susan, I'm sorry."

"For what?"

"I was forgetting for a minute that you're an employee. That was completely inappropriate."

Amidst the popping and booming sounds, his words were too much to process. She was still reeling from how his kiss had made her feel, and she couldn't think why he was looking so upset.

Unless he wished he hadn't done it.

"Come on," he said, and pulled her to her feet. He didn't hold her hand, though; as soon as he was sure she was steady, he stepped a foot away. Too far! her heart called, wanting her to grab on to him. But she squashed the feelings down.

A minute later, she was in his truck and headed to his house. He drove like a silent statue, a muscle twitching in his jaw.

He pulled up in the driveway and stared straight ahead. "We'll talk tomorrow. Again, I apologize."

She looked at him, confused. Clearly she was being dismissed.

Was he angry at himself for having let his feelings go out of control? Did he even *have* feelings, or had that been just a guy thing, driven by testosterone rather than his heart?

She wanted to ask him about it, but suddenly, there was no closeness available for such a discussion.

And she was just a little too fragile to push it tonight, when her lips still tingled from his kiss, her fingertips still remembered the way his strong jaw had felt beneath them.

She'd have to face what had just happened, but not tonight.

The next morning, Sam was in his office trying to put out a few fires before his employee party when there was a hesitant knock on the door.

"Come in." He tried to ignore the way his heart leaped, but it was next to impossible. His heart knew it was Susan; Mindy wouldn't have knocked, and who else would be in the house? And his heart was very interested in being near the woman who'd kissed him back so sweetly last night.

Sure enough, it was her. Dressed in another faded

red, white and blue T-shirt and short jeans and wearing a worried frown. When their eyes met, she blushed and looked away. "We have a problem."

"What's wrong?"

"I just talked to Pammy. The one who's doing the kids' entertainment for the party? Only...she can't do it."

"What do you mean?" He felt relieved that she was all business this morning. Maybe that would help his racing pulse slow down.

"They had a death in the family and they all have to rush down to West Virginia to the funeral. And since it's a family-run business, that's pretty much everyone."

He blew out a breath, thinking of all his employees with families. They looked forward to this event as a time when they could kick back and relax, bring the kids, knowing it would be fun for everyone.

"Any ideas?" he asked. Because if there was one thing he'd learned about Susan, it was that she was good in an emergency.

"As a matter of fact, yes!" A smile broke out on her face, and Sam's mouth went dry. When she was excited about something, she was pretty much irresistible.

"What's the idea?" he asked, his voice a little hoarse.

"Let's get dogs from Troy's rescue to come be the entertainment."

"No." He shook his head. "That won't work."

"Why not?"

"Dogs, instead of a clown and a dunking tank and carnival games?"

She waved a hand impatiently. "Kids like real things better than all that," she said. "If you don't believe me, ask Mindy which she'd rather see."

"Oh, I know what Mindy would choose," he said, mock-glaring at her. "She's been on me nonstop about getting a dog. It's almost like someone put her up to it." He stepped closer.

Susan's eyes darkened and her breathing quickened. "That's an argument for another day," she said primly. "And it proves my point: kids love dogs."

"It's not safe," he explained, stepping back from her dangerous appeal and half sitting on the edge of his desk. "There are liability issues. If someone got bitten, it would be on Hinton Enterprises, and bad PR as well. And more than that, I like to take care of my employees, not put them at risk."

Susan nodded, sinking down to perch on his leather client seat. "Can't we post a warning? And Troy wouldn't bring any dogs who weren't friendly."

Sam shrugged. "A warning might solve the liability issue, but…"

"But you don't like change," she said.

He opened his mouth to argue and then closed it again. "You're right, I don't. We've had Pammy do the kids' entertainment for ten years."

"But sometimes, change has to happen," she said gently. "Pammy can't help it that she's unavailable this year. Her grandma passed."

Troy felt like a heel. "I'll send flowers," he said, making a note to himself.

"Write down, 'Puppy for Mindy's birthday,'" she suggested.

He looked up at her. She was messing with him! "Don't you ever take anything seriously?"

"Yes. Like the fact that an only child like Mindy needs a pet."

"We don't have time for a puppy."

"People manage!" She waved a hand. "There are dog walkers. Doggie day cares. Daisy was saying that new woman in town, your special friend, might start one."

"We're losing focus. Isn't there an easier way to entertain kids? You're the expert in that. Think of something!" He stood and started pacing back and forth in front of his desk, filled with restless energy.

"Yes, and I had an expert idea," she said. "The dogs. Let me go with it, Sam. It'll work great, you'll see. You won't be disappointed."

She didn't get it, how important this business, these people, were to him. How he wanted things to stay the same for them, wanted them to be safe. He stopped directly in front of her, crossing his arms. "No."

"It's community service," she teased, cocking her head to one side. "Helping animals. Doesn't that make Hinton Enterprises look good?" She edged neatly out of the chair and went around behind it, creating a barrier between them. She leaned on the back of the chair, her eyes sparkling.

He frowned away the energy her smile evoked in him. "You sure you didn't have training as a lawyer?"

"Just four or five dogs," she said, ignoring his question. "And Troy would be there the whole time."

Sam felt as if he was losing a business negotiation, which never happened. But then again, he never sat across the table from a negotiator like Susan.

She raised an eyebrow at him. "Embrace the change, Sam. Sometimes, it can be a good thing."

He sighed. "If Troy can be there the whole time," he said grudgingly, "I guess we can give it a try."

Chapter 8

Susan slipped out midmorning and power-walked to the park in downtown Rescue River. Hopefully, the materials to set up for Sam's work picnic would be here. Hopefully, Daisy would be, too, to help her.

Hopefully, Sam wouldn't be anywhere nearby.

She didn't need the distraction of her boss, kisser *extraordinaire*.

Last night had been amazing, wonderful. Her heart, which she kept so carefully guarded beneath her mouthy exterior, had shown itself to be the marshmallow that it was and melted.

And as a result, Sam's coldness and dismissal afterward had bludgeoned said heart.

Back to the old way, the independent way. She'd decided it last night, and kept herself busy putting out fires and getting the new kids' entertainment organized this morning. Their little argument had fanned the attraction flames a bit, but she'd stayed businesslike and she was proud of it.

As she got to the park, she was glad to see that the large tent was up and the tables there. Sam spared no expense for his workers, but at the same time, he didn't want it to be overly fancy. He just wanted everyone to feel comfortable and have fun. So her job was to add a touch of down home to the whole thing.

"Hey!" Daisy strolled toward her, yawning. "Where's the coffee?"

Knowing her friend, Susan had stopped at the Chatterbox and picked up two cups. "Here's yours, black with sweetener." She handed it over.

Daisy sank down on a bench beside the tent while Susan opened all the boxes.

"Here's our centerpieces," Susan said, holding up a bunch of kids' tractors. "Sam had me order enough so that every kid can take one home. We'll march them along the green runners so it looks like they're, you know, on a farm."

"Sweet." Daisy took a long drink of coffee.

And it *was* sweet. Sam was good to his employees. An amazing boss, an amazing man. A real catch.

Just not for her.

To distract herself from the sudden ache in her heart, Susan looked around. There was a father and son tossing a softball while a nearby mom spread a red-and-white plastic tablecloth over the picnic table. At one of the park's pavilions, two pregnant women sprawled on benches while their husbands fired up the park's grills and a couple of babies played at their feet.

And there was Fiona, the new mom in town, pushing her youngest on the swings while her other three children kicked a ball nearby.

Susan had talked to her mom this morning. Apparently Donny was doing well at camp, but her mom sounded not so great. Surprisingly lonely. She'd even asked about how Susan was doing and how she liked her new job, whether she needed anything. It was an uncharacteristically maternal call, and Susan wondered what was going on with her mother.

Thinking about her family made her miss them. Susan sighed. "Holidays can be hard for us single folks."

Daisy didn't answer, and when Susan glanced over, she saw that her friend's eyes were filled with tears.

"What's wrong, honey?" Susan asked, sinking down onto the bench beside her.

Daisy shook her head. "I'm so tired of being single, but I just can't get into dating."

"Not even Dion?"

Daisy stared at her as if she'd grown two heads. "No!"

"Why not?"

"We're friends. I don't want to mess up a good friendship by trying to go romantic."

"But friendship is a good basis—"

"No way."

"Keep praying about it," Susan said, because obviously her friend wasn't open to discussing the topic further, "and I will, too."

"Pray about yourself while you're at it," Daisy advised, "because you and Sam have some major vibes going on between you."

Heat climbed into Susan's cheeks. "It's obvious?"

"To me, it is, because I know both of you so well,"

Daisy said. "What's going on between the two of you, anyway?"

Susan contemplated telling her best friend about the kiss. For about ten seconds. But Daisy was protective of her brother and Susan wasn't at all sure about how she felt about it, so she clamped her jaw shut and got busy unpacking tractor centerpieces.

"Susan? Are you seriously not going to answer?"

"Nothing's going on," Susan said firmly.

A welcome distraction came in the form of Xavier, who jumped into Daisy's lap. A minute later, Angelica appeared with baby Emmie in her arms, breathless. "Hey, guys," she said.

"Where's Mindy?" Xavier asked.

"She'll be here soon, with her dad. Which makes me think we'd better get more done."

"Oh, Sam will be worrying, all right," Daisy said.

"Hey," Angelica said. "Is Mindy all set for camp?"

"I think so," Susan said. "It's next weekend, right?"

"That's right," Angelica said, "but when I mentioned it to Sam, he didn't seem to know anything about it."

"I told him," Susan said. "He wrote the check. I'll talk to him about it." But uneasiness clenched her stomach. The camp was one Xavier was attending for a week, with Angelica, and they had a special program where younger siblings and relatives could come for a weekend. She and Angelica had discussed it, and while she'd explained the details to Sam, he'd been distracted. She'd been surprised when he said it was okay.

Hopefully, this was just a little misunderstanding she could clear up quickly when he arrived, and then she could fade into the background and refill bowls of potato chips and play with Mindy.

They soon had the tent decorated in patriotic, farm decor. Just in time, because the caterers arrived to put out the food, all-American hot dogs and hamburgers, plus a taco bar and tamales.

She and Daisy sank down at a picnic table with cold drinks.

"I'm sweating already," Daisy said.

"Me, too." Susan fanned herself with a napkin.

"Any thoughts of getting work done?" came a stern voice behind them.

The hairs on Susan's arms stood on end. Sam.

Daisy raised her eyebrows at Susan, ignoring her brother. "Somebody's cranky. Wonder what's wrong with him?"

He kissed me and he regrets it. Susan shrugged. "Who knows?"

Mindy, who'd come with Sam but stopped at the swings where Xavier was, ran up to them. "Daddy, Xavier says I can ride with them to camp. And I'm going to stay in a tent!"

Sam looked down at her and then his face focused. "Camp? What camp?"

Mindy looked worriedly at Susan. "I'm going to that camp with Xavier. Right?"

"Right," she said reassuringly, and turned to Sam. Best to get this over with now. "It's that special-needs camp. Xavier goes every summer, as a cancer survivor. They have a program for kids with limb differences. We talked about this."

"No, we didn't. When is it and where?"

"It's next weekend, or at least, Mindy's part is only for the weekend. In West Virginia."

Sam's eyes widened. "She's not going to sleepaway camp in West Virginia. She's five!"

"Daddy! I'm almost six!" Mindy drew a big six in the air to make sure everyone understood.

Susan squatted down. "I'll explain it all to Daddy. You run and keep Xavier company, okay?"

"Okay," Mindy said doubtfully, and ran off.

Sam's face was tight and closed as she led him over to a quieter part of the park.

"We talked about this. It's a done deal." Even as she spoke, guilt clutched at her. Sam had been distracted with Helen's arrival, the evening after they'd gone to the lake. He'd gotten a phone call when she'd been explaining the details, and he'd signed the check amidst a lot of other household expenses.

He shook his head. "I didn't okay her sleeping away. She's way too young."

"They have programs for younger kids who go with relatives. Angelica's going." She paused for emphasis. "Sam, I think it'll be good for her. She needs to meet other kids with limb differences."

"No."

Susan drew in her breath and counted to ten. "She's going to be very disappointed. She wants to go with Xavier. And Angelica will be there the whole time."

"Parents can go?"

She nodded, knowing exactly what he would say.

"Then I'll go."

"Sam." She touched his arm. "Troy and Angelica think it'll be best if you don't go."

"Troy and Angelica aren't Mindy's parents. And neither are you."

That truth hit her like a whip to the heart. She needed

to watch herself, because her feelings as Mindy's nanny had begun to overflow their professional boundaries. It was all too easy to love the little girl. Easy to care too much about Mindy's dad, too, who was currently glaring at her, intent on putting her in her place.

She swallowed her hurt feelings. "I know that! I'm just someone who cares about her and has a role taking care of her. And who knows what kids with special needs, need."

He glared. "If I'm not going, then Mindy can't, either."

She threw up her hands, exasperated. "Fine. It's your money you're wasting. And it's you who can explain to Mindy why she can't go. I'm going to..." She looked around. "Set up the salt and pepper shakers at a perfect angle because I'm sure the control-freak boss of Hinton Enterprises will come in and redo it if I don't."

She spun and stormed into the tent.

Soon Sam was back in charming boss mode, and Susan watched him and marveled at his self-control. He'd been furious at her five minutes ago, but now he was all professional.

And it was clear his employees loved him. They crowded around him, and teased, but with respect; they listened to everything he had to say.

There was a moment when she thought the dog thing was going to be a disaster. Just when he'd stood to make his traditional speech, a squirrel had run past the dog crates and the dogs had gone haywire with barking, drowning out whatever Sam was saying.

But Sam responded graciously, with a joke, while Troy got the dogs under control, and then Sam continued his speech without a hitch.

Several people expressed interest in adopting dogs. And the local paper had come to cover the event and snapped more pictures of the dogs than anything else. Undoubtedly, there'd be a feel-good story featuring Hinton Enterprises in the paper tomorrow.

The downside, if you were looking at it from Sam's point of view, was that Mindy fell in love with a little black-and-white mutt with a bandage on one leg. While Mindy cradled it, Troy explained to Sam how it was non-shedding and, at three years old, already house-trained. "It'll probably always have a limp, though," Troy had said.

"It's got a hurt paw, like me," Mindy had said, cuddling the dog.

Susan's heart squeezed, and she looked up at Sam. The raw love for his little girl that shone out of his eyes almost hurt. She had a feeling that Mindy would end up with that little dog as a birthday present.

As the party went on, Sam seemed to let go of control a little bit and relax. The children played with the dogs and enjoyed the park and the play equipment, running hard, making up games. That gave the adults space to linger over their plates of food, talking and laughing. Aside from a few teenagers, no one seemed to have their cell phones out.

It was an old-fashioned type of picnic that could have just as easily taken place fifty years ago. A perfect kind of event for an old-fashioned, close-knit community like Rescue River, and Susan was proud of her part in organizing it.

Until the topic of Sam's being single came up. "We think Mr. Hinton needs a girlfriend," said Eduardo, a good-looking, thirtysomething groundsman at Hinton

Enterprises. He sometimes moonlighted for Sam, helping with the landscaping around the house, and seemed
to hold a privileged position among the Hinton workers; right now, he was sitting at a table with Sam and
five or six other employees.

Sam's father, who'd been sitting at an adjoining table
with Susan and Daisy, spoke up. "That's exactly what
he needs. But not just a girlfriend, a wife."

"And a mama for his little girl," one of the older sec-
retaries said.

"Hey, what about Susan?" someone said, and the
group at the picnic table turned to look at her. "She's
single, and she already takes care of Mindy."

"Good call," Eduardo said. *"Muy bonita."*

Totally mortified, Susan stared at the ground. She
knew she should come up with some kind of a joke to
make the moment go by easily, but for the life of her,
she couldn't think of one.

"You people need to stick to business, and so do I."
Sam's voice was strained.

"But Daddy," Mindy chimed in, climbing up into
Sam's lap, "I *do* want a mommy!"

The images evoked by those sweet words made Susan's cheeks flame and her heart ache with longing. To
be wanted, needed, cherished. To finally have a real
home.

She stole a glance at Sam's clenched jaw. Obviously,
his employees' suggestions hadn't induced the same images and longings in him. And he wasn't finding the
gentle jokes funny, either.

If only the ground would open up and swallow her.

Sam stood under a giant oak tree in the Rescue River

Park, talking to a group of five or six longtime employees who didn't seem to want to leave.

Even while he listened and laughed with them, he couldn't help watching Susan.

Apparently, she'd recovered just fine from that awkward moment with his employees. She was tying garbage bags and helping to carry heavy food trays to the truck. When a little boy ran up crying, she squatted down to listen, then took his hand and walked back to the tent to find the tractor he'd left on a table.

As he watched, Eduardo approached her, spoke for a minute, then gave her a friendly handshake that, to Sam's eyes, went on a little bit too long and was accompanied by a little too much eye contact.

He tamped the jealousy down. He didn't want Susan as a long-term part of his life, so why feel bad when other men admired her? She was totally inappropriate for him. Just witness this whole ridiculous camp situation. His blood pressure rose just thinking of Mindy going to camp.

Marie would never have allowed it.

But Marie's gone, and you have to move on.

That new voice inside him was unfamiliar and unwelcome, but Sam was honest enough to know that it spoke truth. He had to stop focusing on Marie, had to let her go.

But if he did that, would his life be as it had been for the past twenty-four hours—crazy and emotional? Going from the intense excitement of kissing Susan to the low of feeling guilty, like a bad boss hitting on his employee? Angry about the camp. Embarrassed by his workers' jokes.

He didn't want such an exciting life, couldn't handle it. He wanted life on an even keel. Stable. Comfortable.

As he bid goodbye to the final couple of workers, his father approached. He'd stayed in the background during the picnic, letting Sam have center stage, but Sam had been conscious of him, as always. Though his father's health didn't permit him to run Hinton Enterprises anymore, he'd started the company and cared about its success, and Sam always respected his opinions.

"What did you think?" he asked his dad.

His father clapped him on the back. "Another good picnic," he said. "You have a way with the workers. They like you."

"Thanks." He knew what his father wasn't saying; the workers liked Sam better than they'd liked his father. Personality difference, and maybe the struggles of starting something from the ground up. His father wasn't an easy man to get along with.

Sam knew he wasn't always easy, either, but he at least could laugh at himself—usually—and listen to other people's ideas, talents his father had never mastered.

Since his father was so hard to please, his approving remarks about the event felt good.

They turned together to stroll back toward the almost-empty tent. Just in time to see Mindy run to Susan, hug her legs and get lifted into her arms.

"Looks like those two are close," Mr. Hinton remarked.

Sam nodded slowly. "It sure does."

"You worried about that?" Mr. Hinton asked.

"A little," Sam admitted. "But Mindy needs women

in her life. She's attached to Daisy, and now to Angelica, but those two aren't always around. Susan fills in the gaps, that's all."

"Are you sure that's all?" His father's thick eyebrows came together, and though he was a good head shorter than Sam, his expression was enough to make Sam feel ashamed, as if his father had seen that moment under the street lamp.

"It has to be," he said. "Things couldn't work between us."

Mr. Hinton nodded, looking relieved. "I didn't think she was your type, but I was starting to wonder. Figured you'd do the right thing." He shook his head. "Back in my day, races didn't mix. Oh, we always had a lot of different colors in Rescue River, but for marrying, they stuck to themselves. Times might be changing, but it's hard for me to keep up."

"Dad," Sam said automatically. "What a person looks like doesn't matter, you know that. We're all of the same value to God."

His father frowned at him. "Never thought to hear you spouting religion at me."

Sam laughed. "Surprise myself sometimes," he said.

As his father walked off, Sam sank down on a park bench rather than interrupting the moment between Mindy and Susan. He needed to think.

He probably needed to pray, too, but this wasn't the time or the place.

Still, under the stars, he thought about his goal of finding a mother for Mindy and made a decision.

He wouldn't try so hard to replace Marie anymore. It wasn't working, and it wasn't possible.

But a woman like Susan wasn't possible, either. He wasn't the man to handle it.

Instead, he'd focus on being the best single dad he could be.

People did that. Look at his employee, Eduardo; he'd been a single parent for years. And several other dads at Mindy's school were going it alone.

Anyway, Susan was way too young for him.

He'd go forward single and let Mindy's nurturing needs be filled by his female relatives, by teachers, by the church.

It wasn't what Marie had wanted, and looking up into the starry sky, he shot an apology her way. "I'm sorry, Marie," he whispered. "I don't think I can keep my promise, at least not right now."

He let out a huge sigh as sadness overwhelmed him.

The quest to remarry had helped him get by, had given him a goal. Without it, emptiness and loneliness pushed at him like waves lapping the shore.

He had to find his center again, his stability. Had to get right with God. Had to learn to go on alone.

It was the only thing he could do, but it didn't feel good. Just for a minute, he let his head sink down into his hands and mourned the loss of a dream.

The next morning, Sam broke all of his own Sunday morning rules, flipping on a mindless TV show for Mindy and handing her a donut. Then he ushered Susan into his office.

She was wearing close-fitting black pants and a jade-green sleeveless shirt that showed off her tanned, shapely arms. Jade earrings swung from her ears, giving her a carefree vibe. But her expression was closed tight.

During the night, he'd gotten over some of his anger about the camp situation. He probably hadn't listened carefully enough to what she'd been telling him. Half the time, when Susan talked to him, he got caught up in her honeysuckle perfume and her shiny hair and her lively, sparkling dark eyes; it wasn't surprising that he might have missed some of the details she'd shared with him.

Now that he'd made a new commitment to staying single, maybe he could pay more attention to what she had to say.

And today, he just had to keep a cool, professional distance, make her see reason and get her on his side, so that she could help him explain to Mindy that she wouldn't be going to camp.

"Sit down," he said, ushering her to the same chair she'd sat in the day he'd interviewed her. Thinking of that day almost made him chuckle. When he'd suspected she'd be a handful to work with, he hadn't been wrong.

She perched warily on the edge of the seat. "We only have half an hour before we should leave for church," she said. "Or at least, I'm going to church. Are you?"

He nodded. "There'll be time. He spread his hands and gave her a friendly-but-impersonal smile. "I guess when I agreed to Mindy going to camp, I wasn't really listening," he said. "I'm sorry about that, but I really do think she's too young to go."

Susan nodded, and for the first time he noticed that there were dark circles under her eyes. "I lay awake thinking about it, and I want you to know I feel bad about what happened. I should have made sure I had your full attention about such an important decision."

Relief washed over him. This wasn't going to be as hard as he'd feared. "I'm glad you see it my way."

"Well, but I don't exactly see it your way," she said, flashing a smile at him. "You were wrong, too, not to pay attention about your child's summer plans. Now Mindy has a spot at the camp and some other child doesn't. It wouldn't be right to back out."

He hadn't thought of that. "I'll pay for the place," he said, waving his hand in an effort to dismiss her concern. Wanting to dismiss it himself, and not quite succeeding.

"It's not just that, Sam," she said quietly. "Mindy needs this camp. She needs to go where other kids with limb differences are. She needs to see what's possible for her and what's positive. For example, why doesn't she have an artificial limb?"

"We tried that when she was little. She hated it."

"From what I've read, that's common," she said. "But now that she's a little older, she might want one. And I'm sure the technology has advanced. It's something she can learn about at the camp, get a feel for it, see some kids with artificial limbs and others managing without."

He had to admit, Susan had a point. "In that case, maybe she should go. And—" he said to cut off Susan's expression of victory. "I should go, too."

She bit her lip and shook her head, looking regretful. "I thought of that. I mean, of getting you a space there, too. The problem is that the camp is entirely full. There are no more spaces for adults. I checked online last night, and they texted me a confirmation this morning. No more space."

He frowned. "Then she can't go."

"Sam." Susan leaned forward. "Why don't you want her to, really?"

The question floated in the air.

"I wish you hadn't talked to her about it so much," he heard himself blustering, knowing he was avoiding giving her an answer.

She nodded slowly. "I'm sorry. I should have made sure you understood what you were signing." Her voice was contrite. "And the last thing I want to do is cause Mindy to be disappointed. I...I really have no vested interest in this happening, Sam. For what mistakes I've made, I apologize."

Her accepting responsibility took the wind out of his sails. "I made mistakes, too," he said grudgingly. "I get too caught up in my work and don't pay attention to other people enough. You're...not the first person who's told me that."

"Anyone can get distracted," she said with a shrug. "So you're not perfect."

"That's it?" he asked. "You're not going to yell at me?"

She looked amused. "No. Should I?"

He settled back and stared at her, then down at his desk. That was new to him. Susan admitted her own mistakes, and she accepted that he made mistakes, too.

Hashing things out with someone like Susan, openly flawed, was actually a little more comfortable than arguing with someone practically perfect, like Marie.

Guilt washed over him. The very thought that there was something as good as, even better than, being with Marie seemed disloyal.

"Hey." Susan grabbed an old ruler that was sitting on

the edge of his desk and gave his hand a light, playful whack. "What's going on in there? You never answered my question. Why are you so afraid to let Mindy go to camp with her aunt and cousin?"

He grabbed the ruler, pointed it at her and met her eyes. "I do have my reasons, young lady."

She lifted an eyebrow, waiting.

"The main reason is…" He started, then paused.

"Spill it."

He looked out the window, watching the leaves rustle in the slight breeze. "The main reason is that I don't like her to be so far out of my sight."

"Out of your control, hmm?" She was laughing at him. "Get used to it, Dad. She's growing up."

He smiled ruefully. "I'm not ready for that."

"Are you really going to be so lonely?" she asked in a teasing voice. "If it's too much to face alone, I can keep you company."

"Oh, is that so?" His whole body felt sharp with interest and surprise and…something else.

A pretty pink blush flamed across her cheeks. She picked up his tape holder and studied it with intense interest.

His hand shot out to cover hers. "A date? Maybe at Chez La Ferme?"

She dropped the tape holder and tried to pull her hand back, but he held on until she met his eyes.

"Are you asking me out?"

"Would you go?"

Their eyes met and held. Their hands were pressed together, too, and it didn't seem like either of them was breathing.

Then she pulled back and looked away, and he let her go.

"Now it's you who hasn't answered my question," he said, barely recognizing his own throaty voice. "Will you go out with me?"

"I don't...I don't know."

He leaned forward, not sure if he should press his advantage or retract the question. He knew what he *wanted* to do, but was it the right thing? "I shouldn't be asking you out when you're an employee. I don't mean to put any pressure on you, at all. You have your job whether you say yes or no. Nothing would change."

Her dark eyes flashed up to meet him. "Thanks for that," she said. "I appreciate your being so careful, considering that I'm just a temporary nanny. And...well, it's true that I don't have plans for the weekend."

Triumph surged through him, but he tamped it down.

"And I've never actually eaten at Chez La Ferme."

"So what you're saying is..." He prompted.

"Yes," she said, her voice a little bit breathy. "Yes, I'll go out with you."

And she stood, spun and hurried out of the room, leaving Sam to wonder what on earth he'd been thinking to ask Susan out.

Chapter 9

The next Friday afternoon, Susan climbed the stairs to her over-the-garage apartment, arguing with Daisy the whole way. Quiet Fern was following along, shaking her head.

"It doesn't make sense for me to get all dressed up. This is Sam! He's seen me in my sweats, in my ratty jeans, without makeup…"

"But you're going to Chez La Ferme," Fern said hesitantly. "That's super dressy, right?"

"Exactly!" Daisy said, her voice triumphant. "You can't wear ratty jeans to Chez La Ferme."

"They fired me once, what more can they do to me?" Susan asked as she opened the door. "Come on in. Not like I have a choice about it."

"I'm sorry, Susan," Fern said, looking stricken. "If you don't want us here…"

"Fern. You're fine. It's *her* I don't want." Susan flung an arm toward her best friend. "Because she's got some kind of an agenda that I don't share."

Daisy ignored her, walked over to the refrigerator and pulled out sodas.

"Make yourself at home, why don't you?" Susan said sarcastically. But the truth was, she was glad to have the other two women around. She was way too antsy about her date with Sam tonight.

Why had she offered to keep him company? Why had he jumped on the idea and upped the ante to a real date at Chez La Ferme? Maybe it was just something to do, and after all, he did sort of own the restaurant. Maybe this was all just business.

She'd run into Daisy at the library and made the mistake of confiding the reason for her anxiety. Daisy had taken one look at her and insisted on coming back to help her get dressed. Since Fern was leaving work at the same time, they'd talked her into coming along.

Now, Susan tore open a bag of BBQ potato chips and started pouring them into a bowl, only to have Daisy snatch the bag away. "No. Uh-uh. You're not eating those and then going on a date."

"Why not?" Susan asked.

Daisy and Fern looked at each other and burst out laughing.

"What?" Susan looked from one to the other.

"It's just," Fern said, still chuckling, "if you would happen to get close enough to kiss…"

"Your breath would reek like a third grader's," Daisy finished.

"We're not getting close enough to kiss," Susan said as heat climbed up her face.

"Here." Daisy found a bag of pretzels and tossed it to her. "Have these instead. Fern and I will eat the stinky chips."

"Well, actually," Fern said, blushing, "I think I'll stick to pretzels, too."

Daisy's eyebrows shot up. "Plans with Carlo tonight?"

"We like to watch movies on Friday nights, and it's my turn to pick."

"What are you watching?"

Fern grinned. "*Casablanca*. What's not to like? There's manly war drama for Carlo and romance for me."

"Fine," Daisy said, grabbing the bag of chips. "So I'm the only one without plans. I get the whole bag. Now, what are you wearing tonight?"

"I don't know." Susan looked at the pretzels but had no appetite. She took a sip of diet soda instead. "I have, like, one fancy dress, and I haven't worn it in a year at least. I don't know if it even fits."

"Let's see it," Daisy ordered.

Susan walked back to her bedroom and pulled out the turquoise silk. With a mandarin collar and buttons up the front, it fit snugly and had a perfectly modest hemline...until you noticed the slit that revealed a little leg.

But was that too dressy? This was Sam. She rummaged in her closet and pulled out a plain black skirt. She carried both garments out. "I'm thinking the skirt," she said.

Both Fern and Daisy said "no" at the same time.

"Wear the blue one," Daisy ordered.

"It's gorgeous," Fern agreed.

"But it's Sam, and it's Rescue River. Won't I feel way out of place?"

"You used to work at Chez La Ferme, right? Don't people dress up to go there?"

Susan thought back and nodded, reluctantly. Even Miss Minnie Falcon had worn a beaded dress when she'd come to the restaurant, and most of the men wore suits.

"What's Sam wearing?" Fern asked.

Susan shrugged. "I don't know." Truthfully, they hadn't seen much of each other since that weighted conversation that had led to this date. She wouldn't have thought they were on, except he'd sent her a text message confirming the time. And he'd washed his sleek black sports car and parked it in the driveway, so evidently they weren't going in her car. As if, Susan thought, giggling a little hysterically.

"I'll text him," Daisy offered.

"No!" Susan grabbed for her phone.

"Why not?"

"I don't want him to think I care what we wear!"

"Because…"

"Because I don't want it to seem like a real date!" Her voice broke on the last word and she sank down onto the couch, focusing on pinching a thread off the blue dress while she pulled herself together.

"Hey," Daisy said, coming to sit next to her. "You sound really upset. What's wrong?"

Susan swallowed the lump in her throat. "My dad sent me this dress because he said I had nothing decent to wear on dates with a real good prospect. So that's where I did wear it: on dates with my ex-fiancé."

"Oh." Daisy nodded.

"You were engaged?" Fern asked, her voice sympathetic.

Susan waved her hand impatiently. "Ancient history. It didn't work out because he wanted a dishrag of a wife. Like all businesspeople." She shot a glare at Daisy. "Like Sam, so don't go matching me up permanently with him."

"Who said anything about that?"

"Nobody!" Heat clamped into Susan's cheeks. Nobody had said anything about a permanent connection between her and Sam, so why had she mentioned it? What was she thinking?

"Don't you want to get married someday?" Fern asked quietly.

"No!" Susan said. "Marriage sucks the life out of women."

"It doesn't have to," Fern said. "I'm really looking forward to marrying Carlo."

Way to put your foot in your mouth, Susan. "I'm just going on my mom's example. I'm sorry," Susan apologized. "What you and Carlo have seems wonderful. But for me...for women in my family...marriage is the path to destruction."

"Nothing like being melodramatic," Daisy said, looking up from her phone.

"I'm not being melodramatic. I'm afraid I'll lose myself and then he'll leave! Just like what happened to my mom."

The comment hung in the air.

"Oooh," Fern said. "That does sound scary."

Daisy shook her head. "The past doesn't have to repeat itself. You're a completely different woman from your mom." Her phone buzzed and she glanced down at it. "Sam's wearing a suit, by the way."

"You asked him?" Susan practically shouted.

"So you should wear the blue dress. Go put it on, since you're not going to eat."

Susan drew in her breath and let it out in a sigh, then did what her friend said.

Buttoning the cuffs of a new dress shirt—cuff links would probably be excessive for a woman like Susan—Sam looked in the mirror and thought of his teary departure from Mindy just a few hours ago.

Oh, Angelica had comforted her, all too well. It made him realize how much Mindy needed a female figure in her life. And while he wanted to go forward with his plan to be single, this whole camp thing had put him back in doubt. Mindy needed a mom.

And there was the additional question: with Mindy gone, what was he supposed to do with himself this weekend? He didn't even get to go pick Mindy up because Troy was going to the camp to visit Xavier and had offered to bring Mindy home.

I'll keep you company, Susan had said in her throaty voice. He used water to tame his unruly hair and then decided he should shave after all, and took off the shirt so he wouldn't get anything on it. Man, he was acting like a teenager. He'd been on so many dates. Why was this one such a big deal?

Because it's Susan.

Susan, who was completely inappropriate for him. Susan, who wouldn't fall into line easily with any of his plans, for Mindy or otherwise. Susan, who was way too full of opinions and ideas of her own.

Susan, whose hair was like silk and whose laughter was like jazz music, rich and complex.

Susan, the very thought of whom made his heart rate speed up.

He had it bad.

Susan sat back in her soft and comfortable chair at Chez La Ferme. "You really want to hear that story?" she asked.

"I'm curious why your engagement ended, but if you don't want to talk about it, it's okay. I want this evening to be fun for you, not bringing up unpleasant memories."

"No, it's okay." Susan was surprised at how comfortable she felt. Oh, there'd been a few awkward moments at first, like when he'd come to her door. She'd seen Sam in a suit before, but tonight, knowing he'd dressed up for her, she found him devastatingly handsome.

And when he'd seen her, he'd offered a simple "You look great," but the way his eyes had darkened had sent the heat rushing to her cheeks.

Men didn't usually look at her that way, as if she was gorgeous. It took some getting used to, but…she *could* get used to it. Could learn to love it.

Even so, she'd gone into the meal with her guard up, determined to keep her distance. But Sam, with his pleasant, non-threatening conversation, gentle questions and self-deprecating jokes, had ruthlessly displayed his charm, causing her to drop that guard right back down.

"So, your engagement?" he prompted.

She'd keep it light, in line with the rest of the evening. "We actually broke up in Infinite. That super-exclusive department store in LA?"

He looked surprised. "I'm familiar with it."

"Well then, you can imagine the scene. Frank, his mother, the high-powered registry consultant and me, in their bridal registry salon." She squirmed, remembering. "Not my kind of place."

"You seem more the casual type."

"Exactly. But he and his mom and the consultant were trying to get me to register for formal china and super-expensive linens, stuff none of my friends could afford." She shook her head. "I saw my mom's life flashing before my eyes, you know? Trying to live up to somebody else's dream, trying to make a man happy when he couldn't be pleased."

He nodded, actually seeming interested in her rambling story. "What did you do?"

"Well, I...I'd read about how you can just have charitable donations at your wedding instead of gifts."

"That's usually something older couples do, right? People that already have what they need to set up housekeeping?"

She shrugged. "We had what we needed. Especially compared to the kids who could benefit from donations to Children International, which is the group I decided I wanted our guests to donate to. Frank made plenty of money."

"Okay..."

"So I...kind of stood up and said we were done at Infinite, that we weren't going to do a bridal registry after all."

He arched an eyebrow. "I guess that didn't go over well."

"It didn't." She reflected back on the scene, the horror on the saleswoman's face, the identical disapproval on Frank's and his mother's. "It wasn't that they didn't like charity, it was that such things weren't done among their friends. We ended up yelling—well, I did—and I got kicked out of Infinite, and Frank was totally embarrassed, and then he didn't want to marry me anymore."

"And were you heartbroken?" he asked, the tiniest twinkle in his eye.

"No." She'd been hurt, of course, and her mother had been furious, but mostly, she'd felt relieved. "It made me realize how different we were, and that I could never have made him happy." And she was done talking about it and wanted to change the subject. "I ate too much tonight. That was really good."

He waved for the check and smiled at her. "I overdid it, too. Maybe we need a walk?"

"Sure."

"Was everything okay, you guys?" Tawny, their server, asked as she handed Sam the check. "It's so great to see you guys here! I can't get over it. And I'm learning how to stand up for myself better, Susan. What you did to that one jerk really made a difference to me."

Sam's pen, signing the check, slowed down, and he glanced up at Susan and raised an eyebrow.

She felt herself blushing. "I'm glad," she said, smiling at the girl, who did seem a little more mature than at the beginning of the summer. "You did a good job tonight. You're a better waitress than I'll ever be."

"Aw, thank you!"

Tawny hurried away as Max, the restaurant owner and Susan's former boss, approached their table. "I trust everything was satisfactory, Mr. Hinton?"

He looked up, winked at her. "Ask the lady."

Which put her former boss in the position of having

to treat her as a valued customer. Ha! It felt so gratifying that she had to be gracious about it. "It was fantastic, Max. And it's a lot easier from this side of the table. Tawny's a good waitress."

After another minute of small talk, Sam made some subtle sign of dismissal and turned to Susan. "Ready for a walk?" he asked with just the faintest hint of wolfishness.

Suddenly, she wasn't sure, but she didn't want to let her nerves show. "Sounds good."

He held her elbow as she stood and helped her drape her lacy shawl around her shoulders. "How are your shoes?" he asked, looking down.

She held one out for him to see and was glad she'd painted her toenails to match her dress. "Wedges. Very comfortable."

"Good." He ushered her out of the restaurant with a hand on her back, nodding to a couple of patrons.

"You know," she said as soon as they were out in the parking lot, "we might've just started a whole lot of gossip."

"I didn't see Miss Minnie Falcon," Sam said with a smile.

"No, but that lady with the white updo? That's one of Miss Minnie's best friends. She'll describe us, and the news will be all over the Senior Towers." She frowned. "Not to mention that Tawny's a talker."

"You think people are that interested?"

"In you, yes. Everyone cares about who the local millionaire takes to dinner." By unspoken agreement, they'd started strolling away from town, down a dirt road between two fields, one planted with corn and one with soybeans. The rural fragrances blew on a warm breeze, pungent.

"I've taken a good number of guests to dinner there," Sam said. "It shouldn't be that noteworthy."

"Good to know I'm part of a crowd." She meant the remark to be a joke, but it came out sounding hurt.

He heard it, clearly, and put an arm around her shoulders. "I can truthfully say I've never had more fun." He squeezed her to his side. "You're a great conversationalist. I really like being with you."

"Thanks." Timidly, she put an arm around his waist, and her heart rate shot into the stratosphere, so she let it drop, pretending she'd just meant a quick hug. "I had a good time, too." She hesitated, then added, "I'm glad we're friends."

He turned to face her and took her hands in his. "Is that what we are, Susan? Friends?"

She looked up at him, noticing the way the moonlight highlighted the planes of his face. "Aren't we?"

He drew in a breath. "I'm…trying to figure that out." He looked to the side, across the cornfield, for a long moment and then looked back at her. "The thing is, I can't seem to get around this feeling I have for you. I've tried. I've told myself we're opposites, that it wouldn't work. I've tried to connect with women who are more my type. But it's not working, and I've got to admit to myself…" He leaned in. "I've got to admit, I'm falling in love with you."

Susan's heart fluttered madly, like a caged songbird, and she couldn't seem to catch her breath. This was the moment she'd never thought to have. Shouldn't she be thrilled? Why did she feel so confused?

She replayed what he'd said in her mind.

"I know you're your own woman and think your own way," he went on, "but I'm wondering if you might put some of that aside for Mindy and me."

The mention of Mindy pushed Susan's questions away for a minute. Mindy was a wonderful little girl, so easy to love.

But Sam… She looked up at him, biting her lip.

His smile told her he already knew what her reaction would be.

Because after all, when did the poor teacher from a messed-up family say no to the handsome millionaire?

He leaned down as if he was going to kiss her, and she took a giant step back. Back from him, and back from the confusion he was causing her.

Having her hands free from his felt better. Safer. She propped one on her hip. "So you overcame your scruples and fell in love against your better judgment? And I'm supposed to be grateful, and give up being my own woman, and put my own needs and plans aside?"

"I didn't mean it that way." Behind him, clouds skittered across the moon.

Her heart was still pounding, almost as if she was afraid. But she wasn't afraid, was she? She was angry. "Haven't you ever read *Pride and Prejudice*?"

Her tone pushed the romantic expression from his eyes. "No."

"Well, if you had, you'd know that this type of a declaration leaves a little bit to be desired," she snapped.

He shook his head as if to clear it. "Wait. I did something wrong, and I have no idea what it is."

"Seriously, Sam?" She put her hands on her hips. "You practically told me how bad you feel about…" She couldn't say it. Couldn't acknowledge that he'd said he was falling in love with her.

Couldn't *believe* it.

"Wait a minute." He put his hands on her shoulders, trapping her. "I'm not saying I was right to try to date a certain type of woman. I'm just saying that getting over my past tendencies has been a process. And at the other side of the process…" He bent his head to one side and a crooked smile came onto his face. "At the other side of the process, was you."

She bit her lip. "I wasn't just standing here waiting for you, Sam. I'm not going to fall into your arms just because you've figured a few things out."

"And I wouldn't expect you to." He squeezed her shoulders, then let them go and took her hand, urging her to walk a little further. "I know it'll take time and courtship and compromise. I'm just hoping we can do that, is all."

And drat if she didn't still hear that certainty in his voice. She could read his thoughts: *there's no way Susan could say no to me.*

She walked along the dirt road beside him, fuming. This was exactly why she didn't want to get involved with a man. All this scary emotion, all this confusion. All this feeling of hearing his words and trying to interpret what he meant. It made her stomach hurt.

Best to just be alone. She'd always said it, always known it about herself, and here was exhibit A.

She walked faster.

Until she felt a hand on her shoulder, pressing down, stopping her. "Susan. Wait."

"What?" she asked impatiently without turning around.

Sam stepped in front of her so she couldn't proceed. He looked down at her. "What I really want," he said, "is to kiss you."

She opened her mouth to refuse, and she was going to, for sure. But then she saw that a muscle was twitching under his eye.

Was he nervous?

Sam, the millionaire, nervous?

She cocked her head to one side, looking at him. He'd certainly put on a good show of being the dominant, successful male, but now that she studied him, she could see other signs. The hand he brushed through his hair. The slight uncertainty in his eyes. The way that when his hand reached out to touch her cheek, she could see it trembling just a little.

Now that was different. Sam was so accustomed to putting on a show of confidence in the business world that maybe he didn't know how to conduct himself in the personal world. Maybe he was used to pushing and acting cocky because that's what worked in doing deals. Maybe he didn't know how annoying that trait was when you were trying to declare your feelings to a woman.

"Do you…do you have any of those feelings for me, too?" He was still touching her cheek. And there was still a slight quiver in his hand. "Look, I don't pretend to understand you, or to know exactly how to make this work—"

She reached up and pulled his face down to hers and kissed him.

At least she started to. She started to assume the leadership role, but he quickly took it back, and their

connection was a give and take, sweet and intense and...
electrifying.

Susan didn't want it to stop, but she felt as if she
might pass out if it went on, so she took a step back and
stared at him. "Wow."

He nodded slowly, never letting go of her eyes.
"Wow."

Then he pulled her to his side and put an arm around
her shoulders and they walked together in the direction of the car.

Just like before, only everything was completely different.

Everything was new.

Driving home, the air in the car felt pregnant with
possibilities. Susan had never felt anything like those
moments with Sam. Not when she was engaged; not on
any other dates. Not ever.

And the slight bit of insecurity that he'd shown made
her feel as if she knew him better than ever before. That
she'd gotten to know another side of the arrogant millionaire. A side she liked better. A side she wanted to
know better.

When they pulled up to the house, she wondered if
he'd kiss her again. Wondered if her heart could stand
it, or if it would race right out of control.

But there was no chance to find out. Because there,
sitting in the glow of the headlights, was a familiar
figure. "Sam?" she asked, hearing the shrillness at her
own voice. "What on earth is my mother doing here?"

Chapter 10

Still reeling from the intensity of kissing Susan, from the emotions that swelled his heart, Sam climbed out of the car, looking from Susan to her mother and back again. Two more different women could scarcely be imagined.

Where Susan looked funky and individualistic, her mother looked perfectly proper. Hair in a neat, curly style, impeccable makeup, nails done.

He opened the car door for Susan and reached down to help her climb out. Sports cars weren't always the easiest for women to navigate in a dress.

"I'm sorry to just show up here," Mrs. Hayashi said, hurrying toward them, then stopping a few feet away. "I tried to call when I got in to Columbus, but I couldn't get through."

Susan fumbled in her purse for her phone. "I'm sorry, Mom. It was off."

"You've been out? Somewhere dressy?" There were questions in the older woman's voice. "What have you gotten on your shoes, Susie?"

Susan looked down, and so did Sam. "We took a walk," Susan said, coloring deeply.

The two women still hadn't hugged.

Mrs. Hayashi shot him a quick glance, and heat rose in Sam's face, too. Of course, a mother would wonder where her daughter's employer had taken her, and why, and what his intentions were.

If only he knew the answers.

The moon cast a silvery light, making jewels across Susan's dark hair. A chorus of cicadas chirped in rising and falling waves, punctuated by a dog barking somewhere down the road. New-mown grass sent its tangy summer smell from next door.

"Well, I'm forgetting my manners." The woman approached Sam and held out her hand. "I'm Madolyn Hayashi, Susie's mom. It was so kind of you to send me that airline ticket—"

"You *sent* her an *airline* ticket?" Susan's jaw dropped.

"I had the extra miles," Sam tried to explain. "And I overheard you talking about how you wanted to do that. I just thought I could speed it up a little and give you a nice surprise."

Susan shot him a glare, and he had the feeling that, if her mother weren't here, she'd have kicked him. "Mom," she said, "I was going to send you a ticket next week. I've been saving. You didn't have to take his."

"It was no problem." Sam wasn't sure what he'd done wrong. Was Susan upset that he'd sent her mom a ticket without telling her? Or was it that she didn't want her mom around?

"It was supposed to be for you to take a vacation," Susan went on. "For you to do something relaxing, now that you have a break from Donny."

"Oh, honey, I wanted to see you, not go to a spa!" Almost hesitantly, she stepped closer.

And then the two women lurched into a hug that started out awkward and then lingered long enough to get close. "I missed you so much," Mrs. Hayashi said finally, stepping back to hold Susan's hands. "Especially since Donny's away. I started thinking about things, things I've done wrong."

"Mom..." Susan's face twisted in a complicated expression of love and exasperation and sorrow.

"I know our relationship hasn't been the best, and I wanted to see you, to try to fix things. I had the means, thanks to your boss, so yesterday I just packed up my things and called the airlines, and today...here I am. You don't mind, do you?"

"Mom, I'm glad you're here," Susan said, her eyes shiny in that way Sam was learning meant she was trying not to cry. "If this is where you want to be, I'm glad you came."

Sam had been listening, arms crossed, and thinking at the same time. Susan's mother's words made him reflect about parenting: how quickly it all went by, how little time you really had with your kids. Look at Mindy, away at camp. The first of many times she'd wave and run away. She'd go farther and farther in the years to come.

Susan and her mother had a chance to renew their relationship, right now. And suddenly it came to him, brilliant in its perfect simplicity. "Tell you what," he said, "for once, you *can* have it both ways. There's a spa and resort just an hour away. I have an ownership interest in it, and I'd like to get you two a room and some spa treatments there. You can go pamper yourselves and reconnect."

And the side benefit was that he could figure out what on earth he was doing, kissing Susan.

"No way!" Susan turned away from her mother to face him, hands on hips. "You've already done enough for us, Sam. We couldn't possibly accept."

"I want you to," he said. Even more than with Marie, who'd grown up wealthy, he found he liked providing special things for Susan, who wasn't so used to it. Susan didn't expect people to do things for her; she almost had the reverse of the entitlement mentality he'd seen among so many of his younger workers. "Just take me up on the offer in the spirit it's meant. No obligations, no strings. I just want you to enjoy some time with your mom."

"No!" She was shaking her head. "It's not... We're not..." She lifted her hands, palms up, clearly at a loss to explain.

"Susie." Her mother put a perfectly manicured hand on Susan's shoulder. "It makes him feel good to do it. Men like to do nice things for women."

Susan's eye-roll was monumental, and for just a minute, he could completely picture her as a teenager.

"Let him help us," Mrs. Hayashi urged.

"Besides," Susan went on, twisting away from her mother in another teenager-like motion, "what about Mindy?"

"I just decided I'm going to take a week off to spend with her. Take her to the zoo, hang out at the pool. I miss her like crazy, having her away for the weekend, and I want to spend some extra time with her."

"That is so sweet," Mrs. Hayashi said. "I think that's wonderful."

Susan obviously didn't share the belief, but the slump of her shoulders let him know she realized she was defeated.

Good. She didn't get enough pampering in her life, that much was obvious.

And time off work would let him do some thinking about where his life was going and what he was doing. He might even go to that men's prayer breakfast Dion and Troy were always bugging him about.

Yes, a week off might give him some more perspective on his life.

"Daddy, I'm gonna listen to Mr. Eakin's story, okay?" Mindy said two evenings later.

"Sure, that's fine."

It was the Senior Towers open house, and the elders had gone all out to get the community to stop in and see what went on there. There were storytelling and craft booths, a used-book sale and a table set up to match senior volunteers with community needs.

Sam had relished spending the day with Mindy, hearing her exuberance about her camping experience, sharing simple summer pleasures like swimming and cooking out and the playground in the park.

At the same time, he had to acknowledge that it was hard to keep a five-year-old entertained. Especially one who was getting super excited about her upcoming birthday. He had a renewed respect for teachers and day care workers and nannies.

And for Susan.

In fact, he'd been thinking a lot about Susan.

Without her, the house was quiet, maybe a little lonely. There was less color and excitement.

He realized that he missed her in a completely different way than he'd missed Marie.

Marie had been stability and deep married love. She'd been the mother of his child. And her death had ripped a hole in his heart and in their home, one he and Mindy had been struggling to fix ever since.

Susan was excitement and spice. Her absence didn't hurt in the same way that the loss of Marie had, of course, partly because they knew Susan was coming back, and partly because his and Mindy's relationship with her was just beginning. It wasn't at all clear where it would go.

A lot of that, he realized, depended on him. There was something between him and Susan, something electric. But could he let go of the past for long enough to experience it and see where it led? Could he let go of at least some of his plans for a life as similar as possible to what he and Marie had planned together, what they'd always wanted?

"Sam Hinton." A clawlike hand grasped his arm, and he turned to see Miss Minnie Falcon, his old Sunday school teacher, glaring at him.

"Hey, Miss Minnie," he said. "How are you doing?"

"I'd be more at peace if I knew what was going on over in that mansion of yours."

"What do you mean?"

"I heard you took that nanny of yours out on a date." She looked at him as if he'd pocketed the Sunday school funds.

"I heard the same," came a male voice, one he dreaded because it was always critical and negative. Gramps Camden had issues with Sam's father, but didn't seem to be able to make a distinction between the generations. He always took his ire out on Sam. "Hi, Mr. Camden," Sam said, restraining his sigh.

"What are your intentions toward our Susan?" the older man asked. "I hope you're not taking advantage. She's a real nice girl."

"Yes, she is," Miss Minnie agreed. "Very active in the church. Very helpful, and has a mind of her own."

"Which I wouldn't have figured you to like," Gramps said. "Your father never did."

"Hey, hey," Sam said, trying to still the gossip. "We went out for a friendly dinner. That's all."

"At Chez La Ferme?" Minnie sounded scandalized. "Why, you probably spent over fifty dollars on that dinner. That's hardly something you do with just friends. Or should I say, it's hardly something a poor schoolteacher can afford."

"But a rich businessman can," Gramps said. "Question is, why would he want to?"

"Are you courting her?" Miss Minnie asked.

Sam looked from one to the other and felt a confessional urge similar to one he'd felt years ago, in Sunday school. He gave up trying to say anything but the truth. "I don't know," he admitted. "We're so different. I don't know where it could go, but I do like her."

"How's she feel about you?" Gramps asked. "I warned her about your family. She's probably on her guard, as well she should be."

Sam thought, momentarily, of the way her eyes had

softened as he'd leaned down to kiss her. "I think she's as confused as I am."

Miss Minnie frowned. "We've all got our eyes on you, young man."

"And as the man," Gramps said, "it's your job to get yourself un-confused. Figure out what you're doing. Don't string her along."

The old man was right, Sam reflected as he collected Mindy and headed home. The whole town of Rescue River knew what was going on, and he didn't want to cause gossip or hurt Susan's reputation.

He needed to make some decisions, and fast. Before the decisions made themselves for him. He just didn't know what to do.

Susan stood in the giant Rural America Outlet Store with her mother, looking through the little girls' clothing section.

Susan held up a colorful romper. "Mindy would look adorable in this!"

Her mother eyed her speculatively. "You've gotten close to her."

"Even being away for these few days, I've really missed that child." Susan couldn't wait to find out how Mindy had done at camp and to hear her stories of her week with her daddy.

"So get it," her mother said after feeling the fabric and squinting at the price tag. "It's a good bargain. But we should also get her something fun and glittery. Maybe a nail polish set." She led the way out of the clothing department and toward the makeup aisles.

"That's too grown-up," Susan protested, following

along past counters of jewelry and watches. "She's only five."

"Turning six, right?" Her mother smiled back at her. "Little girls that age love girly stuff. Even you did, back then."

As they reached the nail polish rack, Susan extended her freshly pedicured foot, showing off her new sparkly pink nail polish. "I did well with the girly stuff this week, didn't I?"

"Kicking and screaming, but yes." Her mother handed her a set of pale colors in a cartoonish box obviously meant for little girls. "What about these?"

Susan studied it. "Well, Sam will shoot me for buying it, but you're right, Mindy will love some nail polish."

"Then let's get it." Her mother took the polish set from her, checked the price and dropped it into their basket with the satisfied smile of an experienced bargain hunter.

The fun of shopping together was one of many rediscoveries Susan had made during the week. They'd gotten spa treatments and giggled through yoga classes and cried through the sappy chick flicks they both loved. In between, they'd done a little bit of real talking: about Donny, about Susan's father and about the mistakes they'd both made during Susan's stormy adolescence.

One conversation in particular stood out—the one about when Susan's father had left.

"I held on to him long after the love had died," her mother admitted, "with guilt about leaving me with you kids, and with pressure about how he didn't make enough money. I wasn't a good wife, Susie, and after he left, I tried to sway you kids against him."

"You tried so hard to make him happy, though," Susan had protested. "All those Japanese dinners, all your own needs suppressed."

"Which was my choice," Susan's mother declared. "I should have gotten a job and a life, especially after Donny was in school. The truth is, I was depressed and anxious, and I took it out on all of you."

Susan had hugged her mother. "I took out plenty on you, too," she said. "Some of the things I said to you as a teenager! I'm so sorry, Mom."

"Oh, every teenager does that, especially girls. I don't blame you for rebelling."

After that, they'd kept things light, but the tension and awkwardness that had hindered their connection for years was mostly gone. Susan felt better about their relationship than she ever had before, and for that, she was grateful to Sam Hinton.

Twenty minutes after they'd paid for their purchases, they were back at Sam's house, sneaking their bundles past the pool where Sam, Mindy and Mindy's grandparents were setting up for the birthday party that would occur later that day.

"Now, take the time to wrap these nicely," Susan's mother urged as she poured them both sodas. "You know, you really ought to get some decent dishes. You're an adult woman."

"Mindy will rip through this paper in two seconds. It doesn't matter how it looks."

"A nice package, as nice as the other guests bring, will impress Sam, though," Mom said. "You know, you just might get him to marry you. He's got that look in his eye."

"Mom!"

"He's a great catch," her mother said, coming over to kneel beside the box of wrapping paper Susan was rummaging through. "Look how wealthy and how generous with his money. A good father. You should consider it, sweetie."

Susan felt as if she was choking. "I don't want to do what you did! Look how that turned out!"

Susan's mother's face went sad. "Oh, Susie, it was so complicated between your father and me. You're not going to have the same situation—"

"I don't want to have a marriage that explodes and causes all that pain. I made a decision to stay single, and I'm sticking to it." She was, too. No doubt about it. What had happened between her and Sam, that night of their date, had been temporary insanity.

"Don't be stubborn. You're just like your father in that regard. Just…" Her mother looked off out the window and sighed. "Just choose the right man, the man who truly loves you, who looks at you like you're made of precious gems." She stroked Susan's hair. "And then communicate with him. Don't lose yourself like I did."

"So can I wrap the gift the way I want to?" Susan asked in exasperation.

"It doesn't hurt to show your softer side. You do have one."

So they wrapped the gifts in pink paper, elegantly, to rival Rescue River's finest. And then her mother brushed Susan's hair for her and put a little braid in it.

"You were always the best with my hair, Mom," Susan said, leaning back against her mother's stomach. "I'm so glad you came."

"I'm glad, too." Her mother placed a kiss on top of her head. "And now I'm going to the airport. My van is coming…" She consulted her phone. "Oh my, they're out front now."

"You're leaving already? So soon?"

Her mother clasped her by her shoulders. "You're on your own, you're on your way. You don't need me."

"But I don't want you to go," Susan said, feeling unexpectedly teary.

Sun slanted through the windows. Outside, car doors slammed and excited kids' voices rang out. It sounded as if a lot of people were coming to Mindy's party, and Susan wondered when Sam had planned it. And how he'd managed without her.

Her mother pulled her to her feet. "You have a party to get ready for. Go do that. And come for a visit soon, okay?"

"I will," Susan said. "Let me help carry your bags."

Her mother waved the offer aside. "I only have one bag, and I left it downstairs. Go get ready for your party."

Susan opened her arms, and her mother came to her in a fierce hug that made them both cry a little. And then her mother gave a jaunty wave and hurried down the stairs.

Party noise drifted through the screen door, and all of a sudden, Susan didn't want to be out of the action anymore. She needed to be a part of this important day in Sam and Mindy's life.

She changed into shorts and a sleeveless blouse, and hurried down the stairs, and immediately understood how Sam had gotten the party planned so fast.

Helen was greeting the well-dressed parents and children, and Ralph was directing a truck containing two

ponies to an appropriate unloading spot—the pad behind the garage, where Susan kept her car.

Susan walked slowly toward the gathering, holding
her nicely wrapped gift, which suddenly seemed cheap.
Uncertainty clawed at her, and then she saw Mindy.

Mindy spotted her at the same time and started running. What could Susan do but kneel down and open
her arms?

"There you are! I knew you'd come back in time!" she
crowed, loud enough for everyone to hear. "Grandma
and Daddy said you might not, but I knew you would!"

"I wouldn't miss it, sweetheart," Susan said, bury-
ing her nose in the sweaty, baby-shampoo scent of Mindy's hair.

"Guess what! I got my new little dog! Only," Mindy
said frowning, "Uncle Troy said we had to shut her upstairs in her crate cuz the party's too much excitement
for her. But that's only while she's a new dog."

So he'd gotten her a dog. *Good job, Sam.* "I can't
wait to see her! Maybe after the party."

"You know what?" Mindy said in a serious voice,
as if she was figuring something out. "You know what
I really want for my birthday?"

The intensity of Mindy's voice had most of the others quieting down to hear.

"What, honey?" Susan asked.

Mindy put a hand on her hip and touched Susan's
face with her half arm. "I want *you* to be my new
mommy!"

Chapter 11

Sam heard his daughter's words ring out, clear as a bell. *I want you to be my new mommy.* So, apparently, did everyone else at the party, because a hush fell over the yard.

He knew who his daughter was talking to without even looking. Susan.

The silence was replaced by the buzz of adult conversation that seemed to include a fair share of gossip and curious glances.

He looked toward where he'd heard Mindy's voice and saw that Susan had squatted down in front of her, talking quickly, smiling and laughing, redirecting Mindy's attention to the modest gift in her hand, to the clown who was setting up shop in the driveway.

We have a clown? Sam thought blankly.

Mindy was smiling and laughing as Susan talked to

her, so that was all right. Mindy's words had to have
been embarrassing to Susan, since everyone had heard,
but as usual, her focus had gone immediately to Mindy
and making sure she was okay and handling it.

In the direction of the pool area, he heard the sound
of sniffling and turned to see his mother-in-law fumbling for a napkin and wiping her eyes. She wasn't one
to break down, especially when she had a party to run,
but Mindy's words had obviously struck a nerve.

They'd struck a nerve in him, too. Trust a little kid
to lay out everything so baldly and clearly. She wanted
a new mommy. And she'd decided she wanted Susan.

Which had to go totally against Helen's grain. He
strode over to see what he could do for his grieving
mother-in-law.

Former mother-in-law.

As he bent to put an arm around Helen, he caught
Susan studying him, her eyes thoughtful.

Sam blew out a breath. Everything was coming to
a head now. Mindy, Helen, Susan. It was an emotional
triangle he couldn't figure out how to manage, couldn't
fix. He, who could easily run a complex business, had
no idea what to do, no idea how to arrange his personal life.

"Helen, you don't want to make a scene in front of
all of these folks," said Ralph, patting his wife's arm
and looking every bit as confused as Sam felt.

"You get those ponies set up," Helen snapped at her
husband. "I have to talk to Sam."

After making sure that everyone had access to food
and drink, and that Lou Ann Miller was supervising any
kids who wanted to swim, Sam led Helen to the shelter

beside the pool house. Bushes blocked it from the rest of the house and there was some privacy.

"Hey," he said once he'd got her seated on a picnic bench and found her a can of soda and a napkin to blow her nose. "You're going to be okay." He was terrible at this, terrible at comforting. He remembered all the times he'd tried and failed to comfort Marie. The one thing he'd been able to do to make her feel better, at the end of her life, was the promise. The promise that now dragged at his soul.

"You promised!" It was as if Helen read his mind. "Sam, you promised you'd marry someone like her, someone who would fulfill her legacy. And instead you've come up with…that woman."

"I don't know where the relationship with Susan is going," Sam said truthfully, all of a sudden realizing that he did, in fact, have a relationship with her.

"That woman can't cook, she wants to work rather than staying home, and she says the wrong thing all the time. She's so…different."

"That's for sure," Sam agreed. "Susan is different."

"Marie would hate her!"

Sam thought about it and decided that, yes, it was probably true. Marie would at least be made very insecure by Susan. But Marie *was* insecure, and that was what had made her such a perfectionist. And her insecurity had everything to do with her mother's demanding standards.

He didn't want to raise Mindy like that.

"She'd be a horrible mother. And you promised you'd marry someone like Marie."

Sam sighed heavily. "It's true. If I want to keep my promise to Marie, I…I can't marry Susan." As he said it, he felt trapped in a cage made of his own beliefs, the beliefs he'd always held about what made a good marriage, a good home, a good life.

Desperate for freedom, he lifted his head from his hands…and saw Susan and Mindy standing in the shelter's gateway.

And from the look on Susan's face, she'd overheard every word.

She squatted down and whispered something to Mindy. As Mindy ran toward him and Helen, Susan turned and left, almost at a run.

"Come on, Daddy, the kids all want to ride ponies and swim and nobody knows what to do!"

He had to take control of his child's party. He stood and walked out, feeling dazed, looking for Susan. But she was nowhere to be seen.

Susan's world spun as she thought about what she'd overheard. *I can't marry Susan.*

Marie would hate her.

She fell backward on her bed, staring up at the ceiling, eyes dry, stomach cold. She lay there for a long time while the sounds of the ongoing party drifted up to her.

It's fine, she told herself. It wasn't as if he'd proposed.

But if he'd made some kind of promise about what kind of woman to marry—and who made that kind of promise, anyway?—then what was he doing kissing her?

It was like her dad, saying one thing and doing another. Men were so unreliable.

And what of what Helen had said, about how bad she was at household duties? Hadn't she proven that to be true?

Just like her ex-fiancé, Sam didn't want a woman like her.

Her foolish dreams crashed down around her and she squeezed her eyes shut, willing herself not to cry. She was a strong woman, and she would survive this. After just a little period of mourning.

Her phone buzzed with a text from Daisy. *Where are you?*

Susan ignored it. Clicked off her phone.

The ache in her chest was huge, as if someone had dug a hole there with a blunt shovel. It hurt so much that she couldn't move, couldn't think. *God, help*, she prayed, unable to find more words.

In response, she felt a small soothing rush of love.

She'd always gone to church, read her Bible when there was a study group to push her, talked over her questions with friends like Daisy. She'd felt God's call for her vocation as a teacher. She knew she was saved.

But she'd never thought much about being loved by God. She'd never *felt* it, not deep inside. Now, the small soothing trickle grew to a warm glow.

Her father had only loved her conditionally, and he'd abandoned her. They spoke rarely by phone, and only at his instigation. Never when she needed him.

Her heavenly Father was different. He was here, waiting for her to reach out. *Rest in me*, He seemed to say.

Her hurt about Sam didn't evaporate. In fact, knowing God loved her seemed to unfreeze the tears, and they trickled down the sides of her face and into her hair. She'd never have a future with Sam and Mindy, and the cold truth of that stabbed into her like an icicle, letting her know that somewhere inside, she'd been nursing a dream to life.

Now that dream was pierced, deflated, gone.

Finally, a long while later, she dragged herself out of bed and looked out the window. Most of the kids were inside, no doubt eating birthday cake. The clown was packing up to go. He'd removed his red wig and rubbery nose, but his smile was still painted on.

She watched him pack his clown supplies into his rusty car trunk. He looked tired.

Could she keep a smile pasted on in the face of what she'd heard?

No.

She pulled out her suitcase and hauled a couple of boxes out of the closet. She opened the suitcase on her bed.

She'd started to dream, to hope. Crazy, stupid hope.

And a little girl would suffer because of it. "I want you to be my new mommy," Mindy had said earlier today, and the words, and the notion, had thrilled Susan way too much.

But she could never, ever be Mindy's new mommy. Because Sam had made a promise.

She opened her dresser drawers and started throwing clothes randomly into the suitcase, blinking against the tears that kept blurring her vision. From the open window, she heard car doors slamming, adults calling to one another. The parents were starting to arrive. The party was almost over.

She heard steps coming up the porch stairs, double time. "There you are!" Mindy said, rushing in. "Come see all my presents!" Then she seemed to notice something on Susan's face. She stopped still and looked around the room. "Whatcha doing?"

Susan's heart was breaking. Rip the bandage off quickly, she told herself. "I have to go away," she said.

"But you just got back from a trip."

"No, I mean...I can't stay here anymore."

"Why not?"

Why not indeed, when she loved this little girl almost as much as she loved her difficult, obstinate father? "It's just not working out. But I'll still see you lots, honey. I'll see you at school."

"I don't want you to go."

Susan couldn't help it; she knelt to hug the little girl. "I'm sorry, honey. I don't want to go either, but it's for the best."

Mindy's shoulders shook a little, but she didn't sob out loud. So she was starting to learn self-control. Growing up more each day.

Susan hugged the child tighter, but she struggled out of Susan's arms and ran down the stairs without looking back.

"Whoa there!" came Sam's voice, drifting up through the windows. "C'mere, sweetie. What's wrong?"

Panic rose in Susan at the thought of facing Sam. She needed to get this done fast. She'd just take a few things for now and send for the rest, because staying to pack and move would be too painful. Maybe this way, she could avoid seeing Sam or upsetting Mindy again.

She didn't even have an idea of where to go. Maybe to the little motel in outside of town, until she could figure something else out. Maybe she could go spend the rest of the summer with her mom, drop in unexpectedly just as Mom had done on her.

Heavy steps climbed the wooden stairs, and there was a knock on the open screen door. "Susan?"

She sucked in a breath. Sam. She'd moved too slowly, lost her chance of easy escape. "Come in," she said, feeling as if she was made of stone.

"What's going on here?" he asked, stopping at the door of her bedroom.

"I'm leaving."

"Why?"

What could she say? Because I've fallen in love with you and staying will break my heart? And Mindy's heart, too, because it can't be permanent?

Men were not dependable. She'd always known it, but for a while, Sam had seemed to defy the norm. But he'd proven, too, that he couldn't be trusted, that she'd be better off alone.

"It's just not working out," she said, and found the strength from somewhere to snap her suitcase closed.

He stood in the doorway as if he was frozen there.

She had to leave now or she'd never be able to. "Excuse me," she said, and slipped sideways past him. She trotted out the door and down the stairs.

Sam didn't know how long he stood there after Susan left. But finally standing got to be too much of an effort and he sank down onto her bed. Collapsed down to rest his head on her pillow. Inhaled her scent of honeysuckle, and his throat tightened.

Why had she gone? Was it just that she was flighty, transient, easily bored? Had his and Mindy's life proven too dull for her? Now that she'd earned enough money to send her brother to camp and make things up with her mom, had she gotten everything she could out of him?

But that *wasn't* it. Or at least, it wasn't all. She'd overheard what he'd said to Helen, and it had hurt her.

Having her gone had been bad enough when it was just for a week, but the expression on her face when she'd left had suggested that this time, it was permanent. She'd left for good.

Maybe she was oversensitive. Maybe he'd been right: he needed to stick to his kind of woman. Someone solid and stable and from his background. Someone who valued home and family over excitement. Someone who was in it for the long haul.

But the idea of finding someone else, a clone of the stable, boring blondes he'd dated over the past year, made him squeeze his eyes shut in despair.

He didn't want that. But he'd made a promise.

He was well and truly trapped.

"Hey, Sam!" He heard voices calling outside the window at the same time his cell phone buzzed.

He didn't have the energy to pick it up, but his wretched sense of duty made him look at the screen. Daisy. He texted back a question mark, having no heart for more.

Is Mindy with you? she texted.

He hit the call button, and Daisy answered immediately. "Do you have Mindy?"

"No. She was down on the driveway a few minutes ago."

"Well, everyone's gone, and I don't see her anywhere."

Sam stood and strode to the window. He scanned the yard. He didn't see her, either.

He did see Susan's car. Susan and Daisy were standing by it together. So she hadn't left yet.

"I'm on my way down," he said, and clicked off the phone.

Susan followed Daisy back into the house she'd thought she was leaving forever.

"Maybe she just fell asleep somewhere," Daisy was saying. "Or maybe Troy and Angelica took her home? Would they do that? I'll call them."

She was starting to place the call when Susan put a hand on her friend's arm. "I think I know why she's missing," she said. "It's my fault."

"What?"

So she filled Daisy in on the skeleton details of how she'd been packing and Mindy had found her and gotten upset.

"I'm going to want to hear more about this later," Daisy said, "but for now, let's find Mindy."

A quick survey of the house revealed nothing. They'd already checked the pool, of course, but they went back to look around the pool house. The place where Susan had heard about Sam's promise. Where he'd broken her heart. But there was no time for self-indulgence now.

My prickly independence hurt a little girl, she thought as she searched the woods at the edge of Sam's property. *I need to do something about that. If only I hadn't just run up and packed, Mindy wouldn't be missing.*

They checked in with Sam, who was white-faced and tight-lipped, searching the property lines as well. Phone calls were made, and within minutes Fern and Carlo,

Troy and Angelica came back, with Lou Ann Miller to watch Mercy and Xavier.

"I shouldn't have jumped into packing," Susan lamented as she, Fern and Angelica walked back into the fields behind Sam's property, calling Mindy's name. "I always think I'm just going to run away. If I hadn't done that, she wouldn't be missing."

Fern patted her arm. "Don't forget the time Mercy went missing. Only it was the dead of winter out at the skating pond. I totally blamed myself, but I've come to realize these things happen. We'll find her."

"It's true," Angelica said, giving her a quick side-arm hug. "Don't blame yourself. We all make mistakes with kids."

"You guys are the best," Susan said, gripping each of their hands, not bothering to hide her tears. She couldn't even pretend to be an island now. She needed her friends.

They met up with the men and Daisy in front of the house. "She just can't have gotten far," Troy was saying. "Look, Angelica and I will head to the surrounding houses."

"We'll check the library and the downtown," Carlo said, "just in case she took off running."

Sam shook his head. "I have this feeling she's somewhere in the house. I'm going to search this place from top to bottom. But let's get Dion involved, just in case."

At that, Susan's heart twisted. Everyone else looked half-sick, too, reminded of what could happen to missing little girls.

Daisy made the call to Dion, and then she, Susan and Sam started methodically going through the house. Susan realized anew how huge it was, how many spots there were for a little girl to hide. They searched each floor together, checking in with the other searchers.

Dion came in his cruiser and drove the neighborhoods.

The basement yielded nothing, and the main floor didn't, either. Susan thought she saw a head of blond hair in the playroom, but it was just a doll.

Upstairs, they went through Mindy's bedroom and all the closets, and then started on the spare bedrooms. Nothing.

But as they headed back downstairs, Susan heard a sound, like a sob, behind the sunroom door, that mysterious door that always remained closed.

"Did you hear that?" she asked.

"What? Where?"

Susan indicated the closed door.

"She wouldn't go in there," Sam said. "She's scared of it, because—" He broke off.

"Didn't you ever change it?" Daisy looked at Sam.

"Not yet," he said, and opened the door.

Inside was a beautiful, multi-windowed sunroom with wicker furniture and a rattan carpet, decorated in rust and brown and cream. Autumn colors.

In the center of the room was a hospital bed.

In a flash it came to Susan: this must be the place where Marie had died.

There was a bump in the covers of the bed. And there, sleeping restlessly, with the occasional hiccupping sob, was Mindy. Her new little black-and-white dog slept in her arms.

They all three looked at each other. Daisy bit her lip, tears in her eyes. "You have to get rid of that bed, Sam. You have to open this place up."

He nodded without speaking, and from the way his throat was working, Susan could see that he could barely restrain tears, himself.

"Thank the Lord we found her." Daisy hugged both of them.

Sam picked Mindy up and carried her to her bedroom while Daisy and Susan called the others.

"Now, what's this about you packing? Why were you leaving?" Daisy asked as they walked out to meet the others.

Fern fell into step beside them.

"It's time for girl talk," Daisy told her. "Susan was thinking of leaving."

Fern winced. "I remember when you guys talked sense into me," she said. She beckoned to Angelica, and the four of them headed into the living room, which looked to be the most secluded place right now.

"It's not that I need sense talked into me," Susan said, sinking into one of the formal living room chairs. She was too broken down to lie or conceal her feelings. "I love him. And I love Mindy. But he's never going to be able to commit to someone like me. I heard him say it." She shrugged. "I guess I'm just too different from him, not his type."

"Do I look like Carlo's type?" Fern asked. "I'm a librarian, and he's a mercenary, or at least he used to be. What could we have in common? But love is strange."

Angelica leaned forward and took Susan's hand. "It's hard to trust in men after you've been hurt," she said. "But it's so, so worth it."

"Just stay a little longer," Daisy urged. "Talk to Sam."

Susan wanted to take in what they were saying, but her heart was aching and her head was confused.

They talked a few minutes longer, and then Troy and Carlo called from the foyer and everyone started to leave.

Susan stayed, alone, sitting on the couch in the gathering darkness, too drained to move. "Thank You for letting us find her, Father," she prayed. "I'm sorry I'm so messed up. Please, help me to change so I can find love and do what's important."

She sat without tuning on a lamp, listening to the murmur of Sam talking to Dion on the porch, feeling alternating waves of sadness and God's healing love wash over her.

Finally, she curled up on her side on the narrow couch, tucked a hard, uncomfortable pillow beneath her head, and fell asleep.

Chapter 12

Sam sank down onto the wicker armchair on the front porch, waving to Troy and Angelica as they drove away, tooting their horn.

Only Dion remained, his cruiser parked out on the street. "You okay, my man?"

Sam stared out at the night sky. "Not really."

"Rough day." Dion sat down in the other chair, propped his hands behind his head and put his feet up on the wicker coffee table. "Now's the time you wish for a woman to bring you a tall iced tea."

"Tea's in the refrigerator," Sam offered. "I think."

"Exactly. That would require effort."

They sat together for a few minutes in a comfortable silence.

"Sorry I made you search the streets," Sam said finally. "Mindy never goes in the sunroom."

"The room where your wife died?"

Sam nodded. "I…just keep the door closed."

Dion nodded, tipping the chair back on two legs. "I did that for a while myself. At the house we shared, and in my heart."

"And you stopped? How?"

Dion shrugged, still staring out into the gathering darkness. "Time, man. Time, and prayer." He leveled a stern look at Sam. "You've had enough time, but you could use some help on the prayer side."

"I'm coming to the men's breakfast," Sam protested.

"Which I'm glad of. But you might need a private consult with the Lord."

Sam smiled at the terminology. "I know I do."

"Marie was a good woman," Dion said, and then paused.

Sam knew a "but" was coming. "But what?"

"But I'm guessing she must've been a little hard to live with."

A few weeks ago, that remark would have surprised him and roused his defenses. Now he just nodded. "She was pretty tense."

"Grew up that way, I guess."

"Exactly." Sam thought about his in-laws. Marie had never really broken away from them enough to have her own life. Everything had been colored by their insistence on perfection, on image. It wasn't that they were bad people, just a little misguided about what was important. "They were…controlling."

"Sounds like someone I know."

"What?"

"Look in the mirror, my man." Dion gave him a look.

"Everyone knows you're a dominant alpha-jerk. It's a wonder you have so many friends."

He knew he was controlling, but he'd never put it all together like that. "Is that why Marie married me?"

Dion spread his hands, palms up. "I hate to say it, but she kind of married her mother."

"Hey!"

Dion stood up, clapped him hard on the back. "Think about it, my man. How long you gonna force yourself to live in the past? Don't you remember you can be a new creation?"

And he waved and headed down the long front walk to his cruiser.

Restless, Sam stood and went inside. He checked on Mindy, who was sleeping peacefully, her new little dog beside her. The rule he'd made, no dogs in bed, was obviously not going to stick.

And then he went downstairs to the room where they'd found her. Marie's room. Or Mommy's room, as they'd called it when Marie was alive.

He sat in the chair where he'd spent so much time, right beside the hospital bed where she'd lain as the strength had slowly left her body. Talking to her, trying to cheer her up, reading with her, watching the house and garden shows she'd loved.

Even though the shows had bored him to tears, he'd kept watching them religiously for the first year after her death, because he'd felt closer to her that way. But, he realized, he hadn't seen one in six or eight months.

Dion was right. There came a time to move on.

He leaned forward, elbows on knees, hands clasped together. It was a prayer position, but he wasn't talking to God, not yet. He was talking to Marie. Telling her how sad he was that their dream hadn't worked out. How sorry that he'd been a controlling replica of her parents, that he hadn't encouraged her to spread her wings and fly. Letting her know that he couldn't keep the promise he'd made.

After a while, he stopped telling her anything and just sat. Just invoked the Lord's presence, asking for help. Confessing his sins there, too.

And as he sat, in prayerful meditation, a realization came to him.

Marie was with Christ. He'd prepared for her a room in His mansion. He'd promised that He'd see her face to face.

Oh, Sam had known that, but he hadn't *known* it. Hadn't really felt it.

Marie was happy now, happier than she'd ever been in life. Free of her failing body. Free of her insecurities. Free to love.

Marie had moved on to a new life, one he couldn't even imagine.

And likewise, she hadn't been able to imagine that he would move on, that life would change, that Mindy would grow beyond toddlerhood and would maybe need something, and someone, new. Maybe Sam would, too.

With the promises of Christ, Sam could move on, just as Marie had.

He sat until the tears had mostly stopped falling. Grabbed a tissue from the box Marie had always kept by her bed, a box that hadn't been used or changed out since she'd died.

He wiped his face and blew his nose and felt like an idiot, but a cleansed one. A healed one.

He took a deep breath, opened the door wide and went to find Susan.

Earlier, he'd seen that Susan's car was still behind the garage apartment. She hadn't left with Daisy, so she must have gone back to stay in her apartment. Which was good, because he had things he wanted to say to her.

But the apartment was dark, and she wasn't there, and fear gripped his heart.

What if she'd found another ride, sometime when he wasn't looking? What if she'd left? Left, before he could tell her all the things he wanted to tell her?

He walked back into the house, exhaustion hitting him hard. It had been a long and stressful day, full of fear and joy, sadness and closure. What he wanted at the end of this long day—at the end of any long day—was to be with the woman he loved. But she wasn't here.

As Sam walked through the house, hoping to hear Susan's voice, he seemed to see it with new eyes. It had been Marie's pride and joy; she'd loved inviting her friends here, serving tea, hosting her book club. At one time, the place had been his dream, too, full of stability and love, a home base that ran as smoothly as a business.

Now, it felt empty, lifeless, sad. Was this even the house he wanted to live in? Was it the right place for Mindy to grow up, formal as it was and full of sad memories?

Desolation gripped him hard.

He felt like just collapsing into bed, but he had responsibilities. He finished his walk-through of the house, just as he did every night, shutting off lights, locking doors, checking to make sure nothing was

amiss. He picked up some cups and a few stray cup-
cake wrappers that remained from the party. Feeling
utterly alone.

And then he saw her.

Curled up on the couch like a young girl, her fist at
her mouth, silky black hair spread over her shoulders.
In sleep, the determination and spark and movement
weren't there, and she looked totally vulnerable.

Totally lovely.

Joy was surging in his heart that she hadn't left him,
that she was still in the house. She was still in reach.
There was a chance.

He pulled up an ottoman and sat beside her, but just
watching her sleep felt creepy. So he touched her arm,
patted her awake. "Hey."

She opened her eyes slowly, and Sam got a momentary vision of what it might be like to watch her wake
up every day. His heart ached with longing to be the
man who saw that, who was there with her.

"I fell asleep," she said, looking around. "What time
is it?"

"It's late," he said. "Ten or so."

Susan stretched and pushed herself up into a semi-re-
clining position, propped on pillows, rubbing her arms.

"You're cold," he said, and looked for an afghan or
throw. Finding none, he went to the front closet and
found one of his sweatshirts. "Here," he said, tucking
it gently around her shoulders.

She blinked. "What time did you say it was? And
hey, are we even allowed to put our feet on this couch?"

"We are now," he said.

She grabbed her phone and studied it. "If I go now,
I can get a seat." She started to stand up.

"Wait. What seat?"

"On a plane to California," she said, putting her feet down and brushing her hands over her messy hair. "There's this online standby thing, and it looks like I have a seat if I can claim it by eleven. I've got to go."

He put a hand on her knee. "Susan. Wait."

"If you're going to yell at me, don't bother. I already know I made a mess of things." She was fumbling for her shoes, checking her phone again, looking anywhere but his face.

"What did you make a mess of?"

She stopped fussing and looked at him. "It was because of me that Mindy hid," she said. "She found me packing and got upset. I think she felt like it was another mother figure leaving her alone." She shook her head rapidly. "I'm so sorry I did that to her."

"Why were you packing to leave?" If it was because she didn't care, then he had to let her go.

"Because," she said slowly, "Because I heard what you said to Helen. That you could never marry me, that you made a promise."

"Ah." He took her hands. "I was afraid that was the problem." And he explained about the promise.

"You're right that I'm never going to be that person," she said. "And I don't want to break Mindy's heart. Or mine. I need to go now, before we get more attached."

"Wait." He shook his head slowly. "I've realized something now. That promise is something that helped me to grieve, stopped me from moving on too soon. But it doesn't hold now. It's like the old law and the new."

"What do you mean?" She sounded troubled.

"Susan, one thing you've helped me see is that I

needed to change. I don't have an easy time with change, never have. I'm the steady, boring, rock-solid type."

One side of her mouth quirked up. "Never boring. And steady's not so bad."

"Steady is okay, but I've seen that change is part of life. There's a new way. I'm a new creation."

She raised an eyebrow. "You mean like a new creation in Christ? You're talking religious, and that's not like you."

"It's like me now," he said. "I've recommitted. I've stopped blaming Him for what happened. With God's help, I'm back."

"Oh, Sam, I'm so happy for you!" She threw her arms around him.

Susan felt happy for Sam and more peaceful for herself, but she still had to get going. She talked to Sam for a few minutes, hearing about his conversation with Dion, glad to know he was getting right with the Lord.

But seeing his handsome face lose some of its tension, seeing the light in his eyes that hadn't been there before, just made him more attractive.

"Look," she said finally, "this is wonderful, but I really have to go. If I start driving in the next ten minutes, I can get to the airport just in time to catch this flight."

His lips tightened, but he nodded and followed her to the door. "Your purse, your phone?" he said, looking out for her, making sure she had what she needed.

She swallowed hard as she walked out of the house, because this was truly goodbye. "I'll send for my stuff," she said.

His hands clapped down on her shoulders, turning

her to face him. Behind him, his giant mansion shone in the moonlight.

The mansion that had become home to her.

Looking up at him, thinking of Mindy in the house behind him, just about broke her heart.

"I don't want you to go. I want you to stay."

She shook her head. "It's just hurting Mindy," she said. "And me."

"Why is it hurting you?" he asked, touching her chin to make her look at him.

He was going to make her say it, but what did it matter now? She was already hurting and she was leaving. "Because I've fallen in love with you and Mindy. With this life we're playing at. I want to have it for real, but I can't."

"Why not? Susan, what you just said makes me the happiest man in the world." He sank down to his knees. "I want to marry you. I don't know how or when, I know Mindy and I have a little more healing work to do, but I think we can do it with your help. I want you to be Mindy's new mommy. And my wife. Especially my wife."

"But your promise to Marie…"

He shook his head. "I've made my peace with that. With her. I'm not held to it anymore."

"For real?" She wanted to believe it, but she wasn't sure she could trust him. Was he just saying that? Could people really heal from a loss like the one he and Mindy had sustained?

"I am completely, totally sure." He swept her into his arms and carried her over to the lawn swing she'd insisted they get.

"Sam!"

"No near neighbors to see," he said. "And I want to prove to you just how much I love you."

He cradled her against his chest and kissed her tenderly, and Susan's last shreds of doubt wafted away on the gentle night breeze. Eagerly, she kissed him back and then stroked his hair and looked into his eyes.

"Does that mean yes?" he asked, sounding a little insecure.

She laughed out loud. "When does the nanny ever say no to the millionaire?"

"This is a serious moment!" He shook his head, then traced a finger along her cheek. "And I take nothing for granted."

"I'm sorry," she giggled, her heart almost bursting with joy, her soul singing. Daisy had been right: God's plan for her, for all of them, was bigger and deeper and richer than their human minds could imagine. "I'm just so happy. And it's totally a yes."

Epilogue

"I can't believe you let her do a beauty pageant," Susan said as she and Sam approached the Rescue River community center, hand in hand. Mindy ran ahead of them, wearing a poufy pink dress and scuffed cowboy boots.

Sam chuckled. "It's a different kind of pageant, you'll see."

Susan looked around at other families approaching with their daughters of various ages. Some were dressed in customary pageant gear, but others wore shorts or jeans. Susan noticed one girl in a traditional Chinese cheongsam dress and two other girls, one looking Indian and the other redheaded, wearing matching saris.

"The main rule is that the girls wear what they like. Mindy feels beautiful in that dress. But they're not judged on how they look."

"Then what are they judged on?"

"You'll see."

"I'll take your word for it," Susan said, snuggling closer to Sam's side. "I know it makes her grandma happy, so I'm glad we're here." In the two months since they'd declared their love for each other, Susan had been learning a lot about compromise and communication—and about being loved for exactly who she was.

"Look," Mindy cried, "They have crafts! And I see Miss Fern!"

Sam and Susan followed Mindy to an area where several tables stocked with art supplies were set up. The directions, printed large and bold, instructed participants to make art about something they wanted to do when they were older.

"Hey," Fern greeted them as she pulled out a huge sheet of paper. "You've got plenty of time, honey," she said as she handed it to Mindy. "Make whatever you like, just something you want to do when you're older. There are other art tables with other topics, when you're done here. Do you want a smock to cover that pretty dress?"

Mindy plunged her arms into a smock and sat down beside Fern's daughter, who was vigorously painting.

"Looks like Dad's one of the judges again," Sam observed, looking toward the stage where the judges' tables were being set up. "Last year, he almost came to blows with Gramps Camden."

Helen approached, brushing a hand over her granddaughter's shoulders before turning to Sam and Susan. "We put Lou Ann Miller in between. We're hoping that keeps everyone on good behavior. Hi, Susan."

"Hi." Susan returned the wary greeting and then, impulsively, hugged the older woman. They were starting to forge a relationship, but it would be a slow process. "You were right," Susan said, determined to do her part. "She does look beautiful in her dress, and this is a great event for girls."

When they released the hug and stepped back, Helen's eyes were shiny. "I just want Mindy to be happy," she said. "And I want to be a part of her life."

"Of course you do. You're a huge part of her life, and you always will be."

After an hour of mingling and following Mindy from art table to art table, the formal ceremony began. Susan sat back and listened, impressed, to the girls of all ages talking about the required topics, sometimes displaying art to go alongside. Finally, it was Mindy's turn, and as she walked confidently up to the stage, Sam gripped Susan's hand.

It was as if she could read his mind: he was nervous for Mindy, wanting her to do well, wanting her to feel good about it. Susan felt the same way. She loved the little girl more each day.

"Something I did that was hard," Mindy said into the microphone, speaking clearly, "was I went into my mommy-who-died's room. I used to be scared in there but now I'm not cuz I have my puppy." She held up a picture of Bonz. "I went in there and was brave to tell my mommy who died that I want a new mommy, and she said it was okay."

There was a collective sigh and a spontaneous round of applause.

"And something I like to do," Mindy said, "is hug people. I can hug just as good as anybody else even though I just have one hand."

Another collective "aww."

"I want to show that, for this pageant, but I have to get my daddy and my Miss Susan to come up here," she said, "cuz they're gonna get married."

Gasps and murmurs filled the room, and Sam looked at Susan. "Guess the secret's out. You game?"

"Of course." It had been an open secret, really; in a town like Rescue River, you couldn't hide a relationship very well.

So they went up front and Mindy proved that she could, indeed, hug as well as anyone else. And as the applause swelled for the three of them, standing there hugging each other tightly, Susan felt the invisible Master who'd been guiding them together from the beginning, and looked up through tears to offer praise.

* * * * *

We hope you enjoyed reading

The Cowboy's Lady

by *New York Times* bestselling author

DEBBIE MACOMBER

and

Small-Town Nanny

by *USA TODAY* bestselling author

LEE TOBIN McCLAIN

Both were originally Harlequin series stories!

From passionate, suspenseful and dramatic
love stories to inspirational or historical,
Harlequin offers different lines to
satisfy every romance reader.

New books in each line are available every month.

LOVE INSPIRED

INSPIRATIONAL ROMANCE

Uplifting stories of faith, forgiveness and hope.

SPECIAL EXCERPT FROM

❧

LOVE INSPIRED
INSPIRATIONAL ROMANCE

*Suddenly a father after a toddler is abandoned on his
doorstep, Corbin Beck has no idea how to care for a little
boy. But town troublemaker Samantha Alcorn is looking to
turn over a new leaf…and hiring her as his live-in nanny
could solve both their problems.*

Read on for a sneak preview of
Child on His Doorstep,
the next book in Lee Tobin McClain's
Rescue Haven *miniseries.*

"I'm sorry I was distant before. That was just me being foolish."

Samantha didn't ask what he was talking about; she obviously knew. "What was going on?"

Corbin debated finding some intellectual way to say it, but he wasn't thinking straight enough. "I got turned upside down by that kiss."

"Yeah. Me, too." She glanced at him and then turned to put a stack of plates away.

"It was intense."

"Uh-huh."

Now that he had brought up the topic, he wasn't sure where he wanted to go with it. For him to go into the fact that he couldn't get involved with her because she was an alcoholic… Suddenly, that felt judgmental and mean and not how he wanted to talk to her.

Maybe it wasn't how he wanted to be with her, either, but he wasn't ready to make that alteration to his long-held set of values about who he could get involved with. And until he did, he obviously needed to keep a lid on his feelings.

So he talked about something they would probably agree on. "I was never so scared in my life as when Mikey was lost."

"Me, either. It was awful."

He paused, then admitted, "I just don't know if I'm cut out for taking care of a kid."